Real Life in London, or, The Rambles and Adventures of Bob Tallyho, Esq., and His Cousin the Hon. Tom Dashall – Volume I

Pierce Egan

Illustrated by Heath, Alken, Dighton, Rowlandson and others

HULL LIBRARIES	
942.12081	
54072 012710905	
Bertrams	01.11.07
	£17.99
HCL	RW

REAL LIFE IN LONDON

BY PIERCE EGAN

VOL. I / VOL. II

WITH 34 COLOURED PLATES BY ALKEN AND ROWLANDSON

The Illustrated Pocket Library of Plain and Coloured Books

Methuen and Co., London

REAL LIFE IN LONDON.

W. Read, del. et sculpt.

View of Regent Street from Waterloo Place

THE PRINCIPAL CHARACTERS
presented to Public Exhibition, throughout
REAL LIFE IN LONDON.

REAL LIFE IN LONDON

OR, THE RAMBLES AND ADVENTURES OF BOB TALLYHO, ESQ.,
AND HIS COUSIN, THE HON. TOM DASHALL,
THROUGH THE METROPOLIS;
EXHIBITING A LIVING PICTURE OF FASHIONABLE CHARACTERS,
MANNERS, AND AMUSEMENTS IN HIGH AND LOW LIFE
By an AMATEUR

"'Tis pleasant through the loop-holes of retreat
To peep at such a world; to see the stir
Of the great Babel, and not feel the crowd."
—Cowper

REAL LIFE IN LONDON

OR, THE RAMBLES AND ADVENTURES OF BOB TALLYHO, ESQ., AND HIS COUSIN, THE HON. TOM DASHALL, THROUGH THE METROPOLIS; EXHIBITING A LIVING PICTURE OF FASHIONABLE CHARACTERS, MANNERS, AND AMUSEMENTS IN HIGH AND LOW LIFE

BY AN AMATEUR

EMBELLISHED AND ILLUSTRATED WITH A SERIES OF COLOURED PRINTS, DESIGNED AND ENGRAVED BY MESSRS. HEATH, ALKEN, DIGHTON, ROWLANDSON, ETC.

VOLUME I

A NEW EDITION

METHUEN & CO.
LONDON

EMBELLISHED AND ILLUSTRATED WITH A SERIES OF
COLOURED PRINTS, DESIGNED AND ENGRAVED
BY MESSRS. HEATH, AIKEN, DIGHTON,
ROWLANDSON, ETC.
VOLUME I.
A NEW EDITION

NOTE

This Issue, first published in 1905, is founded on the Edition
printed for Jones & Co. in the year 1821

CONTENTS:

Chapter I

Seduction from rural simplicity, Pleasures of the table, Overpowering oratory, A warm dispute, Amicable arrangement.

Chapter II

Philosophical reflections, A great master, Modern jehuism, A coach race, A wood-nymph, Improvements of the age, An amateur of fashion, Theatrical criticism, Reflections.

Chapter III

Hyde Park, and its various characters, Sir F——s B——tt, , Delightful reverie.

Chapter IV

Fresh game sprung, Lord C——e, alias Coal-hole George, Rot at Carlton Palace, Once-a-week man, Sunday promenader, How to raise the wind, Lord Cripplegate and his Cupid, Live fish, Delicacy, A breathless visito.

Chapter V

A fashionable introduction, A sparkling subject, The true spur to genius, An agreeable surprise, A serious subject, A pleasant fellow, Lively gossip, Living in style, Modern good breeding, Going to see "you know who."

Chapter VI

Early morning amusements, Frightening to death, Improvements of the age, Preparing for a swell, The acmé of barberism, A fine specimen of the art, Duels by Cupid and Apollo, Fashionable news continued, Low niggardly notions, Scenes from Barber-Ross-a, A snip of the superfine, The enraged Managers, Cutting out, and cutting up, The whipstitch mercury, All in the wrong again, A Venus de Medicis, Delicacy alarmed.

Chapter VII

Preparing for a ramble, A man of the town, Bond Street, A hanger on, A man of science, Dandyism, Dandy heroism, Inebriety reproved, My uncle's card, St James's Palace, Pall Mall-Waterloo Place, etc, An Irish Paddy Incorrigible prigs, A hue and cry, A capture, A wake, with an Irish howl, Vocabulary of the new school, Additional company.

Chapter VIII

*Public Office, Bow Street, Irish generosity, A bit
of gig, "I loves fun," A row with the Charleys,
Judicial sagacity, Watch-house scenes, A rummish
piece of business The Brown Bear well baited,
Somerset House, An importunate customer
Peregrinations proposed.*

Chapter IX

*The Bonassus, A Knight of the New Order, Medical
quacks, Medical (not Tailors') Boards, Superlative
modesty, Hard pulling and blowing, Knightly
medicals Buffers and Duffers, Extremes of
fortune, Signs of the Times, Expensive spree,
The young Cit, All in confusion, Losses and
crosses, Rum customers, A genteel hop, Max
and music, Amateurs and actors, A well-known
character, Championship, A grand spectacle,
Adulterations, More important discoveries, Wonders
of cast-iron and steam, Shops of the new school,
Irish paper-hanging.*

Chapter X

*Heterogeneous mass, Attractions of the theatre,
Tragedy talk, Authors and actors, Chancery
injunctions, Olympic music, Dandy larks and
sprees, The Theatre, Its splendid establishment,
Nymphs of the saloon, Torments of love and gout,
Prostitution, A shameful business, Be gone,
dull care, Convenient refreshment, A lushy cove,
The sleeper awake, All on lire, A short
parley.*

Chapter XI

Fire, confusion and alarm, Snuffy tabbies and boosy kids, A cooler for hot disputes, An overturned Charley, Resurrection rigs, Studies from life, An agreeable situation, A nocturnal visit to a lady, Sharp's the word, Frolicsome fellows, Retirement.

Chapter XII

Tattersall's, Friendly dealings, Laudable company, The Sportsman's exchange, An unlimited order, How to ease heavy pockets, Body-snatchers and Bum-traps, The Sharps and the Flats, A secret expedition, A pleasant rencontre, Accommodating friends, The female banker, A buck of the first cut, A highly finished youth, An addition to the party.

Chapter XIII

A promenade, Something the matter, Quizzical hits, London friendship, Fashion versus Reason, Dinners of the Ton, Brilliant mob of a ball-room, What can the matter be? Something-A-Miss.

Chapter XIV

The centre of attraction, The circulating library, Library wit, Fitting on the cap, Breaking up, Gaming, Hells-Greeks-Black-legs, How to become a Greek, Valuable instructions, Gambling-house à la Française, Visitors' cards, Opening scene, List of Nocturnal Hells, Rouge et Noir Tables, Noon-day Hells, Hell broke up, and the devil to pay, A story, Swindling Jews, Ups and downs, High fellows, Mingled company, Severe studies.

Chapter XV

Newspaper recreations, Value of Newspapers, Power of imagination, Rich bill of fare, Proposed Review of the Arts, Demireps and Cyprians, Dashing characters, Female accommodations, Rump and dozen, Maggot race for a hundred, Prime gig, larks and sprees, Female jockeyship, Delicate amusements for the fair sex, Female life in London, Ciphers in society, Ciphers of all sorts, Hydraulics, Watery humours, General street engagement, Harmon restored.

Chapter XVI

The double disappointment, Heading made easy, Exhibition of Engravings, How to cut a dash, Dashing attitude, costume, etc, A Dasher-Street-walking, etc, Dancing—"all the go," Exhibition, Somerset House, Royal Academy, Somerset House, The Sister Arts Character-Caricature, etc, Moral tendency of the Arts, Fresh game sprung, Law and Lawyers, Law qualifications, Benchers, Temple Libraries-Church, St Dunstan's Bell-thumpers, Political Cobbler, Coffee-houses, Metropolitan accommodations, Chop-house delights and recreations, Daffy's Elixir, Blue Ruin, etc, The Queen's gin-Shop.

Chapter XVII

Globe Coffee-house, A humorous sort of fellow, A Punster, Signals and Signs, Disconcerted Professors, A learned Butcher, A successful stratagem, A misconception, A picture of London, All in high glee.

Chapter XVIII

A Slap at Slop, A Nondescript, Romanis, Bow steeple-Sir Chris Wren, The Temple of Apollo, Caricatures, Rich stores of literature, Pulpit oratory, Seven reasons, Street impostors and impositions, Impudent beggars, Wise men of the East, A Royal Visitor and Courtier reproved, Confusion of tongues, Smoking and drinking, Knights of the Round Table, The joys of milling, Noses and nosegays, A Bumpkin in town, Piggish propensities, Joys of the bowl.

Chapter XIX

Jolly boys, Dark-house Lane, A breeze sprung up, Business done in a crack, Billingsgate, Refinements in language, Real Life at Billingsgate, The Female Fancy, The Custom House, Long Room, etc, Greeting mine host, A valuable customer, A public character.

Chapter XX

The Tower of London, Confusion of titles, Interior of the Trinity House, Rag Fair commerce, Itinerant Jews and Depredators, Lamentable state of the Jews, Duke's Place and Synagogue, Portuguese Jews, Bank of England, An eccentric character, Lamentable effects of forgery, Singular alteration of mind, Imaginary wealth, Joint Stock Companies, Auction Mart-Courtois, Irresistible arguments, Wealth without pride, Royal Exchange, A prophecy fulfilled, Lloyd's-Gresham Lecture, etc, The essential requisite, Egress by storm.

Chapter XXI

*Incident "ad infinitum," A distressed Poet,
Interesting calculations, Ingenuity in puffing,
Blacking maker's Lauréat, Miseries of literary
pursuits, Suttling house, Horse Guards, Merits of
two heroes, Hibernian eloquence, A pertinacious
Disputant, Peace restored-Horse Guards, Old
habits-The Miller's horse, Covent Garden-Modern Drury,
A more than Herculean labour, Police Office scene,
Bartholomew Fair, A Knight of the Needle,
Variance of opinion, A visit to the Poet, Produce
of literary pursuits, Quantum versus Quality,
Publishing by subscription, Wealth and ignorance,
Mutual gratification .*

Chapter XXII

*Symptoms of alarm, Parties missing, A strange
world, Wanted, and must come, Expectation alive,
A cure for melancholy, Real Life a game, The
game over, Money-dropping arts, Dividing a prize,
The Holy Alliance broke up, New method of Hat
catching, Dispatching a customer, Laconic
colloquy, Barkers, A mistake corrected,
Pawnbrokers, The biter bit, Miseries of
prostitution, Wardrobe accommodations, New species
of depredation.*

Chapter XXIII

*The Lock-up House, Real Life with John Doe, etc,
Every thing done by proxy, Lottery of marriage,
Sharp-shooting and skirmishing, A fancy sketch,
The universal talisman, living within bounds, How
to live for ten years, An accommodating host, Life
in a lock-up house.*

Chapter XXIV.

A successful election, Patriotic intentions, Political dinner, Another bear-garden, Charley's theatre, . Bear-baiting sports, The coronation, Coronation splendour.

Chapter XXV.

Fancy sports, . Road to a fight, New sentimental journey, Travelling chaff, Humours of the road, Lads of the fancy, Centre of attraction, A force march, Getting to work, True game, The sublime and beautiful, All's well-good night.

Chapter XXVI.

Promenading reflections, Anticipation, Preliminary observations, Characters in masquerade, Irish sympathy, Whimsicalities of character, Masquerade characters, The watchman, New characters, The sport alive, Multifarious amusements, Doctors disagree, Israelitish honesty.

Chapter XXVII.

Ideal enjoyments, A glance at new objects, Street-walking nuisances, Cries of London-Mud-larks, etc. The Monument, London Stone, General Post-Office, Preparations for returning, So endeth the volume.

LIST OF ILLUSTRATIONS

Titlepage
Frontispiece
Titlepage
Hyde-park
Epson Racers
Fives Court
The Kings Levee
Catching a Charley Napping
Drury Lane Theatre
Tom and Bob at Drury Lane
Tattersall's
A Modern Hell
Somerset House
Road to a Fight
Real Life at Billingsgate
Political Dinner
The Country Squire
Grand Coronation Dinner
Road to a Fight
A Private Turn-up
Masquerade

Real Life in London - Volume I

CHAPTER I

Triumphant returning at night with the spoil,
Like Bachanals, shouting and gay:
How sweet with a bottle and song to refresh,
And lose the fatigues of the day.
With sport, wit, and wine, fickle fortune defy,
Dull 'wisdom all happiness sours;
Since Life is no more than a passage at best,
Let's strew the way over with flowers.

"THEY order these things better in London," replied the Hon. Tom Dashall, to an old weather-beaten sportsman, who would fain have made a convert of our London *Sprig of Fashion* to the sports and delights of rural life. The party were regaling themselves after the dangers and fatigues of a very hard day's fox-chace; and, while the sparkling glass circulated, each, anxious to impress on the minds of the company the value of the exploits and amusements in which he felt most delight, became more animated and boisterous in his oratory—forgetting that excellent regulation which forms an article in some of the rules and orders of our *"Free and Easies"* in London, "that no more than three gentlemen shall be allowed to speak at the same time." The whole party, consisting of fourteen, like a pack in full cry, had, with the kind assistance of the "rosy god," become at the same moment most animated, not to say vociferous, orators. The young squire, Bob Tally ho, (as he was called) of Belville Hall, who had recently come into possession of this fine and extensive domain, was far from feeling indifferent to the pleasures of a sporting life, and, in the chace, had even acquired the reputation of being a "keen sportsman:" but the regular intercourse which took place between him and his cousin, the Hon. Tom Dashall, of Bond Street notoriety, had in some measure led to an indecision of character, and often when perusing the lively and fascinating descriptions which the latter drew of the passing scenes in the gay metropolis, Bob would break out into an involuntary exclamation of—"Curse me, but after all, this only is Real Life;"—while, for the moment, horses, dogs, and gun, with the whole paraphernalia of sporting, were annihilated.

Indeed, to do justice to his elegant and highly-finished friend, these pictures were the production of a master-hand, and might have made a dangerous impression on minds more stoical and determined than that of Bob's. The opera, theatres, fashionable pursuits, characters, objects, &c. all became in succession the subjects of his pen; and if lively description, blended with irresistible humour and sarcastic wit, possessed any power of seduction, these certainly belonged to Bob's honourable friend and relative, as an epistolary correspondent. The following Stanzas were often recited by him with great feeling and animation:—

> *Parent of Pleasure and of many a groan,*
> *I should be loath to part with thee, I own,*
> *Dear Life!*
> *To tell the truth, I'd rather lose a wife,*
> *Should Heav'n e'er deem me worthy of possessing*
> *That best, that most invaluable blessing.*
> *I thank thee, that thou brought'st me into being;*
> *The things of this our world are well worth seeing;*
> *And let me add, moreover, well worth feeling;*
> *Then what the Devil would people have?*
> *These gloomy hunters of the grave,*
> *For ever sighing, groaning, canting, kneeling.*
> *Some wish they never had been born, how odd!*
> *To see the handy works of God,*
> *In sun and moon, and starry sky;*
> *Though last, not least, to see sweet Woman's charms,—*
> *Nay, more, to clasp them in our arms,*
> *And pour the soul in love's delicious sigh,*
> *Is well worth coming for, I'm sure,*
> *Supposing that thou gav'st us nothing more.*
> *Yet, thus surrounded, Life, dear Life, I'm thine,*
> *And, could I always call thee mine,*
> *I would not quickly bid this world farewell;*
> *But whether here, or long or short my stay,*
> *I'll keep in mind for ev'ry day*
> *An old French motto, "Vive la bagatelle!"*
> *Misfortunes are this lottery-world's sad blanks;*
> *Presents, in my opinion, not worth thanks.*

The pleasures are the twenty thousand prizes,
Which nothing but a downright ass despises.

It was not, however, the mere representations of Bob's friend, with which, (in consequence of the important result,) we commenced our chapter, that produced the powerful effect of fixing the wavering mind of Bob—No, it was the air—the manner—the *je ne sais quoi*, by which these representations were accompanied: the curled lip of contempt, and the eye, measuring as he spoke, from top to toe, his companions, with the cool elegant sang froid and self-possession displayed in his own person and manner, which became a *fiat* with Bob, and which effected the object so long courted by his cousin.

After the manner of Yorick (though, by the bye, no sentimentalist) Bob thus reasoned with himself:—"If an acquaintance with London is to give a man these airs of superiority—this ascendancy—elegance of manners, and command of enjoyments—why, London for me; and if pleasure is the game in view, there will I instantly pursue the sport."

The song and toast, in unison with the sparkling glass, followed each other in rapid succession. During which, our elegant London visitor favoured the company with the following effusion, sung in a style equal to (though unaccompanied with the affected airs and self-importance of) a first-rate professor:—

SONG.

If to form and distinction, in town you would bow,
Let appearance of wealth be your care:
If your friends see you live, not a creature cares how,
The question will only be, Where?
A circus, a polygon, crescent, or place,
With ideas of magnificence tally;
Squares are common, streets queer, but a lane's a disgrace;
And we've no such thing as an alley.
A first floor's pretty well, and a parlour so so;
But, pray, who can give themselves airs,
Or mix with high folks, if so vulgarly low
To live up in a two pair of stairs?

The garret, excuse me, I mean attic floor,
(That's the name, and it's right you should know it,)
Would he tenantless often; but genius will soar,
And it does very well for a poet.

These amusements of the table were succeeded by a most stormy and lengthened debate, (to use a parliamentary phrase) during which, Bob's London friend had with daring heroism opposed the whole of the party, in supporting the superiority of Life in London over every pleasure the country could afford. After copious libations to Bacchus, whose influence at length effected what oratory had in vain essayed, and silenced these contending and jarring elements, "grey-eyed Morn" peeped intrusively amid the jovial crew, and Somnus, (with the cart before the horse) stepping softly on tip-toe after his companion, led, if not by, at least accompanied with, the music of the nose, each to his snoring pillow.

——"Glorious resolve!" exclaimed Tom, as soon as his friend had next morning intimated his intention,—"nobly resolved indeed!— "What! shall he whom Nature has formed to shine in the dance and sparkle in the ring—to fascinate the fair—lead and control the fashions—attract the gaze and admiration of the surrounding crowd!—shall he pass a life, or rather a torpid existence, amid country bumpkins and Johnny-raws? Forbid it all ye powers that rule with despotic sway where Life alone is to be found,—forbid it cards—dice—balls—fashion, and ye gay et coteras,—forbid"—— "Pon my soul," interrupted Bob, "you have frightened me to death! I thought you were beginning an Epic,—a thing I abominate of all others. I had rather at any time follow the pack on a foundered horse than read ten lines of Homer; so, my dear fellow, descend for God's sake from the Heroics."

Calmly let me, at least, begin Life's chapter,
Not panting for a hurricane of rapture;
Calm let me step—not riotous and jumping:
With due decorum, let my heart
Try to perform a sober part,
Not at the ribs be ever bumping—bumping.
Rapture's a charger—often breaks his girt,

Runs oft", and flings his rider in the dirt.

"However, it shall be so: adieu, my dear little roan filly,—Snow-ball, good by,—my new patent double-barrelled percussion—ah, I give you all up!—Order the tandem, my dear Tom, whenever you please; whisk me up to the fairy scenes you have so often and admirably described; and, above all things, take me as an humble and docile pupil under your august auspices and tuition." Says Tom, "thou reasonest well."

The rapidity with which great characters execute their determinations has been often remarked by authors. The dashing tandem, with its beautiful high-bred bits of blood, accompanied by two grooms on horsebaek in splendid liveries, stood at the lodge-gate, and our heroes had only to bid adieu to relatives and friends, and commence their rapid career.

Before we start on this long journey of one hundred and eighty miles, with the celerity which is unavoidable in modern travelling, it may be prudent to ascertain that our readers are still in company, and that we all start fairly together; otherwise, there is but little probability of our ever meeting again on the journey;—so now to satisfy queries, remarks, and animadversions.

"Why, Sir, I must say it is a new way of introducing a story, and appears to me very irregular.—What! tumble your hero neck and heels into the midst of a drunken fox-hunting party, and then carry him off from his paternal estate, without even noticing his ancestors, relatives, friends, connexions, or prospects—without any description of romantic scenery on the estate—without so much as an allusion to the female who first kindled in his breast the tender passion, or a detail of those incidents with which it is usually connected!—a strange, very strange way indeed this of commencing."

"My dear Sir, I agree with you as to the deviation from customary rules: but allow me to ask,—is not one common object—amusement, all we have in view? Suppose then, by way of illustration, you were desirous of arriving at a given place or object, to which there were several roads, and having traversed one of these till the monotony of the scene had rendered every object upon it dull and wearisome, would you quarrel with the traveller who pointed out another road, merely because it was a new one? Considering the impatience of our young friends, the one to return to scenes in which alone he can live, and the other to realize ideal dreams of happiness, painted in all the glowing tints that a warm imagination and youthful fancy can pourtray, it will be impossible longer to continue the argument. Let me, therefore, entreat you to cut it short—accompany us in our rapid pursuit after Life in London; nor risk for the sake of a little peevish criticism, the cruel reflection, that by a refusal, you would, probably, be in *at the death* of the Author—by Starvation."

CHAPTER II

*"The panting steed the hero's empire feel,
Who sits triumphant o'er the flying wheel,
And as he guides it through th' admiring throng,
With what an air he holds the reins, and smacks the silken thong!"*

ORDINARY minds, in viewing distant objects, first see the obstacles that intervene, magnify the difficulty of surmounting them, and sit down in despair. The man of genius with his mind's-eye pointed steadfastly, like the needle towards the pole, on the object of his ambition, meets and conquers every difficulty in detail, and the mass dissolves before him as the mountain snow yields, drop by drop, to the progressive but invincible operation of the solar beam. Our honourable friend was well aware that a perfect knowledge of the art of driving, and the character of a *"first-rate whip,"* were objects worthy his ambition; and that, to hold four-in-hand—turn a corner in style—handle the reins in form—take a fly off the tip of his leader's ear—square the elbows, and keep the wrists pliant, were matters as essential to the formation of a man of fashion as *dice or milling*: it was a principle he had long laid down and strictly adhered to, that whatever tended to the completion of that character, should be acquired to the very acmé of perfection, without regard to ulterior consequences, or minor pursuits.

In an early stage, therefore, of his fashionable course of studies, the whip became an object of careful solicitate; and after some private tuition, he first exhibited his prowess about twice a week, on the box of a Windsor stage, tipping coachy a crown for the indulgence and improvement it afforded. Few could boast of being more fortunate during a noviciate: two overturns only occurred in the whole course of practice, and except the trifling accident of an old lady being killed, a shoulder or two dislocated, and about half a dozen legs and arms broken, belonging to people who were not at all known in high life, nothing worthy of notice may be said to have happened on these occasions. 'Tis true, some ill-natured remarks appeared in one of the public papers, on the "conduct of coachmen entrusting the reins to young practitioners, and thus endangering the lives of his majesty's subjects;" but these passed off like other philanthropic suggestions of the day, unheeded and forgotten.

The next advance of our hero was an important step. The mail-coach is considered the school; its driver, the great master of the art—the *Phidias* of the statuary—the *Claude* of the landscape-painter. To approach him without preparatory instruction and study, would be like an attempt to copy the former without a knowledge of anatomy, or the latter, while ignorant of perspective. The standard of excellence—the model of perfection, all that the highest ambition can attain, is to approach as near as possible the original; to attempt a deviation, would be to *bolt out of the course, snap the curb, and run riot.* Sensible of the importance of his character, accustomed to hold the reins of arbitrary power; and seated where will is law, the mail-whip carries in his appearance all that may be expected from his elevated situation. Stern and sedate in his manner, and given to taciturnity, he speaks sententiously, or in monosyllables. If he passes on the road even an humble follower of the profession, with four tidy ones in hand, he views him with ineffable contempt, and would consider it an irreparable disgrace to appear conscious of the proximity. Should it be a country gentleman of large property and influence, and he held the reins, and handled the whip with a knowledge of the art, so to "get over the ground," coachy might, perhaps, notice him *"en passant,"* by a slight and familiar nod; but it is only the peer, or man of first-rate sporting celebrity, that is honoured with any thing like a familiar mark of approbation and acquaintance; and these, justly appreciating the proud distinction, feel higher gratification by it than any thing the monarch could bestow: it is an inclination of the head, not forward, in the manner of a nod, but towards the off shoulder, accompanied with a certain jerk and elevation from the opposite side. But here neither pen nor pencil can depict; it belongs to him alone whose individual powers can nightly keep the house in a roar, to catch the living manner and present it to the eye.

"— —*A merrier man*

Within the limit of becoming mirth,
I never spent an hour's talk withall:

His eye begets occasion for his wit;
For every object that the one doth catch
The other turns to a mirth-moving jest."

And now, gentle reader, if the epithet means any thing, you cannot but feel disposed to good humour and indulgence: Instead of rattling you off, as was proposed at our last interview, and whirling you at the rate of twelve miles an hour, exhausted with fatigue, and half *dead* in pursuit of *Life*, we have proceeded gently along the road, amusing ourselves by the way, rather with drawing than driving. 'Tis high time, however, we made some little progress in our journey: "Come Bob, take the reins—push on—keep moving—touch up the leader into a hand-gallop—give Snarler his head—that's it my tight one, keep out of the ruts—mind your quartering—not a gig, buggy, tandem, or tilbury, have we yet seen on the road—what an infernal place for a human being to inhabit!—curse me if I had not as lief emigrate to the back settlements of America: one might find some novelty and amusement there—I'd have the woods cleared—cut out some turnpike-roads, and, like Palmer, start the first mail"— —"Stop, Tom, don't set off yet to the Illinois—here's something ahead, but what the devil it is I cant guess—why it's a barge on wheels, and drove four-in-hand."—"Ha, ha—barge indeed, Bob, you seem to know as much about coaches as Snarler does of Backgammon: I suppose you never see any thing in this quarter but the old heavy Bridgewater—why we have half a dozen new launches every week, and as great a variety of names, shape, size, and colour, as there are ships in the navy—we have the heavy coach, light coach, Caterpillar, and Mail—the Balloon, Comet, Fly, Dart, Regulator, Telegraph, Courier, Times, High-flyer, Hope, with as many others as would fill a list as long as my tandem-whip. What you now see is one of the *new patent safety-coaches*—you can't have an overturn if you're ever so disposed for a spree. The old city cormorants, after a gorge of mock-turtle, turn into them for a journey, and drop off in a nap, with as much confidence of security to their neck and limbs as if they had mounted a rocking-horse, or drop't into an arm-chair."— "Ah! come, the scene improves, and becomes a little like Life—here's a dasher making up to the Safety—why its—no, impossible—can't be—gad it is tho'—the Dart, by all that's good! and drove by Hellfire Dick!—there's a fellow would do honour to any box—drove the

Cambridge Fly three months—pass'd every thing on the road, and because he overturned in three or four hard matches, the stupid rascals of proprietors moved him off the ground. Joe Spinum, who's at Corpus Christi, matched Dick once for 50, when he carried five inside and thirteen at top, besides heavy luggage, against the other Cambridge—never was a prettier race seen at Newmarket—Dick must have beat hollow, but a d——d fat alderman who was inside, and felt alarmed at the velocity of the vehicle, moved to the other end of the seat: this destroyed the equilibrium—over they went, into a four-feet ditch, and Joe lost his match. However, he had the satisfaction of hearing afterwards, that the old cormorant who occasioned his loss, had nearly burst himself by the concussion."

"See, see!—Dick's got up to, and wants to give the Safety the go by—gad, its a race—go it Dick—now Safety—d——d good cattle both—lay it in to 'em Dick—leaders neck and neck—pretty race by G——! Ah, its of no use Safety—Dick wont stand it—a dead beat—there she goes—all up—over by Jove "——"I can't see for that tree—what do you say Tom, is the race over?"—"Race, ah! and the coach too—knew Dick would beat him—would have betted the long odds the moment I saw it was him."

The tandem had by this time reached the race-course, and the disaster which Tom had hardly thought worth noticing in his lively description of the sport, sure enough had befallen the *new 'patent Safety*, which was about mid way between an upright and a side position, supported by the high and very strong quicksett-hedge against which it hath fallen. Our heroes dismounted, left Flip at the leader's head, and with Ned, the other groom, proceeded to offer their services. Whilst engaged in extricating the horses, which had become entangled in their harness, and were kicking and plunging, their attention was arrested by the screams and outrageous vociferations of a very fat, middle-aged woman, who had been jerked from her seat on the box to one not quite so smooth—the top of the hedge, which, with the assistance of an old alder tree, supported the coach. Tom found it impossible to resist the violent impulse to risibility which the ludicrous appearance of the old lady excited, and as no serious injury was sustained, determined to enjoy the fun.

"If e'er a pleasant mischief sprang to view,
At once o'er hedge and ditch away he flew,
Nor left the game till he had run it down."

Approaching her with all the gravity of countenance he was master of—"Madam," says he, "are we to consider you as one of the Sylvan Deities who preside over these scenes, or connected in any way with the vehicle?"—"Wehicle, indeed, you *hunhuman-brutes*, instead of assisting a poor distressed female who has been chuck'd from top of that there *safety-thing*, as they calls it, into such a dangerous *pisition*, you must be chuckling and grinning, must you? I only wish my husband, Mr. Giblet, was here, he should soon wring your necks, and pluck some of your fine feathers for you, and make you look as foolish as a peacock without his tail." Mrs. Giblet's ire at length having subsided, she was handed down in safety on *terra firma*, and our heroes transferred their assistance to the other passengers. The violence of the concussion had burst open the coach-door on one side, and a London *Dandy*, of the exquisite genus, lay in danger of being pressed to a jelly beneath the weight of an infirm and very stout old farmer, whom they had pick'd up on the road; and it was impossible to get at, so as to afford relief to the sufferers, till the coach was raised in a perpendicular position. The farmer was no sooner on his legs, than clapping his hand with anxious concern into an immense large pocket, he discovered that a bottle of brandy it contained was crack'd, and the contents beginning to escape: "I ax pardon, young gentleman," says he, seizing a hat that the latter held with great care in his hand, and applying it to catch the liquor—"I ax pardon for making so free, but I see the hat is a little out of order, and can't be much hurt; and its a pity to waste the liquor, such a price as it is now-a-days."—"Sir, what do you mean, shouldn't have thought of your taking such liberties indeed, but makes good the old saying—impudence and ignorance go together: my hat out of order, hey! I'd have you to know, Sir, that *that there* hat was bought of Lloyd, in Newgate-street,{1} only last Thursday,-and cost eighteen shillings; and if you look at the book in his *vindow* on hats, dedicated to the head, you'll find that this here hat is a real exquisite; so much for what you know about hats, my old fellow—I burst my stays all to pieces in saving it from being squeezed out of shape, and now this old brute has made a brandy-bottle of it."—"Oh! oh! my young Miss in disguise," replied the farmer, "I thought I smelt a rat when the Captain left the coach, under pretence of walking up the hill—what, I suppose you are bound for Gretna, both of you, hey young Lady?"

Every thing appertaining to the coach being now righted, our young friends left the company to adjust their quarrels and pursue their journey at discretion, anxious to reach the next town as expeditiously as possible, where they purposed sleeping for the night. They mounted the tandem, smack went the whip, and in a few minutes the stage-coach and its motley group had disappeared.

Having reached their destination, and passed the night comfortably, they next morning determined to kill an hour or two in the town; and were taking a stroll arm in arm, when perceiving by a playbill, that an amateur of fashion from the theatres royal, Drury Lane and Haymarket, was just *come in*, and would shortly *come out*,

> *1 It would be injustice to great talents, not to notice, among other important discoveries and improvements of the age, the labours of Lloyd, who has classified and arranged whatever relates to that necessary article of personal elegance, the Hat. He has given the world a volume on the subject of Hats, dedicated to their great patron, the Head, in which all the endless varieties of shape, dependent before on mere whim and caprice, are reduced to fixed principles, and designated after the great characters by which each particular fashion was first introduced. The advantages to gentlemen residing in the country must be incalculable: they have only to refer to the engravings in Mr. Lloyd's work, where every possible variety is clearly defined, and to order such as may suit the rank or character in life they either possess, or wish to assume. The following enumeration comprises a few of the latest fashions: —The Wellington—The Regent—The Caroline—The Bashful—The Dandy—The Shallow—The Exquisite—The Marquis —The New Dash—The Clerieus—The Tally-ho—The Noble Lord— The Taedum—The Bang-up—The Irresistible—The Bon Ton—The Paris Beau—The Baronet—The Eccentric—The Bit of Blood, &c.*

in a favourite character, they immediately directed their steps towards a barn, with the hope of witnessing a rehearsal. Chance introduced them to the country manager, and Tom having asked several questions about this candidate, was assured by Mr. Mist:

"Oh! he is a gentleman-performer, and very useful to us managers, for he not only finds his own dresses and properties, but 'struts and frets his hour on the stage without any emoluments. His aversion to salary recommended him to the lessee of Drury-lane theatre, though his services had been previously rejected by the sub-committee."

"Can it be that game-cock, the gay Lothario," said Tom, "who sports an immensity of diamonds?"—

Of Coates's frolics he of course well knew, Rare pastime for the ragamuffin crew! Who welcome with the crowing of a cock, This hero of the buskin and sock.

"Oh! no," rejoined Mr. Mist, "that cock don't crow now: this gentleman, I assure you, has been at a theatrical school; he was instructed by the person who made Master Betty a young Roscius."

Tom shook his head, as if he doubted the abilities of this instructed actor. To be a performer, he thought as arduous as to be a poet; and if *poeta nascitur, non fit*—consequently an actor must have natural abilities.

"And pray what character did this gentleman enact at Drury-lane Theatre?"

"Hamlet, Prince of Denmark," answered Mr. Mist—"Shakespeare is his favourite author."

"And what said the critics—'to be, or not to be'—I suppose he repeated the character?"

"Oh! Sir, it was stated in the play-bill, that he met with great applause, and he was announced for the character again; but, as the Free List was not suspended, and our amateur dreaded some hostility from that quarter, he performed the character by proxy, and repeated it at the Little Theatre in the Haymarket."

"Then the gentlemen of the Free List," remarked Bob, "are free and easy?"

"Yes—yes—they laugh and cough whenever they please: indeed, they are generally excluded whenever a full house is expected, as *ready money* is an object to the poor manager of Drury-lane Theatre. The British Press, however, is always excepted."

"The British press!—Oh! you mean the newspapers," exclaimed Tom—"then I dare say they were very favourable to this Amateur of Fashion?"

"No—not very—indeed; they don't join the manager in his puffs, notwithstanding his marked civility to them: one said he was a methodist preacher, and sermonized the character—another assimilated him to a school-boy saying his lesson—in short, they were very ill-natured—but hush—here he is—walk in, gentlemen, and you shall hear him rehearse some of King Richard"—

"King Richard!" What ambition! thought Bob to himself—"late a Prince, and now—a king!"

"I assure you," continued Mr. Mist, "that all his readings are new; but according to my humble observation, his action does not always suit the word—for when he exclaims—' may Hell make crook'd my mind,' he looks up to Heaven"—

"Looks up to Heaven!" exclaimed Tom; "then this London star makes a solecism with his eyes."

Our heroes now went into the barn, and took a private corner, when they remained invisible. Their patience was soon exhausted, and Bob and his honourable cousin were both on the fidgits, when the representative of King Richard exclaimed—

"Give me a horse——"

"—Whip!" added Tom with stunning vociferation, before King Richard could bind up his wounds. The amateur started, and betrayed consummate embarrassment, as if the horsewhip had actually made its entrance. Tom and his companion stole away, and left the astounded monarch with the words—"twas all a dream."

While returning to the inn, our heroes mutually commented on the ambition and folly of those amateurs of fashion, who not only sacrifice time and property, but absolutely take abundant pains to render themselves ridiculous. "Certainly," says Tom, "this cacoethes ludendi has made fools of several: this infatuated youth though not possessed of a single requisite for the stage, no doubt flatters himself he is a second Kean; and, regardless of his birth and family, he will continue his strolling life

> *Till the broad shame comes staring in his face,*
> *And critics hoot the blockhead as he struts."*

Having now reached the inn, and finding every thing adjusted for their procedure, our heroes mounted their vehicle, and went in full gallop for Real Life in London.

CHAPTER III

"Round, round, and round-about, they whiz, they fly,
With eager worrying, whirling here and there,
They know, nor whence, nor whither, where, nor why.
In utter hurry-scurry, going, coming,
Maddening the summer air with ceaseless humming."

OUR travellers now approached at a rapid rate, the desideratim of their eager hopes and wishes: to one all was novel, wonderful, and fascinating; to the other, it was the welcome return to an old and beloved friend, the separation from whom had but increased the ardour of attachment.—"We, now," says Dashall, "are approaching Hyde-Park, and being Sunday, a scene will at once burst upon you, far surpassing in reality any thing I have been able to pourtray, notwithstanding the flattering compliments you have so often paid to my talents for description."

They had scarcely entered the Park-gate, when Lady Jane Townley's carriage crossed them, and Tom immediately approached it, to pay his respects to an old acquaintance. Her lady-ship congratulated him on his return to town, lamented the serious loss the *beau-monde* had sustained by his absence, and smiling archly at his young friend, was happy to find he had not returned empty-handed, but with a recruit, whose appearance promised a valuable accession to their select circle. "You would not have seen me here," continued her ladyship, "but I vow and protest it is utterly impossible to make a prisoner of one's self, such a day as this, merely because it is Sunday—for my own part, I wish there was no such thing as a Sunday in the whole year—there's no knowing what to do with one's self. When fine, it draws out as many insects as a hot sun and a shower of rain can produce in the middle of June. The vulgar plebeians flock so, that you can scarcely get into your barouche without being hustled by the men-milliners, linen-drapers, and shop-boys, who have been serving you all the previous part of the week; and wet, or dry, there's no bearing it. For my part, I am *ennuyée*, beyond measure, on that day, and find no little difficulty in getting through it without a fit of the horrors.

"What a legion of counter-coxcombs!" exclaimed she, as we passed Grosvenor-gate. "Upon the plunder of the till, or by overcharging some particular article sold on the previous day, it is easy for these *once-a-week* beaux to hire a tilbury, and an awkward groom in a pepper and salt, or drab coat, like the *incog.* of the royal family, to mix with their betters and sport their persons in the drive of fashion: some of the monsters, too, have the impudence of bowing to ladies whom they do not know, merely to give them an air, or pass off their customers for their acquaintance: its very distressing. There!" continued she, "there goes my plumassier, with gilt spurs like a field-officer, and riding as importantly as if he were one of the Lords of the Treasury; or—ah! there, again, is my banker's clerk, so stiff and so laced up, that he might pass for an Egyptian mummy—the self-importance of these puppies is insufferable! What impudence! he has picked up some groom out of place, with a cockade in his hat, by way of imposing on the world for a *beau militaire*. What will the world come to! I really have not common patience with these creatures. I have long since left off going to the play on a Saturday night, because, independently of my preference for the Opera, these insects from Cornhill or Whitechapel, shut up their shops, cheat their masters, and commence their airs of importance about nine o'clock. Then again you have the same party crowding the Park on a Sunday; but on the following day, return, like school boys, to their work, and you see them with their pen behind their ear, calculating how to make up for their late extravagances, pestering you with lies, and urging you to buy twice as much as you want, then officiously offering their arm at your carriage-door."

Capt. Bergamotte at this moment came up to the carriage, perfumed like a milliner, his colour much heightened by some vegetable dye, and resolved neither to "blush unseen," nor "waste his sweetness on the desert air." Two false teeth in front, shamed the others a little in their ivory polish, and his breath savoured of myrrh like a heathen sacrifice, or the incense burned in one of their temples. He thrust his horse's head into the carriage, rather abruptly and indecorously, (as one not accustomed to the haut-ton might suppose) but it gave no offence. He smiled affectedly, adjusted his hat, pulled a lock of hair across his forehead, with a view of shewing the whiteness of the latter, and next, that the glossiness of the former must have owed its lustre to at least two hours brushing, arranging, and perfuming; used his quizzing-glass, and took snuff with a flourish. Lady Townley condescended to caress the horse, and to display her lovely white arm ungloved, with which she patted the horse's neck, and drew a hundred admiring eyes.

The exquisite all this time brushed the animal gently with a highly-scented silk handkerchief, after which he displayed a cambric one, and went through a thousand little playful airs and affectations, which Bob thought would have suited a fine lady better than a lieutenant in his Majesty's brigade of guards. Applying the lines of an inimitable satire, (The Age of Frivolity) to the figure before him, he concluded:

> *"That gaudy dress and decorations gay,*
> *The tinsel-trappings of a vain array.*
> *The spruce trimm'd jacket, and the waving plume,*
> *The powder'd head emitting soft perfume;*
> *These may make fops, but never can impart*
> *The soldier's hardy frame, or daring heart;*
> *May in Hyde-Park present a splendid train,*
> *But are not weapons for a dread campaign;*
> *May please the fair, who like a tawdry beau,*
> *But are not fit to check an active foe;*
> *Such heroes may acquire sufficient skill*
> *To march erect, and labour through a drill;*
> *In some sham-fight may manfully hold out,*
> *But must not hope an enemy to rout."*

Although he talked a great deal, the whole amount of his discourse was to inform her Ladyship that (*Stilletto*) meaning his horse, (who in truth appeared to possess more fire and spirit than his rider could either boast of or command,) had cost him only 700 guineas, and was *prime blood*; that the horse his groom rode, was *nothing but a* good one, *and had run at the* Craven—that he had been prodigiously fortunate that season on the turf—that he was a bold rider, and could not bear himself without a fine high spirited animal—and, that being engaged to dine at three places that day, he was desperately at a loss to know how he should act; but that if her Ladyship dined at any one of the three, he would certainly join that party, and *cut* the other two.

At this moment, a mad-brained ruffian of quality, with a splendid equipage, came driving by with four in hand, and exclaimed as he flew past, in an affected tone,—"All! Tom, my dear fellow,—why where the devil have you hid yourself of late?" The speed of his cattle prevented the possibility of reply. "Although you see him in such excellent trim," observed Tom to Lady Jane, "though his cattle and equipage are so well appointed, would you suppose, it, he has but just made his appearance from the Bench after *white-washing?* But he is a noble spirited fellow," remarked the exquisite, "drives the best horses, and is one of the first whips in town; always gallant and gay, full of life and good humour; and, I am happy to say, he has now a dozen of as fine horses as any in Christendom, *bien entendu,* kept in my name." After this explanation of the characters of his friend and his horses, he kissed his hand to her Ladyship, and was out of sight in an instant, "Adieu, adieu, thou dear, delightful sprig of fashion!" said Lady Jane, as he left the side of the carriage.—"Fashion and folly," said Tom, half whispering, and recalling to his mind the following lines:—

> *"Oh! Fashion, to thy wiles, thy votaries owe*
> *Unnumber'd pangs of sharp domestic woe.*
> *What broken tradesmen and abandon'd wives*
> *Curse thy delusion through their wretched lives;*
> *What pale-faced spinsters vent on thee their rage,*
> *And youths decrepid e're they come of age."*

His moralizing reverie was however interrupted by her Ladyship, who perceiving a group of females decked in the extreme of Parisian fashions, "there," said she, "there is all that taffeta, feathers, flowers, and lace can do; and yet you see by their loud talking, their being unattended by a servant, and by the bit of straw adhering to the pettycoat of one of them, that they come all the way from Fish Street Hill, or the Borough, in a hackney-coach, and are now trying to play off the airs of women of fashion."

Mrs. Marvellous now drew up close to the party. "My dear Lady Jane," said she, "1 am positively suffocated with dust, and sickened with vulgarity; but to be sure we have every thing in London here, from the House of Peers to Waterloo House. I must tell you about the trial, and Lady Barbara's mortification, and about poor Mr. R.'s being arrested, and the midnight flight to the Continent of our poor friend W——."

With this brief, but at the same time comprehensive introduction, she lacerated the reputation of almost all her acquaintance, and excited great attention from the party, which had been joined by several during her truly interesting intelligence. Every other topic in a moment gave way to this delightful amusement, and each with volubility contributed his or her share to the general stock of slander.

Scandal is at all times the *sauce piquante* that *currys* incident in every situation; and where is the fashionable circle that can sit down to table without made dishes?—Character is the good old-fashioned roast beef of the table, which no one touches but to mangle and destroy.

> *"Lord! who'd have thought our cousin D*
> *Could think of marrying Mrs. E.*
> *True I don't like such things to tell;*
> *But, faith, I pity Mrs. L,*
> *And was I her, the bride to vex,*
> *I would engage with Mrs. X.*
> *But they do say that Charlotte U,*
> *With Fanny M, and we know who,*
> *Occasioned all, for you must know*
> *They set their caps at Mr. O.*
> *And as he courted Mrs. E,*
> *They thought, if she'd have cousin D,*
> *That things might be by Colonel A*
> *Just brought about in their own way."*

Our heroes now took leave, and proceeded through the Park. "Who is that fat, fair, and forty-looking dame, in the landau?" says Bob.— "Your description shews," rejoined his friend, "you are but a novice in the world of fashion—you are deceived, that lady is as much made up as a wax-doll. She has been such as she now appears to be for these last five and twenty years; her figure as you see, rather en-bon point, is friendly to the ravages of time, and every lineament of age is artfully filled up by an expert fille de chambre, whose time has been employed at the toilette of a celebrated devotee in Paris. She drives through the Park as a matter of course, merely to furnish an opportunity for saying that she has been there: but the more important business of the morning will be transacted at her boudoir, in the King's Road, where every luxury is provided to influence the senses; and where, by daily appointment, she is expected to meet a sturdy gallant. She is a perfect Messalina in her enjoyments; but her rank in society protects her from sustaining any injury by her sentimental wanderings.

"Do you see that tall handsome man on horseback, who has just taken off his hat to her, he is a knight of the ... ribbon; and a well-known flutterer among the ladies, as well as a vast composer of pretty little nothings."—"Indeed! and pray, cousin, do you see that lady of quality, just driving in at the gate in a superb yellow vis-à-vis,—as you seem to know every body, who is she?"

"Ha! ha! ha!" replied Tom, almost bursting with laughter, yet endeavouring to conceal it, "that Lady of Quality, as you are inclined to think her, a very few years since, was nothing more than a pot-girl to a publican in Marj'-le-bone; but an old debauchee (upon the look out for defenceless beauty) admiring the fineness of her form, the brilliancy of her eye, and the symmetry of her features, became the possessor of her person, and took her into keeping, as one of the indispensable appendages of fashionable life, after a month's ablution at Margate, where he gave her masters of every description. Her understanding was ready, and at his death, which happened, luckily for her, before satiety had extinguished appetite, she was left with an annuity of twelve hundred pounds—improved beauty—superficial accomplishments—and an immoderate share of caprice, insolence, and vanity. As a proof of this, I must tell you that at an elegant entertainment lately given by this dashing cyprian, she demolished a desert service of glass and china that cost five hundred guineas, in a fit of passionate ill-humour; and when her paramour intreated her to be more composed, she became indignant—called for her writing-desk in a rage—committed a settlement of four hundred a year, which he had made but a short time previously, to the flames, and asked him, with, a self-important air, whether he dared to suppose that *paltry* parchment gave him an authority to direct her actions?"

"And what said the lover to this severe remonstrance?"

"Say,—why he very sensibly made her a low bow, thanked her for her kindness, in releasing him from his bond, and took his leave of her, determined to return no more."

"Turn to the right," says Tom, "and yonder you will see on horseback, that staunch patriot, and friend of the people, Sir——, of whom you must have heard so much."

"He has just come out of the K——B——, having completed last week the term of imprisonment, to which he was sentenced for a libel on Government, contained in his address to his constituents on the subject of the memorable Manchester Meeting."

"Ah! indeed, and is that the red-hot patriot?—well, I must say I have often regretted he should have gone to such extremes in one or two instances, although I ever admired his general character for firmness, manly intrepidity, and disinterested conduct."

"You are right, Bob, perfectly right; but you know, 'to err is human, to forgive divine,' and however he may err, he does so from principle. In his private character, as father, husband, friend, and polished gentleman, he has very few equals—no superior.

"He is a branch of one of the most ancient families in the kingdom, and can trace his ancestors without interruption, from the days of William the Conqueror. His political career has been eventful, and perhaps has cost him more, both in pocket and person, than any Member of Parliament now existing. He took his seat in the House of Commons at an early age, and first rendered himself popular by his strenuous opposition to a bill purporting to regulate the publication of newspapers.

"The next object of his determined reprehension, was the Cold-Bath-Fields Prison, and the treatment of the unfortunates therein confined. The uniformly bold and energetic language made use of by the honourable Baronet upon that occasion, breathed the true spirit of British liberty. He reprobated the unconstitutional measure of erecting what he termed a *Bastile* in the very heart of a free country, as one that could neither have its foundation in national policy, nor eventually be productive of private good. He remarked that prisons, at which private punishments, cruel as they were illegal, were exercised, at the mercy of an unprincipled gaoler—cells in which human beings were exposed to the horrors of heart-sickening solitude, and depressed in spirit by their restriction to a scanty and exclusive allowance of bread and water, were not only incompatible with the spirit of the constitution, but were likely to prove injurious to the spirit of the people of this happy country; for as Goldsmith admirably remarks,

> "Princes and Lords may nourish or may fade,
> A breath can make them as a breath hath made,
> But a bold peasantry their country's pride,
> When once destroyed can never be supplied."

"*And if this be not tyranny*" continued the philanthropic orator, "*it is impossible to define the term. I promise you here* that I will persevere to the last in unmasking this wanton abuse of justice and humanity." His invincible fortitude in favour of the people, has rendered him a distinguished favourite among them: and though by some he is termed a visionary, an enthusiast, and a tool of party, his adherence to the rights of the subject, and his perseverance to uphold the principles of the constitution, are deserving the admiration of every Englishman; and although his fortune is princely, and has been at his command ever since an early age, he has never had his name registered among the fashionable gamesters at the clubs in St. James's-street, Newmarket, or elsewhere. He labours in the vineyard of utility rather than in the more luxuriant garden of folly; and, according to general conception, may emphatically be called an honest man. "But come," said Tom, "it is time for us to move homeward—the company are drawing off I see, we must shape our course towards Piccadilly."

They dashed through the Park, not however without being saluted by many of his fashionable friends, who rejoiced to see that the Honourable Tom Dashall was again to be numbered among the votaries of Real Life in London; while the young squire, whose visionary orbs appeared to be in perpetual motion, dazzled with the splendid equipages of the moving panorama, was absorbed in reflections somewhat similar to the following:

> *"No spot on earth to me is half so fair*
> *As Hyde-Park Corner, or St. James's Square;*
> *And Happiness has surely fix'd her seat*
> *In Palace Yard, Pall Mall, or Downing Street:*
> *Are hills, and dales, and valleys half so gay*
> *As bright St. James's on a levee day?*
> *What fierce ecstatic transports fire my soul,*
> *To hear the drivers swear, the coaches roll;*
> *The Courtier's compliment, the Ladies' clack,*
> *The satins rustle, and the whalebone crack!"*

CHAPTER IV

"Together let us beat this ample field
Try what the open, what the covert yield:
The latent tracts, the giddy heights explore
Of all who blindly creep, or sightless soar;
Eye nature's walks, shoot folly as it flies,
And catch the manners living as they rise."

IT was half past five when the Hon. Tom Dashall, and his enraptured cousin, reached the habitation of the former, who had taken care to dispatch a groom, apprizing Mrs. Watson, the housekeeper, of his intention to be at home by half past six to dinner; consequently all was prepared for their reception. The style of elegance in which Tom appeared to move, struck Tallyho at once with delight and astonishment, as they entered the drawing-room; which was superbly and tastefully fitted up, and commanded a cheerful view of Piccadilly. "Welcome, my dear Bob!" said Tom to his cousin, "to all the delights of Town—come, tell me what you think of its first appearance, only remember you commence your studies of Life in London on a dull day; to-morrow you will have more enlivening prospects before you." "'Why in truth," replied Bob, "the rapidity of attraction is such, as at present to leave no distinct impressions on my mind; all appears like enchantment, and I am completely bewildered in a labyrinth of wonders, to which there appears to be no end; but under your kind guidance and tuition I may prove myself an apt scholar, in unravelling its intricacies." By this time they had approached the window.

"Aye, aye," says Dashall, "we shall not be long, I see, without some object to exercise your mind upon, and dispel the horrors.

"Oh for that Muse of fire, whose burning pen
Records the God-like deeds of valiant men!
Then might our humble, yet aspiring verse,
Our matchless hero's matchless deeds rehearse."

Bob was surprised at this sudden exclamation of his cousin, and from the introduction naturally expected something extraordinary, though he looked around him without discovering his object.

"That," continued Tom, "is a Peer"—*pointing to a gig just turning the corner*, "of whom it may be said:*

> To many a jovial club that Peer was known,
> With whom his active wit unrivall'd shone,
> Choice spirit, grave freemason, buck and blood,
> Would crowd his stories and bon mots to hear,
> And none a disappointment e'er need fear
> His humour flow'd in such a copious flood."

"It is Lord C——, who was formerly well known as the celebrated Major H——, the companion of the now most distinguished personage in the British dominions! and who not long since became possessed of his lordly honours. Some particulars of him are worth knowing. He was early introduced into life, and often kept both good and bad company, associating with men and women of every description and of every rank, from the highest to the lowest—from St. James's to St. Giles's, in palaces and night-cellars—from the drawing-room to the dust-cart. He can drink, swear, tell stories, cudgel, box, and smoke with any one; having by his intercourse with society fitted himself for all companies. His education has been more practical than theoretical, though he was brought up at Eton, where, notwithstanding he made considerable progress in his studies, he took such an aversion to Greek that he never would learn it. Previous to his arrival at his present title, he used to be called Honest George, and so unalterable is his nature, that to this hour he likes it, and it fits him better than his title. But he has often been sadly put to his shifts under various circumstances: he was a courtier, but was too honest for that; he tried gaming, but he was too honest for that; he got into prison, and might have wiped off, but he was too honest for that; he got into the coal trade, but he found it a black business, and he was too honest for that. At drawing the long bow, so much perhaps cannot be said—but that you know is habit, not principle; his courage is undoubted, having fought three duels before he was twenty years of age.

Being disappointed in his hope of promotion in the army, he resolved, in spite of the remonstrances of his friends, to quit the guards, and solicited an appointment in one of the Hessian corps, at that time raising for the British service in America, where the war of the revolution was then commencing, and obtained from the Landgrave of Hesse a captain's commission in his corps of Jagers.

Previous to his departure for America, finding he had involved himself in difficulties by a profuse expenditure, too extensive for his income, and an indulgence in the pleasures of the turf to a very great extent, he felt himself under the necessity of mortgaging an estate of about 11,000L. per annum, left him by his aunt, and which proved unequal to the liquidation of his debts. He remained in America till the end of the war, where he distinguished himself for bravery, and suffered much with the yellow fever. On his return, he obtained an introduction to the Prince of Wales, who by that time had lanched into public life, and became one of the jovial characters whom he selected for his associates; and many are the amusing anecdotes related of him. The Prince conferred on him the appointment of equerry, with a salary of 300L. a year; this, however, he lost on the retrenchments that were afterwards made in the household of His Royal Highness. He continued, however, to be one of his constant companions, and while in his favour they were accustomed to practice strange vagaries. The Major was always a wag, ripe and ready for a *spree or a lark*.

> *"To him a frolic was a high delight,*
> *A frolic he would hunt for, day and night,*
> *Careless how prudence on the sport might frown."*

At one time, when the favourite's finances were rather low, and the *mopusses ran taper*, it was remarked among the 60 vivants of the party, that the Major had not for some time given them an invitation. This, however, he promised to do, and fixed the day—the Prince having engaged to make one. Upon this occasion he took lodgings in Tottenham-court Road—went to a wine-merchant—promised to introduce him to the royal presence, upon his engaging to find wine for the party, which was readily acceded to; and a dinner of three courses was served up. Three such courses, perhaps, were never before seen; when the company were seated, two large dishes appeared; one was placed at the top of the table, and one at the bottom; all was anxious expectation: the covers being removed, exhibited to view, a baked shoulder of mutton at top, and baked potatoes at the bottom. They all looked around with astonishment, but, knowing the general eccentricity of their host, they readily fell into his humour, and partook of his fare; not doubting but the second course would make ample amends for the first. The wine was good, and the Major apologized for his accommodations, being, as he said, a family sort of man, and the dinner, though somewhat uncommon, was not such an one as is described by Goldsmith:

> *"At the top, a fried liver and bacon were seen;*
> *At the bottom was tripe, in a swinging tureen;*
> *At the sides there were spinach and pudding made hot;*
> *In the middle a place where the pasty—was not."*

At length the second course appeared; when lo and behold, another baked shoulder of mutton and baked potatoes! Surprise followed surprise—but

> *"Another and another still succeeds."*

The third course consisted of the same fare, clearly proving that he had in his catering studied quantity more than variety; however, they enjoyed the joke, eat as much as they pleased, laughed heartily at the dinner, and after bumpering till a late hour, took their departure: it is said, however, that he introduced the wine-merchant to his Highness, who afterwards profited by his orders.{1}

> *1 This remarkable dinner reminds us of a laughable*
> *caricature which made its appearance some time ago upon the*
> *marriage of a Jew attorney, in Jewry-street, Aldgate, to the*
> *daughter of a well-known fishmonger, of St. Peter's-alley,*
> *Cornhill, when a certain Baronet, Alderman, Colonel, and*
> *then Lord Mayor, opened the ball at the London Tavern, as*
> *the partner of the bride; a circum-stance which excited*
> *considerable curiosity and surprise at the time. We know the*
> *worthy Baronet had been a hunter for a seat in Parliament,*
> *but what he could be hunting among the children of Israel*

is, perhaps, not so easily ascertained. We, however, are not speaking of the character, but the caricature, which represented the bride, not resting on Abraham's bosom, but seated on his knee, surrounded by their guests at the marriage-feast; while to a panel just behind them, appears to be affixed a bill of fare, which runs thus:

First course, Fish!

Second course, Fish!!

Third course, Fish!!!

Perhaps the idea of the artist originated in the anecdote above recorded.

It is reported that the Prince gave him a commission, under an express promise that when he could not shew it, he was no longer to enjoy his royal favour. This commission was afterwards lost by the improvident possessor, and going to call on the donor one morning, who espying him on his way, he threw up the sash and called out, "Well, George, commission or no commission?" "No commission, by G— —, your Highness?" was the reply.

"Then you cannot enter here," rejoined the prince, closing the window and the connection at the same time.

"His Lordship now resides in the Regent's Park, and may almost nightly be seen at a public-house in the neighbourhood, where he takes his grog and smokes his pipe, amusing the company around him with anecdotes of his former days; we may, perhaps, fall in with him some night in our travels, and you will find him a very amusing and sometimes very sensible sort of fellow, till he gets his grog on board, when he can be as boisterous and blustering as a coal-heaver or a bully. His present fortune is impaired by his former imprudence, but he still mingles with the sporting world, and a short time back had his pocket picked, at a *milling* match, of a valuable gold repeater. He has favoured the world with several literary productions, among which are Memoirs of his own Life, embellished with a view of the author, suspended from (to use the phrase of a late celebrated auctioneer) a *hanging wood*; and a very elaborate treatise on the Art of Rat-catching. In the advertisement of the latter work, the author engages it will enable the reader to "clear any house of these noxious vermin, however much infested, excepting only a certain great House in the neighbourhood of St. Stephen's, Westminster."{1}

> 1 *It appears by the newspapers, that the foundation of a certain great house in Pall Mall is rotten, and giving-way. The cause is not stated; but as it cannot arise from being top-heavy, we may presume that the rats have been at work there. Query, would not an early application of the Major's recipe have remedied the evil, and prevented the necessity of a removal of a very heavy body, which of course, must be attended with a very heavy expense? 'Tis a pity an old friend should have been overlooked on such an occasion.*

"Do you," said Tom, pointing to a person on the other side of the way, "see that young man, walking with a half-smothered air of indifference, affecting to whistle as he walks, and twirling his stick? He is a *once-a-week man*, or, in other words, a *Sunday promenader*—Harry Hairbrain was born of a good family, and, at the decease of his father, became possessed of ten thousand pounds, which he sported with more zeal than discretion, so much so, that having been introduced to the gaming table by a pretended friend, and fluctuated between poverty and affluence for four years, he found himself considerably in debt, and was compelled to seek refuge in an obscure lodging, somewhere in the neighbourhood of Kilburn, in order to avoid the *traps*; for, as he observes, he has been among the *Greeks and pigeons*, who have completely *rook'd* him, and now want to crow over him: he has been at hide and seek for the last two months, and, depending on the death of a rich old maiden aunt who has no other heir, he eventually hopes to *'diddle 'em.'*"

This narrative of Hairbrain was like Hebrew ta Tallyho, who requested his interesting cousin, as he found himself at *falt, to try back*, and put him on the *right scent*.

"Ha! ha! ha!" said Tom, "we must find a new London vocabulary, I see, before we shall be able to converse intelligibly; but as you are now solely under my tuition, I will endeavour to throw a little light upon the subject.

"Your *once-a-week man, or Sunday promenader*, is one who confines himself, to avoid confinement, lodging in remote quarters in the vicinity of the Metropolis, within a mile or two of the Bridges, Oxford Street, or Hyde-Park Corner, and is constrained to waste six uncomfortable and useless days in the week, in order to secure the enjoyment of the seventh, when he fearlessly ventures forth, to recruit his ideas—to give a little variety to the sombre picture of life, unmolested, to transact his business, or to call on some old friend, and keep up those relations with the world which would otherwise be completely neglected or broken.

"Among characters of this description, may frequently be recognised the remnant of fashion, and, perhaps, the impression of nobility not wholly destroyed by adversity and seclusion—the air and manners of a man who has outlived his century, with an assumption of *sans souci* pourtrayed in his agreeable smile, murmur'd through a low whistle of 'Begone dull care,' or 'No more by sorrow chased, my heart,' or played off by the flourishing of a whip, or the rapping of a boot that has a spur attached to it, which perhaps has not crossed a horse for many months; and occasionally by a judicious glance at another man's carriage, horses, or appointments, which indicates taste, and the former possession of such valuable things. These form a part of the votaries of Real Life in London. This however," said he (observing his cousin in mute attention) "is but a gloomy part of the scene; yet, perhaps, not altogether uninteresting or unprofitable."

"I can assure you," replied Tallyho, "I am delighted with the accurate knowledge you appear to have of society in general, while I regret the situation of the actors in scenes so glowingly described, and am only astonished at the appearance of such persons."

"You must not be astonished at appearances," rejoined Dashall, "for appearance is every thing in London; and I must particularly warn you not to found your judgment upon it. There is an old adage, which says 'To *be* poor, and *seem* poor, is the Devil all over.' Why, if you meet one of these *Sunday-men*, he will accost you with urbanity and affected cheerfulness, endeavouring to inspire you with an idea that he is one of the happiest of mortals; while, perhaps, the worm of sorrow is secretly gnawing his heart, and preying upon his constitution. Honourable sentiment, struggling with untoward circumstances, is destroying his vitals; not having the courage to pollute his character by a jail-delivery, or to condescend to *white-washing*, or some low bankrupt trick, to extricate himself from difficulty, in order to stand upright again.

"A *once-a-week man, or Sunday promenader*, frequently takes his way through bye streets and short cuts, through courts and alleys, as it were between retirement and a desire to see what is going on in the scenes of his former splendour, to take a sly peep at that world from which he seems to be excluded."

"And for all such men," replied Bob, "expelled from high and from good society, (even though I were compelled to allow by their own imprudence and folly) I should always like to have a spare hundred, to send them in an anonymous cover."

"You are right," rejoined Tom, catching him ardently by the hand, "the sentiment does honour to your head and heart; for to such men, in general, is attached a heart-broken wife, withering by their side in the shade, as the leaves and the blossom cling together at all seasons, in sickness or in health, in affluence or in poverty, until the storm beats too roughly on them, and prematurely destroys the weakest. But I must warn you not to let your liberality get the better of your discretion, for there are active and artful spirits abroad, and even these necessities and miseries are made a handle for deception, to entrap the unwary; and you yet have much to learn—Puff lived two years on sickness and misfortune, by advertisements in the newspapers."

"How?" enquired Bob.

"You shall have it in his own words," said Dashall.

> *"I suppose never man went through such a series of*
> *"calamities in the same space of time! Sir, I was five*

"times made a bankrupt and reduced from a state of
"affluence, by a train of unavoidable misfortunes! then
"Sir, though a very industrious tradesman, I was twice
"burnt out, and lost my little all both times! I lived
"upon those fires a month. I soon after was confined by a
"most excruciating disorder, and lost the use of my limbs!
"That told very well; for I had the case strongly attested,
"and went about col—called on you, a close prisoner
"in the Marshalsea, for a debt benevolently contracted
"to serve a friend. I was afterwards twice tapped
"for a dropsy, which declined into a very profitable
"consumption! I was then reduced to—0—no—then,
"I became a widow with six helpless children—after
"having had eleven husbands pressed, and being left
"every time eight months gone with child, and without
"money to get me into an hospital!"

"Astonishing!" cried Bob, "and are such things possible?"

"A month's residence in the metropolis," said Dashall, "will satisfy your enquiries. One ingenious villain, a short time back, had artifice enough to defraud the public, at different periods of his life, of upwards of one hundred thousand pounds, and actually carried on his fraudulent schemes to the last moment of his existence, for he defrauded Jack Ketch of his fee by hanging himself in his cell after condemnation."{1}

Just as a tilbury was passing, "Observe," said Tom, "the driver of that tilbury is the celebrated Lord Cripplegate with his usual equipage—his blue cloak with a scarlet lining, hanging loosely over the vehicle, gives an air of importance to his appearance, and he is always attended by that boy, who has been denominated his cupid; he is a nobleman by birth, a gentleman by courtesy, and a gamester by profession. He exhausted a large estate upon *odd and even, sevens the main*, &c. till having lost sight of the *main chance*, he found it necessary to curtail his establishment and enliven his prospects, by exchanging a first floor for a second, without an opportunity of ascertaining whether or not these alterations were best suited to his high notions or exalted taste; from which in a short time he was induced, either by inclination or necessity, to take a small lodging in an obscure street, and to sport a gig and one horse, instead of a curricle and pair; though in former times he used to drive four in hand, and was acknowledged to be an excellent whip. He still, however, possessed money enough to collect together a large quantity of halfpence, which in his hours of relaxation he managed to turn to good account, by the following stratagem:—He distributed his halfpence on the floor of his little parlour in straight lines, and ascertained how many it would require to cover it; having thus prepared himself, he invited some wealthy spendthrifts (with whom he still had the power of associating) to sup with him, and he welcomed them to his habitation with much cordiality. The glass circulated freely, and each recounted his gaming or amorous adventures till a late hour, when the effects of the bottle becoming visible, he proposed, as a momentary suggestion, to name how many halfpence laid side by side would carpet the floor; and offered to lay a large

> 1 Charles Price, the well-known impostor, whose extensive
> forgeries on the Bank of England rendered him notorious, may
> serve as a practical illustration of Puff, for he, at
> several periods of his life, carried on his system of fraud
> by advertisements, and by personating the character of a
> clergyman collecting subscriptions under various pretences.
> His whole life is marked with determined and systematic
> depravity. He hanged himself in Tothil-fields Bridewell,
> where he was confined, at the age of fifty-five.

wager, that he would guess the nearest. Done! done! was echoed round the room. Every one made a deposit of 100L. and every one made a guess equally certain of success; and his lordship declaring he had a large lot of halfpence by him, though, perhaps, not enough, the experiment was to be tried immediately—'twas an excellent hit! The room was cleared, to it they went, the halfpence were arranged rank and file in military order, when it appeared that his lordship had certainly guessed (as well he might) nearest to the number: the consequence was, an immediate alteration of his lordship's residence and appearance: he got one step in the world by it, he gave up his second-hand gig for one warranted new; and a change in his vehicle may pretty generally be considered as the barometer of his pocket.

"Do you mark, he is learing at that pretty girl on the other side of the way? he is fond of the wenches, and has been a true votary of fashion. Perhaps there is not a more perfect model of Real Life in London than might be furnished from the memoirs of his lordship! He is rather a good looking man, as he sits, and prides himself on being a striking likeness of his present majesty; but, unfortunately, has a lameness which impedes him in the ardour of his pursuit of game, although it must be acknowledged he has been a game one in his time. The boy you see with him is reported to be his own son, who is now employed by him as an assistant in all his amorous adventures."

"His own son!" exclaimed Bob.

"Aye, and (if so) a merrily begotten one, I'll be bound for it," continued Tom; "such things will happen, and his lordship has kept a very pretty assortment of servant girls. But the introduction of this youth to public notice was somewhat curious. It is said, that having a large party of *bon vivants* to dine with him, on sitting down to table, and taking the cover off one of the dishes, a plump and smiling infant appeared. A sweet little *Cupid* by

— —! (exclaimed his lordship) I'll be his father!—I'll

take care of him!—call Rose, and tell her to look out for a nurse for him. Thus taking upon himself the character of parent and protector as well as parson. Young *Cupid* was christened in libations of claret, and furnished a fund of amusement for the evening. How young Cupid came there, I believe has not yet been satisfactorily ascertained:

> *Who seeks a friend, should come disposed*
> *T' exhibit, in full bloom disclosed,*
> *The graces and the beauties*
> *That form the character he seeks;*
> *For 'tis an union that bespeaks*
> *Reciprocated duties.*

And thus it has proved with *Cupid*, himself the offspring of an illicit amour, is now constantly engaged in promoting others.

"His lordship had three brothers, *Billingsgate! Hellgate!* and *Newgate!* whose names are adorned with a similarity of perfections in the Temple of Fame; but they are consigned to the tomb of the Capulets, and we will not rake up the ashes of the dead."{1}

At this moment a loud knocking was heard at the door, and Mr. Sparkle was ushered into the drawing-room, which he entered, as it were, with a hop, step, and jump, and had Tom Dashall by the hand almost before they could turn round to see who it was.

"My dear fellow!" exclaimed Sparkle, almost out of breath, "where have you been to? Time has been standing still since your departure!—there has been a complete void in nature—how do you do?—I beg pardon, (turning to Bob) you will excuse my rapture at meeting my old friend, whom I have lost so long, that I have almost lost myself—egad, I have run myself out of breath—cursed unlucky I was not in the Park this morning to see you first, but I have just heard all about you from Lady Jane, and lost no time in paying my respects—what are you going to do with yourself?"

> 1 *There was a delicate propriety in this conduct of the Hon. Tom Dashall which cannot but be admired; for although they were alone, and speaking to each other in perfect confidence, it was always his desire to avoid as much as possible making bad worse; he had a heart to feel, as well as a head to think; and would rather lend a hand to raise a fellow-creature from the mud than walk deliberately over him; besides, he foresaw other opportunities would arise in which, from circumstances, he would almost be compelled to draw his Cousin's attention again to the persons in question, and he was always unwilling to ex-haust a subject of an interesting nature without sonic leading occurrence to warrant it.*

At this moment dinner was announced. "Come," said Tom, "let us refresh a bit, and after dinner I will tell you all about it. We are travellers, you know, and feel a little fatigued. *Allons, allons.*" And so saying, he led the way to the dinner-room.

"Nothing could be more *apropos*," said Sparkle, "for although I have two engagements beforehand, and have promised a visit to you know who in the evening, they appear like icicles that must melt before the sun of your re-appearance: so I am your's." And to it they went. Tom always kept a liberal table, and gave his friends a hearty welcome. But here it will be necessary, while they are regaling themselves, to make our readers a little acquainted with Charles Sparkle, Esq.; for which purpose we must request his patience till the next chapter.

CHAPTER V

"Place me, thou great Supreme, in that blest state,
Unknown to those the silly world call Great,
Where all my wants may be with ease supply'd,
Yet nought superfluous to pamper pride."

IT will be seen in the previous chapter, that the formal ceremony of a fashionable introduction, such as—"Mr. Sparkle, my friend Mr. Robert Tallyho, of Belville Hall; Mr. Tallyho, Mr. Charles Sparkle," was altogether omitted; indeed, the abrupt entrance of the latter rendered it utterly impossible, for although Sparkle was really a well-bred man, he had heard from Lady Jane of Tom's arrival with his young friend from the country. *Etiquette* between themselves, was at all times completely unnecessary, an air of gaiety and freedom, as the friend of Dashall, was introduction enough to Bob, and consequently this point of good breeding was wholly unnoticed by all the party; but we are not yet sufficiently acquainted with our readers to expect a similar mode of proceeding will be overlooked; we shall therefore lose no time in giving our promised account of Mr. Sparkle, and beg to introduce him accordingly.

Mr. Reader, Mr. Sparkle; Mr. Sparkle, Mr. Reader.

Hold, Sir, what are you about? You have bewildered yourself with etiquette, and seem to know as little about *Life in London* as the novice you have already introduced—By the way, that introduction was one of the most extraordinary I ever met with; this may be equally so for ought I know; and I really begin to suspect you are an extraordinary fellow yourself. How can you introduce me, of whom you know nothing?

Egad, I believe you have me there—"a palpable hit, my Lord," (or my Lady, for I certainly cannot say which;) I was getting myself into an awkward dilemma, but I hate suspicion—

"Suspicion ever haunts the guilty mind."

Methinks I see a frown, but I meant no offence, and if you throw down my book in a rage, you will perhaps not only remain ignorant of Mr. Sparkle, but, what is more important, of those other numerous fashionable characters in high and low life—of those manners—incidents—amusements—follies—vices, &c. which, combined together, form the true picture of Real Life in the Metropolis.

> *"He who hath trod th' intricate maze,*
> *Exploring every devious way,*
> *Can best direct th' enquiring gaze,*
> *And all the varied scenes display."*

Mr. Author, you are a strange rambler.

Admitted, Sir, or Ma'am, I am a rambler, who, with your permission, would willingly not be impeded in my progress, and under such expectations I shall proceed.

Charles Sparkle was the son and only child of a Right Hon. Member of Parliament, now no more, whose mother dying soon after his birth, was left destitute of that maternal kindness and solicitude which frequently has so much influence in forming the character of the future man.

His father, a man of eccentric turn of mind, being appointed soon afterwards to a diplomatic situation abroad, left the care of his son's education to an elderly friend of his, who held a situation of some importance under the then existing government, with an injunction to conceal from the boy the knowledge of his real parent, and to bring him up as his own child.

This important trust was executed with tenderness and fidelity; the boy grew in strength, and ripened in intelligence, and being accustomed to consider his protector as his parent, the father, upon returning to England, determined not to undeceive him, until he should arrive at years of discretion; and with this view Mr. Orford was instructed at a proper age to send him to Oxford.

Charles, however had contracted before this period, habits and acquaintances in London, that were completely in opposition to the dictates and inclinations of his supposed father. He became passionately fond of literary amusements, music, and drawing, which served to occupy his morning hours: but his evenings were devoted to the company of vitiated associates, who did not fail to exercise their influence over his youthful passions, and he frequently engaged himself in unlucky and improvident adventures, which involved him in pecuniary difficulties far beyond his stipulated income. These circumstances were no sooner made known to the supposed parent, than they excited his displeasure, and being carried to an unpardonable extent, he was, at the age of eighteen, literally banished the house of his protector, and compelled to take an obscure lodging in the vicinity of London; the rent of which was paid for him, and a scanty allowance of one guinea sent to him regularly every Saturday night. Thus secluded from his old associates, it will not be wondered at that he contrived to form new ones, and having purchased an old harpsicord, turned the musical instruction he had received to occasional account; he also wrote some political pamphlets which were well received. But this solitary and dependent life was wholly unsuited to the gaiety in which he had hitherto moved. It had, however, the effect of drawing forth talent, which perhaps would never, but for this circumstance, have been discovered; for

> *"Many a gem, of purest ray serene,*
> *The dark unfathom'd caves of ocean bear;*
> *Full many a flower is born to blush unseen,*
> *And waste its sweetness on the desert air."*

His writings, &c. under the name of Oribrd, were recognised by the real father, as the productions of a promising son: at his instigation, and upon a promise of reform, he was again restored to his former home, and shortly after entered as a gentleman commoner of St. Mary's, Oxford; but not till he had, by some means or other, made the discovery that Orford was not his real name. Congenial spirits are naturally fond of associating, and it was here that he first became acquainted with the Hon. Tom Dashall: they were constant companions and mutual assistants to each other, in all their exercises as well as all their vagaries; so as to cement a friendship and interest in each other's fate, up to the moment of which we are now speaking.

Orford, however, was at that time more impetuous and less discreet in the pursuit of his pleasures than his honourable friend, and after obtaining the distinction of Bachelor of Arts, was in consequence of his imprudence and irregularities, after frequently hair-breadth escapes, expelled the college. This circumstance, however, appeared of little consequence to him. He hired a gig at Oxford, promising to return in a few days, and came up to London, but had not effrontery enough to venture into the presence of his reputed father. On arrival in town, he put up at an inn in the Borough, where he resided till all the money he had was exhausted, and till, as he emphatically observes, he had actually eaten his horse and chaise.

In the mean time, the people at Oxford found he was expelled; and as he had not returned according to appointment, he was pursued, and eventually found: they had no doubt of obtaining their demand from his friends, and he was arrested at the suit of the lender; which was immediately followed by a retainer from the inn-keeper where he had resided in town. Application was made to Mr. Orford for his liberation, without effect; in consequence of which he became a resident in the rules of the King's Bench, as his friends conceived by this means his habits would be corrected and his future conduct be amended, his real father still keeping in the back ground.

While in this confinement, he again resorted to the produce of his pen and his talent for musical composition, and his friend Tom, at the first vacation, did not fail to visit him. During this time, in the shape of donation, from Mr. Orford he received occasional supplies more than equal to his necessities, though not to his wishes. While here, he fished out some further clue to the real parent, who visited him in disguise during his confinement as a friend of Mr. Orford: still, however, he had no chance of liberation, till, being one day called on by Mr. Orford, he was informed he was at perfect liberty to leave his present abode, and was directed to go with him immediately; a coach was called, and he heard the direction given to drive to Bedford Square, where they arrived just time enough to learn that the Right Hon. S. S. had breathed his last, after a lingering illness.

Upon alighting from the coach, and receiving this information, they were ushered into the drawing-room, and presently joined by a clergyman who had been the chaplain of the deceased, who acquainted our adventurer of the death of his parent—that by will he was entitled to 10,000L. per annum, and a handsome estate in Wiltshire. This sudden reverse of fortune to Sparkle—the change from confinement to liberty, from indigence to affluence—awakened sensations more easily to be conceived than described. He wept, (perhaps the first tears of sincerity in his life;) his heart was subdued by an overwhelming flood of affection for that unknown being, whom he now found had been his constant guardian angel, alternately taking Orford and the reverend Divine by the hand, and hiding his head in the bosom of his reputed father. At length they led him to the room in which were the remains of his lamented parent.

There are perhaps few circumstances better calculated to impress awe on the youthful mind than the contemplation of those features in death which have been respected and revered while living. Such respect had ever been entertained by Charles Sparkle for the supposed friend of Mr. Orford, from whom he had several times received the most kind and affectionate advice; and his sensations upon discovering that friend to be no other than his own father, may be more easily conceived than described—he was at once exalted and humbled, delighted and afflicted. He threw himself in an agony of feeling by the bed-side, fell on his knees, in which he was joined by the clergyman and Orford, where he remained some time.

After the first paroxysms of grief had subsided, young Sparkle, who had already felt the strongest impression that could possibly be made on a naturally good heart, gave orders for the funeral of his deceased father, and then proceeded to make other arrangements suitable to the character he was hereafter to sustain through life, went down to Wiltshire, and took possession of his estate, where for a time he secluded himself, and devoted his attention to the perusal of the best authors in the English, French, and Italian language, under the superintendence of the reverend Divine, who had been a resident for many years with his father.

But a life in the country could not long have superior charms for a young man who had already seen much to admire, as well as much to avoid, in the metropolis. The combination however of theoretical information he had derived from books, as well as the practical observations he had made during his residence in London, fitted him at once for the gayest and most distinguished circles of metropolitan society. He therefore arranged with Mr. Orford, who had formerly acted as his parent, to continue with him in the capacity of steward, and for the last two years of his life had been almost a constant resident at "Long's Hotel", in Bond Street, not choosing to have the charge of an establishment in town; and the early friendship and attachment which had been cultivated at Oxford being again renewed, appeared to grow with their growth, and strengthen with their strength.

Sparkle had still a large portion of that vivacity for which he was so remarkable in his younger days. His motives and intentions were at all times good, and if he indulged himself in the pursuits of frolic and fun, it was never at the expence of creating an unpleasant feeling to an honest or honourable mind. His fortune was ample. He had a hand to give, and a heart to forgive; no "malice or hatred were there to be found:" but of these qualifications, and the exercise of them, sufficient traits will be given in the ensuing pages. No man was better *up* to the rigs of the town; no one better *down* to the manoeuvres of the *flats*, and *sharps*. He had mingled with life in all companies; he was at once an elegant and interesting companion; his views were extensive upon all subjects; his conversation lively, and his manners polished.

Such, gentle reader, is the brief sketch of Charles Sparkle, the esteemed friend of the Hon. Tom Dashall, and with such recommendations it will not be wondered at if he should become also the friend of Tally-ho; for, although living in the height of fashionable splendour, his mind was at all times in consonance with the lines which precede this chapter; yet none could be more ready to lend a hand in any pleasant party in pursuit of a bit of *gig. A mill at Moulsey Hurst—a badger-bait, or bear-bait—a main at the Cock-pit—a smock-race—*or a scamper to the Tipping hunt, ultimately claimed his attention; while upon all occasions he was an acute observer of life and character.

> *"His years but young, but his experience old,*
> *His heart unmellow'd, though his judgment ripe,*
> *And in a word, (for far behind his worth*
> *Come all the praises that we now bestow)*
> *He is complete in conduct and in mind,*
> *With all good grace, to grace a gentleman."*

But dinner is over, and we must now accompany our triumvirate to the drawing-room, where we find them seated with bottles, glasses, &c. determined to make a quiet evening after the fatigues of the journey, and with a view to prepare themselves for the more arduous, and to Tally-ho more interesting, pursuits in the new world, for such he almost considered London.

"Yes," said Sparkle, addressing himself to Bob, with whom a little previous conversation had almost rendered him familiar, "London is a world within itself; it is, indeed, the only place to see life—it is the "*multum in parvo,*" as the old song says,

> *"Would you see the world in little,*
> *Ye curious here repair;"*

it is the acmé of perfection, the "*summum bonum*" of style—indeed, there is a certain affectation of style from the highest to the lowest individual."

"You are a merry and stylish fellow," said Tom; we should have been hipp'd without you, there is a fund of amusement in you at all times."

"You are a bit of a wag," replied Sparkle, "but I am up to your gossip, and can serve you out in your own style."

"Every body," says Tallyho, "appears to live in style."

"Yes," continued Sparkle, "*living in style* is one of the most essential requisites for a residence in London; but I'll give you my idea of living in style, which, by many, is literally nothing more than keeping up appearances at other people's expence: for instance, a Duchess conceives it to consist in taking her breakfast at three o'clock in the afternoon—dining at eight—playing at Faro till four the next morning—supping at five, and going to bed at six—and to eat green peas and peaches in January—in making a half-curtsey at the creed, and a whole one to a scoundrel—in giving fifty guineas to an exotic capon for a pit-ticket—and treating the deserved claims of a parental actor with contempt—to lisp for the mere purpose of appearing singular, and to seem completely ignorant of the Mosaic law—to be in the reverse of extremes—to laugh when she could weep, and weep when she could .dance and be merry—to leave her compliment cards with her acquaintance, whom at the same moment she wishes she may never see again—to speak of the community with marked disrespect, and to consider the sacrament a bore!"

"Admirable!" said Tom.

"Wonderful, indeed!" exclaimed Tallyho.

"Aye, aye, London is full of wonders—there is a general and insatiate appetite for the marvellous; but let us proceed: Now we'll take the reverse of the picture. The Duke thinks he does things in style, by paying his debts of honour contracted at the gaming-table, and but very few honourable debts—by being harsh and severe to a private supplicant, while he is publicly a liberal subscriber to a person he never saw—by leaving his vis-a-vis at the door of a well-known courtesan, in order to have the credit of an intrigue—in making use of an optical glass for personal inspection, though he can ascertain the horizon without any—by being or seeming to be, every thing that is in opposition to nature and virtue—in counting the lines in the Red Book, and carefully watching the importation of *figurantes* from the Continent—in roundly declaring that a man of fashion is a being of a superior order, and ought to be amenable only to himself—in jumbling ethics and physics together, so as to make them destroy each other—in walking arm in arm with a sneering jockey—talking loudly any thing but sense—and in burning long letters without once looking at their contents;... and so much for my Lord Duke."

"Go along Bob!" exclaimed Tom.

Tallyho conceiving himself addressed by this, looked up with an air of surprise and enquiry, which excited the risibility of Dashall and Sparkle, till it was explained to him as a common phrase in London, with which he would soon become more familiar. Sparkle continued.

"The gay young Peerling, who is scarcely entitled to the honours and immunities of manhood, is satisfied he is *doing things in style*, by raising large sums of money on *post-obit* bonds, at the very moderate premium of 40 per cent.—in *queering* the clergyman at his father's table, and leaving the marks of his finger and thumb on the article of matrimony in his aunt's prayer-book—in kicking up a row at the theatre, when he knows he has some roaring bullies at his elbow, though humble and dastardly when alone—in keeping a dashing *impure*, who publicly squanders away his money, and privately laughs at his follies—in buying a phaeton as high as a two pair of stairs window, and a dozen of spanking bays at Tattersall's, and in dashing through St. James's Street, Pall Mall, Piccadilly, and Hyde Park, thus accompanied and accoutred, amidst the contumelies of the coxcombs and the sighs of the worthy. And these are pictures of high life, of which the originals are to be seen daily.

"The haberdasher of Cheapside, whose father, by adherence to the most rigid economy, had amassed a competence, and who transmitted his property, without his prudence, to his darling son, is determined to shew his spirit, by buying a *bit of blood*, keeping his gig, his girl, and a thatched cottage on the skirts of Epping Forest, or Sydenham Common; but as keeping a girl and a gig would be a nothing unless all the world were *up to it*, he regularly drives her to all the boxing-matches, the Epping hunt, and all the races at Barnet, Epsom, Egham, and Ascot Heath, where he places himself in one of the most conspicuous situations; and as he knows his racing, &c. must eventually distinguish his name in the Gazette with a whereas! he rejoices in the progress and acceleration of his own ruin, and, placing his arms akimbo, he laughs, sings, swears, swaggers, and vociferates—'What d'ye think o' that now,—is'nt this doing it in stile, eh?'

"Prime of life to go it, where's a place like London? Four in hand to-day, the next you may be undone."

Real Life in London - Volume I

EPSOM RACES, Shewing Bob how to drive a Tandem.

"Well, Sir, the mercer's wife, from Watling Street, thinks living in style is evinced by going once a year to a masquerade at the new Museodeum, or Argyle Rooms; having her daughters taught French, dancing, and music—dancing a minuet at Prewterers' Hall, or Mr. Wilson's{1} annual benefit—in getting a good situation in the green boxes—going to Hampstead or Copenhagen House in a glass coach on a Sunday—having card-parties at home

> 1 Mr. Wilson's flaming bills of "Dancing at the Old Bailey," which are so profusely stuck up about the city, are said to have occasioned several awkward jokes and blunders; among others related, is that of a great unintellectual Yorkshire booby, who, after staring at the bills with his mouth open, and his saucer eyes nearly starting out of his head with astonishment, exclaimed, "Dang the buttons on't, I zee'd urn dangling all of a row last Wednesday at t' Ould Bailey, but didn't know as how they call'd that danzing,—by gum there be no understanding these here Lunnun folk!"

during Lent, declaring she never drinks any thing else but the *most bestest* gunpowder tea, that she has a most *screwciating* cold, and that the country air is always *salubrus*, and sure to do her good.

"So much for living in style, and good breeding."

> "That's your true breeding—that's your sort my boys—
> Fun, fire, and pathos—metre, mirth, and noise;
> To make you die with laughter, or the hiccups,
> Tickle your favourites, or smash your tea-cups."

"By the way, in former times the term *good-breeding* meant a combination of all that was amiable and excellent; and a well-bred person would shrink from an action or expression that could possibly wound the feelings of another; its foundation was laid in truth, and its supporting pillars were justice and integrity, sensibility and philanthropy; but

> "In this gay age—in Taste's enlighten'd times,
> When Fashion sanctifies the basest crimes;
> E'en not to swear and game were impolite,

Since he who sins in style must sure be right."

A well-bred person must learn to smile when he is angry, and to laugh even when he is vexed to the very soul.

"It would be the height of *mauvaise honte* for a wellbred person to blush upon any occasions whatever; no young lady blushes after eleven years of age; to study the expression of the countenance of others, in order to govern your own, is indispensably necessary.

"In former times, no well-bred person would have uttered a falsehood; but now such ideas are completely exploded, and such conduct would now be termed a *bore*. My Lord Portly remarks, 'It is a cold day.' 'Yes, my Lord, it is a very cold day,' replies Major Punt. In two minutes after, meeting Lord Lounge, who observes he thinks the weather very warm—'Yes, very warm, my Lord,' is the reply—thus contradicting himself almost in the same breath. It would be perfectly inconsistent in a well-bred man to think, for fear of being absent. When he enters or leaves a drawing-room, he should round his shoulders, drop his head, and imitate a clown or a coachman. This has the effect of the best *ruse de guerre*—for it serves to astonish the ladies, when they afterwards discover, by the familiarity of his address, and his unrestrained manners, what a well-bred man he is; for he will address every fair one in the room in the most enchanting terms, except her to whom in the same party he had previously paid the most particular attention; and on her he will contrive to turn his back for the whole evening, and if he is a man of fashion, he will thus cause triumph to the other ladies, and save the neglected fair one from envious and slanderous whisperings."

"An admirable picture of living in style, and good breeding, indeed!" cried Tom. "The game is in view and well worth pursuit; so hark forward! hark forward! my boys."

Sparkle, now recollecting his engagement—with "you know who" as he significantly observed in the last Chapter, withdrew, after promising to take a stroll by way of killing an hour or two with them in the morning; and Tom and his Cousin soon after retired to rest—

"Perchance to sleep, perchance to dream."

CHAPTER VI

"The alarm was so strong.
So loud and so long,
'Twas surely some robber, or sprite,
Who without any doubt
Was prowling about
To fill ev'ry heart with affright."

THE smiles of a May morning, bedecked with the splendid rays of a rising sun, awakened Tallyho about five o'clock, and being accustomed to rise early in the country, he left the downy couch of soft repose, and sought his way down stairs. Not a sound of any kind was to be heard in the house, but the rattling of the carts and the coaches in the streets, with the deep-toned accompaniment of a dustman's bell, and an occasional *ab libitum* of "Clothes—clothes sale," gave Bob an idea that all the world was moving. However he could find nobody up; he walked into the drawing-room, amused himself for some time by looking out of the window, indulging his observations and remarks, without knowing what to make of the moving mass of incongruities which met his eye, and wondering what time the servants of the house would wake: he tried the street-door, but found it locked, bolted, and chained; and if he had known where to have found his friend Tom, he would have aroused him with *the View halloo.*

"It is strange," thought he to himself, "all the world seems abroad, and yet not a soul stirring here!" Then checking the current of his reflections, "But this," said he, "is Life in London. Egad! I must not make a noise, because it will not be *good breeding.*" In this wray he sauntered about the house for near two hours, till at last espying his portmanteau, which had been left in the passage by the servants the previous evening—"I'll carry this up stairs," said he, "by way of amusement;" and carelessly shouldering the portmanteau, he was walking deliberately up stairs, when his ears were suddenly attracted by a loud cry of "Murder, murder, thieves, murder!" and the violent ringing of a bell. Alarmed at these extraordinary sounds, which appeared to be near him at a moment when he conceived no soul was stirring, he dropped his portmanteau over the banisters, which fell, (demolishing in its way an elegant Grecian patent lamp with glass shades, drops, &c.) into the passage below with a hideous crash, while the cry of Murder, thieves, murder, was repeated by many voices, and rendered him almost immoveable. In the next moment, the butler, the cook, the groom, and indeed every person in the house, appeared on the stair-case, some almost in a state of nudity, and shrinking from each other's gaze, and all armed with such weapons as chance had thrown in their way, to attack the supposed depredator.

Among the rest, fortunately for Tallyho, (who stood balancing himself against the banisters in a state of indecision whether he should ascend or descend) Tom Dashall in his night-gown burst out of his room in alarm at the noise, with a brace of pistols, one in his hand in the very act of cocking it, and the other placed in convenient readiness under his left arm. "Why, what the devil is the matter?" vociferated he, and at that moment his eye caught the agitated figure of his Cousin Bob, on the half-landing place below him. At the sound of his well-known voice, the innocent and unsuspecting cause of this confusion and alarm looked up at his friend, as if half afraid and half ashamed of the occurrence, and stammered out, "Where is the thief?—Who is murdered?—I'll swear there is something broke somewhere—tell me which way to go!" Tom looked around him at the group of half-clad nymphs and swains, (who were now huddling together, conceiving their security lay in combination, and finding all eyes were placed with astonishment and wonder on Bob) began to see through what had happened, and burst into an immoderate fit of laughter; which relieved the frightened damsels, but so confounded poor Tallyho, that he scarcely knew whether he was standing on his head or his heels. "Why," said Tom, addressing himself to his Cousin, "you will get yourself murdered if you go wandering about people's houses at the dead of the night in this manner—are you asleep or awake?—who have you made an assignation with—or where are you going to—what are you up to, Master Bobby, eh?— These tricks won't do here!"

> *"Is't Love's unhallow'd flame invites to roam,*
> *And bids you from your pillow creep?*

Or say, why thus disturb my peaceful home,
Like Macbeth, who doth murder sleep."

Tallyho was unable to reply: he looked down over the banister—he looked up at the risible features of Tom Dashall, who was almost bursting at the ludicrous situation in which he found his friend and his servants. "Come," said Tom, "there are no thieves—all's right"— to the servants, "you may quiet your minds and go to business. Bob, I'll be down with you presently." Upon this, the stair-case was cleared in an instant of all but the unfortunate Tallyho; and peace appeared to be restored in the family, but not to Bob's mind, conceiving he had committed a gross violation of good breeding, and shewn but a bad specimen of his aptitude to become a learner of London manners. It must be confessed, it was rather an awkward commencement; however, in a few minutes, recovering himself from the fright, he crawled gently down the stairs, and took a survey of the devastation he had made—cursed the lamp, d——d the portmanteau—then snatching it from the ruin before him, and again placing his luggage on his shoulder, he quietly walked up stairs to his bed-room.

It is much to be lamented in this wonderful age of discovery and continual improvement, that our philosophers have not yet found out a mode of supplying the place of glass (as almost every thing else) with cast-iron. The substitution of gas for oil has long been talked of, as one of national importance, even so much so, that one man, whose ideas were as brilliant as his own experiments, has endeavoured to shew that its produce would in a short time pay off the national debt!{1}

"A consummation devoutly to be wished;" and experience has taught the world at large there is nothing impossible, nor is there any one in existence more credulous than honest John Bull. But we are

1 *Mr. Winsor, the original lecturer on the powers of gas, in Pall Mall.*

digressing from the adventure of the lamp, however it was occasioned, by clearly proving it was not a *patent safety-lamp*: and that among the luxuries of the Hon. Tom Dashall's habitation, gas had not yet been introduced, will speedily be discovered.

Upon arriving in his bed-room, wondering within himself how he should repair the blundering mistake, of which he had so unluckily been the unwilling and unconscious author, he found himself in a new dilemma, as the receptacle of the oil had fallen with the lamp, and plentifully bedewed the portmanteau with its contents, so that he had now transferred the savoury fluid to his coat, waistcoat, cravat, and shirt. What was to be done in such a case? He could not make his appearance in that state; but his mortifications were not yet at an end—

"Hills over hills, and Alps on Alps arise."

The key of his portmanteau was missing; he rummaged all his pockets in vain—he turned them inside out—it was not here—it was not there; enraged at the multiplicity of disappointments to which he was subjected, he cut open the leathern carriage of his wardrobe with a penknife; undressed, and re-dressed himself; by which time it was half-past eight o'clock. His Cousin Tom, who had hurried down according to promise, had in the mean time been making enquiry after him, and now entered the room, singing,

"And all with attention would eagerly mark:
When he cheer'd up the pack—Hark! to Rockwood hark! hark!"

At the sight of Dashall, he recovered himself from his embarrassment, and descended with him to the breakfast-parlour.

"Did you send to Robinson's?" enquired Tom of one of the servants, as they entered the room. "Yes, Sir," was the reply; "and Weston's too?" continued he; being answered in the affirmative, "then let us have breakfast directly." Then turning to Bob, "Sparkle," said he, "promised to be with us about eleven, for the purpose of taking a stroll; in the mean time we must dress and make ready."—"Dress," said Bob, "Egad! I have dressed and made ready twice already this morning." He then recounted the adventures above recorded; at which Dashall repeatedly burst into fits of immoderate laughter.

Breakfast being over, a person from Mr. Robinson's was announced, and ushered into the room.

A more prepossessing appearance had scarcely met Bob's eye—a tall, elegant young man, dressed in black, cut in the extreme of fashion, whose features bespoke intelligence, and whose air and manner were indicative of a something which to him was quite new. He arose upon his entrance, and made a formal bow; which was returned by the youth. "Good morning, gentlemen."—"Good morning, Mr. R——," said Tom, mentioning a name celebrated by

Pope in the following lines:

> "But all my praises, why should lords engross?
> Bise, honest Muse, and sing the man of Boss."

"I am happy to have the honour of seeing you in town again, Sir! The fashionables are mustering very strong, and the prospect of the approaching coronation appears to be very attractive." During this time he was occupied in opening a leathern case, which contained combs, brushes, &c.; then taking off his coat, he appeared in a jacket with an apron, which, like a fashionable *pinafore* of the present day, nearly concealed his person, from his chin to his toes. "Yes," replied Dashall, "the coronation is a subject of deep importance just now in the circles of fashion," seating himself in his chair, in readiness for the operator,{1} who, Bob now discovered, was no other than the *Peruquier*.

> 1 *The progress of taste and refinement is visible in all situations, and the language of putting has become so well understood by all ranks of society, that it is made use of by the most humble and obscure tradesmen of the metropolis. One remarkable instance ought not to be omitted here. In a narrow dirty street, leading from the Temple towards Blackfriars, over a small triangular-fronted shop, scarcely big enough to hold three persons at a time, the eye of the passing traveller is greeted with the following welcome information, painted in large and legible characters, the letters being each nearly a foot in size:—*

HAIR CUT AND MODERNIZED!!!

This is the true "Multum in parvo "—a combination of the "Utile et dulce," the very acme of perfection. Surely, after this, to Robinson, Vickery, Boss, and Cryer, we may say—"Ye lesser stars, hide your diminished heads."

The art of puffing may be further illustrated by the following specimen of the Sublime, which is inserted here for the information of such persons as, residing in the country, have had no opportunity of seeing the original. "R— — makes gentlemen's and ladies' perukes on an entire new system; which for lightness, taste, and ease, are superior to any other in Europe. He has exerted the genius and abilities of the first artists to complete his exhibition of ornamental hair, in all its luxuriant varieties, where the elegance of nature and convenience of art are so blended, as at once to rival and ameliorate each other. Here his fair patrons may uninterruptedly examine the effects of artificial tresses, or toupees of all complexions, and, in a trial on themselves, blend the different tints with their own!"

The strife for pre-eminence in this art is not however confined to this country; for we find an instance recorded in an American newspaper, which may perhaps be equally amusing and acceptable:—

"A. C. D. La vigne, having heard of the envious expressions uttered by certain common barbers, miserable chin-scrapers, and frizulary quacks, tending to depreciate that superiority which genius is entitled to, and talents will invariably command, hereby puts them and their vulgar arts at defiance; and, scorning to hold parley with such sneaking imps, proposes to any gentleman to defend and maintain, at his shop, the head quarters of fashion, No. 6, South Gay Street, against all persons whomsoever, his title to supremacy in curlery, wiggery, and razory, to the amount of one hundred

*dollars and upwards. As hostile as he is to that low style
of puffery adopted by a certain adventurer, 'yclept Higgins,
Lavigne cannot avoid declaring, in the face of the world,
that his education has been scientifical; that after having
finished his studies at Paris, he took the tour of the
universe, having had the rare fortune of regulating the
heads of Catherine the Second, and the Grand Turk; the King
of Prussia, and the Emperor of China; the Mamelukes of
Egypt, and the Dey of Algiers; together with all the ladies
of their respective Courts. He has visited the Cape of Good
Hope, India, Java, Madagascar, Tartary, and Kamschatka,
whence he reached the United States by the way of Cape Horn.
In England he had previously tarried, where he delivered
Lectures on Heads in great style. He has at last settled in
Baltimore, determined to devote the remainder of his days to
the high profession to which his des-tiny has called him;
inviting all the literati, the lovers of the arts and
sciences, to visit him at his laboratory of beauty, where he
has separate rooms for accommodating ladies and gentlemen,
who desire to adorn their heads with hairudition. "Can
France, England—nay, the world itself, produce such
another specimen of puffing and barberism?*

"And pray," continued Tom, "what is there new in the haut ton? Has there been any thing of importance to attract attention since my absence? "Nothing very particular," was the reply—"all very dull and flat. Rumour however, as usual, has not been inactive; two or three trifling faux pas, and—oh!—yes—two duels—one in the literary world: two authors, who, after attacking each other with the quill, chose to decide their quarrel with the pistol, and poor Scot lost his life! But how should authors understand such things? The other has made a great noise in the world—You like the Corinthian cut, I believe, Sir?"

"I believe so too," said Tom—"but don't you cut the duel so short—who were the parties?"

"Oh! aye, why one, Sir, was a celebrated leader of ton, no other than Lord Shampêtre, and the other Mr. Webb, a gentleman well known:

it was a sort of family affair. His lordship's gallantry and courage, however, were put to the test, and the result bids fair to increase his popularity. The cause was nothing very extraordinary, but the effect had nearly proved fatal to his Lordship."

"What, was he wounded?" enquired Tom.

"It was thought so at first," replied the *Peruquier*, "but it was afterwards discovered that his Lordship had only fainted at the report of his opponent's pistol."

"Ha! ha! ha!" said Tom, "then it was a bloodless battle—but I should like to know more of the particulars."

"Hold your head a little more this way, Sir, if you please—that will do, I thank you, Sir;—why, it appears, that in attempting to fulfil an assignation with Mr. Webb's wife, the husband, who had got scent of the appointment, as to place and time, lustily cudgelled the dandy Lord Whiskerphiz, and rescued his own brows from certain other fashionable appendages, for which he had no relish. His Lordship's whiskers were injured, by which circumstance some people might conceive his features and appearance must have been improved, however that was not his opinion; his bones were sore, and his mind (that is to say, as the public supposed) hurt. The subject became a general theme of conversation, a Commoner had thrashed a Lord!—flesh and blood could not bear it—but then such flesh and blood could as little bear the thought of a duel—Lord Polly was made the bearer of a challenge—a meeting took place, and at the first fire his Lordship fell. A fine subject for the caricaturists, and they have not failed to make a good use of it. The fire of his Lordship's features was so completely obscured by his whiskers and mustachios, that it was immediately concluded the shot had proved mortal, till Lord Polly (who had taken refuge for safety behind a neighbouring tree) advancing, drew a bottle from his pocket, which, upon application to his nose, had the desired effect of restoring the half-dead duellist to life and light. The Seconds interfered, and succeeded in bringing the matter to a conclusion, and preventing the expected dissolution of Shampetre, who, report says, has determined not to place himself in such a perilous situation again. The fright caused him a severe illness, from which he has scarcely yet recovered sufficiently to appear in public—I believe that will do, Sir; will you look in the glass—can I make any alteration?"

"Perhaps not in your story," replied Tom; "and as to my head, so as you do not make it like the one you have been speaking of, I rely solely on your taste and judgment."

The Peruquier made his bow—"Sir, your politeness is well known!" then turning to Tallyho, "Will you allow me the honour of officiating for you, Sir?"

"Certainly," replied Bob, who by this time had seen the alteration made in his Cousin's appearance, as well as been delighted with the account of the duel, at which they all laughed during the narration—and immediately prepared for action, while Dashall continued his enquiries as to the fashionable occurrences during his absence.

"There have been some other circumstances, of minor importance," continued the Peruquier—"it is said that a certain Lord, of high military character, has lost considerable sums of money, and seriously impaired his fortune—Lord —— and a friend are completely ruined at hazard—there was a most excellent mill at Moulsey Hurst on Thursday last, between the Gas-light man, who appears to be a game chicken, and a prime hammerer—he can give and take with any man—and Oliver—Gas beat him hollow, it was all Lombard-street to a china orange. The Masked Festival on the 18th is a subject of considerable attraction, and wigs of every nature, style, and fashion, are in high request for the occasion—The Bob, the Tye, the Natural Scratch, the Full Bottom, the Queue, the Curl, the Clerical, the Narcissus, the Auricula, the Capital, the Corinthian, the Roman, the Spanish, the French, the Dutch—oh! we are full of business just now. Speaking of the art, by the by, reminds me of a circumstance which occurred a very short time back, and which shows such a striking contrast between the low-bred citizens, and the True Blues of the West!—have the kindness to hold your head a little on one side, Sir, if you please—a little more towards the light, if you please—that will do excellently—why you'll look quite another thing!—From the country, I presume?" "You are right," said Bob, "but I don't want a wig just yet."

"Shall be happy to fit you upon all occasions—masquerade, ball, or supper, Sir: you may perhaps wish to go out, as we say in the West, in coy.—happy to receive your commands at any time, prompt attention and dispatch."

"Zounds! you are clipping the wig too close," said Tom, impatient to hear the story, "and if you go on at this rate, you won't leave us even the *tail* (tale)."

"Right, Sir, I take—'and thereby hangs a tale.' The observation is in point, *verbum sat*, as the latinist would say. Well, Sir, as I was saying, a citizen, with a design to outdo his neighbours, called at one of the first shops in London a very short time since, and gave particular orders to have his *pericranium* fitted with a wig of the true royal cut. The dimensions of his upper story were taken—the order executed to the very letter of the instructions—it fitted like wax—it was nature—nay it soared beyond nature—it was the perfection of art—the very acmé of science! Conception was outdone, and there is no power in language to describe it. He was delighted; his wife was charmed with the idea of a new husband, and he with his new wig; but

> "Now comes the pleasant joke of all,
> 'Tis when too close attack'd we fall."

The account was produced—-would you believe it, he refused to have it—he objected to the price."

"The devil take it!" said Tom, "object to pay for the acme of perfection; this unnaturally natural wig would have fetched any money among the collectors of curiosities."

"What was the price?" enquired Bob.

"Trifling, Sir, very trifling, to an artist 'of the first water,' as a jeweller would say by his diamonds—only thirty guineas!!!"

"Thirty guineas!" exclaimed Bob, starting from his seat, and almost overturning the *modernizer* of his head.

Then, recollecting Sparkle's account of Living in Style, and Good Breeding, falling gently into his seat again.

"Did I hurt you, Sir?" exclaimed the Peruquier.

Dashall bit his lip, and smiled at the surprise of his Cousin, which was now so visibly depicted in his countenance.

"Not at all," replied Tallyho.

"In two minutes more, Sir, your head will be a grace to; Bond Street or St. James's; it cuts well, and looks well; and if you will allow me to attend you once a month, it will continue so."

Tom hummed a tune, and looked out of the window; the other two were silent till Bob was released. Tom *tip'd the blunt*, and the interesting young man made his congé, and departed.

"A very interesting and amusing sort of person," said Bob.

"Yes," replied Tom, "he is a walking volume of information: he knows something of every thing, and almost of every body. He has been in better circumstances, and seen a great deal of life; his history is somewhat remarkable, and some particulars, not generally known, have excited a considerable portion of interest in his fate among those who are acquainted with them. He is the son, before marriage, of a respectable and worthy tradesman, a celebrated vender of bear's grease,{1} lately deceased, who

> 1 *The infallibility of this specimen cannot possibly be doubted, after reading the following*
>
> *Advertisement:*
> *"Bear's grease has virtues, many, great and rare;*
> *To hair decay'd, life, health, and vigour giving;*
>
> *'Tis sold by — —, fam'd for cutting hair,*
>
> *At — —. — — — — — — — — — — — — — — — living.*
>
> *Who then would lose a head of hair for trying?*

A thousand tongues are heard 'I won't,' replying;

T— —r no doubt with bear's grease can supply
A thousand more, when they're dispos'd to buy.

No deception!—Seven Bears publicly exhibited in seven months, and not an agent on the globe's surface.—Sold upon oath, from 1L. to 10s. 6d. The smallest child will direct to — —, near the church—a real Bear over the door, where a good peruke is charged 1L.. 10s. equal to those produced by Mr. T., at B— —ss's, for 2L. 12s. 6d.—Scalp 10s. 6d. and 6d. only for hair-cutting—never refusing one shilling.

N. B. Bear's-grease effects wonders for the knees &c. of horses."

resided in the vicinity of Cornhill, and was for many years brought up under his roof as his nephew; in which situation, the elegance of his person, the vivacity of his disposition, and the general information he acquired, became subjects of attraction. His education was respectable for his situation, and his allowance liberal. His father however marrying a young lady of some property, and he, 'gay, light, and airy,' falling into bad hands, found his finances not sufficient to support the company he kept, and by these means involved himself in pecuniary difficulties, which, however, (if report say true) were more than once or twice averted by the indulgent parent. In the course of time, the family was increased by two sons, but he continued the flower of the flock. At length it was intended by his father to retire, in part, from business, and leave its management to this young man, and another who had been many years in his service, and whose successful endeavours in promoting his interest were well deserving his consideration; and the writings for this purpose were actually drawn up. Previous however to their execution, he was dispatched to Edinburgh, to superintend an extensive concern of his father's in that city, where, meeting with an amiable young lady with some expectations, he married without the consent of his parent, a circumstance which drew down upon him the good man's displeasure.

"Not at all dismayed at this, he almost immediately left his father's shop, and set up business for himself in the same neighbourhood, where he continued for two or three years, living, as it was supposed, upon the produce of his matrimonial connexion. At length, however, it was discovered that he was insolvent, and bankruptcy became the consequence. Here he remained till affairs were arranged, and then returned to London with his wife and two children.

"In the mean time, the legitimate family of his father had become useful in the business, and acquainted with his former indiscretions, which, consequently, were not likely to be obliterated from the old gentleman's recollection. Without money and without prospect, he arrived in London, where, for some unliquidated debt, he was arrested and became a resident in the King's Bench, from which he was liberated by the Insolvent Debtor's Act. Emancipated from this, he took small shops, or rather rooms, in various parts of the city, vainly endeavouring to support the character he had formerly maintained. These however proved abortive. Appeals to his father were found fruitless, and he has consequently, after a series of vicissitudes, been compelled to act as a journeyman.

In the career of his youth, he distinguished himself as a dashing, high-spirited fellow. He was selected as fuegel man to a regiment of Volunteers, and made himself conspicuous at the celebrated O. P. row, at the opening of Covent Garden Theatre, on which occasion he attracted the notice of the Caricaturists,{1} and was generally known in the circles of High Life, by his attendance on the first families on behalf of his father.

But perhaps the most remarkable circumstance took place at his deceased parent's funeral. Being so reduced at that time as to have no power even of providing the necessary apparel to manifest the respect, gratitude, and affection, he had ever entertained for the author of his being; and as a natural son has no legal claims upon his father, so naturally nothing was left for him; he applied by letter to the legitimates for a suit of mourning, and permission to attend the remains of their common father to the last receptacle of mortality, which being peremptorily refused, he raised a subscription, obtained clothing, with a gown and hatband, and, as the melancholy procession was moving to the parish church, which was but a few yards distance, he rushed from his hiding-place, stationed himself immediately in the front of the other attendants upon the occasion, and actually accompanied the corpse as chief mourner, having previously concerted with his own mother to be upon the spot. When the body was deposited in the vault, he took her by the hand, led her down the steps, and gave some directions to the bearers as to the situation of the coffin, while the other mourners, panic-struck at the extraordinary circumstances in which they found themselves, turned about and walked in mournful silence back, ruminating on the past with amazement, and full of conjecture for the future.

> 1 A caricature of a similar nature to the one alluded to by
> Dashall in this description, was certainly exhibited at the
> time of the memorable O. P. row, which exhibited a young man
> of genteel appearance in the pit of Covent Garden Theatre,
> addressing the audience. It had inscribed at the bottom
> of it,
>
> Is this Barber-Ross-a?
>
> in allusion (no doubt) to the tragedy of Barbarossa.

"It was an extraordinary situation for all parties," said Bob; "but hold, who have we here?—Egad! there is an elegant carriage drawn up to the door; some Lord, or Nobleman, I'll be bound for it—We can't be seen in this deshabille, I shall make my escape." And saying this, he was hastening out of the room.

"Ha! ha! ha!" exclaimed Tom, "you need not be so speedy in your flight. This is one of the fashionable requisites of London, with whom you must also become acquainted; there is no such thing as doing without them—dress and address are indispensables. This is no other than one of the decorators."

"Decorators!" continued Bob, not exactly comprehending him.

"Monsieur le Tailleur—'Tin Mr. W— —, from Cork Street, come to exhibit his Spring patterns, and turn us out with the new cut—so pray remain where you are."

"Tailor—decorator," said Bob—"Egad! the idea is almost as ridiculous as the representation of the taylor riding to Brentford."

By this time the door was opened, and Mr. W. entered, making his bow with the precision of a dancing-master, and was followed by a servant with pattern-books, the other apparatus of his trade. The first salutations over, large pattern-books were displayed upon the table, exhibiting to view a variety of fancy-coloured cloths, and measures taken accordingly. During which time, Tom, as on the former occasion, continued his enquiries relative to the occurrences in the fashionable world.

"Rather tame, Sir, at present: the Queen's unexpected visit to the two theatres was for a time a matter of surprise—the backwardness of Drury Lane managers to produce 'God Save the King,' has been construed into disloyalty to the Sovereign—and a laughable circumstance took place on his going to the same house a few nights back, which has already been made the subject of much merriment, both in conversation and caricature. It appears that Mr. Gloss'em, who is a *shining character* in the theatrical world, at least among the minors of the metropolis; and whose father was for many years a wax-chandler in the neighbourhood of Soho, holds a situation as clerk of the cheque to the Gentlemen Pensioners of his Majesty's household, as well as that of Major Domo, manager and proprietor of a certain theatre, not half a mile from Waterloo Bridge.

A part of his duty in the former capacity is to attend occasionally upon the person of the King, as one of the appendages of Royalty; in which *character* he appeared on the night in question. The servants of the attendants who were in waiting for their masters, had a room appropriated to their use. One of these latter gentry, no other than Gloss'em's servant, being anxious to have as near a view of the sacred person of his Majesty as his employer, had placed himself in a good situation at the door, in order to witness his departure, when a Mr. Winpebble, of mismanaging notoriety, and also a ponderous puff, assuming managerial authority, espying him, desired the police-officers and guards in attendance to turn out the lamp-lighter's boy, pointing to Gloss'em's servant. This, it seems, was no sooner said than done, at the point of the bayonet. Some little scuffle ensued—His Majesty and suite departed—Hold up your arm, Sir."

"But did the matter end there?" enquired Dashall.

"O dear, no—not exactly."

"Because if it did," continued Tom, "in my opinion, it began with a wax taper, and ended in the smoke of a farthing rushlight. You have made it appear to be a gas-receiver without supplies."

"I beg pardon," said Mr. W.; "the pipes are full, but the gas is not yet turned on."

This created a laugh, and Mr. W. proceeded:—

"The next day, the servant having informed his Master of the treatment he had received, a gentleman was dispatched from Gloss'em to Winpebble, to demand an apology: which being refused, the former, with a large horsewhip under his arm, accosted the latter, and handsomely belaboured his shoulders with lusty stripes. That, you see, Sir, sets the gas all in a blaze.—That will do, Sir.—Now, Sir, at your service," addressing himself to Tallyho.

"Yes," said Tom, "the taper's alight again now; and pray what was the consequence?"

"Winpebble called for assistance, which was soon obtained, and away they went to Bow-street. Manager Taper, and Manager Vapour—the one blazing with fire, and the other exhausted with thrashing;—'twas a laughing scene. Manager Strutt, and Manager Butt, were strutting and butting each other. The magistrate heard the case, and recommended peace and quietness between them, by an amicable adjustment. The irritated minds of the now two enraged managers could not be brought to consent to this. Gloss'em declared the piece should be repeated, having been received with the most rapturous applause. Winpebble roundly swore that the piece was ill got up, badly represented, and damn'd to all intents and purposes—that the author had more strength than wit—and though not a friend to injunctions himself, he moved for an injunction against Gloss'em; who was at length something like the renowned John Astley with his imitator Rees:

"This great John Astley, and this little Tommy Rees, Were both bound over to keep the King's Peas."

Gloss'em was bound to keep the peace, and compelled to find security in the sum of twenty pounds. Thus ended the farce of *The Enraged Managers—Drury Lane in a Blaze, or Bow Street bewildered.*"

"Ha! ha! ha! an animated sort of vehicle for public amusement truly," said Tom, "and of course produced with new scenery, music, dresses, and decorations; forming a combination of attractions superior to any ever exhibited at any theatre—egad! it would make a most excellent scene in a new pantomime."

"Ha! ha! ha!" said Mr. W. "true, Sir, true; and the duel of Lord Shampetre would have also its due portion of effect; but as his Lordship is a good customer of mine, you must excuse any remarks on that circumstance."

"We have already heard of his Lordship's undaunted courage and firmness, as well as the correctness of his aim."

"He! he! he!" chuckled W.; "then I fancy your information is not very correct, for it appears his lordship displayed a want of every one of those qualities that you impute to him; however, I venture to hope no unpleasant measures will result from the occurrence, as I made the very pantaloons he wore upon the occasion. It seems he is considerably *cut up*; but you must know that, previous to the duel, I was consulted upon the best mode of securing his sacred person from the effects of a bullet: I recommended a very high waistband lined with whale-bone, and well padded with horse-hair, to serve as a breast-plate, and calculated at once to produce warmth, and resist penetration. The pantaloons were accordingly made, thickly overlaid with extremely rich and expensive gold lace, and considered to be stiff enough for any thing—aye, even to keep his Lordship erect. But what do you suppose was the effect of all my care? I should not like to make a common talk of it, but so it certainly was: his Lordship had no objection to the whalebone, buckram, &c. outside of him, but was fearful that if his antagonist's fire should be well-directed, his tender body might be additionally hurt by the splinters of the whalebone being carried along with it, and actually proposed to take them off before the dreadful hour of appointment came on. In this however he was fortunately overruled by his Second, who, by the by, was but a goose in the affair, and managed it altogether very badly, except in the instance of being prompt with the smelling-bottle, which certainly was well-timed; and it would have been a hissing hot business, but for the judicious interference of the other Second."

A loud laugh succeeded this additional piece of information relative to the *affair of honour*; and Snip having finished his measurement, colours were fixed upon, and he departed, promising to be punctual in the delivery of the new habiliments on the next day.

"I am now convinced," said Bob, "of the great importance and utility of a London tradesman, and the speed of their execution is wonderful!"

"Yes," replied Tom, "it is only to be equalled by the avidity with which they obtain information, and the rapidity with which they circulate it—why, in another half hour your personal appearance, the cut of your country coat, your complexion and character, as far as so short an interview would allow for obtaining it, will be known to all his customers—they are generally quick and acute discerners. But come, we must be making ready for our walk, it is now half-past ten o'clock—Sparkle will be here presently. It is time to be dressing, as I mean to have a complete ramble during the day, take a chop somewhere on the road, and in the evening, my boy, we'll take a peep into the theatre. Lord Byron's tragedy of Marino Faliero is to be performed to-night, and I can, I think, promise you a treat of the highest kind."

Tallyho, who had no idea of dressing again, having already been obliged to dress twice, seemed a little surprised at the proposition, but supposing it to be the custom of London, nodded assent, and proceeded to the dressing-room. As he walked up stairs he could not help casting his visual orbs over the banisters, just to take a bird's eye view of the scene of his morning disasters, of which, to his great astonishment and surprise, not a vestige remained—a new lamp had been procured, which seemed to have arisen like a phoenix from its ashes, and the stone passage and stairs appeared as he termed it, "as white as a cauliflower." At the sight of all this, he was gratified and delighted, for he expected to find a heap of ruins to reproach him. He skipped, or rather vaulted up the stairs, three or four at a stride, with all the gaiety of a race-horse when first brought to the starting-post. The rapid movements of a Life in London at once astonished and enraptured him; nor did he delay his steps, or his delight, until he had reached the topmost story, when bursting open the door, lie marched boldly into the room. Here again he was at fault; a female shriek assailed his ear, which stopped his course, and looking around him, he could not find from whence the voice proceeded. "Good God!" continued the same voice, "what can be the meaning of this intrusion?—Begone, rash man." In the mean time, Tom, who was in a room just under the one into which he had unfortunately made so sudden an entrance, appeared at the door.

"What the devil is the matter now?" said Tom; when spying his cousin in the centre of the room, without seeming to know whether to return or remain, he could not restrain his laughter. Tallyho looked up, like one in a dream—then down—then casting his eyes around him, he perceived in the corner, peeping out from the bed-curtains in which she had endeavoured to hide her almost naked person, the head of the old Housekeeper. The picture was moving, and at the same time laughable. The confusion of Bob—the fright of the Housekeeper, and the laughter of Tom, were subjects for the pencil of a Hogarth!

"So," said Tom, "you are for springing game in all parts of the house, and at all times too. How came you here?"—"Not by my appointment, Sir," replied the old lady, who still remained rolled up in the curtain. "I never did such a thing in all my born days: I'm an honest woman, and mean to remain so. I never was so ashamed in all my life."

"I believe the house is enchanted," cried Bob; "d—— me, I never seem to step without being on a barrel of gunpowder, ready to ignite with the touch of my foot. I have made some cursed blunder again, and don't seem to know where I am."

"Come, come," said Dashall, "that won't do—I'm sure you had some design upon my Housekeeper, who you hear by her own account is a good woman, and won't listen to your advances."

By this time the servants had arrived at the door, and were alternately peeping in, wondering to see the two gentlemen in such a situation, and secretly giggling and enjoying the embarrassment of the old woman, whose wig lay on the table, and who was displaying her bald pate and shrivelled features from the bed-curtains, enveloped in fringe and tassels, which only served to render them still more ludicrous.

Bob affected to laugh; said it was very odd—he could not account for it at all—stammered out something like an apology—begg'd pardon—it was—a mistake—he really took it for his own room—he never was so bewildered in his life—was very sorry he should cause so much alarm—but really had no sort of intention whatever.

"Well," said Dashall, "the best reparation you can now make for your intrusion is a speedy retreat. Time is escaping, so come along;" and taking him by the arm, they walked down the stairs together, and then proceeded to re-fit without further obstruction, in order to be ready for Sparkle, who was expected every minute.

The first day of Bob's residence in London had already been productive of some curious adventures, in which he, unfortunately as he considered, had sustained the principal character—a character not altogether suitable to is inclinations or wishes, though productive of much merriment to his ever gay and sprightly Cousin, who had witnessed the embarrassment of his pupil upon his first entrance into Life with ungovernable laughter. It was to him excellent sport, while it furnished a good subject of speculation and conversation among the servants below, but was not so well relished by the affrighted old house-keeper. Indeed, the abrupt entrance of a man into her bed-chamber had so deranged her ideas, that she was longer than usual in decking her person previous to her re-appearance. The tender frame of the old lady had been subjected to serious agitations at the bare idea of such a visit, and the probable imputations that might in consequence be thrown upon her sacred and unspotted character; nor could she for some time recover her usual serenity.

Such was the situation of the parties at the moment we are now describing; but as our Heroes are preparing for an extensive, actual survey of men, manners, and tilings, we shall for the present leave them in peace and quietness, while we proceed to the next chapter.

CHAPTER VII

What shows! and what sights! what a round of delights
You'll meet in the gay scene of London;
How charming to view" amusements still new,
Twenty others you'll find soon as one's done.
At the gay scene at Court—Peers and gentry resort,
In pleasure you'll never miss one day:
There's the Opera treat, the parade in Bond Street,
And the crowd in Hyde Park on a Sunday.

TOM, whose wardrobe was extensive, found no difficulty, and lost no time in preparing for the promenade; while, on the other hand, Tallyho was perplexed to know how to tog himself out in a way suitable to make his appearance in the gay world of fashion. Dashall had therefore rapidly equipped himself, when, perceiving it was half-past eleven, he was the more perplexed to account for the absence of Sparkle; for although it was an early hour, yet, upon such an occasion as that of initiating a new recruit, it was very extraordinary that he should not have been prompt. However, he entered Tallyho's room, and found him looking out of the window in a posture of rumination, probably revolving in his mind the events of the morning.

"Come," said Tom, as he entered, "'tis time to be on the move, and if Sparkle don't show in a few minutes, we'll set sail and call in upon him at Long's, in Bond Street. Perhaps he is not well, or something prevents his appearance—we'll make it in our way, and we have a fine day before us."

"I am at your service," replied Bob, who could not help viewing the elegance of his Cousin's appearance: the style of his dress, and the neatness with which his garments fitted him, were all subjects of admiration, and formed so strong a contrast with his own as almost to excite envy. He had however attired himself in a way that befits a fashionable country gentleman: a green coat, white waistcoat, buckskin breeches, and boots, over which a pair of leggings appeared, which extended below the calf of the leg and half up the thigh, surmounted with a *Lily Shallow*. Such was the costume in which he was destined to show off; and thus equipped, after a few minutes they emerged from the house in Piccadilly on the proposed ramble, and proceeded towards Bond Street.

The first object that took their particular attention was the Burlington Arcade. "Come," said Tom, "we may as well go this way," and immediately they passed the man in the gold-laced hat, who guards the entrance to prevent the admission of boys and improper persons. The display of the shops, with the sun shining through the windows above, afforded much for observation, and attracted Bob from side to side—to look, to wonder and admire. But Tom, who was intent upon finding his friend Sparkle, urged the necessity of moving onward with more celerity, lest he should be gone out, and consequently kept drawing his Cousin forward. "Another and a better opportunity will be afforded for explanation than the present, and as speed is the order of the day, I hope you will not prove disorderly; we shall soon reach Long's, and when we have Sparkle with us, we have one of the most intelligent and entertaining fellows in the world. He is a sort of index to every thing, and every body; his knowledge of life and character, together with a facetiousness of whim and manner, which he has in delineating them, are what we call in London—*Prime and bang up to the mark*. There is scarcely a Lane, Court, Alley, or Street, in the Metropolis, but what he knows, from the remotest corners of Rag-Fair, to the open and elegant Squares of the West, even to Hyde Park Corner. Memory, mirth, and magic, seem at all times to animate his tongue, and, as the Song says,

> "He is the hoy for bewitching 'em,
> Whether good-humour'd or coy."

Indeed, he is the admiration of all who know him; wit, whim, frolic, and fun, are constant companions with him, and I really believe, in a dungeon or a palace, he would always appear the same."

By this time they had reached Bond Street, in their way to which, each step they had taken, the streets and avenues of every description appeared to Bob to be crowded to an excess; the mingling cries which were vociferated around them produced in his mind uncommon sensations. The rattling of the carriages, the brilliance of the shops, and the continual hum of the passengers, contributed to heighten the scene.

"Bond Street," said Dashall, "is not one of the most elegant streets in the vicinity of London, but is the resort of the most fashionable people, and from about two o'clock till five, it is all bustle—all life—every species of fashionable vehicle is to be seen dashing along in gay and gallant pride. From two to five are the fashionable shopping-hours, for which purpose the first families resort to this well-known street—others, to shew their equipage, make an assignation, or kill a little time; which is as much a business with some, as is the more careful endeavours of others to seize him in his flight, and make the most of his presence. The throng is already increasing; the variety, richness, and gaiety of the shops in this street, will always be attractive, and make it a popular rendezvous of both sexes. It will shortly be as crowded as Rag Fair, or the Royal Exchange; and the magic splendour has very peculiar properties.

"It makes the tradesman forget—while he is cheating a lovely and smiling Duchess—that in all probability her ladyship is endeavouring to cheat him. It makes the gay and airy, the furbelowed and painted lady of the town, forget that she must pay a visit to her uncle,{1} in order to raise the wind before she can make her appearance at the theatre at half-price. It makes the dashing prisoner forget, that while "he is sporting his figure in the bang-up style of appearance, he is only taking his ride on a day-rule from the King's Bench. It makes the Lord who drives four-in-hand forget his losses of the night before at some of the fashionable gaming-houses. It makes one adventurer forget that the clothes in which he expects to obtain respect and attention, are more than likely to be paid for in Newgate; another for a time forgets that *John Doe* and *Richard Roe* have expelled him from his

> 1 *My Uncle is a very convenient and accommodating sort of friend, who lives at the sign of the Three Balls, indicative of his willingness to lend money upon good security, for the payment of enormous interest. The original meaning of the sign has puzzled the curious and antiquarians, and the only*

probable meaning they can discover is, that it implies the chances are two to one against any property being redeemed after being once committed to the keeping of this tender hearted and affectionate relative.

lodgings; and a third that all his worldly possessions are not equal to the purchase of a dinner. It is an *ignis fatuus*—a sort of magic lantern replete with delusive appearances—of momentary duration—an escape to the regions of noise, tumult, vanity, and frivolity, where the realities of Life, the circumstances and the situation of the observer, are not suffered to intrude.

"But to be seen in this street at a certain hour, is one of the essentials to the existence of *haut-ton*—it is the point of attraction for greetings in splendid equipages, from the haughty bend or familiar nod of arrogance, to the humble bow of servility. Here mimicry without money assumes the consequential air of independence: while modest merit creeps along unheeded through the glittering crowd. Here all the senses are tantalized with profusion, and the eye is dazzled with temptation, for no other reason than because it is the constant business of a fashionable life—not to live in, but out of self, to imitate the luxuries of the affluent without a tithe of their income, and to sacrifice morality at the altar of notoriety."

"Your description of this celebrated street, of which I have heard so much," said Tallyho, "is truly lively."

"But it is strictly true," continued Tom.

They had now arrived at Long's, and found a barouche and four waiting at the door. Upon entering, the first person they met was Lord Cripplegate, whom they passed, and proceeded to the coffee-room; in one of the boxes of which Tom immediately directed his Cousin's attention to a well-dressed young man, who was reading the newspaper, and sipping his coffee—"Take notice of him," said Tom.

Bob looked at him for a moment, marked his features, and his dress, which was in the extreme of fashion; while Tom, turning to one of the Waiters, enquired for his friend Sparkle.

"He has not been here since yesterday morning!" said the Waiter.

"I have been waiting for him these two hours!" exclaimed the young Sprig of Fashion, laying down the newspaper almost at the same moment, "and must wait till he comes—Ah! Mr. Dashall, how d'ye do?—-very glad to see you—left all well in the country, I hope!—Mr. Sparkle was to have met me this morning at eleven precisely, I should judge he is gone into the country."

"It must have been late last night, then," said Dashall, "for he left us about half-past ten, and promised also to meet us again this morning at eleven; I can't think what can have become of him—but come," said he, taking Bob by the arm, "we must keep moving—Good morning—good morning." And thus saying, walked directly out of the house, turning to the right again towards Piccadilly.

"There is a remark made, I think by Goldsmith," said Tom, "that one half of the world don't know how the other half lives; and the man I spoke to in the coffee-room, whose name I am unacquainted with, though his person is recognized by almost every body, while his true character, residence, and means of subsistence, remain completely in obscurity, from what I have seen of him, I judge is what may be termed a *hanger on*."

"A hanger on," said Bob—"what can that mean? I took him for a man of property and high birth—but I saw you take so little notice of him."

"Ah! my good fellow, I have already cautioned you not to be duped by appearances. A *hanger on* is a sort of sycophant, or toad-eater, and, in the coffee-houses and hotels of London, many such are to be found—men who can *spin out a long yarn*, tell a tough story, and tip you *a rum chant*—who invite themselves by a freedom of address bordering on impudence to the tables and the parties of persons they know, by pretending to call in by mere accident, just at the appointed time: by assuming great confidence, great haste, little appetite, and much business; but, at the same time, requiring but little pressure to forego them all for the pleasure of the company present. What he can have to do with Sparkle I am at a loss to conceive; but he is an insinuating and an intriguing sort of fellow, whom I by no means like, so I cut him."

Bob did not exactly understand the meaning of the word cut, and therefore begged his Cousin to explain.

"The cut," said Tom, "is a fashionable word for getting rid, by rude or any means, of any person whose company is not agreeable. The art of *cutting* is reduced to a system in London; and an explanatory treatise has been written on the subject for the edification of the natives.{1} But I am so bewildered to think what can have detained Sparkle, and deprived us of his company, that I scarcely know how to think for a moment on any other subject at present."

   1 Vide a small volume entitled "The Cutter."

"It is somewhat strange!" cried Bob, "that he was not with you this morning."

"There is some mystery in it," said Tom, "which time alone can unravel; but however, we will not be deprived of our intended ramble." At this moment they entered Piccadilly, and were crossing the road in their way to St. James's Street, when Dashall nodded to a gentleman passing by on the opposite side, and received a sort of half bow in return. "That," said Tom, "is a curious fellow, and a devilish clever fellow too—for although he has but one arm, he is a man of science."

"In what way?" enquired Bob.

"He is a pugilist," said Tom—"one of those courageous gentlemen who can queer the daylights, tap the claret, prevent telling fibs, and pop the noddle into chancery; and a devilish good hand he is, I can assure you, among those who

> ——"can combat with ferocious strife,
> And beat an eye out, or thump out a life;
> Can bang the ribs in, or bruise out the brains,
> And die, like noble blockheads, for their pains."

FIVES COURT Tom & Bob, studying Real Life among the Millers

"Having but one arm, of course he is unable to figure in the ring—though he attends the mills, and is a constant visitor at the Fives Court exhibitions, and generally appears *a la Belcher*. He prides himself upon flooring a novice, and hits devilish hard with the glove. I have had some lessons from this amateur of the old English science, and felt the force of his fist; but it is a very customary thing to commence in a friendly way, till the knowing one finds an opportunity which he cannot resist, of shewing the superiority he possesses. So it was with Harry and me, when he put on his glove. I use the singular number, because he has but one hand whereon to place a glove withal. Come, said he, it shall only be a little innocent spar. I also put on a glove, for it would not be fair to attack a one-armed man with two, and no one ought to take the odds in combat. To it we went, and I shewed *first blood*, for he tapped *the claret* in no time.

"Neat *milling we had*, what with *clouts on the nob*, Home hits in the *bread-basket*, clicks in the gob, And plumps in the daylights, a prettier treat Between two *Johnny Raws* 'tis not easy to meet."

"I profited however by Harry's lessons, and after a short time was enabled to return the compliment with interest, by sewing up one of his *glimmers*.

"This is St. James's Street," continued he, as they turned the corner rather short; in doing which, somewhat animated by the description he had just been giving, Tom's foot caught the toe of a gentleman, who was mincing along the pathway with all the care and precision of a dancing-master, which had the effect of bringing him to the ground in an instant as effectually as a blow from one of the fancy. Tom, who had no intention of giving offence wantonly, apologized for the misfortune, by—"I beg pardon, Sir," while Bob, who perceived the poor creature was unable to rise again, and apprehending some broken bones, assisted him to regain his erect position. The poor animal, or nondescript, yclept Dandy, however had only been prevented the exercise of its limbs by the stiffness of certain appendages, without which its person could not be complete—the *stays*, lined with whalebone, were the obstacles to its rising. Being however placed in its natural position, he began in an affected blustering tone of voice to complain that it was d——d odd a gentleman could not walk along the streets without being incommoded by puppies—pulled out his quizzing glass, and surveyed our heroes from head to foot—then taking from his pocket a smelling bottle, which, by application to the nose, appeared to revive him, Tom declared he was sorry for the accident, had no intention, and hoped he was not hurt. This, however, did not appear to satisfy the offended Dandy, who turned upon his heel muttering to himself the necessity there was of preventing drunken fellows from rambling the streets to the annoyance of sober and genteel people in the day-time.

Dashall, who overheard the substance of his ejaculation, broke from the arm of Bob, and stepping after him without ceremony, by a sudden wheel placed himself in the front of him, so as to impede his progress a second time; a circumstance which filled Mr. Fribble with additional alarm, and his agitation became visibly' depicted on his countenance.

"What do you mean?" cried Dashall, with indignation, taking the imputation of drunkenness at that early hour in dudgeon. "Who, and what are you, Sir?{1} Explain instantly, or by the honour of a gentleman, I'll chastise this insolence."

> 1 "What are you?" is a formidable question to a dandy of the present day, for
>
> > "Dandy's a gender of the doubtful kind;
> > A something, nothing, not to be defined;
> > 'Twould puzzle worlds its sex to ascertain,
> > So very empty, and so very vain."
>
> It is a fact that the following examination of three of these non-descripts took place at Bow Street a very short time back, in consequence of a nocturnal fracas. The report was thus given:
>
> "Three young sprigs of fashion, in full dress, somewhat damaged and discoloured by a night's lodging in the cell of

a watch-house, were yesterday brought before Mr. Birnie, charged with disorderly conduct in the streets, and with beating a watchman named Lloyd.

"Lloyd stated that his beat was near the Piazza, and at a very late hour on Thursday night, the three defendants came through Covent Garden, singing, and conducting themselves in the most riotous manner possible. They were running, and were followed by three others, all in a most uproarious state of intoxication, and he thought proper to stop them; upon which he was floored san-ceremonie, and when he recovered his legs, he was again struck, and called 'a b— —y Charley,' and other ungenteel names.   He called for the assistance of some of his brethren, and the defendants were with some trouble taken to the watch-house. They were very jolly on the way, and when lodged in durance, amused themselves with abusing the Constable of the night, and took especial care that no one within hearing of the watch-house should get a wink of sleep for the remainder of the night.

Mr. Birnie.—"Well young gentleman, what have you to say to this?" The one who undertook to be spokesman, threw himself in the most familiar manner possible across the table, and having fixed himself perfectly at his ease, he said, "The fact was, they had been dining at a tavern, and were rather drunk, and on their way through the Piazza, they endeavoured by running away to give the slip to their three companions, who were still worse than themselves. The others, however called out Stop thief! and the watchman stopped them; whereat they naturally felt irritated, and certainly gave the watchman a bit of a thrashing."

Mr. Birnie.—"How was he to know you were not the thieves? He did quite right to stop you, and I am very glad he has brought you here—Pray, Sir, what are you?" Defendant.—"I am nothing, Sir." Mr. Birnie (to another).—"And what are you?" Defendant.—"Why, Sir, I am—I am, Sir, nothing." Mr. Birnie.—"Well, this is very fine. Pray, Sir, (turning to *the third, who stood twirling his hat) will you do me the favour to tell what you are?"*

This gentleman answered in the same way. "I am, as my friends observed, nothing."

Mr. Birnie.—"Well, gentlemen, I must endeavour to make something of you. Here, gaoler, let them he locked up, and I shall not part with them until I have some better account of their occupations."

We have heard it asserted, that Nine tailors make a man. How many Dandies, professing to be Nothing, may be required to accomplish the proposed intention of making Something, may (perhaps by this time) be discovered by the worthy Magistrate. We however suspect he has had severe work of it.

"Leave me alone," exclaimed the almost petrified Dandy.

"Not till you have given me the satisfaction I have a right to demand," cried Tom. "I insist upon an explanation and apology—or demand your card—who are you, Sir? That's my address," instantly handing him a card. "I am not to be played with, nor will I suffer your escape, after the insulting manner in which you have spoken, with impunity."

Though not prepared for such a rencontre, the Dandy, who now perceived the inflexible temper of Tom's mind—and a crowd of people gathering round him—determined at least to put on as much of the character of a man as possible, and fumbled in his pocket for a card; at length finding one, he slipped it into Tom's hand. "Oh, Sir," said he, "if that's the case, I'm your man, *demmee*,—how, when, or where you please, 'pon honor." Then beckoning to a hackney coach, he hobbled to the door, and was pushed in by coachee, who, immediately mounted the box and flourishing his whip, soon rescued him from his perilous situation, and the jeers of the surrounding multitude.

Tom, who in the bustle of the crowd had slipped the card of his antagonist into his pocket, now took Bob's arm, and they pursued their way down St. James's Street, and could not help laughing at the affair: but Tallyho, who had a great aversion to duelling, and was thinking of the consequences, bit his lips, and expressed his sorrow at what had occurred; he ascribed the hasty imputation of drunkenness to the irritating effects of the poor creature's accident, and expressed his hope that his cousin would take no further notice of it. Tom, however, on the other hand, ridiculed Bob's fears—told him it was a point of honour not to suffer an insult in the street from any man—nor would he—besides, the charge of drunkenness from such a thing as that, is not to be borne. "D— —n it, man, drunkenness in the early part of the day is a thing I abhor, it is at all times what I would avoid if possible, but at night there may be many apologies for it; nay in some cases even to avoid it is impossible. The pleasures of society are enhanced by it—the joys of love are increased by the circulation of the glass—harmony, conviviality and friendship are produced by it—though I am no advocate for inebriety, and detest the idea of the beast—

> "Who clouds his reason by the light of day,
> And falls to drink, an early and an easy prey."

"Well," said Bob, "I cannot help thinking this poor fellow, who has already betrayed his fears, will be inclined to make any apology for his rudeness to-morrow."

"If he does not," said Tom, "I'll wing him, to a certainty—a jackanapes—a puppy—a man-milliner; perhaps a thing of shreds and patches—he shall not go unpunished, I promise you; so come along, we will just step in here, and I'll dispatch this business at once: I'll write a challenge, and then it will be off my hands." And so saying, they entered a Coffee-house, where, calling for pen, ink and paper, Tom immediately began his epistle, shrewdly hinting to his Cousin, that he expected he would act as his Second. "It will be a fine opportunity for introducing your name to the gay world—the newspapers will record your name as a man of ton. Let us see now how it will appear:—On — — last, the Honourable Tom Dashall, attended by his Cousin, Robert Tallyho, Esq. of Belleville Hall, met— ah, by the bye, let us see who he is," here he felt in his pocket for the card.

Bob, however, declared his wish to decline obtaining popularity by being present upon such an occasion, and suggested the idea of his calling upon the offender, and endeavouring to effect an amicable arrangement between them.

"Hallo!" exclaimed Tom with surprise, as he drew the card from his pocket, and threw it on the table—"Ha, ha, ha,—look at that."

Tallyho looked at the card without understanding it. "What does it mean?" said he.

"Mean," replied Tom, "why it is a Pawnbroker's duplicate for a Hunting Watch, deposited with his uncle this morning in St. Martin's Lane, for two pounds—laughable enough—well, you may dismiss your fears for the present; but I'll try if I can't find my man by this means—if he is worth finding—at all events we have found a watch."

Bob now joined in the laugh, and, having satisfied the Waiter, they sallied forth again.

Just as they left the Coffee-house, "Do you see that Gentleman in the blue great coat, arm in arm with another? that is no other than the — —. You would scarcely conceive, by his present appearance, that he has commanded armies, and led them on to victory; and that having retired under the shade of his laurels, he is withering them away, leaf by leaf, by attendance at the *hells*{1} of the metropolis; his unconquerable spirit still actuating him in his hours of relaxation. It is said that the immense sum awarded to him for his prowess in war, has been so materially reduced by his inordinate passion for play, that although he appears at Court, and is a favourite, the demon Poverty stares him in the face. But this is a vile world, and half one hears is not to be believed. He is certainly extravagant, fond of women, and fond of wine; but all these foibles are overshadowed with so much glory as scarcely to remain perceptible. Here is the Palace," said Tom, directing his Cousin's attention to the bottom of the street.

Bob was evidently struck at this piece of information, as he could discover no mark of grandeur in its appearance to entitle it to the dignity of a royal residence.

"It is true," said Tom, "the outside appearance is not much in its favour; but it is venerable for its antiquity, and for its being till lately the place at which the Kings of this happy Island have held their Courts. On the site of that palace originally stood an hospital, founded before the conquest, for fourteen leprous females, to whom eight brethren were afterwards added, to assist in the performance of divine service."

"Very necessary," said Bob, "and yet scarcely sufficient."

> 1 Hells—The abode or resort of black-legs or gamblers, where they assemble to commit their depredations on the unwary. But of these we shall have occasion to enlarge elsewhere.

"You seem to quiz this Palace, and are inclined to indulge your wit upon old age. In 1532, it was surrendered to Henry viii. and he erected the present Palace, and enclosed St. James's Park, to serve as a place of amusement and exercise, both to this Palace and Whitehall. But it does not appear to have been the Court of the English Sovereigns, during their residence in town, till the reign of Queen Ann, from which time it has been uniformly used as such.

"It is built of brick; and that part which contains the state apartments, being only one story high, gives it a regular appearance outside. The State-rooms are commodious and handsome, although there is nothing very superb or grand in the decorations or furniture.

"The entrance to these rooms is by a stair-case which opens into the principal court, which you now see. At the top of the stair-case are two rooms; one on the left, called the Queen's, and the other the King's Guard-room, leading to the State-apartments. Immediately beyond the King's Guard-room is the Presence-chamber, which contains a canopy, and is hung with tapestry; and which is now used as a passage to the principal rooms.

"There is a suite of five rooms opening into each other successively, fronting the Park. The Presence-chamber opens into the centre room, which is denominated the Privy-chamber, in which is a canopy of flowered-crimson velvet, generally made use of for the King to receive the Quakers.

"On the right are two drawing-rooms, one within the other. At the upper end of the further one, is a throne with a splendid canopy, on which the Kings have been accustomed to receive certain addresses. This is called the Grand Drawing-room, and is used by the King and Queen on certain state occasions, the nearer room being appropriated as a kind of ante-chamber, in which the nobility, &c. are permitted to remain while their Majesties are present in the further room, and is furnished with stools, sofas, &c. for the purpose. There are two levee-rooms on the left of the privy-chamber, on entering from the King's guard-room and presence-chamber, the nearer one serving as an ante-chamber to the other. They were all of them, formerly, meanly furnished, but at the time of the marriage of our present King, they were elegantly fitted up. The walls are now covered with tapestry, very beautiful, and of rich colours—tapestry which, although it was made for Charles II. had never been used, having by some accident lain unnoticed in a chest, till it was discovered a short time before the marriage of the Prince.

"The canopy of the throne was made for the late-Queen's birth-day, the first which happened after the union of Great Britain and Ireland. It is made of crimson velvet, with very broad gold lace, embroidered with crowns set with fine and rich pearls. The shamrock, emblematical of the Irish nation, forms a part of the decorations of the British crown, and is executed with great taste and accuracy.

"The grand drawing-room contains a large, magnificent chandelier of silver, gilt, but I believe it has not been lighted for some years; and in the grand levee-room is a very noble bed, the furniture of which is of Spitalfields manufacture, in crimson velvet. It was first put up with the tapestry, on the marriage of the present King, then Prince of Wales.

"It is upon the whole an irregular building, chiefly consisting of several courts and alleys, which lead into the Park. This, however, is the age of improvement, and it is said that the Palace will shortly be pulled down, and in the front of St. James's Street a magnificent triumphal arch is to be erected, to commemorate the glorious victories of the late war, and to form a grand entrance to the Park.

"The Duke of York, the Duke of Clarence, the King's servants, and many other dignified persons, live in the Stable-yard."

"In the Stable-yard!" said Bob, "dignified persons reside in a Stable-yard, you astonish me!"

"It is quite true," said Tom, "and remember it is the Stable-yard of a King."

"I forgot that circumstance," said Bob, "and that circumstances alter cases. But whose carriage is this driving with so much rapidity?"

"That is His Highness the Duke of York, most likely going to pay a visit to his royal brother, the King, who resides in a Palace a little further on: which will be in our way, for it is yet too early to see much in the Park: so let us proceed, I am anxious to make some inquiry about my antagonist, and therefore mean to take St. Martin's Lane as we go along."

With this they pursued their way along Pall Mall. The rapidity of Tom's movements however afforded little opportunity for observation or remark, till they arrived opposite Carlton House, when he called his Cousin's attention to the elegance of the new streets opposite to it.

"That," said he, "is Waterloo Place, which, as well as the memorable battle after which it is named, has already cost the nation an immense sum of money, and must cost much more before the proposed improvements are completed: it is however, the most elegant street in London. The want of uniformity of the buildings has a striking effect, and gives it the appearance of a number of palaces. In the time of Queen Elizabeth there were no such places as Pall Mall, St. James's-street, Piccadilly, nor any of the streets or fine squares in this part of the town. That building at the farther end is now the British Fire-office, and has a pleasing effect at this distance. The cupola on the left belongs to a chapel, the interior of which for elegant simplicity is unrivalled. To the left of the centre building is a Circus, and a serpentine street, not yet finished, which runs to Swallow Street, and thence directly to Oxford Road, where another circus is forming, and is intended to communicate with Portland Place; by which means a line of street, composed of all new buildings, will be completed. Of this dull looking place (turning to Carlton House) although it is the town-residence of our King, I shall say nothing at present, as I intend devoting a morning, along with you, to its inspection. The exterior has not the most lively appearance, but the interior is magnificent."—During this conversation they had kept moving gently on.

Bob was charmed with the view down Waterloo Place.

"That," said his Cousin, pointing to the Arcade at the opposite corner of Pall Mall, "is the Italian Opera-house, which has recently assumed its present superb appearance, and may be ranked among the finest buildings in London. It is devoted to the performance of Italian operas and French ballets, is generally open from December to July, and is attended by the most distinguished and fashionable persons. The improvements in this part are great. That church, which you see in the distance over the tops of the houses, is St. Martin's in the fields."

"In the fields," inquired Bob; "what then, are we come to the end of the town?"

"Ha! ha! ha!" cried Tom—"the end—no, no,—I was going to say there is no end to it—no, we have not reached any thing like the centre."

THE KING'S LEVEE. Tom & Bob gratifying their Curiosity at the Expence of their Pockets.

"*Blood an owns, boderation and blarney,*" (said an Irishman, at that moment passing them with a hod of mortar on his shoulder, towards the new buildings, and leaving an ornamental patch as he went along on Bob's shoulder) "but I'll be a'ter *tipping turnups*{l} to any b——dy rogue that's tip to saying—*Black's the white of the blue part of Pat Murphy's eye*; and for that there matter," dropping the hod of mortar almost on their toes at the same time, and turning round to Bob—"By the powers! I ax the Jontleman's pardon—tho' he's not the first Jontleman that has carried mortar—where is that *big, bully-faced blackguard* that I'm looking after?" During this he brushed the mortar off Tallyho's coat with a snap of his fingers, regardless of where or on whom he distributed it.

The offender, it seemed, had taken flight while Pat was apologizing, and was no where to be found.

"Why what's the matter?" inquired Tom; "you seem in a passion."

"Och! not in the least bit, your honour! I'm only in a d——d rage. By the mug of my mother—arn't it a great shame that a Jontleman of Ireland can't walk the streets of London without having *poratees and butter-milk* throw'd in his gums?"—Hitching up the waistband of his breeches—"It won't do at all at all for Pat: its a reflection on my own native land, where—

> "*Is hospitality,*
> *All reality,*
> *No formality*
> *There you ever see;*
> *The free and easy*
> *Would so amaze ye,*
> *You'd think us all crazy,*
> *For dull we never be.*"

These lines sung with an Irish accent, to the tune of "Morgan Rattler," accompanied with a snapping of his fingers, and concluded with a something in imitation of

> 1 *Tipping Turnups—This is a phrase made use of among the prigging fraternity, to signify a turn-up—which is to knock down.*

an Irish jilt, were altogether so truly characteristic of the nation to which he belonged, as to afford our Heroes considerable amusement. Tom threw him a half-crown, which he picked up with more haste than he had thrown down the mortar in his rage.

"Long life and good luck to the Jontleman!" said Pat. "Sure enough, I won't be after drinking health and success to your Honour's pretty picture, and the devil pitch into his own cabin the fellow that would be after picking a hole or clapping a dirty patch on the coat of St. Patrick—whiskey for ever, your Honour, huzza—

> *"A drop of good whiskey*
> *Would make a man frisky."*

By this time a crowd was gathering round them, and Tom cautioned Bob in a whisper to beware of his pockets. This piece of advice however came too late, for his *blue bird's eye wipe*{1} had taken flight.

"What," said Bob, "is this done in open day?" "Are you all right and tight elsewhere?" said Tom—"if you are, toddle on and say nothing about it.—Open day!" continued he, "aye, the system of *frigging*{2}

> 1 *Blue bird's eye wipe—A blue pocket handkerchief with white spots.*

> 2 *A cant term for all sorts of thieving. The Life of the celebrated George Barrington, of Old Bailey notoriety, is admirably illustrative of this art; which by a more recent development of Hardy Vaux, appears to be almost reduced to a system, notwithstanding the wholesomeness of our laws and the vigilance of our police in their administration. However incredible it may appear, such is the force of habit and association, the latter, notwithstanding he was detected and transported, contrived to continue his depredations during*

his captivity, returned, at the expiration of his term, to his native land and his old pursuits, was transported a second time, suffered floggings and imprison-ments, without correcting what cannot but be termed the vicious propensities of his nature. He generally spent his mornings in visiting the shops of jewellers, watch-makers, pawnbrokers, &c. depending upon his address and appearance, and determining to make the whole circuit of the metropolis and not to omit a single shop in either of those branches. This scheme he actually executed so fully, that he believes he did not leave ten untried in London; for he made a point of commencing early every day, and went regularly through it, taking both sides of the way. His practice on entering a shop was to request to look at gold seals, chains, brooches, rings, or any other small articles of value, and while examining them, and looking the shopkeeper in the face, he contrived by sleight of hand to conceal two or three, sometimes more, as opportunities offered, in the sleeve of his coat, which was purposely made wide. In this practice he succeeded to a very great extent, and in the course of his career was never once detected in the fact, though on two or three occa-sions so much suspicion arose that he was obliged to exert all his effrontery, and to use very high language, in order, as the cant phrase is, to bounce the tradesman out of it; his fashionable appearance, and affected anger at his insinuations, always had the effect of inducing an apology; and in many such cases he has actually carried away the spoil, notwithstanding what passed between them, and even gone so far as to visit the same shop again a second and a third time with as good success as at first. This, with his nightly attendance at the Theatres and places of public resort, where he picked pockets of watches, snuff-boxes, &c. was for a length of time the sole business of his life. He was however secured, after secreting himself for a time, convicted, and is now transported for life—as he conceives, sold by another cele-brated Prig, whose real *name was Bill White, but better known by the title of Conky Beau.*

will be acted on sometimes by the very party you are speaking to—the expertness with which it is done is almost beyond belief."

Bob having ascertained that his handkerchief was the extent of his loss, they pursued their way towards Charing Cross.

"A line of street is intended," continued Tom, "to be made from the Opera House to terminate with that church; and here is the King's Mews, which is now turned into barracks."

"Stop thief! Stop thief!" was at this moment vociferated in their ears by a variety of voices, and turning round, they perceived a well-dressed man at full speed, followed pretty closely by a concourse of people. In a moment the whole neighbourhood appeared to be in alarm. The up-stairs windows were crowded with females—the tradesmen were at their shop-doors—the passengers were huddled together in groups, inquiring of each other—"What is the matter?—who is it?—which is him?—what has he done?" while the pursuers were increasing in numbers as they went. The bustle of the scene was new to Bob—Charing Cross and its vicinity was all in motion.

"Come," said Tom, "let us see the end of this—they are sure to *nab*{1} my gentleman before he gets much

  1 Nabbed or nibbled—Secured or taken.

farther, so let us *brush*{1} on." Then pulling his Cousin by the arm, they moved forward to the scene of action.

As they approached St. Martin's Lane, the gathering of the crowd, which was now immense, indicated to Tom a capture.

"Button up," said he, "and let us see what's the matter."

"*Arrah be easy*" cried a voice which they instantly recognized to be no other than Pat Murphy's. "I'll hold you, my dear, till the night after Doomsday, though I can't tell what day of the year that is. Where's the man wid the *gould-laced skull-cap*? Sure enough I tought I'd be up wi' you, and so now you see I'm down upon you."

At this moment a Street-keeper made way through the crowd, and Tom and Bob keeping close in his rear, came directly up to the principal performers in this interesting scene, and found honest Pat Murphy holding the man by his collar, while he was twisting and writhing to get released from the strong and determined grasp of the athletic Hibernian.

Pat no sooner saw our Heroes, than he burst out with a lusty "Arroo! arroo! there's the sweet-looking jontleman that's been robbed by a dirty *spalpeen* that's not worth the tail of a rotten red-herring. I'll give charge of dis here pick'd bladebone of a dead donkey that walks about in God's own daylight, dirting his fingers wid what don't belong to him at all at all. So sure as the devil's in his own house, and that's London, you've had your pocket pick'd, my darling, and that's news well worth hearing"—addressing himself to Dashall.

By this harangue it was pretty clearly understood that Murphy had been in pursuit of the pickpocket, and Tom immediately gave charge.

The man, however, continued to declare he was not the right person—"That, so help him G——d, the Irishman had got the wrong bull by the tail—that he was a b——dy *snitch*{2} and that he would *sarve him out*{3}—that he wished

1 Brush—Be off.

2 Snitch—A term made use of by the light-fingered tribe,
to signify an informer, by whom they have been impeached or
betrayed—So a person who turns king's evidence against his
accomplices is called a Snitch.

3 Serve him out—To punish, or be revenged upon any person
for any real or supposed injury.

he might meet him out of St. Giles's, and he would *wake*{ 1} him with an *Irish howl.*"

> 1 *Wake with an Irish howl — An Irish Wake, which is no unfrequent occurrence in the neighbourhood of St. Giles's and Saffron Hill, is one of the most comically serious ceremonies which can well be conceived, and certainly baffles all powers of description. It is, however, considered indispensable to wake the body of a de-ceased native of the sister kingdom, which is, by a sort of mock lying in state, to which all the friends, relatives, and fellow countrymen and women, of the dead person, are indiscriminately admitted; and among the low Irish this duty is frequently performed in a cellar, upon which occasions the motley group of assembled Hibernians would form a subject for the pencil of the most able satirist.*
>
> *Upon one of these occasions, when Murtoch Mulrooney, who had suffered the sentence of the law by the common hangman, for a footpad robbery, an Englishman was induced by a friend of the deceased to accompany him, and has left on record the following account of his entertainment:—*
>
> *"When we had descended (says he) about a dozen steps, we found ourselves in a subterraneous region, but fortunately not uninhabited. On the right sat three old bawds, drinking whiskey and smoking tobacco out of pipes about two inches long, (by which means, I conceive, their noses had become red,) and swearing and blasting between each puff. I was immediately saluted by one of the most sober of the ladies, and invited to take a glass of the enlivening nectar, and led to the bed exactly opposite the door, where Murtoch was laid out, and begged to pray for the repose of his precious shoul. This, however, I declined, alleging that as the parsons were paid for praying, it was their proper business. At this moment a coarse female voice exclaimed, in a sort of*

yell or Irish howl, 'Arrah! by Jasus, and why did you die, honey? — Sure enough it was not for the want of milk, meal, or tatoes.'

"In a remote corner of the room, or rather cellar, sat three draymen, five of his majesty's body guards, four sailors, six haymakers, eight chairmen, and six evidence makers, together with three bailiffs' followers, who came by turns to view the body, and take a drop of the cratur to drink repose to the shoul of their countryman; and to complete the group, they were at-tended by the journeyman Jack Ketch. The noise and confusion were almost stupefying — there were praying — swearing — crying-howling — smoking — and drinking.

"At the head of the bed where the remains of Murtoch were laid, was the picture of the Virgin Mary on one side, and that of St. Patrick on the other; and at the feet was depicted the devil and some of his angels, with the blood running down their backs, from the flagellations which they had received from the disciples of Ketigern. Whether the blue devils were flying around or not, I could not exactly discover, but the whiskey and blue ruin were evidently powerful in their effects.

"One was swearing — a second counting his beads — a third descanting on the good qualities of his departed friend, and about to try those of the whiskey — a fourth evacuating that load with which he had already overloaded himself — a fifth, declaring he could carry a fare, hear mass, knock down a member of parliament, murder a peace officer, and after all receive a pension: and while the priest was making an assignation with a sprightly female sprig of Shelalah, another was jonteelly picking his pocket. I had seen enough, and having no desire to continue in such company, made my escape with as much speed as I could from *this animated group of persons, assembled as they were upon so solemn an occasion."*

With conversation of this kind, the party were amused up St. Martin's lane, and on the remainder of the road to Bow-street, followed by many persons, some of whom pretended to have seen a part of the proceedings, and promised to give their evidence before the magistrate, who was then sitting.

On arriving in Bow Street, they entered the Brown Bear,{1} a public-house, much frequented by the officers, and in which is a strong-room for the safe custody of prisoners, where they were shewn into a dark back-parlour, as they termed it, and the officer proceeded to search the man in custody, when lo and behold! the handkerchief was not to be found about him.

Pat d——d the devil and all his works—swore "by the fiery furnace of Beelzebub, and that's the devil's own bed-chamber, that was the man that nibbled the Jontleman's *dive*,{2} and must have *ding'd away the wipe*,{3} or else what should he *bolt*{4} for?—that he was up to the *rum slum*,{5}

   1 *A former landlord of the house facetiously christened it the Russian Hotel, and had the words painted under the sign of Bruin.*

   2 *Nibbled the Jontleman's dive—Picked the gentleman's pocket.*

   3 *Ding'd away the wipe—Passed away the handkerchief to another, to escape detection. This is a very common practice in London: two or three in a party will be near, without appearing to have the least knowledge of, or connexion with each other, and the moment a depredation is committed by one, he transfers the property to one of his pals, by whom it is conveyed perhaps to the third, who decamps with it to some receiver, who will immediately advance money upon it; while, if any suspicion should fall upon the first, the*

second will perhaps busy himself in his endeavours to secure the offender, well knowing no proof of possession can be brought against him.

4 Bolt—Run away; try to make an escape.

5 Rum slum—Gammon—queer talk or action, in which some fraudulent intentions are discoverable or suspected.

and down upon the *kiddies*{1}—and sure enough you're *boned,*{2} my dear boy."

Some of the officers came in, and appeared to know the prisoner well, as if they had been acquainted with each other upon former official business; but as the lost property was not found upon him, it was the general opinion that nothing could be done, and the accused began to exercise his wit upon Murphy, which roused Pat's blood:

"For the least thing, you know, makes an Irishman roar."

At length, upon charging him with having been caught *blue-pigeon flying,*{3} Pat gave him the lie in his teeth—swore he'd fight him for all the *blunt*{4} he had about him, "which to be sure," said he, "is but a sweet pretty half-a-crown, and be d——d to you—good luck to it! Here goes," throwing the half-crown upon the floor, which the prisoner attempted to pick up, but was prevented by Pat's stamping his foot upon it, while he was *doffing his jacket,*{5} exclaiming—

"Arrah, be after putting your dirty fingers in your pocket, and don't spoil the King's picture by touching it—devil burn me, but I'll *mill your mug to muffin dust*{6} before I'll give up that beautiful looking bit; so tip us your mauley,{7} and no more blarney."

1 Down upon the Kiddies—To understand the arts and manouvres of thieves and sharpers.

2 Boned—Taken or secured.

s Blue pigeon flying—The practice of stealing lead from houses, churches, or other buildings. A species of

*depredation very prevalent in London and its vicinity, and
which is but too much encouraged by the readiness with which
it can be disposed of to the plumbers in general.*

4 Blunt—A flash term for money.

5 Doffing his Jacket—Taking off his jacket.

*6 Mill your mug to muffin dust—The peculiarity of the Irish
character for overstrained metaphor, may perhaps, in some
degree, account for the Hibernian's idea of beating his head
to flour, though he was afterwards inclined to commence his
operations in the true style and character of the prize
ring, where*

*"Men shake hands before they box, Then give each other
plaguy knocks, With all the love and kindness of a brother."
7 Tip us your mauley—Give me your hand. Honour is so sacred
a thing with the Irish, that the rapid transition from a
violent expression to the point of honour, is no uncommon
thing amongst them; and in this instance it is quite clear
that although he meant to mill the mug of his opponent to
muffin dust, he had a notion of the thing, and intended to
do it in an honourable way.*

During this conversation, the spectators, who were numerous, were employed in endeavouring to pacify the indignant Hibernian, who by this time had buffid it, or, in other words, *peeled in prime twig*,{1} for a regular *turn to*.{2} All was noise and confusion, when a new group of persons entered the room—another capture had been made, and another charge given. It was however with some difficulty that honest Pat Murphy was prevailed upon to remain a little quiet, while one of the officers beckoned Dashall out of the room, and gave him to understand that the man in custody, just brought in, was a well-known *pal*{3} of the one first suspected, though they took not the least notice of each other upon meeting. In the mean time, another officer in the room had been searching the person of the last captured, from whose bosom he drew the identical handkerchief of Bob; and the Irishman recollected seeing him in the crowd opposite the Opera House.

This cleared up the mystery in some degree, though the two culprits affected a total ignorance of each other. The property of the person who had given the last charge was also discovered, and it was deemed absolutely necessary to take them before the Magistrate. But as some new incidents will arise on their introduction to the office, we shall reserve them for the next Chapter.

> 1 *Buff'd it, or peeled in prime twig — Stripped to the skin in good order. The expressions are well known, and frequently in use, among the sporting characters and lovers of the fancy.*
>
> 2 *Turn to, or set to — The commencement of a battle.*
>
> 3 *Pal — A partner or confederate.*

CHAPTER VIII

Houses, churches, mixt together,
Streets unpleasant in all weather;
Prisons, palaces contiguous,
Gates, a bridge—the Thames irriguous;
Gaudy things, enough to tempt ye,
Showy outsides, insides empty;
Bubbles, trades, mechanic arts,
Coaches, wheelbarrows, and carts;
Warrants, bailiffs, bills unpaid,
Lords of laundresses afraid;
Rogues, that nightly rob and shoot men,
Hangmen, aldermen, and footmen;
Lawyers, poets, priests, physicians,
Noble, simple, all conditions;
Worth beneath a thread-bare cover,
Villainy bedaubed all over;
Women, black, red, fair, and grey,
Prudes, and such as never pray;
Handsome, ugly, noisy still,
Some that will not, some that will;
Many a beau without a shilling,
Many a widow not unwilling;
Many a bargain, if you strike it:—
This is London—How d'ye like it?

ON entering the Public Office, Bow-street, we must leave our readers to guess at the surprise and astonishment with which the Hon. Tom Dashall and his Cousin beheld their lost friend, Charles Sparkle, who it appeared had been kindly accommodated with a lodging gratis in a neighbouring watch-house, not, as it may readily be supposed, exactly suitable to his taste or inclination. Nor was wonder less excited in the mind of Sparkle at this unexpected meeting, as unlooked for as it was fortunate to all parties. There was however no opportunity at the present moment for an explanation, as the worthy Magistrate immediately proceeded to an investigation of the case just brought before him, upon which there was no difficulty in deciding. The charge was made, the handkerchief sworn to, and the men, who were well known as old hands upon the town, committed for trial. The most remarkable feature in the examination being the evidence of Pat Murphy, who by this time had recollected that the man who was taken with the property about his person, was the very identical aggressor who had offended him while the hod of mortar was on his shoulder, before the conversation commenced between himself and Tom opposite the Opera-house.

"Sure enough, your Honour," said he, "its a true bill. I'm an Irishman, and I don't care who knows it—I don't fight under false colours, but love the land of potatoes, and honour St. Patrick. That there man with the *blue toggery*{1} tipp'd me a bit of blarney, what did not suit my stomach. I dropp'd my load, which he took for an order to quit, and so *mizzled*{2} out of my way, or by the big bull of Ballynafad, I'd have powdered his wig with brick-dust, and bothered his bread-basket with a little human kindness in the shape of an Irishman's fist; and then that there other dirty end of a shelalah, while the Jontleman—long life to your Honour, (bowing to Tom Dashall)—was houlding a bit of conversation with Pat Murphy, *grabb'd*{3} his pocket-handkerchief, and was after shewing a leg,{4} when a little boy that kept his oglers upon 'em, let me into the secret, and let the cat out of the bag by bawling—Stop thief! He darted off like a cow at the sound of the bagpipes, and I boulted a'ter him like a good'un; so when I came up to him, Down you go, says I, and down he was; and that's all I know about the matter."

As the prisoners were being taken out of court, the Hibernian followed them. "Arrah," said he, "my lads, as I have procured you a lodging for nothing, here's the half-a-crown, what the good-looking Jontleman gave me; it may sarve you in time of need, so take it along with you, perhaps you may want it more than I do; and if you know the pleasure of spending money that is honestly come by, it may teach you a lesson that may keep you out of the clutches of Jock Ketch, and save

> 1 Blue toggery—*Toggery is a flash term for clothing in general, but is made use of to describe a blue coat.*

2 Mizzled—Ran away.

3 Grabb'd—Took, or stole.

4 Shewing a leg—or, as it is sometimes called, giving leg-bail—making the best use of legs to escape detection.

you from dying in a horse's night-cap{1}—there, be off wid you."

The Hon. Tom Dashall, who had carefully watched the proceedings of Pat, could not help moralizing upon this last act of the Irishman, and the advice which accompanied it. "Here," said he to himself, "is a genuine display of national character. Here is the heat, the fire, the effervescence, blended with the generosity and open-heartedness, so much boasted of by the sons of Erin, and so much eulogized by travellers who have visited the Emerald Isle." And slipping a sovereign into his hand, after the execution of a bond to prosecute the offenders, each of them taking an arm of Sparkle, they passed down Bow-street, conversing on the occurrences in which they had been engaged, of which the extraordinary appearance of Sparkle was the most prominent and interesting.

"How in the name of wonder came you in such a scrape?" said Tom.

"Innocently enough, I can assure you," replied Sparkle—"with my usual luck—a bit of gig, a lark, and a turn up.{2}

> "... 'Twas waxing rather late,
> And reeling bucks the street began to scour,
> While guardian watchmen, with a tottering gait,
> Cried every thing quite clear, except the hour."

1 Horse's night-cap—A halter.

2 A bit of gig—a lark—a turn up—are terms made use of to signify a bit of fun of any kind, though the latter more generally means a fight. Among the bucks and bloods of the Metropolis, a bit of fun or a lark, as they term it, ending in a milling match, a night's lodging in the watch-house, and a composition with the Charleys in the morning, to avoid exposure before the Magistrate, is a proof of high spirit—a prime delight, and serves in many cases to stamp a man's character. Some, however, who have not courage enough to brave a street-row and its consequences, are fond of fun of other kinds, heedless of the consequences to others. "Go it, my boys," says one of the latter description, "keep it up, huzza! I loves fun—for I made such a fool of my father last April day:—but what do you think I did now, eh?—Ha! ha! ha!—I will tell you what makes me laugh so: we were keeping it up in prime twig, faith, so about four o'clock in the morning 1 went down into the kitchen, and there was Dick the waiter snoring like a pig before a blazing fire—done up, for the fellow can't keep it up as we jolly boys do: So thinks 1, I'll have you, my boy—and what does I do, but I goes softly and takes the tongs, and gets a red hot coal as big as my head, and plumpt it upon the fellow's foot and run away, because I loves fun, you know: So it has lamed him, and that makes me laugh so—Ha! ha! ha!—it was what I call better than your rappartees and your bobinâtes. I'll tell you more too: you must know I was in high tip-top spirits, faith, so I stole a dog from a blind man—for I do loves fun: so then the blind man cried for his dog, and that made me laugh heartily: So says I to the blind man—Hallo, Master, what a you a'ter, what is you up to? does you want your dog?—Yes, Sir, says he. Now only you mark what I said to the blind man—Then go and look for him, old chap, says I—Ha! ha! ha!—that's your sort, my boy, keep it up, keep it up, d— — me.   That's the worst of it, I always turn sick when I think of a Parson—I always do; and my brother he is a parson too, and he hates to hear any body swear: so you know I always swear like a trooper when I am near him, on purpose to roast him. I went to dine with him one day last week, and there was my sisters, and two or three more of what you call your modest women; but I sent 'em all from the table, and then laugh'd at 'em, for I loves fun, and that was fun alive 0. And so there was nobody in the room but my brother and me, and I begun to swear most sweetly: I never swore so well in all my life—I swore all my new oaths; it would have done you good to have heard me swear; till at last my brother looked frightened, and d— — me that was good fun. At last, he lifted up his hands and eyes to Heaven, and calls out O tempora, O mores! But I was not to be done so. Oh! oh! Brother, says I, what you think to frighten me by calling all your family about you; but I don't care for you, nor your family neither—so stow it— I'll mill the whole troop—Only bring your Tempora and Mores here, that's all—let us have fair play, I'll tip 'em the Gas in a flash of lightning—I'll box 'em for five pounds, d— — me: here, where's Tempora and Mores, where are they? My eyes, how he did stare when he see me ready for a set to— I never laugh'd so in my life—he made but two steps out of the room, and left me master of the field. What d'ye think of that for a lark, eh?—Keep it up—keep it up, d— — me, says I—so I sets down to the table, drank as much as I could—then I mix'd the heel-taps all in one bottle, and broke all the empty ones—then bid adieu to Tempora and Mores, and rolled home in a hackney-coach in prime and plummy order, d— — me."

"Coming along Piccadilly last night after leaving you, I was overtaken at the corner of Rupert-street by our old college-companion Harry Hartwell, pursuing his way to the Hummums, where it seems he has taken up his abode. Harry, you remember, never was exactly one of us; he studies too much, and pores everlastingly over musty old volumes of Law Cases, Blackstone's Commentaries, and other black books, to qualify himself for the black art, and as fit and proper person to appear at the Bar. The length of time that had elapsed since our last meeting was sufficient inducement for us to crack a bottle together; so taking his arm, we proceeded to the place of destination, where we sat talking over past times, and indulging our humour till half-past one o'clock, when I sallied forth on my return to Long's, having altogether abandoned my original intention of calling in Golden-square. At the corner of Leicester-square, my ears were assailed with a little of the night music—the rattles were in full chorus, and the Charleys, in prime twig,{1} were mustering from all quarters.

Real Life in London - Volume I

TOM & BOB Catching a Charley Napping.

"The street was all alive, and I made my way through the crowd to the immediate scene of action, which was rendered peculiarly interesting by the discovery of a dainty bit of female beauty shewing fight with half a dozen watchmen, in order to extricate herself from the grasp of these guardians of our peace. She was evidently under the influence of the Bacchanalian god, which invigorated her arm, without imparting discretion to her head, and she laid about her with such dexterity, that the old files{2} were fearful of losing their prey; but the odds were fearfully against her, and never did I feel my indignation more aroused, than when I beheld a sturdy ruffian aim a desperate blow at her head with his rattle, which in all probability, had it taken the intended effect, would have sent her in search of that peace in the other world, of which she was experiencing so little in this. It was not possible for me to stand by, an idle spectator of the destruction of a female who appeared to have no defender, whatever might be the nature of the offence alleged or committed. I therefore warded off the blow with my left arm, and with my right gave him a well-planted blow on the conk,{3} which sent him piping into the kennel. In a moment I was surrounded and charged with a violent assault upon the charley,{4} and interfering with the guardians of the night in the execution of their duty. A complete diversion took place from the original object of their fury, and in the bustle to secure me, the unfortunate girl made her escape, where to, or how, heaven

> 1 *Prime twig—Any thing accomplished in good order, or with dexterity: a person well dressed, or in high spirits, is considered to be in prime twig.*

> 2 *Old Jiles—A person who has had a long course of experience in the arts of fraud, so as to become an adept in the manouvres of the town, is termed a deep file—a rum file, or an old file.*

> 3 *Conk—The nose.*

> 4 *Charley—A watchman.*

only knows. Upon finding this, I made no resistance, but marched boldly along with the scouts{1} to St. Martin's watch-house, where we arrived just as a hackney coach drew up to the door.

"Take her in, d———n her eyes, she shall *stump up the rubbish*{2} before I leave her, or give me the address of her *flash covey*,{3} and so here goes." By this time we had entered the watch-house, where I perceived the awful representative of justice seated in an arm chair, with a good blazing fire, smoking his pipe in consequential ease. A crowd of Charleys, with broken lanterns, broken heads, and other symptoms of a row, together with several casual spectators, had gained admittance, when Jarvis entered, declaring—By G——he wouldn't be choused by any wh———re or cull in Christendom, and he would make 'em come down pretty handsomely, or he'd know the reason why: "And so please your Worship, Sir"—then turning round, "hallo," said he, "Sam, what's becom'd of that there voman—eh—vhat, you've been playing booty eh, and let her escape." The man to whom this was intended to be addressed did not appear to be present, as no reply was made. However, the case was briefly explained.

"But, by G——, I von't put any thing in Sam's vay again," cried Jarvey.{4} For my own part, as I knew nothing of the occurrences adverted to, I was as much in the dark as if I had gone home without interruption. The representations of the Charleys proved decisive against me—in vain I urged the cause of humanity, and the necessity I felt of protecting a defenceless female from the violence of accumulating numbers, and that I had done no more than every man ought to have done upon such an occasion. *Old puff and swill*, the lord of the night, declared that I must have acted with malice afore-thought—that I was a pal in the concern, and that I had been instrumental in the design of effecting a rescue; and, after a very short deliberation, he concluded that I must be a notorious rascal, and desired me to make up my mind to remain with him for the remainder of the night. Not relishing this, I proposed to send for bail, assuring him of my

1 Scouts—Watchmen.

3 *Stump up the rubbish—Meaning she (or he) shall pay, or find money.*

3 *Flash covey—A fancy man, partner or protector*

4 *Jarvey—A coachman.*

attendance in the morning; but was informed it could not be accepted of, as it was clearly made out against me that I had committed a violent breach of the peace, and nothing at that time could be produced that would prove satisfactory. Under these circumstances, and partly induced by a desire to avoid being troublesome in other quarters, I submitted to a restraint which it appeared I could not very well avoid, and, taking my seat in an armchair by the fire-side, I soon fell fast asleep, from which I was only aroused by the occasional entrances and exits of the guardians, until between four and five o'clock, when a sort of general muster of the Charleys took place, and each one depositing his nightly paraphernalia, proceeded to his own habitation. Finding the liberation of others from their duties would not have the effect of emancipating me from my confinement, which was likely to be prolonged to eleven, or perhaps twelve o'clock, I began to feel my situation as a truly uncomfortable one, when I was informed by the watch-house keeper, who resides upon the spot, that he was going to *turn in*,{1} that there was fire enough to last till his wife turn'd out, which would be about six o'clock, and, as I had the appearance of a gentleman, if there was any thing I wanted, she would endeavour to make herself useful in obtaining it. "But Lord," said he, "there is no such thing as believing any body now-a-days—there was such sets out, and such manouvering, that nobody knew nothing of nobody."

"I am obliged to you, my friend," said I, "for this piece of information, and in order that you may understand something of the person you are speaking to beyond the mere exterior view, here is half-a-crown for your communication."

"Why, Sir," said he, laying on at the same moment a shovel of coals, "this here makes out what I said—Don't you see, said I, that 'are Gentleman is a gentleman every inch of him, says I—as don't want nothing at all no more nor what is right, and if so be as how he's got himself in a bit of a hobble, I knows very well as how he's got the tip{2} in his pocket, and does'nt want for spirit to pull it out—Perhaps you might like some breakfast, sir?"

> 1 Turn in—*Going to bed. This is a term most in use among seafaring men.*
>
> 2 *Tip is synonymous with blunt, and means money.*

"Why yes," said I—for I began to feel a little inclined that way.

"O my wife, Sir," said he, "will do all you want, when she rouses herself."

"I suppose," continued I, "you frequently have occasion to accommodate persons in similar situations?"

"Lord bless you! yes, sir, and a strange set of rum customers we have too sometimes—why it was but a few nights ago we had 'em stowed here as thick as three in a bed. We had 'em all upon the *hop*{1}—you never see'd such fun in all your life, and this here place was as full of curiosities as Pidcock's at Exeter Change, or Bartlemy-fair—Show 'em up here, all alive alive O!"

"Indeed!" said I, feeling a little inquisitive on the subject; "and how did this happen?"

"Why it was a *rummish* piece of business altogether. There was a large party of dancing fashionables all met together for a little jig in St. Martin's lane, and a very pretty medley there was of them. The fiddlers wagg'd their elbows, and the lads and lasses their trotters, till about one o'clock, when, just as they were in the midst of a quadrille, in burst the officers, and quickly changed the tune. The appearance of these gentlemen had an instantaneous effect upon all parties present: the cause of their visit was explained, and the whole squad taken into custody, to give an account of themselves, and was brought here in hackney-coaches. The delicate Miss and her assiduous partner, who, a short time before had been all spirits and animation, were now sunk in gloomy reflections upon the awkwardness of their situation; and many of our inhabitants would have fainted when they were informed they would have to appear before the Magistrate in the morning, but for the well-timed introduction of a little drap of the *cratur*, which an Irish lady ax'd me to fetch for her. But the best of the fun was, that in the group we had a Lord and a Parson! For the dignity of the one, and the honour of the other, they were admitted to bail—Lord have mercy upon us! said the Parson—Amen, said the Lord; and this had the desired effect upon the Constable of the night, for he let them off on the sly, you understand: But my eyes what work there was in the morning! sixteen Jarveys, full of live lumber,

1 Hop—A dance.

were taken to Bow-street, in a nice pickle you may be sure, dancing-pumps and silk-stockings, after setting in the watch-house all night, and surrounded by lots of people that hooted and howled, as the procession passed along, in good style. They were safely landed at the Brown Bear, from which they were handed over in groups to be examined by the Magistrate, when the men were discharged upon giving satisfactory accounts, and the women after some questions being put to them. You see all this took place because they were dancing in an unlicensed room. It was altogether a laughable set-out as ever you see'd—the Dandys and the Dandyzettes—the Exquisites—the Shopmen—the Ladies' maid and the Prentice Boys—my Lord and his Reverence—mingled up higgledy-piggledy, pigs in the straw, with Bow-street Officers, Runners and Watchmen—Ladies squalling and fainting, Men swearing and almost fighting. It would have been a pleasure to have kick'd up a row that night, a purpose to get admission—you would have been highly amused, I'll assure you—good morning, Sir." And thus saying, he turned the lock upon me, and left me to my meditations. In about a couple of hours the old woman made her appearance, and prepared me some coffee; and at eleven o'clock came the Constable of the night, to accompany me before the Magistrate.

"Aware that the circumstances were rather against me, and that I had no right to interfere in other persons' business or quarrels, I consulted him upon the best mode of making up the matter; for although I had really done no more than becomes a man in protecting a female, I had certainly infringed upon the law, in effecting the escape of a person in custody, and consequently was liable to the penalty or penalties in such cases made and provided. On our arrival at the Brown Bear, I was met by a genteel-looking man, who delivered me a letter, and immediately disappeared. Upon breaking the seal, I found its contents as follows:

Dear Sir, Although unknown to me, I have learned enough of your character to pronounce you a trump, a prime cock, and nothing but a good one. I am detained by John Doe and Richard Roe with their d——d *fieri facias,* or I should be with you. However, I trust you will excuse the liberty I take in requesting you will make use of the enclosed for the purpose of shaking yourself out of the hands of the scouts and their pals. We shall have some opportunities of meeting, when I will explain: in the mean time, believe me I am

Your's truly,

Tom.

"With this advice, so consonant with my own opinion, I immediately complied; and having satisfied the broken-headed Charley, and paid all expences incurred, I was induced to walk into the office merely to give a look around me, when by a lucky chance I saw you enter. And thus you have a full, true, and particular account of the peregrinations of your humble servant."

Listening with close attention to this narrative of Sparkle's, all other subjects had escaped observation, till they found themselves in the Strand.

"Whither are we bound?" inquired Sparkle.

"On a voyage of discoveries," replied Dashall, "and we just wanted you to act as pilot."

"What place is this?" inquired Bob.

"That," continued Sparkle, "is Somerset-house. It is a fine old building; it stands on the banks of the Thames, raised on piers and arches, and is now appropriated to various public offices, and houses belonging to the various offices of the Government."

"The terrace, which lies on the river, is very fine, and may be well viewed from Waterloo Bridge. The front in the Strand, you perceive, has a noble aspect, being composed of a rustic basement, supporting a Corinthian order of columns crowned with an attic in the centre, and at the extremities with a balustrade. The south front, which looks into the court, is very elegant in its composition.

"The basement consists of nine large arches; and three in the centre open, forming the principal entrance; and three at each end, filled with windows of the Doric order, are adorned with pilasters, entablatures, and pediments. On the key-stones of the nine arches are carved, in alto relievo, nine colossal masks, representing the Ocean, and the eight main Rivers of England, viz. *Thames, Humber, Mersey, Dee, Medway, Tweed, Tyne, and Severn*, with appropriate emblems to denote their various characters.

"Over the basement the Corinthian order consists of ten columns upon pedestals, having their regular entablature. It comprehends two floors, and the attic in the centre of the front extends over three intercolomniations, and is divided into three parts by four colossal statues placed on the columns of the order. It terminates with a group consisting of the arms of the British empire, supported on one side by the Genius of England, and by Fame, sounding the trumpet, on the other. These three open arches in the front form the principal entrance to the whole of the structure, and lead to an elegant vestibule decorated with Doric columns.

"The terrace, which fronts the Thames, is spacious, and commands a beautiful view of part of the river, including Blackfriars, Waterloo, and Westminster Bridges. It is reared on a grand rustic basement, having thirty-two spacious arches. The arcade thus formed is judiciously relieved by projections ornamented with rusticated columns, and the effect of the whole of the terrace from the water is truly grand and noble. There is however, at present, no admission for the public to it; but, in all probability, it will be open to all when the edifice is completed, which would form one of the finest promenades in the world, and prove to be one of the first luxuries of the metropolis.

"That statue in the centre is a representation of our late King, George the Third, with the Thames at his feet, pouring wealth and plenty from a large Cornucopia. It is executed by Bacon, and has his characteristic cast of expression. It is in a most ludicrous situation, being placed behind, and on the brink of a deep area.

"In the vestibule are the rooms of the Royal Society, the Society of Antiquarians, and the Royal Academy of Arts, all in a very grand and beautiful style. Over the door of the Royal Academy is a bust of Michael Angelo; and over the door leading to the Royal Society and Society of Antiquarians, you will find the bust of Sir Isaac Newton.

"The Government-offices, to which this building is devoted, are objects of great astonishment to strangers, being at once commodious and elegant, and worthy the wealth of the nation to which they belong. The hall of the Navy office is a fine room with two fronts, one facing the terrace and river, and the other facing the court. On the right is the Stamp-office: it consists of a multitude of apartments: the room in which the stamping is executed is very interesting to the curious. On the left you see the Pay-office of the Navy.

"The principal thing to attract notice in this edifice is the solidity and completeness of the workmanship in the masonry, and indeed in every other part."

After taking a rather prolonged view of this elegant edifice, they again sallied forth into the Strand, mingling with all the noise and bustle of a crowded street, where by turns were to be discovered, justling each other, parsons, lawyers, apothecaries, projectors, excisemen, organists, picture-sellers, bear and monkey-leaders, fiddlers and bailiffs. The barber and the chimney-sweeper were however always observed to be careful in avoiding the touch of each other, as if contamination must be the inevitable consequence.

"My dear fellow!" exclaimed a tall and well-dressed person, who dragged the Honourable Tom Dashall on one side—"you are the very person I wanted—I'm very glad to see you in town again—but I have not a moment to spare—the blood-hounds are in pursuit—this term will be ended in two days, then comes the long vacation—liberty without hiring a horse—you understand—was devilishly afraid of being nabb'd just now—should have been dished if I had—lend me five shillings—come, make haste."

"Five shillings, Diddler, when am I to be paid? you remember—' When I grow rich' was the reply."

"Know—yes, I know all about it—but no matter, I'm not going to settle accounts just now, so don't detain me, I hate Debtor and Creditor. Fine sport to-morrow, eh—shall be at the Ring—in cog.—take no notice—disguised as a Quaker—Obadiah Lankloaks—d——d large beaver hat, and hide my physog.—Lend me what silver you have, and be quick about it, for I can't stay—thank you, you're a d——a good fellow, Tom, a trump—shall now pop into a hack, and drive into another county—thank ye—good day—by by."

During this harangue, while Tost was counting his silver, the ingenious Mr. Diddler seized all he had, and whipping it speedily into his pocket, in a few minutes was out of his sight.

Sparkle observing Dashall looking earnestly after Diddler, approached, and giving him a lusty slap on the shoulder—"Ha! ha! ha!" exclaimed he, "what are you done again?"

"I suppose so," said Dashall; "confound the fellow, he is always borrowing: I never met him in my life but he had some immediate necessity or other to require a loan of a little temporary supply, as he calls it."

"I wonder," said Sparkle, "that you are so ready to lend, after such frequent experience—how much does he owe you?"

"Heaven only knows," continued Tom, "for I do not keep account against him, I must even trust to his honour—so it is useless to stand here losing our time—Come, let us forward."

"With all my heart,", said Sparkle, "and with permission I propose a visit to the Bonassus, a peep at St. Paul's, and a chop at Dolly's."

This proposition being highly approved of, they continued their walk along the Strand, towards Temple Bar, and in a few minutes were attracted by the appearance of men dressed in the garb of the Yeomen of the Guards, who appeared active in the distribution of hand-bills, and surrounded a house on the front of which appeared a long string of high and distinguished names, as patrons and patronesses of the celebrated animal called the Bonassus. Crossing the road in their approach to the door, Tallyho could not help admiring the simple elegance of a shop-front belonging to a grocer, whose name is Peck.

"Very handsome and tasty, indeed," replied Sparkle; "that combination of marble and brass has a light and elegant effect: it has no appearance of being laboured at. The inhabitant of the house I believe is a foreigner, I think an Italian; but London boasts of some of the most elegant shops in the world." And by this time they entered the opposite house.

CHAPTER IX

"In London my life is a ring of delight,
In frolics I keep up the day and the night;
I snooze at the Hummums till twelve, perhaps later,
I rattle the bell, and I roar up the Waiter;
'Your Honour,' says he, and he makes me a leg;
He brings me my tea, but I swallow an egg;
For tea in a morning's a slop I renounce,
So I down with a glass of good right cherry-bounce.
With—swearing, tearing—ranting, jaunting—slashing,
smashing—smacking, cracking—rumbling, tumbling
—laughing, quaffing—smoking, joking—swaggering,
Staggering:
So thoughtless, so knowing, so green and so mellow,
This, this is the life of a frolicsome fellow."

UPON entering the house, and depositing their shilling each to view this newly discovered animal from the Apalachian mountains of America, and being supplied with immense long bills descriptive of his form and powers—"Come along (said Sparkle,) let us have a look at the most wonderful production of nature—only seventeen months old, five feet ten inches high, and one of the most fashionable fellows in the metropolis."

"It should seem so," said Tallyho, "by the long list of friends and visitors that are detailed in the commencement of the bill of fare."

"Perhaps," said Tom, "there are more Bon asses than one."

"Very likely (continued Sparkle;) but let me tell you the allusion in this case does not apply, for this animal has nothing of the donkey about him, and makes no noise, as you will infer from the following lines in the Bill:

"As the Bonassus does not roar,
His fame is widely known,
For no dumb animal before

Has made such noise in town."

At this moment the barking of a dog assailed their ears, and suspended the conversation. Passing onward to the den of the Bonassus, they found a dark-featured gentleman of middling stature, with his hair, whiskers, and ears, so bewhitened with powder as to form a complete contrast with his complexion and a black silk handkerchief which he wore round his neck, holding a large brown-coloured dog by the collar, in order to prevent annoyance to the visitors.

"D——n the dog, (exclaimed he) although he is the best tempered creature in the world, he don't seem to like the appearance of the Bonassus "—and espying Sparkle, "Ha, my dear fellow! how are you?—I have not seen you for a long while."

"Why, Sir D—n—ll, I am happy to say I never was better in my life—allow me to introduce you to my two friends, the Hon. Mr. Dashall, and Robert Tallyho—Sir D—n—ll Harlequin."

The mutual accompaniments of such an introduction having passed among them, the Knight, who was upon the moment of departure as they entered, expressed his approbation of the animal he had been viewing, and, lugging his puppy by one hand, and his cudgel in the other, wished them a good morning.

"There is an eccentric man of Title," continued Sparkle.

"I should judge," said Bob, "there was a considerable portion of eccentricity about him, by his appearance. Is he a Baronet?"

"A Baronet," (replied Sparkle) "no, no, he is no other than a *Quack Doctor.*"{1}

> *1 Of all the subjects that afford opportunities for the satiric pen in the Metropolis, perhaps there is none more abundant or prolific than that of Quackery. Dr. Johnson observes, that "cheats can seldom stand long against laughter." But if a judgment is really to be formed from existing facts, it may be supposed that times are so materially changed since the residence of that able writer*

in this sublunary sphere, that the reverse of the position may with greater propriety be asserted. For such is the prevailing practice of the present day, that, according to the opinion of thousands, there is nothing to be done without a vast deal more of profession and pretence than actual power, and he who is the best able to bear laughing at, is the most likely to realize the hopes he entertains of obtaining celebrity, and of having his labours crowned with success. Nothing can be more evident than this in the Medical profession, though there are successful Quacks of all kinds, and in all situations, to be found in London. This may truly be called the age of Quackery, from the abundance of impostors of every kind that prey upon society; and such as cannot or will not think for themselves, ought to be guarded in a publication of this nature, against the fraudulent acts of those persons who make it their business and profit to deteriorate the health, morals, and amusements of the public. But, in the present instance, we are speaking of the Medical Quack only, than which perhaps there is none more remarkable.

The race of Bossys, Brodrums, Solomons, Perkins, Chamants, &c. is filled by others of equal notoriety, and no doubt of equal utility. The Cerfs, the Curries, the Lamerts, the Ruspinis, the Coopers, and Munroes, are all equally entitled to public approbation, particularly if we may credit the letters from the various persons who authenticate the miraculous cures they have performed in the most inveterate, we hail almost said, the most impossible, cases. If those persons are really in existence (and who can doubt it?) they certainly have occasion to be thankful for their escapes, and we congratulate them; for in our estimation Quack Doctors seem to consider the human frame merely as a subject for experiments, which if successful will secure the reputation of the practitioner. The acquisition of fame and fortune is, in the estimation of these philosophers, cheaply purchased by sacrificing the lives of a few of the vulgar, to whom they prescribe gratis; and the slavish obedience of some patients to the Doctor, is really astonishing. It is said that a convalescent at Bath wrote to his Physician in London, to know whether he might eat sauce with his pork; but we have not been able to discover whether he expected an answer gratis; that would perhaps have been an experiment not altogether grateful to the Doctor's feelings.

The practice of advertising and billing the town has become so common, that a man scarcely opens a coal-shed, or a potatoe-stall, without giving due notice of it in the newspapers, and distributing hand-bills: and frequently with great success. But our Doctors, who make no show of their commodities, have no mode of making themselves known without it. Hence the quantity of bills thrust into the hand of the passenger through the streets of London, which divulge the almost incredible performances of their publishers. A high-sounding name, such as The Chevalier de diamant, the Chevalier de Ruspini, or The Medical Board, well bored behind and before, are perhaps more necessary, with a few paper puffs—as "palpable hits, my Lord," than either skill or practice, to obtain notice and secure fame.

The Chevalier de Chamant, who was originally a box-maker, and a man of genius, considering box-making a plebeian occupation, was for deducing a logical position, not exactly perhaps by fair argument, but at all events through the teeth, and was determined, although he could not, like Dr. Pangloss, mend the cacology of his friends, at least to give them an opportunity for plenty of jaw-work. With this laudable object in view, he obtained a patent for making artificial teeth of mineral paste; and in his advertisements condescended not to prove their utility as substitutes for the real teeth, when decayed or wanting, (this was beneath his notice, and would have been a piece of mere plebeian Quackery unworthy of his great genius,) but absolutely assured the world that his mineral teeth were infinitely superior to any production of nature, both for mastication and beauty! How this was relished we know not; but he declared (and he certainly ought to know) that none but silly and timid persons would hesitate for one moment to have their teeth drawn, and substitute his minerals: and it is wonderful to relate, that although his charges were enormous, and the operation (as may be supposed) not the most pleasant, yet people could not resist the ingenious Chevalier's fascinating and drawing puffs; in consequence of which he soon became possessed of a large surplus of capital, with which he determined to speculate in the Funds.

For this purpose he employed old Tom Bish, the Stockbroker, to purchase stock for the amount; but owing to a sudden fluctuation in the market, a considerable depreciation took place between the time of purchase and that of payment; a circumstance which made the Chevalier grin and show his teeth: Determining however, not to become a victim to the fangs of Bulls and Bears, but rather to dive like a duck, he declared the bargain was not legal, and that he would not be bound by it. Bish upon this occasion proved a hard-mouthed customer to the man of teeth, and was not a quiet subject to be drawn, but brought an action against the mineral monger, and recovered the debt. Tom's counsel, in stating the case, observed, that the Defendant would find the law could bite sharper aud hold tighter than any teeth he could make; and so it turned out.

The Chevalier de R—sp—ni is another character who has cut no small figure in this line, but has recently made his appearance in the Gazette, not exactly on so happy an occasion as such a circumstance would be to his brother chip, Dr. D—n—ll, now (we suppose) Sir Francis—though perhaps equally entitled to the honour of knighthood. The Chevalier has for some years looked Royalty in the face by residing opposite Carlton House, and taken every precaution to let the public know that such an important public character was there to be found, by displaying his name as conspicuously as possible on brass plates, &c. so that the visitors to Carlton House could hardly fail to notice him as the second greatest Character of that great neighbourhood. But what could induce so great a man to sport his figure in the Gazette, is as unaccountable as the means by which he obtained such happy celebrity. Had it occurred immediately after the war, it might have been concluded without much stretch of imagination, that the Chevalier, who prides himself on his intimacy with all the great men of the day, had, through the friendship of the Duke of Wellington, made a contract for the teeth and jaw-bones of all who fell at the battle of Waterloo, and that by bringing to market so great a stock at one time, the article had fallen in value, and left the speculating Chevalier so great a loser as to cause his bankruptcy. Whether such is the real cause or not, it is difficult to ascertain what could induce the Chevalier to descend from his dealings with the head to dabble with lower commodities.

Among other modes of obtaining notoriety, usually resorted to by Empirics, the Chevalier used to job a very genteel carriage and pair, but his management was so excellent, that the expenses of his equipage were very trifling; for as it was not intended to run, but merely to stand at the door like a barker at a broker's shop, or a direction-post, he had the loan on very moderate terms, the job-master taking into account that the wind of the cattle was not likely to be injured, or the wheels rattled to pieces by velocity, or smashed by any violent concussion.

The Chevalier had a Son, who unfortunately was not endowed by nature with so much ambition or information as his father; for, frequently when the carriage has been standing at the door, he has been seen drinking gin most cordially with Coachee, without once thinking of the evils of example, or recollecting that he was one of the family. Papa used to be very angry on these occasions, because, as he said, it was letting people know that Coachee was only hired as &job, and not as a family domestic.

For the great benefit and advantage of the community, Medical Boards have recently been announced in various parts of the Metropolis, where, according to the assertions of the Principals, in their advertisements, every disease incident to human nature is treated by men of skilful practice; and among these truly useful establishments, those of Drs. Cooper, Munro, and Co. of Charlotte house, Blackfriars, and Woodstock-house, Oxford-road, are not the least conspicuous. Who these worthies are, it is perhaps difficult to ascertain. One thing however is certain, that Sir F — —s C— —e D—n—ll, M.D. is announced as Treasurer, therefore there can be no doubt but that all is fair above board, for

"Brutus is an honourable man,
So are they all — all honourable men."

And where so much skill derived from experience is exercised, it cannot be doubted but great and important benefits may result to a liberal and enlightened people. Of the establishment itself we are informed by a friend, that having occasion to call on the Treasurer, upon some business, the door was opened by a copper-coloured servant, a good-looking young Indian — not a fuscus Hydaspes, but a serving man of good appearance, who ushered him up stairs, and introduced him to the front room on the first floor, where all was quackery, bronze and brass, an electrical machine, images, pictures and diplomas framed and glazed, and a table covered with books and papers. In a short time, a person of very imposing appearance entered the room, with his hair profusely powdered, and his person, from his chin to his toes, enveloped in a sort of plaid roquelaure, who, apologizing for the absence of the Doctor, began to assure him of his being in the entire confidence of the Board, and in all probability would have proceeded to the operation of feeling the pulse in a very short time, had not the visitor discovered in the features of this disciple of Esculapius a person he had known in former times. 'Why, good God!'

cried he, 'is that you?—What have you done with the Magic-lantern, and the Lecture on Heads?—am I right, or am I in fairy-land?' calling him by his name.   It was in vain to hesitate, it was impossible to escape, the discovery was complete. It was plain however that the dealer in magical delusions had not altogether given up the art of legerdemain, which, perhaps, he finds the most profitable of the two.

Of the worthy Knight himself, (and perhaps the Coopers and Munros have been consumed by the electrical fluid of their own Board) much might be said. He is the inventor of a life-preserver, with which it may be fairly presumed he has effected valuable services to his country by the preservation of Royalty, as a proof of deserving the honour he has obtained. He is patriotic and independent, masonic and benevolent, a great admirer of fancy horses and fancy ladies, a curer of incurables, and has recently published one of the most extraordinary Memoirs that has ever been laid before the public, embellished with two portraits: which of the two is most interesting must be left to the discrimination of those who view them. It must however be acknowledged, that after reading the following extract, ingratitude is not yet eradicated from our nature, since, notwithstanding he has obtained the dignified appellation of Sir Francis, the Gazette says, that "in future no improper person shall be admitted to the honour of knighthood, in consequence of two surreptitious presentations lately"—the one an M.D. the other F.R.C. Surgeons, particularly if it were possible that this Gentleman may be one of the persons alluded to.   For, what says the Memoir?

"The utility of Sir Francis's invention being thus fully established, and its ingenuity universally admired, it excited the interest of the first characters among the nobility, and an introduction to Court was repeatedly offered to Sir Francis on this account. After a previous communication with one of the Royal Family, and also with

the Secretary of State, on the 14th June last, he had the honour of being presented to His Majesty, who, justly appreciating the merit of the discovery, was pleased to confer upon him the honour of knighthood.

"Thus it is pleasing, in the distribution of honours by the hand of the Sovereign, to mark where they are conferred on real merit. This is the true intention of their origin; but it has been too often departed from, and they have been given where no other title existed than being the friend of those who had influence to gain the Royal ear. From the above statement, it will be seen this honour was conferred on Sir Francis by his Majesty for an invention, which has saved since its discovery the lives of many hundreds, and which may be considered as having given the original idea to the similar inventions that have been attempted since that time. Its utility and importance we have also seen acknowledged and rewarded by the two leading Societies in this country, and perhaps in Europe, viz. the Royal Humane, and the Society of Arts. The Sovereign therefore was only recognizing merit which had been previously established; and the honour of knighthood, to the credit of the individual, was conferred by his Majesty in the most liberal and handsome manner, without any other influence being used by Sir Francis than simply preferring the claim."

Thus the subject of Knighthood is to be nursed; and as the Doctor and the Nurse are generally to be recognized together, no one can read this part of the Memoir without exclaiming—Well done, Nussey. But why not Gazetted, after this liberal and hand-some manner of being rewarded? or why an allusion to two surreptitious presentations, the names of which two persons, so pointedly omitted, cannot well be misunderstood? This is but doing things by halves, though no such an observation can be applied to the proceedings of Charlotte-house, where Cooper, Munro, and Co. (being well explained) means two or three persons, viz. a black, a white man, and a mahogany-coloured Knight—a barber by trade, and a skinner by company—a dealer in mercurials—a puff by practice and an advertiser well versed in all the arts of his prototype—a practitioner in panygyric—the puff direct— the puff preliminary—the puff collateral—the puff collusive—and the puff oblique, or puff by implication. Whether this will apply to Sir Charles Althis or not, is perhaps not so easy to ascertain; but as birds of a feather like to flock together, so these medical Knights in misfortune deserve to be noticed in the same column, although the one is said to be a Shaver, and the other a Quaker. It seems they have both been moved by the same spirit, and both follow (a good way off) the profession of medicine.

Among the various improvements of these improving times, for we are still improving, notwithstanding complaint, a learned little Devil, inflated with gas, has suggested a plan for the establishment of a Medical Assurance-office, where person and property might be insured at so much per annum, and the advantages to be derived from such an Institution would be, that instead of the insurance increasing with years, it would grow less and less. How many thousand grateful patients would it relieve annually! but we fear it would be a daily source of sorrow to these knightly medicals, and would by them be considered a devilish hard case.

But hush, here is other company, and I will give you an account of him as we go along."

They now attended the Keeper, who explained the age, height, weight, species, size, power, and propensities of the animal, and then departed on their road towards Temple Bar,—on passing through which, they were overtaken again by Sir Francis, in a gig drawn by a dun-coloured horse, with his puppy between his legs, and a servant by his side, and immediately renewed the previous conversation.

"There he goes again," said Sparkle, "and a rare fellow he is too."

"I should think so," said Bob; "he must have quacked to some good purpose, to obtain the honour of knighthood."

"Not positively that," continued Sparkle; "for to obtain and to deserve are not synonymous, and, if report say true, there is not much honour attached to his obtaining it.

"— —In the modesty of fearful duty,

> *I read as much as from the rattling tongue*
> *Of saucy and audacious eloquence:*
> *Love, therefore, and tongue-tied simplicity,*
> *At least speak most to my capacity."*

And, according to my humble conception, he who talks much about himself, or pays others to talk or write about him, is generally most likely to be least deserving of public patronage; for if a man possesses real and evident abilities in any line of profession, the public will not be long in making a discovery of its existence, and the bounty, as is most usually the case, would quickly follow upon the heels of approbation. But many a meritorious man in the Metropolis is pining away his miserable existence, too proud to beg, and too honest to steal, while others, with scarcely more brains than a sparrow, by persevering in a determination to leave no stone unturned to make themselves appear ridiculous, as a first step to popularity; and having once excited attention, even though it is merely to be laughed at by the thinking part of mankind, he finds it no great difficulty to draw the money out of their pockets while their eyes are riveted on a contemplation of his person or conduct. And there are not wanting instances of effrontery that have elevated men of little or no capacity to dignified situations. If report say true, the present Secretary of the Admiralty, who is admirable for his poetry also, was originally a hair-dresser, residing somewhere in Blackfriar's or Westminster-road; but then you must recollect he was a man who knew it was useless to lose a single opportunity; and probably such has been the case with Sir Daniel Harlequin, who, from keeping a small shop in Wapping, making a blaze upon the water about his Life-preserver, marrying a wife with a red face and a full pocket, retired to a small cottage at Mile End, and afterwards establishing a Medical Board, has got himself dubbed a Knight. To be sure he has had a deal of puffing and blowing work to get through in his progress, which probably accounts for his black looks, not a little increased by the quantity of powder he wears. But what have we here?" finding the bustle of the streets considerably increased after passing Temple Bar.

"Some political Bookseller or other, in all probability," said Tom—"I'll step forward and see." And in passing through the numerous body of persons that crowded on every side, the whole party was separated. Bob, who had hung a little back while his two friends rushed forward, was lingering near the corner of the Temple: he was beckoned by a man across the way, to whom he immediately went.

"Do you happen to want a piece of fine India silk handkerchiefs, Sir? I have some in my pocket that I can recommend and sell cheap—for money must be had; but only keep it to yourself, because they are smuggled goods, of the best quality and richest pattern." During this opening speech, he was endeavouring to draw Tallyho under the archway of Bell-yard, when Sparkle espying him, ran across to him, and taking him by the arm—"Come along (said he;) and if you don't take yourself off instantly, I'll put you in custody," shaking his stick at the other.

All this was like Hebrew to Bob, who, for his part, really conceived the poor fellow, as he termed him, might be in want of money, and compelled to dispose of his article for subsistence.

"Ha, ha, ha," cried Sparkle, "I see you know nothing about them: these are the locusts of the town." At this moment they were joined by the Hon. Tom Dashall.

"Egad!" continued Sparkle, "I just saved your Cousin from being trepanned, and sent for a soldier."

Tallyho appeared all amazement.

"What," cried Tom, "in the wars of Venus then, I suppose I know he has a fancy for astronomy, and probably he was desirous of taking a peep into Shire-lane, where he might easily find the Sun, Moon, and Seven Stars."

"Ha! ha! ha!" replied Sparkle, "not exactly so; but I rescued him from the hands of a Buffer,{1} who would

> 1 Buffers miscalled Duffers—Persons who adopt a species of swindling which is rather difficult of detection, though it is daily practised in London. The term Buffer takes its derivation from a custom which at one time prevailed of carrying Bandanas, sarsnets, French stockings, and silk of various kinds, next the shirts of the sellers; so that upon making a sale, they were obliged to undress in order to come at the goods, or in other words, to strip to the skin, or buff it; by which means they obtained the title of Buffers. This trade (if it may be so termed) is carried on in a genteel manner. The parties go about from house to house, and attend public-houses, inns, and fairs, pretending to sell smuggled goods, such as those already mentioned; and by offering their goods for sale, they are enabled by practice to discover the proper objects for their arts.
>
> Buffers, or Duffers, who are not rogues in the strict sense of the word, only offer to sell their goods to the best advantage, and by this means evade the detection of the police, but are equally subversive or destructive of common honesty under a cloak or disguise; for if they can persuade any person that the article offered is actually better or cheaper than any other person's, they are doing no more than every tradesman does; but then as they pay no rent or taxes to the State, the principal objection to them lies in the mode of operation, and an overstrained recommendation of their goods, which are always, according to their account, of the most superior quality; and they have a peculiar facility of discovering the novice or the silly, to whom walking up with a serious countenance and interesting air, they broach the pleasing intelligence, that they have on sale an excellent article well worth their attention, giving a caution at the same time, that honour and secrecy must be implicitly observed, or it may lead to unpleasantness to both parties. By these means persons from the country are frequently enticed into public-houses to look at their

goods; and if they do not succeed in one way, they are almost sure in another, by having an accomplice, who will not fail to praise the articles for sale, and propose some gambling scheme, by which the party is plundered of his money by passing forged Bank-notes, base silver or copper, in the course of their dealings.

doubtless have fleeced him in good style, if he could only have induced him to attend to his story."

"The mob you see collected there," said the Hon. Tom Dashalll, "is attracted by two circumstances—Money's new Coronation Crop, just lanched—and a broken image of a Highlander, at the door of a snuff-shop; each of them truly important and interesting of course, the elevation of one man, and the destruction of another. The poor Scotchman seems dreadfully bruised, and I suppose is now under the Doctor's hands, for he has two or three plasters on his face."

"Yes," continued Sparkle, "he has been out on a spree,{1} had a bit of a turn-up, and been knock'd down."

Upon hearing this conversation, Tallyho could not help inquiring into the particulars.

"Why the facts are simply as follows," continued

1 *Spree—A bit of fun, or a frolicsome lark.*

Sparkle—"in London, as you perceive, tradesmen are in the habit of exhibiting signs of the business or profession in which they are engaged. The Pawnbroker decorates his door with three gold balls—the Barber, in some places, (though it is a practice almost out of date) hangs out a long pole—the Gold-beater, an arm with a hammer in the act of striking—the Chemist, a head of Glauber, or Esculapius—the Tobacconist, a roll of tobacco, and of late it has become customary for these venders of pulverised atoms called snuff, to station a wooden figure of a Highlander, in the act of taking a pinch of Hardham's, or High-dried, as a sort of inviting introduction to their counters; and a few nights back, a Scotchman, returning from his enjoyments at a neighbouring tavern, stopped to have a little friendly chat with this gentleman's Highlander, and by some means or other, I suppose, a quarrel ensued, upon which the animated young Scotchman took advantage of his countryman—floored him, broke both his arms, and otherwise did him considerable bodily injury, the effects of which are still visible; and Johnny Bull, who is fond of a little gape-seed, is endeavouring to console him under his sufferings."

"Very kind of him, indeed," replied Bob.

"At any rate," said Tom, "the Tobacconist will have occasion to be grateful to the Highlander{1} for some portion of his popularity."

> 1 It is matter of astonishment to some, but not less true, that many tradesmen in the Metropolis have to ascribe both fame and fortune to adventitious circumstances. It is said that Hardham, of Fleet Street, had to thank the celebrated Comedian, Foote, who, in one of his popular characters, introducing his snuffbox, offered a pinch to the person he was in conversation with on the stage, who spoke well of it, and inquired where he obtained it? — "Why, at Hardham's, to be sure." And to this apparently trifling circumstance, Hardham was indebted for his fortune.
>
> The importance of a Highlander to a snuff-shop will appear by a perusal of the following fact: —
>
> A very respectable young man, a Clerk in the office of an eminent Solicitor, was recently brought before Mr. Alderman Atkins, upon the charge of being disorderly. The prisoner, it seemed, on his return home from a social party, where he had been sacrificing rather too freely to the jolly god, was struck with the appearance of a showy wooden figure of a Highlander, at the door of Mr. Micklan's snuff-shop, No. 12, Fleet Street. The young Attorney, who is himself a Scotchman, must needs claim acquaintance with his countryman. He chucked him familiarly under the chin, called him a very pretty fellow, and, in the vehemence of his affection, embraced him with so much violence, as to force him from his station. Mr. Micklan ran to the assistance of

his servant, and in the scuffle the unfortunate Highlander had both his arms dislocated, the frill that adorned his neck damaged, besides other personal injuries, which his living countryman not being in the humour to atone for, Mr. Micklau gave him in charge to the watchman. Before the Magistrate in the morning, the young man appeared heartily sick of his folly, and perfectly willing to make every reparation, but complained of the excessive demand, which he stated to be no less than thirteen guineas. Mr. Micklan produced the remains of the unfortunate Highlander, who excited a compound fracture of both arms, with a mutilation of three or four fingers, and such other bodily wounds, as to render his perfect recovery, so as to resume his functions at Mr. Micklan's door, altogether hopeless. The Highlander, the complainant stated, cost him thirteen guineas, and was entirely new. The sum might seem large for the young gentleman to pay for such a frolic, but it would not compensate him for the injury he should sustain by the absence of the figure; for, however strange it might appear, he did not hesitate to say, that without it he should not have more than half his business. Since he had stationed it at his door, he had taken on an average thirty shillings a day more than he had done previous to exhibiting his attractions.

There being no proof of a breach of the peace, Mr. Alderman Atkins advised the gentleman to settle the matter upon the best terms he could. They withdrew together, and on their return the complainant reported that the gentleman had agreed to take the figure, and furnish him with a new one.

Mr. Alderman Atkins, in discharging the prisoner, recommended to him to get the figure repaired, and make a niche for him in his office, where, by using it as a proper memorial, it would probably save him more than it cost him.

The broken figure has since been exhibited in his old station, and excited considerable notice; but we apprehend he is not yet able to afford all the attractions of his occupation, for he has formerly been seen inviting his friends to a pinch of snuff gratis, by holding a box actually containing that recreating powder in his hand, in the most obliging and condescending manner—a mark of politeness and good breeding well worthy of respectful attention.

"Come," said Sparkle, "we are now in one of the principal thoroughfares of the Metropolis, Fleet Street, of which you have already heard much, and is at all times thronged with multitudes of active and industrious persons, in pursuit of their various avocations, like a hive of bees, and keeping up, like them, a ceaseless hum. Nor is it less a scene of Real Life worth viewing, than the more refined haunts of the noble, the rich, and the great, many of whom leave their splendid habitations in the West in the morning, to attend the money-getting, commercial men of the City, and transact their business.—The dashing young spendthrift, to borrow at any interest; and the more prudent, to buy or to sell. The plodding tradesman, the ingenious mechanic, are exhausting their time in endeavours to realize property, perhaps to be left for the benefit of a Son, who as ardently sets about, after his Father's decease, to get rid of it—nay, perhaps, pants for an opportunity of doing this before he can take possession; for the young Citizen, having lived just long enough to conceive himself superior to his father, in violation of filial duty and natural authority, affects an aversion to every thing that is not novel, expensive, and singular. He is a lad of high spirit; he calls the city a poor dull prison, in which he cannot bear to be confined; and though he may not intend to mount his nag, stiffens his cravat, whistles a sonata, to which his whip applied to the boot forms an accompaniment; while his spurs wage war with the flounces of a fashionably-dressed belle, or come occasionally in painful contact with the full-stretched stockings of a gouty old gentleman; by all which he fancies he is keeping" up the dignity and importance of his character. He does not slip the white kid glove from his hand without convincing the spectator that; his hand is the whiter skin; nor twist his fingers for the introduction of a pinch of Maccaba, without displaying to the best advantage his beautifully chased ring and elegantly painted snuff-box lid; nor can the hour of the day be ascertained without discovering his engine-turned repeater, and hearing its fascinating music: then the fanciful chain, the precious stones in golden robes, and last of all, the family pride described in true heraldic taste and naïveté. Of Peter Pindar's opinion, that

> "Care to our coffin adds a nail,
> But every grin so merry draws one out,"

he thinks it an admirable piece of politeness and true breeding to give correct specimens of the turkey or the goose in the serious scenes of a dramatic representation, or while witnessing her Ladyship's confusion in a crowd of carriages combating for precedence in order to obtain an early appearance at Court. Reading he considers quite a bore, but attends the reading-room, which he enters, not to know what is worth reading and add a little knowledge to his slender stock from the labours and experience of men of letters—no, but to quiz the cognoscenti, and throw the incense over its learned atmosphere from his strongly perfumed cambric handkerchief, which also implies what is most in use for the indulgence of one of the five senses. When he enters a coffee-room, it is not for the purpose of meeting an old friend, and to enjoy with him a little rational conversation over his viands, but to ask for every newspaper, and throw them aside without looking at them—to call the Waiter loudly by his name, and shew his authority—to contradict an unknown speaker who is in debate with others, and declare, upon the honour of a gentleman and the veracity of a scholar, that Pope never understood Greek, nor translated Homer with tolerable justice. He considers it a high privilege to meet a celebrated pugilist at an appointed place, to floor him for a quid,{1} a fall, and a high delight to talk of it afterwards for the edification of his friends—to pick up a Cyprian at mid-day—to stare modest women out of countenance—to bluster at a hackney-coachman—or to upset a waterman in the river, in order to gain the fame of a Leander, and prove himself a Hero.

"He rejects all his father's proposed arrangements for his domestic comforts and matrimonial alliance. He wanders in his own capricious fancy, like a fly in summer, over the fields of feminine beauty and loveliness; yet he declares there is so much versatility and instability about the fair sex, that they are unworthy his professions of regard; and, perhaps, in his whole composition, there is nothing deserving of serious notice but his good-nature. Thus you have a short sketch of a young Citizen."

"Upon my word, friend Sparkle, you are an admirable delineator of Society," said Dashall.

"My drawings are made from nature," continued Sparkle.

"Aye, and very naturally executed too," replied Tom. Having kept walking on towards St. Paul's, they were by this time near the end of Shoe Lane, at the corner of which sat an elderly woman with a basket of mackerel for sale; and as they approached they saw several persons rush from thence into the main street in evident alarm.

"Come up, d——n your eyes," said an ill-favoured fellow with an immense cudgel in his fist, driving an ass laden

1 Quid—A. Guinea.

with brick-dust, with which he was belabouring him most unmercifully. The poor beast, with an endeavour to escape if possible the cudgelling which awaited him, made a sudden turn round the post, rubbing his side against it as he went along, and thereby relieving himself of his load, which he safely deposited, with a cloud of brick-dust that almost blinded the old woman and those who were near her, in the basket of fish. Neddy then made the best of his way towards Fleet-market, and an over-drove bullock, which had terrified many persons, issued almost at the same moment from Shoe Lane, and took the direction for Temple-bar. The whistling, the hooting, the hallooing, and the running of the drovers in pursuit— men, women, and children, scampering to get out of the way of the infuriated beast—the noise and rattling of carriages, the lamentations of the poor fish-fag, and the vociferations of the donkey-driver to recover his neddy—together with a combination of undistinguishable sounds from a variety of voices, crying their articles for sale, or announcing their several occupations—formed a contrast of characters, situations, and circumstances, not easily to be described. Here, a poor half-starved and almost frightened-to-death brat of a Chimney-sweeper, in haste to escape, had run against a lady whose garments were as white as snow—there, a Barber had run against a Parson, and falling along with him, had dropped a pot of pomatum from his apron-pocket on the reverend gentleman's eye, and left a mark in perfect unison with the colour of his garments before the disaster, but which were now of a piebald nature, neither black nor white. A barrow of nuts, overturned in one place, afforded fine amusement for the scrambling boys and girls—a Jew old clothes-man swore upon his conscience he had losht the pest pargain vhat he ever had offered to him in all his lifetime, by dem tam'd bears of bull-drivers—a Sailor called him a gallows *half-hung ould crimp*,{1} d——d his

> 1 Crimp—*Kidnappers, Trappers, or Procurers of men for the Merchant Service; and the East-India company contract with them for a supply of sailors to navigate their ships out and home. These are for the most part Jews, who have made advances to the sailors of money, clothes, victuals, and lodgings, generally to a very small amount, taking care to charge an enormous price for every article. The poor fellows, by these means, are placed under a sort of espionage, if not close confinement, till the ship is ready to receive them; and then they are conducted on board at Gravesend by the Crimp and his assistants, and a receipt taken for them.*
>
> *In this process there is nothing very reprehensible—the men want births, and have no money—the Crimp keeps a lodging-house, and wishes to be certain of his man: he therefore takes him into the house, and after a very small supply of cash, the grand do, is to persuade him to buy watches, buckles, hats, and jackets, to be paid for on his receiving his advance previous to sailing. By this means and the introduction of grog, the most barefaced and unblushing robberies have been committed.*
>
> *With the same view of fleecing the unwary poor fellows, who*
>
> > "... *at sea earn their money like horses,*

To squander it idly like asses on shore,"

they watch their arrival after the voyage, and advance small sums of money upon their tickets, or perhaps buy them out and out, getting rid at the same time of watches, jewellery, and such stuff, at more than treble their real value. Not only is this the case in London, but at all the out-ports it is practised to a very great extent, particularly in war time.

Happy would it be for poor Jack were this all; he is sometimes brought in indebted to the Crimp to a large nominal amount, by what is called a long-shore attorney, or more appropriately, a black shark, and thrown into jail!!! There he lies until his body is wanted, and then the incarcerator négociâtes with him for his liberty, to be permitted to enter on board again.

eyes if he was not glad of it, and, with a sling of his arm, deposited an enormous quid he had in his mouth directly in the chaps of the Israelite, then joined the throng in pursuit; while the Jew, endeavouring to call Stop thief, took more of the second-hand quid than agreed with the delicacy of his stomach, and commenced a vomit, ejaculating with woful lamentations, that he had lost his bag mit all his propertish.

The old mackarel-woman, seeing her fish covered with brick-dust, set off in pursuit of the limping donkey-driver, and catching him by the neck, swore he should pay her for the fish, and brought him back to the scene of action; but, in the mean time, the Street-keeper had seized and carried off the basket with all its contents—misfortune upon misfortune!

"D——n your ass, and you too," said the Fish-woman, "if you doesn't pay me for my fish, I'll *quod*{1} you—that there's all vat I ar got to say."

"Here's a bit of b——dy gammon—don't you see as how I am lost both my ass and his cargo, and if you von't leave

1 Quod—A Jail—to quod a person is to send him to jail.

me alone, and give me my bags again, I'll sarve you out—there now, that's all—bl——st me! fair play's a jewel—let go my hair, and don't kick up no rows about it—see vhat a mob you're a making here—can't you sell your mackarel ready sauced, and let me go ater Neddy?"

"Vhat, you thinks you are a *flat-catching*,{1} do you, Limping Billy—but eh, who has run away with my basket offish?"

"Ha, ha, ha," cried Limping Billy, bursting into a horse-laugh at the additional distress of the old woman, in which he was joined by many of the surrounding spectators; and which so enraged her, that she let go her hold, and bursting through the crowd with an irresistible strength, increased almost to the fury of madness by her additional loss, she ran some paces distance in search of, not only her stock in trade, but her shop, shop-board, and working-tools; while the donkey-driver boisterously vociferated after her—"Here they are six a shilling, live mackarel O."

This taunt of the brick-dust merchant was too much to be borne, and brought her back again with a determination to chastise him, which she did in a summary way, by knocking him backwards into the kennel. Billy was not pleased at this unexpected salute, called her a drunken ——, and endeavoured to get out of her way—"for," said he, "I know she is a b——dy rum customer when she gets lushy."{2} At this moment, a sturdy youth, about sixteen or seventeen years of age, was seen at a short distance riding the runaway-ass back again. Billy perceiving this, became a little more reconciled to his rough usage—swore he never would strike a voman, so help him G——d, for that he was a man every inch of him; and as for Mother Mapps, he'd be d——nd-if he vouldn't treat her with all the pleasure of life; and now he had got his own ass, he vould go along with her for to find her mackarel. Then shaking a cloud of brick-dust from the dry parts of his apparel, with sundry portions of mud from those parts which had most easily reached the kennel, he took the bridle of his donkey, and bidding her come along, they toddled{3} together to a gin-shop in Shoe Lane.

1 Flat-catching—Is an expression of very common use, and seems almost to explain itself, being the act of taking advantage of any person who appears ignorant and unsuspicious.

2 Lushy—Drunk.

3 Toddle—To toddle is to walk slowly, either from infirmity or choice—"Come, let us toddle," is a very familiar phrase, signifying let us be going.

Desirous of seeing an end to this bit of gig—"Come along," said Sparkle, "they'll all be in prime twig presently, and we shall have some fun.

> *"I'm the boy for a bit of a bobbery,*
> *Nabbing a lantern, or milling a pane;*
> *A jolly good lark is not murder or robbery,*
> *Let us be ready and nimble."*

Hark, (said he) there's a fiddle-scraper in the house—here goes;" and immediately they entered.

They had no occasion to repent of their movements; for in one corner of the tap-room sat Billy Waters, a well-known character about town, a Black Man with a wooden leg was fiddling to a Slaughterman from Fleet-market, in wooden shoes, who, deck'd with all the paraphernalia of his occupation, a greasy jacket and night-cap, an apron besmeared with mud, blood, and grease, nearly an inch thick, and a leathern girdle, from which was suspended a case to hold his knives, and his sleeves tuck'd up as if he had but just left the slaughter-house, was dancing in the centre to the infinite amusement of the company, which consisted of an old woman with periwinkles and crabs for sale in a basket—a porter with his knot upon the table—a dustman with his broad-flapped hat, and his bell by his side—an Irish hodman—and two poor girls, who appeared to be greatly taken with the black fiddler, whose head was decorated with an oil-skinned cock'd hat, and a profusion of many coloured feathers: on the other side of the room sat a young man of shabby-genteel appearance, reading the newspaper with close attention, and purring forth volumes of smoke. Limping Billy and Mother Mapps were immediately known, and room was made for their accommodation, while the fiddler's elbow and the slaughterman's wooden shoes were kept in motion.

Max{1} was the order of the day, and the *sluicery*{2} in good request. Mother Mapps was made easy by being informed the Street-keeper had her valuables in charge, which Limping Billy promised he would redeem. "Bring us a

1 *Max* — *A very common term for gin.*

2 *Sluicery* — *A gin-shop or public-house: so denominated from the lower orders of society sluicing their throats as it were with gin, and probably derived from the old song entitled "The Christening of Little Joey," formerly sung by Jemmy Dodd, of facetious memory.*

"*And when they had sluiced their gobs
With striving to excel wit,
The lads began to hang their nobs,**

* *Nobs* — *Heads.*

** *Frows* — *Originally a Dutch word, meaning wives, or girls.*

*** *Velvet* — *The tongue.*

noggin of *white tape,*{1} and fill me a pipe," said he—"d——n my eyes, I knowed as how it vou'd be all right enough, I never gets in no rows whatever without getting myself out again—come, *ould chap,*{2} vet your vistle, and tip it us rum—go it my kiddy, that are's just vat I likes."

"Vat's the reason I an't to have a pipe?" said Mother Mapps.

"Lord bless your heart," said the Donkey-driver, "if I did'nt forget you, never trust me—here, Landlord, a pipe for this here Lady."

"Which way did the bull run?" said the Irishman.

"Bl— —st me if I know," replied Limping Billy, "for I was a looking out for my own ass—let's have the Sprig of Shelalah, *ould Blackymoor*—come, tune up."

The old woman being supplied with a pipe, and the fiddler having rosined his nerves with a glass of *blue ruin*{3} to it they went, some singing, some whistling, and others drumming with their hands upon the table; while Tom, Bob, and Sparkle, taking a seat at the other side of the room, ordered a glass of brandy and water each, and enjoyed the merriment of the scene before them, perhaps more than those actually engaged in it. Bob was alive to every movement and every character, for it was new, and truly interesting: and kept growing more so, for in a few minutes Limping Billy and Mother Mapps joined the Slaughterman in the dance, when nothing could be more grotesque and amusing. Their pipes in their mouths—clapping of hands and snapping of fingers, formed a curious accompaniment to the squeaking of the fiddle—the broad grin of the Dustman, and the preposterous laugh of the

> 1 White Tape—*Also a common term for gin, particularly among the Ladies.*
>
> 2 Ould Chap, or Ould Boy—*Familiar terms of address among flash lads, being a sort of contraction of old acquaintance, or old friend.*
>
> 3 Blue Ruin—*Gin.*

Irishman at the reelers in the centre, heightened the picture—more gin—more music, and more tobacco, soon ad a visible effect upon the party, and reeling became unavoidable. The young man reading the paper, found it impossible to understand what he was perusing, and having finished his pipe and his pint, made his exit, appearing to have no relish for the entertainment, and perhaps heartily cursing both the cause and the effect. Still, however, the party was not reduced in number, for as one went out another came in.

This new customer was a young-looking man, bearing a large board on a high pole, announcing the residence of a Bug-destroyer in the Strand. His appearance was grotesque in the extreme, and could only be equalled by the eccentricities of his manners and conversation. He was dressed in a brown coat, close buttoned, over which he had a red camlet or stuff surtout, apparently the off-cast of some theatrical performer, but with a determination to appear fashionable; for

> *"Folks might as well be dead—nay buried too,*
> *As not to dress and act as others do."*

He wore mustachios, a pair of green spectacles, and his whole figure was surmounted with a fur-cap. Taking a seat directly opposite our party at the same table—"Bring me a pint," said he; and then deliberately searching his pockets, he produced a short pipe and some tobacco, with which he filled it—"You see," said he, "I am obliged to smoke according to the Doctor's orders, for an asthma—so I always smokes three pipes a day, that's my allowance; but I can eat more than any man in the room, and can dance, sing, and act—nothing conies amiss to me, all the players takes their characters from me."

After this introduction—"You are a clever fellow, I'll be bound for it," said Dashall.

"O yes, I acts Richard the Third sometimes—sometimes Macbeth and Tom Thumb. I have played before Mr. Kean: then I acted Richard the Third—'Give me a horse! '—(starting into the middle of the room)—'no, stop, not so—let me see, let me see, how is it?—ah, this is the way—Give me a horse—Oh! Oh! Oh!—then you know I dies."—And down he fell on the floor, which created a general roar of laughter; while Billy Waters struck up, "See the conquering Hero conies!" to the inexpressible delight of all around him—their feet and hands all going at the same time.

Mother Mapps dropp'd her pipe, and d——d the weed, it made her sick, she said.

Limping Billy was also evidently in *queer-street*.

"Come," said Sparkle, "won't you have a drop more?"

"Thank ye, Sir," was the reply; and Sparkle, intent upon having his gig out, ordered a fresh supply, which soon revived the fallen hero of Bosworth-field, and Richard was himself again.

"Now," said he, "I'll sing you a song," and immediately commenced as follows:—

> *"My name's Hookey Walker, I'm known very well,*
> *In acting and eating I others excel;*
> *The player-folks all take their patterns from me,*
> *And a nice pattern too!—Don't you see? don't you see?*
> *Oh! [glancing at his fingers] It will do—it will do.*
>
> *At Chippenham born, I was left quite forlorn,*
> *When my father was dead and my mother was gone;*
> *So I came up to London, a nice little he,*
> *And a nice pattern too!—Don't you see? don't you see?*
> *Oh! it will do—it will do.*
>
> *A courting I went to a girl in our court,*
> *She laugh'd at my figure, and made me her sport;*
> *I was cut to the soul,—so said I on my knee,*
> *I'm a victim of love!—Don't you see? don't you see?*
> *Oh! it won't do—it won't do.*
>
> *Now all day I march to and fro in the street,*
> *And a candle sometimes on my journey I eat;*
> *So I'll set you a pattern, if you'll but agree,*
> *And a nice pattern too! you shall see—you shall see.*
> *Oh! it will do—it will do."*

This Song, which he declared was all *made out of his own head*, was sung with grotesque action and ridiculous grimace, intended no doubt in imitation of Mr. Wilkinson in his inimitable performance of this strange piece of whimsicality. The dancing party was knock'd up and were lobbing their *lollys*,{1} half asleep and half awake, on the table, bowing as it were to the magnanimous influence

1 Lobbing their lollys—Laying their heads.

of *Old Tom*.{1} The Dustman and the Irishman laugh'd heartily; and Das hall, Tallyho, and Sparkle, could not resist the impulse to risibility when they contemplated the group before them. The Bug-destroyer *munched*{2} a candle and *sluiced*{3} his greasy *chops*{4} with *Jacky*{5} almost as fast as they could supply him with it, when Sparkle perceiving the boy was still at the door with the runaway ass,

"Come," said he, "we'll start 'em off home in high style—here, you Mr. Bugman, can you ride?"

"Ride, aye to be sure I can, any of Mr. Astley's horses as well as the Champion of England,"{6} was the reply.

> 1 *Old Tom*—It is customary in public-houses and gin-shops in London and its vicinity to exhibit a cask inscribed with large letters—OLD TOM, intended to indicate the best gin in the house.
>
> 2 *Munched*—Eat.
>
> 3 *Sluiced*—Washed.   See Sluicery.
>
> 4 *Chops*—The mouth.
>
> 5 *Jacky*—A vulgar term for gin.
>
> 6 Any person would almost suspect that Hookey had been reading the newspapers by this allusion; but that certainly could not be the case, for, spurning all education in early life, this representative of the immortal bard—this character of characters from Shakespeare, could neither read nor write, but made all he acted, as he said, from his own head: however, it may fairly be presumed, that in the course of his travels during the day he had heard something of the Champion intended to appear at the approaching Coronation, of whom the following account has recently been circulated through the daily press, and, with his usual consistency, conceived his own innate abilities equal to those which

might be acquired by Mr. Dymocke, though his claims were not equally honourable or advantageous.

Mr. Dymocke, the nephew of the gentleman (who is a Clergyman) entitled by hereditary right to do the service of the Champion to his Majesty, is still in hopes he may be permitted to act under his Uncle's nomination, although he wants a few months of being of age. A petition is before the King on the subject; and Mr. Dymocke, by constant practice at Astley's Hiding-school, is endeavouring to qualify himself for the due fulfilment of the office. On Thursday lie went through his exercise in a heavy suit of armour with great celerity. The horse which will be rode by the Champion has been selected from Mr. Astley's troop. It is a fine animal, pieballed black and white, and is regularly exercised in the part he will have to perform.

"Walk in—walk in, Ladies and Gentlemen, just going to begin—come, Mr. Merryman, all ready—Ladies and Gentlemen, please to observe, this here horse is not that there horse."

"So we laugh at John Bull a little."

"Come, then," continued Sparkle, "another glass—half-a-crown to ride to the bottom of the lane and up Holboru-hill on that donkey at the door, and you shall be our Champion."

"A bargain—a bargain," said the assumed Hookey Walker, rubbing the tallow from his *gills*.{1}

"Here goes then," said Sparkle; then slipping half-a-crown into the boy's hand, desiring him to run as far as the Traveller-office, in Fleet-street, and get him a newspaper, promising to take care of his ass till his return. The lad nibbled the bait, and was off in a *pig's whisper*{2} Sparkle called to Tom and Bob, and putting them up to his scheme, Hookey was quickly mounted, while Dashall and his Cousin, assisted by the Hibernian and Dust-ho, succeeded in getting Mother Mapps out, who was placed in the front of the Champion, astride, with her face towards him and Limping Billy, who though *beat to a stand still*,{3} was after some difficulty lifted up behind. Hookey was then supplied with his board, the pole of which he placed on his foot, in the manner of a spear or lance. Then giving the Irishman and the Dustman some silver, to act as Supporters or Esquires, one on each side, they proceeded along Shoe-lane, preceded by Billy Waters flourishing his wooden-leg and feathers, and fiddling as he went—the Irishman roaring out with Stentorian lungs,

> *"Sure won't you hear*
> *What roaring cheer*
> *Was spread at Paddy's wedding O,*
> *And how so gay*
> *They spent the day,*
> *From the churching to the bedding O.*
> *First book in hand came Father Quipes,*
> *With the Bride's dadda, the Bailey O,*
> *While all the way to church the pipes*
> *Struck up a jilt so gaily O.*

"Kim ap—be after sitting fast in the front there, old Mapps, or you'll make a mud-lark of yourself." The Dustman rang his bell; and thus accompanied with an immense assemblage of boys, girls, men, women, and

1 Gills—*The mouth.*

2 Pig's Whisper—*A very common term for speed.*

3 Beat to a dead stand still—*Means completely unable to assist himself.*

children, collected from all the courts and alleys in the neighbourhood, joining in a chorus of shouts that rent the air, poor Balaam continued to bear his load; while our party, after watching them till nearly out of sight, passed down Harp-alley into Fleet-market," and turning to the right, very soon regained Fleet-Street, laughing heartily at the bull's cookery of mackarel buttered with brick-dust, and very well satisfied with their spree.

Engaged in conversation upon this adventure, they found nothing of interest' or amusement to attract their notice till they arrived at the warehouse of the London Genuine Tea Company, except merely remarking the grand appearance of St. Paul's, from that situation.

"Genuine tea" said Bob; "what can that mean—Is tea any thing but tea?"

"To be sure it is," said Sparkle, "or has been—*any*thing but tea,"{l} strongly marking the latter part of the

> 1 Tea and Coffee—*The adulteration of articles of human food is a practice of the most nefarious description, and cannot be too strongly deprecated, although it has been carried to an alarming extent. There is scarcely an article of ordinary consumption but has been unlawfully adulterated, and in many cases rendered injurious by the infamous and fraudulent practice of interested persons. Bread, which is considered to be the staff of life, and beer and ale the universal beverage of the people of this country, are known to be frequently mixed with drugs of the most pernicious quality. Gin, that favourite and heart-inspiring cordial of the lower orders of society, that it may have the grip, or the appearance of being particularly strong, is frequently adulterated with the decoction of long pepper, or a small quantity of aqua-fortis, a deadly poison. Sugar has been known to be mixed with sand; and tobacco, for the public-houses, undergoes a process for making it strong and intoxicating; but the recent discovery of the nefarious practice of adulterating tea and coffee, articles of the most universal and extensive consumption, deserves particular reprehension.*
>
> *Tea has been adulterated by the introduction of dried sloe leaves; the practice is not very new, but its extensive adoption, and the deleterious properties ascribed to them by physicians, have been, at length, successfully exposed by the conviction of many of the venders, so, it is hoped, as to prevent a repetition of the crime. The sloe leaf, though a spurious commodity when sold as tea, might afford a harmless vegetable infusion, and be recommended to the poor*

*and frugal as a cheap succedaneum for the Chinese vegetable.
The establishment of the Genuine Tea Company on Ludgate-hill
originated in the recent discoveries, promising to sell
nothing but the Unadulterated Tea, and it is sincerely to be
hoped has done some good.*

sentence as he spoke it: "horse-beans have been converted to coffee, and sloe-leaves have been transformed into tea; hog's lard has been manufactured for butter; an ingenious gentleman wishes to persuade us *Periwinkles*{1} are young Lobsters; and another has proposed to extract sugar, and some say brandy, out of pea-shells! London is the mart for inventions and discoveries of all kinds, and every one of its inhabitants appears to have studied something of the art of Legerdemain, to catch the eye and deceive the senses."

"Wonderful!" exclaimed Bob.

"Not more wonderful than true," continued Sparkle; "invention is always on the stretch in London. Here we have cast-iron Bridges{2}—a cast-iron Sugar-house—

*1 Sparkle appears to have been rather sceptical on the
subject of Periwinkles being young Lobsters, though the
opinion is not very new. A gentleman, whose indefatigable
research appears to be deserving of encouragement and
support, has recently issued the following advertisement,
inviting the curious and the learned to inspect the result
of his discoveries, which seems, at least, to warrant
something more than conjecture.*

*"J. Cleghorne having in his possession some specimens which
prove, in his opinion, a circumstance before suggested, but
treated by the scientific as a vulgar error, any known
naturalist willing to view them, by noticing by letter,
within a week, may have J. C. attend with his specimens. The
subject is a curious change in the formation of Lobsters
from various species of the Winkle, the Winkle being
considered the larva;.*

The only advantage J. C. desires from the communication is, the credit of advancing his proofs, and the stimulating further enquiry.—A line addressed to J. Cleghorne, Architectural Engraver, No. 19, Chapman-street, Black-road, Islington, will have immediate attention."

It is sincerely to be hoped that proper notice will be taken of this advertisement, for in times of general scarcity like the present, such a discovery might be turned to great national advantage, by the establishment of proper depots for the cultivation of lobsters, as we have preserves for game, &c.

2 Cast-iron has become an object of general utility. The Southwark or New London Bridge consists of three arches, the centre of which is a span of 240 feet, and the other two 210 feet each; the Vauxhall Bridge consists of nine arches, over a width of 809 feet; and it is a fact, that a Sugar-house is building with cast-iron floors, window-frames, and rafters, to prevent fire. Cast-iron holds fire and resists fire; but it is probable that all its properties and powers are not yet discovered, and that we may some day or other witness the ascension of a cast-iron balloon inflated with steam!

coaches running, and barges, packets, and sailing-boats navigated, by Steam{1}—St. Paul's, as you perceive, without its ball—smoke burning itself, and money burning men's consciences."

"Well done, Sparkle!" cried Tom; "your ideas seem to flow like gas, touch but the valve and off you go; and you are equally diffusive, for you throw a light upon all subjects."

Bob was now suddenly attracted by a full view of himself and his friends at the further end of Everington's{2}

1 Steam—Here is a subject that evaporates as we approach; it soars beyond finite comprehension, and appears to be inexhaustible—every thing is done by it—machinery of every kind is set in motion by it—a newspaper of the most extensive circulation in the kingdom is printed by it, and the paper supplied sheet by sheet to receive the impression.

*Tobacco is manufactured, and sausage-meat cut, by steam—
nay, a celebrated Vender of the latter article had asserted,
that his machinery was in such a state of progressive
improvement, that he had little doubt before long of making
it supply the demands of his customers, and thereby save the
expense of a Shopman; but, it is much to be regretted, his
apparatus made sausage-meat of him before the accomplishment
of his project.*

*Considering the increasing, and by some Philosophers almost
overwhelming population of the country at the present
moment, it is certainly an alarming circumstance, that when
employment is so much required, mechanical science should so
completely supersede it to the injury of thousands,
independent of the many who have lost their lives by the
blowing up of steam-engines. It is a malady however which
must be left to our political economists, who will
doubtless at the same time determine which would prove the
most effectual remedy—the recommendation of Mr. Malthus to
condemn the lower orders to celibacy—the Jack Tars to a
good war—or the Ministers to emigration.*

*2 If an estimate of the wealth or poverty of the nation
were to lie formed from the appearance of the houses in the
Metropolis, no one could be induced to believe that the
latter had any existence among us. The splendour and taste
of our streets is indescribable, and the vast improvements
in the West are equally indicative of the former.*

*The enormous increase of rents for Shops, particularly in
the leading thoroughfares of London, may in a great measure
be attributed to the Linen-drapers. The usual method
practised by some of these gentry, is to take a shop in the
first-rate situation, pull down the old front, and erect a
new one, regardless of expense, a good outside being
considered the first and indispensable requisite. This is
often effected, either upon credit with a builder, or, if
they have a capital of a few hundreds, it is all exhausted*

in external decorations. Goods are obtained upon credit, and customers procured by puffing advertisements, and exciting astonishment at the splendid appearance of the front. Thus the concern is generally carried on till the credit obtained has expired, and the wonder and novelty of the concern has evaporated; when the stock is sold off at 30 per cent, under prime cost for the benefit of the creditors! This is so common an occurrence, that it is scarcely possible to walk through London any day in the year, without being attracted by numerous Linen-drapers' shops, whose windows are decorated with bills, indicating that they are actually selling off under prime cost, as the premises must be cleared in a few days.

The most elegant Shop of this description in the Metropolis is supposed to be one not a hundred miles from Ludgate-hill, the front and fitting up of which alone is said to have cost several thousand pounds. The interior is nearly all of looking-glass, with gilt mouldings; even the ceiling is looking-glass, from which is appended splendid cut-glass chandeliers, which when lighted give to the whole the brilliance of enchantment; however it is not very easy to form an idea of what is sold, for, with the exception of a shawl or two carelessly thrown into the window, there is nothing to be seen, (the stock being all concealed in drawers, cupboards, &c.) except the decorations and the Dandy Shopmen, who parade up and down in a state of ecstasy at the reflection of their own pretty persons from every part of the premises!

This concealment of the stock has occasioned some laughable occurrences. It is said that a gentleman from the country accidentally passing, took it for a looking-glass manufactory, and went in to inquire the price of a glass. The Shopmen gathered round him with evident surprise, assured him of his mistake, and directed him to go to Blades,{1} lower down the Hill. The Countryman was not disconcerted, but, after surveying them somewhat minutely, informed them it was glass he wanted, not cutlery; but as for blades, he thought there were enow there for one street, at least.

Another is said to have been so pleased with a row of grotesque Indian-China jars, which embellish one side of the entrance, and which he mistook for pots de chambre, that after returning home and consulting his rib, he sent an order per post for one of the most elegant pattern to be forwarded to him!

There is a similar Shop to this, though on a smaller scale, to be seen in a great leading thoroughfare at the West end of the Town; the owner of which, from his swarthy complexion and extravagant mode of dress, has been denominated The Black Prince, a name by which he is well known in his own neighbourhood, and among the gentlemen of the cloth. This dandy gentleman, who affects the dress and air of a military officer, has the egregious vanity to boast that the numerous families of rank and fashion who frequent his shop, are principally attracted to view his elegant person, and seems to consider that upon this principally depends the success of his trade.

1 A large Glass-manufacturer.

128—shop, and without observing the other persons about him, saw himself surrounded with spectators, unconscious of being in their company. He look'd up—he look'd down—he gazed around him, and all was inconceivable light. Tom's allusion to the gas flashed upon him in a moment—"What—what is this?" said he—"where, in the name of wonder, am I?" A flash of lightning could not have operated more suddenly upon him. "Why," said Sparkle, "don't you see?

"You are not here, for you are there,"

pointing to his reflection, in the looking-glass.

"Egad," said Bob, under evident surprise, and perhaps not without some apprehension they were playing tricks with him—"I wish you would explain—is this a Drawing-room, or is it the *Phantasmagoria* we have heard so much of in the country?"

"No, no, it is not the Phantasmagoria, but it forms a part of metropolitan magic, which you shall be better acquainted with before we part. That is no other than a Linen-draper's shop, '*papered*,' as an Irishman one day remarked, 'vvid nothing at all at all but looking-glass, my dear '—one of the most superb things of the kind that perhaps ever was seen—But come, I perceive it is getting late, let us proceed directly to Dolly's, take our chop, then a *rattler*,{1} and hey for the Spell."{2}

Bob appeared almost to be spell-bound at the moment, and, as they moved onward, could not help casting

"One longing, lingering look behind."

1 *Rattler*—A coach.

2 *Spell*—*The Play-house; so denominated from its variety of attractions, both before and behind the curtain.*

CHAPTER X

"What various swains our motley walls contain!
Fashion from Moorfields, honour from Chick-lane;
Bankers from Paper-buildings here resort,
Bankrupts from Golden-square and Riches-court;
From the Haymarket canting rogues in grain,
Gulls from the Poultry, sots from Water-lane;
The lottery cormorant, the auction shark,
The full-price master, and the half-price clerk;
Boys, who long linger at the gallery-door,
With pence twice live, they want but twopence more,
Till some Samaritan the twopence spares,
And sends them jumping up the gallery-stairs.
Critics we boast, who ne'er their malice baulk,
But talk their minds—we wish they'd mind their talk;
Big-worded bullies, who by quarrels live,
Who give the lie, and tell the lie they give;
Jews from St. Mary-Axe, for jobs so wary,
That for old clothes they'd even axe St. Mary;
And Bucks with pockets empty as their pate,
Lax in their gaiters, laxer in their gait.
Say, why these Babel strains from Babel tongues?
Who's that calls "Silence" with such leathern lungs?
He, who, in quest of quiet, "Silence" hoots,
Is apt to make the hubbub he imputes."

IN a few minutes they entered Dolly's, from whence, after partaking of a cheerful repast and an exhilarating glass of wine, a coach conveyed them to Drury-lane. ',

"Now," said the Hon. Tom Dashall, "I shall introduce you to a new scene in Real Life, well worth your close observation. We have already taken a promiscuous ramble from the West towards the East, and it has afforded some amusement; but our stock is abundant, and many objects of curiosity are still in view."

BLUE RUIN. Tom & Bob tasting Thompson's Best.

"Yes, yes," continued Sparkle, "every day produces novelty; for although London itself is always the same, the inhabitants assume various forms, as inclination or necessity may induce or compel. The Charioteer of to-day, dashing along with four in hand, may be an inhabitant of the King's-bench to-morrow, and—but here we are, and Marino Faliero is the order of the night. The character of its author is so well known, as to require no observation; but you will be introduced to a great variety of other characters, both in High and Low Life, of an interesting nature."

By this time they had alighted, and were entering the House. The rapid succession of carriages arriving with the company, the splendour of the equipages, the general elegance of the dresses, and the blazing of the lamps, alternately became objects of attraction to Bob, whose eyes were kept in constant motion—while "A Bill of the Play for Covent Garden or Drury Lane," still resounded in their ears.

On arriving at the Box-lobby, Tom, who was well known, was immediately shewn into the centre box with great politeness by the Box-keeper,{1} the second scene of the Tragedy being just over. The appearance of the House was a delicious treat to Bob, whose visual orbs wandered more among the delighted and delightful faces which surrounded him, than to the plot or the progress of the performances before him. It was a scene of splendour of which lie had not the least conception; and Sparkle perceiving the principal objects of attraction, could not resist the impulse to deliver, in a sort of half-whisper, the following lines:—

> *"When Woman's soft smile all our senses bewilders,*
> *And gilds while it carves her dear form on the heart,*
> *What need has new Drury of carvers and gilders?*
> *With nature so bounteous, why call upon art?*

> 1 *The Box-keeper to a public Theatre has many duties to perform to the public, his employer, and himself; but, perhaps, in order to be strictly correct, we ought to have reversed the order in which we have noticed them, since of the three, the latter appears to be the most important, (at least) in his consideration; for he takes care before the*

commencement of the performance to place one of his automaton figures on the second row of every box, which commands a good view of the House, who are merely intended to sit with their hats off, and to signify that the two first seats are taken, till the conclusion of the second act; and so in point of fact they are taken by himself, for the accommodation of such friends as he is quite aware are willing to accommodate him with a quid pro quo.

*How well would our Actors attend to their duties,
Our House save in oil, and our Authors in wit,*

*In lieu of yon lamps, if a row of young Beauties
Glanc'd light from their eyes between us and the Pit.*

*The apples that grew on the fruit-tree of knowledge
By Woman were pluck'd, and she still wears the prize,*

*To tempt us in Theatre, Senate, or College—
I mean the Love-apples that bloom in the eyes.*

*There too is the lash which, all statutes controlling,
Still governs the slaves that are made by the Fair,*

*For Man is the pupil who, while her eye's rolling,
Is lifted to rapture, or sunk in despair."*

Tallyho eagerly listened to his friend's recitation of lines so consonant with his own enraptured feelings; while his Cousin Dashall was holding a conversation in dumb-show with some person at a distance, who was presently recognized by Sparkle to be Mrs. G——den,{1} a well-known frequenter of the House.

"Come," said he, "I see how it is with Tom—you may rely upon it he will not stop long where he is, there is other game in view—he has but little taste for Tragedy fiction, the Realities of Life are the objects of his regard.

"Tis a fine Tragedy," continued he, addressing himself to Tom.

"Yes—yes," replied the other, "I dare say it is, but, upon my soul, I know nothing about it—that is—I have seen it before, and I mean to read it."

"Bless my heart!" said a fat lady in a back seat, "what a noise them 'are gentlemen does make—they talk so loud there 'ant no such thing as seeing what is said—I wonder they don't make these here boxes more bigger, for I declare I'm so scrouged I'm all in a—Fanny, did you bring the rumperella for fear it should rain as we goes home?"

"Hush, Mother," said a plump-faced little girl, who sat along side of her—"don't talk so loud, or otherwise every body will hear you instead of the Performers, and that would be quite preposterous."

"Don't call me *posterous* Miss; because you have been to school, and learnt some *edification*, you thinks you are to do as you please with me."

> 1 Mrs. G— —den, a dashing Cyprian of the first order, well known in the House, a fine, well-made woman, always ready for a lark, and generally well togged.

This interesting conversation was interrupted by loud vociferations of Bravo, Bravo, from all parts of the House, as the drop-scene fell upon the conclusion of the second act. The clapping of hands, the whistling and noise that ensued for a few minutes, appeared to astonish Tallyho. "I don't much like my seat," said Dashall. "No," said Sparkle, "I did not much expect you would remain long—you are a mighty ambitious sort of fellow, and I perceive you have a desire to be exalted."

"I confess the situation, is too confined," replied Tom—"come, it is excessively warm here, let us take a turn and catch a little air."

The House was crowded in every part; for the announcement of a new Tragedy from the pen of Lord Byron, particularly under the circumstances of its introduction to the Stage, against the expressed inclination of its Author, the

> 1 At an early hour on the evening this Tragedy was first

pro-duced at Drury Lane, Hand-bills were plentifully distributed through the Theatre, of which the following is a copy:

"The public are respectfully informed, that the representation of Lord Byron's Tragedy, The Doge of Venice, this evening, takes place in defiance of the injunction from the Lord Chancellor, which was not applied for until the remonstrance of the Publisher, at the earnest desire of the noble Author, had failed in protecting that Drama from its intrusion on the Stage, for which it was never intended."

This announcement had the effect of exciting public expectation beyond its usual pitch upon such occasions. The circumstances were somewhat new in the history of the Drama: the question being, whether a published Flay could be legally brought on the Stage without the consent, or rather we should say, in defiance of the Author. "We are not aware whether this question has been absolutely decided, but this we do know, that the Piece was performed several nights, and underwent all the puffing of the adventurous Manager, as well as all the severity of the Critics. The newspapers of the day were filled with histories and observations upon it. No subject engrossed the conversation of the polite and play-going part of the community but Lord Byron, The Doge of Venice, and Mr. Elliston. They were all bepraised and beplastered—exalted and debased—acquitted and condemned; but it was generally allowed on all hands, that the printed Tragedy contained many striking beauties, notwithstanding its alleged resemblance to Venice Preserved. We are, however, speaking of the acted Tragedy, and the magnanimous Manager, who with such promptitude produced it in an altered shape; and having already alluded to the theatrical puffing so constantly resorted to upon all occasions, we shall drop the curtain upon the subject, after merely remarking, that the Times of the same day has been known to contain the Manager's puff, declaring the piece to have been received with rapturous applause, in direct opposition to the Editor's critique, which as unequivocally pronounced its complete failure!

will of its publisher, and the injunction{1} of the Lord Chancellor, were attractions of no ordinary nature; and

> 1 Injunction—The word injunction implies a great deal, and has in its sound so much of the terrific, as in many instances to paralyze exertion on the part of the supposed offending person or persons. It has been made the instrument of artful, designing, and malicious persons, aided by pettifogging or pretended attorneys, to obtain money for themselves and clients by way of compromise; and in numerous instances it is well known that fear has been construed into actual guilt. Injunctions are become so common, that even penny printsellers have lately issued threats, and promised actual proceedings, against the venders of articles said to be copies from their original drawings, and even carried it so far as to withhold (kind souls!) the execution of their promises, upon the payment of a 5L. from those who were easily to be duped, having no inclination to encounter the glorious uncertainty of the law, or no time to spare for litigation. We have recently been furnished with a curious case which occurred in Utopia, where it appears by our informant, that the laws hold great similarity with our own. A certain house of considerable respectability had imported a large quantity of Welsh cheese, which were packed in wooden boxes, and offered them for sale (a great rarity in Eutopia) as double Gloucester.
>
> It is said that two of a trade seldom agree; how far the adage may apply to Eutopia, will be seen in the sequel. A tradesman, residing in the next street, a short time after, received an importation from Gloucester, of the favourite double production of that place, packed in a similar way, and (as was very natural for a tradesman to do, at least we know it is so here,) the latter immediately began to vend his cheese as the real Double Gloucester. This was an offence beyond bearing. The High Court of Equity was moved,

similar we suppose to our High Court of Chancery, to suppress the sale of the latter; but as no proof of deception could be produced, it was not granted. This only increased the flame already excited in the breasts of the first importers; every effort was made use of to find a good and sufficient excuse to petition the Court again, and at length they found out one of the craft to swear, that as the real Gloucester had been imported in boxes of a similar shape, make, and wood, it was quite evident that the possessor must have bought similar cheeses, and was imposing on the public to their great disadvantage, notwithstanding they could not find a similarity either of taste, smell, or appearance. In the mean time the real Gloucester cheese became a general favourite with the inhabit-ants of Utopia, and upon this, though slender ground, the innocent tradesman was served with a process, enjoining him not to do that, which, poor man, he never intended to do; and besides if he had, the people of that country were not such ignoramuses as to be so deceived; it was merely to restrain him from selling his own real double Gloucester as their Welsh cheeses, purporting, as they did, to be double Gloucester, or of mixing them together (than which nothing could be further from his thoughts,) and charging him at the same time with having sold his cheeses under their name. But the most curious part of the business was, the real cheeseman brought the investigation before the Court, cheeses in boxes were produced, and evidence was brought forward, when, as the charges alleged could not be substantiated, the restraint was removed, and the three importers of Welsh cheese hung their heads, and retired in dudgeon.

the Hon. Tom availed himself of the circumstance to leave the Box, though the truth was, there were other attractions of a more enlivening cast in his view.

"Come," said he, "we shall have a better opportunity of seeing the House, and its decorations, by getting nearer to the curtain; besides, Ave shall have a bird's-eye view of the company in all quarters, from the seat of the Gods to the Pit."

The influx of company, (it being the time of half-price), and the rush and confusion which took place in all parts at this moment, were indescribable. Jumping over boxes and obtaining seats by any means, regardless of politeness or even of decorum—Bucks and Bloods warm from the pleasures of the bottle—dashing Belles and flaming Beaux, squabbling and almost fighting—rendered the amusements before the curtain of a momentary interest, which appeared to obliterate the recollection of what they had previously witnessed. In the mean time, the Gods in the Gallery issued forth an abundant variety of discordant sounds, from their elevated situation. Growling of bears, grunting of hogs, braying of donkeys, gobbling of turkeys, hissing of geese, the catcall, and the loud shrill whistle, were heard in one mingling concatenation of excellent imitation and undistinguished variety: During which, Tom led the way to the upper Boxes, where upon arriving, he was evidently disappointed at not meeting the party who had been seen occupying a seat on the left side of the House, besides having sacrificed a front seat, to be now compelled to take one at the very back part of a side Box, an exchange by no means advantageous for a view of the performance. However, this was compensated in some degree by a more extensive prospect round the House; and his eyes were seen moving in all directions, without seeming to know where to fix, while Sparkle and Bob were attracted by a fight in the Gallery, between a Soldier and a Gentleman's Servant in livery, for some supposed insult offered to the companion of the latter, and which promised serious results from the repeated vociferations of those around them, of "Throw 'em over—throw 'em over;" while the gifts of the Gods were plentifully showered down upon the inhabitants of the lower regions in the shape of orange-peelings, apples, &c. The drawing up of the curtain however seemed to have some little effect upon the audience, and in a moment the Babel of tongues was changed into a pretty general cry of "Down—down in the front—hats off—silence, &c. which at length subsided in every quarter but the Gallery, where still some mutterings and murmurings were at intervals to be heard.

"— —*one fiddle will*
Produce a tiny flourish still."

Sparkle could neither see nor hear the performance—Tom was wholly engaged in observing the company, and Bob alternately straining his neck to get a view of the Stage, and then towards the noisy inhabitants of the upper regions. "We dined at the Hummums," said a finicking little Gentleman just below him—"Bill, and I, and Harry—drank claret like fishes—Harry was half-sprung—fell out with a Parson about chopping logic; you know Harry's father was a butcher, and used to chopping, so it was all prime—the Parson would'n't be convinced, though Harry knock'd down his argument with his knuckles on the table, almost hard enough to split it—it was a bang-up lark—Harry got in a passion, doff'd his toggery, and was going to show fight—so then the Parson sneak'd off—Such a bit of gig.'"

"Silence there, behind."

"So then," continued the Dandy, "we went to the Billiard-rooms, in Fleet Street, played three games, diddled the Flats, bilk'd the Marker, and bolted—I say, when did you see Dolly?"{1}

> 1 *To the frequenters of Drury-lane Theatre, who occasionally lounge away a little of their time between the acts in sipping soda-water, negus, &c. the party here alluded to cannot but be well known—we mean particularly the laffing-boys and the lads of the village. We are aware that fictitious names are assumed or given to the Ladies of Saloon notoriety, originating in particular circum-stances, and we have reason to believe that Dolly K———lly has been so denominated from the propensity she almost invariably manifests of painting, as remarked particularly by one of the parties in conversation.*

"Last night," replied the other—"she'll be here presently—d——nd fine girl, arn't she?"

"Very well," said the first; "a nice plump face, but then she paints so d—n—bly, I hate your painted Dollys, give me natural flesh and blood—Polly H—ward for me."

"Gallows Tom{1} will speak to you in plain terms if you trespass there, my boy; you know he has out-general'd the Captain in that quarter, and came off victorious, so— —"

"Come," said Sparkle, "let us adjourn into the Saloon, for, Heaven knows, it is useless staying here." And taking their arms, they immediately left the Box.

"The theatre," continued he, "is a sort of enchanted island, where nothing appears as it really is, nor what it should be. In London, it is a sort of time-killer, or exchange of looks and smiles. It is frequented by persons of all degrees and qualities whatsoever. Here Lords come to laugh and be laughed at—Knights to learn the amorous smirk and a-la-mode grin, the newest fashion in the cut of his garments, the twist of his body, and the adjustment of his phiz.

"This House{2} was built upon a grand and extensive scale, designed and executed under the inspection of Mr. Benj. Wyatt, the architect, whose skill was powerfully and liberally aided by an intelligent and public spirited Committee, of which the late Mr. Whitbread was the Chairman. It is altogether a master-piece of art, and an ornament to the Metropolis. You perceive the interior is truly delightful, and the exterior presents the idea of solidity and security: it affords sitting room for 2810 persons, that is, 1200 in the Boxes, 850 in the Pit, 480

---

1 It appears that the adoption of fictitious names is not wholly confined to the female visitors of these regions of fashion and folly. Gallows Tom is a character well known, and is a sort of general friend, at all times full of fun, fire, and spirit. We have not been able to discover whether he holds any official situation under government, though it is generally believed he is safely anchored under the crown, a stanch friend to the British constitution—probably more so than to his own. And we should judge from what is to be inferred from the conversation overheard, that he is the acknowledged friend of Miss H— —d. Capt. T— —pe is supposed to hold a Commission in the Navy, a gay and gallant frequenter of the Saloon, and, till a short time back, the chere ami of Miss H— —d.

*2 The building of this Theatre was completed for 112,000L.
Including lamps, furniture, &c. 125,000L.; and including
scent ry, wardrobe, properties, &c. 150,000L.*

in the Lower Gallery, and 280 in the Upper Gallery. The talents of the celebrated Mr. Kean (who has recently left us for the shores of the Atlantic) first blazed forth to astonish the world beneath this roof. Old Drury immortalized the name of Garrick, and has also established the fame of Mr. Kean; and the House at the present moment has to boast of a combination of histrionic{1} talent, rich and excellent."

"Come along, come along," said Tom, interrupting him, "leave these explanations for another opportunity—here is the Saloon. Now for a peep at old particulars. There is no seeing nor hearing the Play—I have no inclination for histories, I am just alive for a bit of gig."

On entering the Saloon, Bob was additionally gratified at viewing the splendour of its decorations. The arched ceiling, the two massy Corinthian columns of *vera antique,* and the ten corresponding pilasters on each side, struck him as particularly beautiful, and he was for some moments lost in contemplation, while his friends Sparkle and Tom were in immediate request to receive the congratulations of their acquaintance.

"Where the d——l have you been to?" was the first question addressed to Dashall—"rusticating, I suppose, to the serious loss of all polished society."

"You are right in the first part of your reply," said Tom; "but, as I conceive, not exactly so in the inference you draw from it."

"Modesty, by Jove! well done Dashall, this travelling appears to improve your manners wonderfully; and I dare say if you had staid away another month, your old friends would not have known you."

This created a laugh among the party, which roused Bob from his reverie, who, turning round rather hastily, trod with considerable force upon the gouty toe of an old debauchee in spectacles, who, in the height of ecstasy, was at that moment entering into a treaty of amity with a pretty rosy-faced little girl, and chucking her under the

1 *The names of Elliston, Pope, Johnston, Powell, Dowton, Munden, Holland, Wallack, Knight, T. Cooke, Oxberry, Smith, Bromley, &c. are to be found on the male list of Performers, and it is sincerely to be hoped that of Mr. Kean will not long be absent. The females are, Mrs. Davison, Mrs. Glover, Miss Kelly, Mrs. Bland, Mrs. Orger, Mrs. Sparks, Miss Wilson, Miss Byrne, Miss Cubitt, &c.*

chin, as a sort of preliminary, to be succeeded by a ratification; for in all probability gratification was out of the question. However this might be, the pain occasioned by the sudden movement of Tallyho, who had not yet learned to trip it lightly along the *mutton walk*,{1} induced the sufferer to roar out most lustily, a circumstance which immediately attracted the attention of every one in the room, and in a moment they were surrounded by a group of lads and lasses.

"Upon my soul, Sir," stammer'd out Bob, "I beg your pardon, I—I—did not mean—"

"Oh! oh! oh!" continued the gouty Amoroso. Mother K——p{2} came running like lightning with a glass of water; the frail sisterhood were laughing, nodding, whispering, and winking at each other; while St——ns,{3} who pick'd up the spectacles the unfortunate victim of the gout had dropp'd, swore that fellow in the green coat and white hat ought to be sent to some dancing-school, to learn to step without kicking people's shins.

Another declared he was a Johnny-raw,{4} just catched, and what could be expected.

Tom, who, however, kept himself alive to the passing occurrences, stepping up to Bob, was immediately recognized by all around him, and passing a significant wink, declared it was an accident, and begged to assist the Old Buck to a seat, which being accomplished, he declared he had not had his shoe on for a week, but as he found himself able to walk, he could not resist the temptation of taking a look around him.

The Hon'ble Tom Dashall & his Cousin Bob in the Lobby at Drury Lane Theatre

Over a bottle of wine the unpleasant impressions made by this unfortunate occurrence appeared to be removed. In the mean time, Tom received a hundred congratulations and salutations; while Sparkle, after a glass or two, was missing.

Dashall informed the friends around him, that his Cousin was a pupil of his, and begged to introduce him

> 1 Mutton Walk—A flash term recently adopted to denominate the Saloon.
>
> 2 A well known fruit-woman, who is in constant attendance, well acquainted with the girls and their protectors, and ready upon all occasions to give or convey information for the benefit of both parties.
>
> 3 St— —ns—A very pretty round-faced young lady-bird, of rather small figure, inclining to be lusty.
>
> 4 Johnny Raw—A country bumpkin.

as a future visitor to this gay scene. This had an instantaneous effect upon the trading fair ones, who began immediately to throw out their lures. One declared he had a sweet pretty brooch; another, that she knew he was a trump by the cut of his jib; a third, that he look'd like a gentleman, for she liked the make of his mug; a fourth, that his hat was a very pretty shaped one, although it was of a radical colour; and while Tom and the ladybird{l} were soothing the pains of the grey-headed wanton, Bob was as busily employed in handing about the contents of the bottle. A second and a third succeeded, and it was not a little astonishing to him that every bottle improved his appearance; for, though not one of his admirers remained long with him, yet the absence of one only brought another, equally attracted by his look and manner: every one declared he was really a gentleman in every respect, and in the course of their short parley, did not fail to slip a card into his hand. By this time he began to grow chatty, and was enabled to rally in turn the observations they made.

He swore he lov'd them all round, and once or twice hummed over,

> *"Dear creatures, we can't do without them,*
> *They're all that is sweet and seducing to man,*
> *Looking, sighing about, and about them,*
> *We doat on them—do for them, all that we can."*

The play being over, brought a considerable influx of company into the Saloon. The regular covies paired off with their covesses, and the moving panorama of elegance and fashion presented a scene that was truly delightful to Bob.

The Ladybird, who had been so attentive to the gouty customer, now wished him a good night, for, said she, "There is my friend,{2} and so I am off." This seemed only to increase the agony of his already agonized toe, notwithstanding which he presently toddled off, and was seen no more for the evening.

"What's become of Sparkle," enquired Tom. "Stole away," was the reply.

"Tipp'd us the double, has he," said Dashall. "Well, what think you of Drury-lane?"

> 1 Lady-bird—A dashing Cyprian.
>
> 2 The term friend is in constant use among accessible
> ladies, and signifies their protector or keeper.

"'Tis a very delightful tragedy indeed, but performed in the most comical manner I ever witnessed in my life."

"Pshaw!" said Bob, "very few indeed, except the critics and the plebs, come here to look at the play; they come to see and be seen."

"Egad then," said Bob, "a great many have been gratified to-night, and perhaps I have been highly honoured, for every person that has passed me has complimented me with a stare."

"Which of course you did not fail to return?"

"Certainly not; and upon my soul you have a choice show of fruit here."

"Yes," continued Tom, "London is a sort of hot-house, where fruit is forced into ripeness by the fostering and liberal sun of Folly, sooner than it would be, if left to its natural growth. Here however, you observe nothing but joyful and animated features, while perhaps the vulture of misery is gnawing at the heart. I could give you histories of several of these unfortunates,{1}

> 1 A life of prostitution is a life fraught with too many
> miseries to be collected in any moderate compass. The mode
> in which they are treated, by parties who live upon the
> produce of their infamy, the rude and boisterous, nay, often
> brutal manner in which they are used by those with whom they
> occasionally associate, and the horrible reflections of
> their own minds, are too frequently and too fatally
> attempted to be obliterated by recourse to the Bacchanalian
> fount. Reason becomes obscured, and all decency and
> propriety abandoned. Passion rules predominantly until it
> extinguishes itself, and leaves the wretched victim of early
> delusion, vitiated both in body and mind, to drag on a
> miserable existence, without character, without friends, and
> almost without hope. There is unfortunately, however, no
> occasion for the exercise of imagination on this subject.
> The annals of our police occurrences, furnish too many
> examples of actual circumstances, deeply to be deplored; and
> we have selected one of a most atrocious kind which recently
> took place, and is recorded as follows:—
>
> Prostitution.
>
> "An unfortunate girl, apparently about eighteen years of
> age, and of the most interesting and handsome person, but

whose attire indicated extreme poverty and distress, applied to the sitting magistrate, Richard Bimie, Esq. under the following circum-stances: — It appeared from the statement, that she had for the last three weeks been living at a house of ill fame in Exeter-street, Strand, kept by a man named James Locke: this wretch had exacted the enormous sum of three guineas per week for her board and lodging, and in consequence of her not being able to pay the sum due for the last week, he threatened to strip her of her cloaths, and turn her naked into the street. This threat he deferred executing until yesterday morning (having in the mean time kept her locked up in a dark room, without any covering whatever,) when in lieu of her cloaths, he gave her the tattered and loathsome garments she then appeared in, which were barely sufficient to preserve common decency, and then brutally turned her into the street. Being thus plunged into the most abject wretchedness, without money or friends, to whom she could apply in her present situation, her bodily strength exhausted by the dissipated life she had led, and rendered more so by a long abstinence from food; her spirits broken and overcome by the bitter and humiliating reflection, that her own guilty conduct debarred her from flying to the fostering arms of affectionate parents, whom she had loaded with disgrace and misery; and the now inevitable exposure of her infamy, it was some time ere her wandering senses were sufficiently composed to determine what course she should pursue in the present emergency, when she thought she could not do better than have recourse to the justice of her country against the villain Lock, who had so basely treated her; and after extreme pain and difficulty, she succeeded in dragging her enfeebled limbs to the Office. During the detail of the foregoing particulars, she seemed overwhelmed with shame and remorse, and at times sobbed so violently as to render her voice inarticulate. Her piteous case excited the attention and sympathy of all present; and it was much to the general satisfaction that Mr. Bimie ordered Humphries, one of the conductors of the Patrol, to fetch Lock to the Office. On being brought there, the necessary proceedings were gone into for the purpose of indicting the house as a common brothel.

"It was afterwards discovered that this unhappy girl was of the most respectable parents, and for the last six years had been residing with her Aunt. About three months ago, some difference having arisen between them, she absconded, taking with her only a few shillings, and the clothes she then wore. The first night of her remaining from home she went to Drury-lane Theatre, and was there pick'd up by a genteel woman dressed in black, who having learned her situation, enticed her to a house in Hart-street, Covent-garden, where the ruin of the poor girl was finally effected. It was not until she had immersed herself in vice and folly that she reflected on her situation, and it was then too late to retract; and after suffering unheard of miseries, was, in the short space of three months, reduced to her present state of wretchedness.

"The worthy Magistrate ordered that proper care should be taken of the girl, which was readily undertaken on the part of the parish.

"The Prisoner set up a defence, in which he said, a friend of the girl's owed him 14L. and that he detained her clothes for it—but was stopped by Mr. Bimie.

"He at first treated the matter very lightly; but on perceiving the determination on the part of the parish to proceed, he offered to give up the things. This however he was not allowed to do."

(who are exercising all their arts to entrap customers) apparently full of life and vivacity, who perhaps dare not approach their homes without the produce of their successful blandishments. But this is not

a place for moralizing—a truce to Old Care and the Blue Devils—
Come on, my boy, let us take a turn in the Lobby—

> *"Banish sorrow, griefs a folly;*
> *Saturn, bend thy wrinkled brow;*
> *Get thee hence, dull Melancholy,*
> *Mirth and wine invite us now.*
>
> *Love displays his mine of treasure,*
> *Comus brings us mirth and song!;*
> *Follow, follow, follow pleasure,*
> *Let us join the jovial throng."*

Upon this they adjourned to the Lobby, where a repetition of similar circumstances took place, with only this difference, that Tally ho having already been seen in the Saloon, and now introduced, leaning upon the arm of his Cousin, the enticing goddesses of pleasure hung around them at every step, every one anxious to be foremost in their assiduities to catch the new-comer's smile; and the odds were almost a cornucopia to a cabbage-net that Bob would be hook'd.

Tom was still evidently disappointed, and after pacing the Lobby once or twice, and whispering Bob to make his observations the subject of future inquiry, they returned to the Saloon, where Sparkle met them almost out of breath, declaring he had been hunting them in all parts of the House for the last half hour.

Tom laugh'd heartily at this, and complimented Sparkle on the ingenuity with which he managed his affairs. "But I see how it is," said he, "and I naturally suppose you are engaged."

"'Suspicion ever haunts the guilty mind,' and I perceive clearly that you are only disappointed that you are not engaged—where are all your *golden*{1} dreams now?"

"Pshaw! there is no such thing as speaking to you," said Tom, rather peevishly, "without feeling a lash like a cart-whip."

1 This was a touch of the satirical which it appears did not exactly suit the taste of Dashall, as it applied to the Ladybird who had attracted his attention on entering the house.

"Merely in return," continued Sparkle, "for the genteel, not to say gentle manner, in which you handle the horse-whip."

"There is something very mulish in all this," said Bob, interrupting the conversation, "I don't understand it."

"Nor I neither," said Tom, leaving the arm of his Cousin, and stepping forward.

This hasty dismissal of the subject under debate had been occasioned by the appearance of a Lady, whose arm Tom immediately took upon leaving that of his cousin, a circumstance which seemed to restore harmony to all parties. Tallyho and Sparkle soon joined them, and after a few turns for the purpose of seeing, and being seen, it was proposed to adjourn to the Oyster-shop directly opposite the front of the Theatre; and with that view they in a short time departed, but not without an addition of two other ladies, selected from the numerous frequenters of the Saloon, most of whom appeared to be well known both to Tom and Sparkle.

The appearance of the outside was very pleasing—the brilliance of the lights—the neat and cleanly style in which its contents were displayed seemed inviting to appetite, and in a very short time a cheerful repast was served up; while the room was progressively filling with company, and Mother P——was kept in constant activity.

Bob was highly gratified with the company, and the manner in which they were entertained.

A vast crowd of dashing young Beaux and elegantly dressed Belles, calling about them for oysters, lobsters, salmon, shrimps, bread and butter, soda-water, ginger-beer, &c. kept up a sort of running accompaniment to the general conversation in which they were engaged; when the mirth and hilarity of the room was for a moment delayed upon the appearance of a dashing Blade, who seemed as he entered to say to himself,

"Plebeians, avaunt! I have altered my plan, Metamorphosed completely, behold a Fine Man! That is, throughout town I am grown quite the rage, The meteor of fashion, the Buck of the age."

He was dressed in the extreme of fashion, and seemed desirous of imparting the idea of his great importance to all around him: he had a light-coloured great-coat with immense mother o' pearl buttons and double capes, Buff or Petersham breeches, and coat of *sky-blue*,{1} his hat cocked on one side, and stout ground-ashen stick in his hand. It was plain to be seen that the juice of the grape had been operative upon the upper story, as he reeled to the further end of the room, and, calling the attendant, desired her to bring him a bottle of soda-water, for he was *lushy*,{2} by G——d; then throwing himself into a box, which he alone occupied, he stretched himself at length on the seat, and seemed as if he would go to sleep.

"That (said Sparkle) is a distinguished Member of the Tilbury Club, and is denominated a Ruffian, a kind of character that gains ground, as to numbers, over the Exquisite, but he is very different in polish.

> 1 *A partiality to these coloured habits is undoubtedly intended to impress upon the minds of plebeian beholders an exalted idea of their own consequence, or to prove, perhaps, that their conceptions are as superior to common ones as the sky is to the earth.*
>
> 2 *The variety of denominations that have at different times been given to drunkenness forms an admirable specimen of ingenuity well worthy of remark. The derivation of Lushy, we believe, is from a very common expression, that a drunken man votes for Lushington; but perhaps it would be rather difficult to discover the origin of many terms made use of to express a jolly good fellow, and no flincher under the*

effects of good fellowship. It is said—that he is drunk, intoxicated, fuddled, muddled, flustered, rocky, reely, tipsy, merry, half-boosy, top-heavy, chuck-full, cup-sprung, pot-valiant, maudlin, a little how came you so, groggy, jolly, rather mightitity, in drink, in his cups, high, in uubibus, under the table, slew'd, cut, merry, queer, quisby, sew'd up, over-taken, elevated, cast away, concerned, half-coek'd, exhilarated, on a merry pin, a little in the suds, in a quandary, wing'd as wise as Solomon.

It is also said, that he has business on both sides of the way, got his little hat on, bung'd his eye, been in the sun, got a spur in his head, (this is frequently used by brother Jockeys to each other) got a crumb in his beard, had a little, had enough, got more than he can carry, been among the Philistines, lost his legs, been in a storm, got his night-cap on, got his skin full, had a cup too much, had his cold tea, a red eye, got his dose, a pinch of snuff in his wig, overdone it, taken draps, taking a lunar, sugar in his eye, had his wig oil'd, that he is diddled, dish'd and done up.

He clips the King's English, sees double, reels, heels a little, heels and sets, shews his hob-nails, looks as if he couldn't help it, takes an observation, chases geese, loves a drap, and cannot sport a right line, can't walk a chalk.

He is as drunk as a piper, drunk as an owl, drunk as David's sow, drunk as a lord, fuddled as an ape, merry as a grig, happy as a king.

"In the higher circles, a Ruffian is one of the many mushroom-productions which the sun of prosperity brings to life. Stout in general is his appearance, but Dame Nature has done little for him, and Fortune has spoilt even that little. To resemble his groom and his coachman is his highest ambition. He is a perfect horseman, a perfect whip, but takes care never to be a perfect gentleman. His principal accomplishments are sporting, swaggering, milling, drawing, and greeking.{1} He takes the ribands in his hands, mounts his box, with Missus by his side—"All right, ya hip, my hearties"—drives his empty mail with four prime tits—cuts out a Johnny-raw—shakes his head, and lolls out his tongue at him; and if he don't break his own neck, gets safe home after his morning's drive.

"He is always accompanied by a brace at least of dogs in his morning visits; and it is not easy to determine on these occasions which is the most troublesome animal of the two, the biped or the quadruped."

This description caused a laugh among the Ladybirds, who thought it vastly amusing, while it was also listened to with great attention by Tallyho.

The Hon. Tom Dashall in the mean time was in close conversation with his mott{2} in the corner of the Box, and was getting, as Sparkle observed, "rather nutty{3} in that quarter of the globe."

The laugh which concluded Sparkle's account of the Tilbury-club man roused him from his sleep, and also attracted the attention of Tom and his inamorata.

"D——n my eyes," said the fancy cove, as he rubbed open his peepers,{4}" am I awake or asleep?—what a h——ll of a light there is!"

> 1 Greeking—An epithet generally applied to gambling and gamblers, among the polished hells of society, principally to be found in and near St. James's: but of this more hereafter.
>
> 2 Mott—A blowen, or woman of the town. We know not from whom or whence the word originated, but we recollect some lines of an old song in which the term is made use of, viz.
>
>> "When first I saw this flaming Mutt,
>> 'Twas at the sign of the Pewter Pot;
>> We call'd for some Purl, and we had it hot,
>> With Gin and Bitters too."
>
> 3 Nutty—Amorous.
>
> 4 An elegant and expressive term for the eyes.

This was followed immediately by the rattling of an engine with two torches, accompanied by an immense concourse of people following it at full speed past the window.

"It is well lit, by Jove," said the sleeper awake, "where ever it is;" and with that he tipp'd the *slavey*{1}1 a tanner,{2} and mizzled.

The noise and confusion outside of the House completely put a stop to all harmony and comfort within.

"It must be near us," said Tom.

"It is Covent Garden Theatre, in my opinion," said Sparkle.

Bob said nothing, but kept looking about him in a sort

of wild surprise.

"However," said Tom, "wherever it is, we must go and have a peep."

"You are a very gallant fellow, truly," said one of the bewitchers—"I thought—"

"And so did I," said Tom—"but 'rest the babe—the time it shall come'—never mind, we won't be disappointed; but here, (said he) as I belong to the Tip and Toddle Club, I don't mean to disgrace my calling, by forgetting my duty." And slipping a something into her hand, her note was immediately changed into,

"Well, I always thought you was a trump, and I likes a man that behaves like a gentleman."

Something of the same kind was going on between the other two, which proved completely satisfactory.

"So then, Mr. Author, it seems you have raised a fire to stew the oysters, and leave your Readers to feast upon the blaze."

"Hold for a moment, and be not so testy, and for your satisfaction I can solemnly promise, that if the oysters are stewed, you shall have good and sufficient notice of the moment they are to be on table— But, bless my heart, how the fire rages!—I can neither spare time nor wind to parley a moment longer—Tom and Bob have already started off with the velocity of a race-horse, and if I lose them, I should cut but a poor figure with my Readers afterward.

"Pray, Sir, can you tell me where the fire is?" 'Really, Sir, I don't know, but I am told it is somewhere by Whitechapel.'

1 Slaveys—Servants of either sex.

2 Tanner—A flash term for a sixpence.

"Could you inform me Madam, whereabouts the fire is?"

'Westminster Road, Sir, as I am informed.' "Westminster, and Whitechapel—some little difference of opinion I find as usual—however, I have just caught sight of Tom, and he's sure to be on the right scent; so adieu, Mr. Reader, for the present, and have no doubt but I shall soon be able to throw further light on the subject."

CHAPTER XI

"Some folks in the streets, by the Lord, made me stare,
So comical, droll, is the dress that they wear,
For the Gentlemen's waists are atop of their backs,
And their large cassock trowsers they tit just like sacks.
Then the Ladies—their dresses are equally queer,
They wear such large bonnets, no face can appear:
It puts me in mind, now don't think I'm a joker,
Of a coal-scuttle stuck on the head of a poker.
In their bonnets they wear of green leaves such a power,
It puts me in mind of a great cauliflower;
And their legs, 1 am sure, must be ready to freeze,
For they wear all their petticoats up to their knees.
They carry large bags full of trinkets and lockets,
'Cause the fashion is now not to wear any pockets;
"While to keep off the flies, and to hide from beholders,
A large cabbage-net is thrown over their shoulders."

IN a moment all was consternation, confusion, and alarm. The brilliant light that illuminated the surrounding buildings presented a scene of dazzling splendour, mingled with sensations of horror not easily to be described. The rattling of engines, the flashing of torches, and the shouting of thousands, by whom they were followed and surrounded, all combined to give lively interest to the circumstance.

It was quickly ascertained that the dreadful conflagration had taken place at an extensive Timber-yard, within a very short distance of the Theatres, situated as it were nearly in the centre, between Covent Garden and Drury Lane. Men, women, and children, were seen running in all directions; and report, with his ten thousand tongues, here found an opportunity for the exercise of them all; assertion and denial followed each other in rapid succession, while the flames continued to increase. Our party being thus abruptly disturbed in their anticipated enjoyments, bade adieu to their Doxies,{1}

1 Doxies—A flash term frequently made use of to denominate ladies of easy virtue.

and rushed forward to the spot, where they witnessed the devouring ravages of the yet unquenched element, consuming with resistless force all that came in its way.

"Button up," said Tom, "and let us keep together, for upon these occasions,

"The Scamps,{1} the Pads,{2} the Divers,{3} are all upon the lay."{4}

The Flash Molishers,{5} in the vicinity of Drury Lane, were out in parties, and it was reasonable to suppose, that where there was so much heat, considerable thirst must also prevail; consequently the Sluiceries were all in high request, every one of those in the neighbourhood being able to boast of overflowing Houses, without any imputation upon their veracity. We say nothing of elegant genteel, or enlightened audiences, so frequently introduced in the Bills from other houses in the neighbourhood; even the door-ways were block'd up with the collectors and imparters of information. Prognostications as to how and where it began, how it would end, and the property that would be consumed, were to be met at every corner—Snuffy Tabbies, and Boosy Kids, some giving way to jocularity, and others indulging in lamentations.

"Hot, hot, hot, all hot," said a Black man, as he pushed in and out among the crowd; with "Hoot awa', the de'il tak your soul, mon, don't you think we are all hot eneugh?—gin ye bring more hot here I'll crack your croon—I've been roasting alive for the last half hoor, an' want to be ganging, but I can't get out."

"Hot, hot, hot, all hot, Ladies and Gentlemen," said the dingy dealer in delicacies, and almost as soon disappeared among the crowd, where he found better opportunities for vending his rarities.

"Lumps of pudding," said Tom, jerking Tallyho by the arm, "what do you think of a slice? here's accommodation for you—all hot, ready dress'd, and well done."

"Egad!" said Bob, "I think we shall be well done ourselves presently."

"Keep your hands out of my pockets, you lousy beggar,"

1 Scamps—Highwaymen.

2 Pads—Foot-pads.

3 Divers—Pickpockets.

4 The Lay—Upon the look-out for opportunities for the exercise of their profession.

5 Flash Molishers—a term given to low Prostitutes.

said a tall man standing near them, "or b— — me if I don't mill you."

"You mill me, vhy you don't know how to go about it, Mr. Bully Brag, and I doesn't care half a farden for you—you go for to say as how I—"

"Take that, then," said the other, and gave him a floorer; but he was prevented from falling by those around him.

The salute was returned in good earnest, and a random sort of fight ensued. The accompaniments of this exhibition were the shrieks of the women, and the shouts of the partisans of each of the Bruisers— the cries of "Go it, little one—stick to it—tip it him—sarve him out— ring, ring—give 'em room—foul, foul—fair, fair," &c." At this moment the Firemen, who had been actively engaged in endeavours to subdue the devouring flames, obtained a supply of water: the engines were set to work, and the Foreman directed the pipe so as to throw the water completely into the mob which had collected round them. This had the desired effect of putting an end to the squabble, and dispersing a large portion of the multitude, at least to some distance, so as to leave good and sufficient room for their operations.

"The Devil take it," cried Sparkle, "I am drench'd."

"Ditto repeated," said Tom.

"Curse the fellow," cried Bob, "I am sopp'd."

"Never mind," continued Tom,

. . . *"By fellowship in woe,*
Scarce half our pain we know."

"Since we are all in it, there is no laughing allowed."

In a short time, the water flowed through the street in torrents; the pumping of the engines, and the calls of the Firemen, were all the noises that could be heard, except now and then the arrival of additional assistance.

Bob watched minutely the skill and activity of those robust and hardy men, who were seen in all directions upon the tops of houses, &c. near the calamitous scene, giving information to those below; and he was astonished to see the rapidity with which they effected their object.

Having ascertained as far as they could the extent of the damage, and that no lives were lost, Tom proposed a move, and Sparkle gladly seconded the motion—"for," said he, "I am so wet, though I cannot complain of being cold, that I think I resemble the fat man who seemed something like two single gentlemen roll'd into one,' and 'who after half a year's baking declared he had been so cursed hot, he was sure he'd caught cold;' so come along."

"Past twelve o'clock," said a Charley, about three parts sprung, and who appeared to have more light in his head than he could shew from his lantern.

"Stop thief, stop thief," was vociferated behind them; and the night music, the rattles, were in immediate use in several quarters—a rush of the crowd almost knock'd Bob off his pins, and he would certainly have fell to the ground, but his nob{1} came with so much force against the bread-basket{2} of the groggy guardian of the night, that he was turn'd keel upwards,{3} and rolled with his lantern, staff, and rattle, into the overflowing kennel; a circumstance which perhaps had really no bad effect, for in all probability it brought the sober senses of the Charley a little more into action than the juice of the juniper had previously allowed. He was dragged from his birth, and his coat, which was of the blanket kind, brought with it a plentiful supply of the moistening fluid, being literally sous'd from head to foot.

Bob fished for the *darkey*{4}—the *musical instrument*{5}—and the post of honour, alias the *supporter of peace*;{6} but he was not yet complete, for he had dropped his *canister-cap*,{7} which was at length found by a flash molisher, and drawn from the pool, full of water, who appeared to know him, and swore he was one of the best fellows on any of the beats round about; and that they had got hold of a Fire-prigger,{8} and bundled{9} him off to St. Giles's watch-house, because he was bolting with a *bag of togs*.

1 Nob—The head.

2 Bread-basket—The stomach.

3 Keel upwards—Originally a sea phrase, and most in use among sailors, &c.

4 Darkey—Generally made use of to signify a dark lantern.

5 Musical instrument—a rattle.

6 Post of honour, or supporter of his peace—Stick, or cudgel.

7 "Canister-cap—& hat.

8 Fire-prigger—No beast of prey can be more noxious to society or destitute of feeling than those who plunder the unfortunate sufferers under that dreadful and destructive calamity, fire. The tiger who leaps on the unguarded passenger will fly from the fire, and the traveller shall be protected by it; while these wretches, who attend on fires, and rob the unfortunate sufferers under pretence of coming to give assistance, and assuming the style and manner of neighbours, take advantage of distress and confusion. Such wretches have a more eminent claim to the detestation of society, than almost any other of those who prey upon it.

9 *Bundled—Took, or conveyed.*

The feeble old scout shook his dripping wardrobe, d——d the water and the boosy kid that wallof'd him into it, but without appearing to know which was him; till Bob stepped up, and passing some silver into his mawley, told him he hoped he was not hurt. And our party then, moved on in the direction for Russel-street, Covent-garden, when Sparkle again mentioned his wet condition, and particularly recommended a glass of Cogniac by way of preventive from taking cold. "A good motion well made (said Tom;) and here we are just by the Harp, where we can be fitted to a shaving; so come along."

Having taken this, as Sparkle observed, very necessary precaution, they pursued their way towards Piccadilly, taking their route under the Piazzas of Covent-garden, and thence up James-street into Long-acre, where they were amused by a circumstance of no very uncommon kind in London, but perfectly new to Tallyho. Two Charleys had in close custody a sturdy young man (who was surrounded by several others,) and was taking him to the neighbouring watch-house "What is the matter?" said Tom.

"Oh, 'tis only a little bit of a dead body-snatcher," said one of the guardians. "He has been up to the resurrection rig.{1} Here," continued he, "I've got the bone-basket,"

> 1 *Resurrection rig—This subject, though a grave one, has been treated by many with a degree of comicality calculated to excite considerable risibility. A late well known humorist has related the following anecdote:*
>
> *Some young men, who had been out upon the spree, returning home pretty well primed after drinking plentifully, found themselves so dry as they passed a public house where they were well known, they could not resist the desire they had of calling on their old friend, and taking a glass of brandy with him by way of finish, as they termed it; and finding the door open, though it was late, were tempted to walk in. But their old friend was out of temper. "What is the matter?" — "Matter enough," replied Boniface; "here have I got an old fool of a fellow occupying my parlour dead drunk,*

and what the devil to do with him I don't know. He can neither walk nor speak."

"Oh," said one of the party, who knew that a resurrection Doctor resided in the next street, "I'll remove that nuisance, if that's all you have to complain of; only lend me a sack, and I'll sell him."

A sack was produced, and the Bacchanalian, who almost appeared void of animation, was without much difficulty thrust into it. "Give me a lift," said the frolicsome blade, and away he went with the load. On arriving at the doctor's door, he pulled the night bell, when the Assistant made his appearance, not un-accustomed to this sort of nocturnal visitant.

holding up a bag, "and it was taken off his shoulder as he went along Mercer-street, so he can't say nothing at all.

"I have brought you a subject—all right."

"Come in. What is it, a man or a woman?"

"A man."

"Down with him—that corner. D——n it, I was fast asleep.

"Call for the sack in the morning, will you, for I want to get to bed."

"With all my heart."

Then going to a drawer, and bringing the customary fee, "Here, (said he) be quick and be off." This was exactly what the other wanted; and having secured the rubbish,{1} the door was shut upon him. This, however, was no sooner done, than the Boosy Kid in the sack, feeling a sudden internal turn of the contents of his stomach, which brought with it a heaving, fell, from the upright situation in which he had been placed, on the floor. This so alarmed the young Doctor, that he ran with all speed after the vender, and just coming up to him at the corner of the street.

"Why, (said he) you have left me a living man!"

"Never mind, (replied the other;) kill him when you want him." And making good use of his heels he quickly disappeared.

A Comedian of some celebrity, but who is now too old for theatrical service, relates a circumstance which occurred to him upon his first arrival in town:—

Having entered into an engagement to appear upon the boards of one of the London Theatres, he sought the metropolis some short time before the opening of the House; and conceiving it necessary to his profession to study life—real life as it is,—he was accustomed to mingle promiscuously in almost all society. With this view he frequently entered the tap rooms of the lowest public houses, to enjoy his pipe and his pint, keeping the main object always in view—

"To catch the manners living as they rise."

Calling one evening at one of these houses, not far from Drury Lane, he found some strapping fellows engaged in conversation, interlarded with much flash and low slang; but decently dressed, he mingled in a sort of general dialogue with them on the state of the weather, politics, &c. After sitting some time in their company, and particularly noticing their persons and apparent character—

> "Come, Bill, it is time to be off, it is getting rather darkish." "Ah, very well (replied the other,) let us have another quart, and then I am your man for a bit of a lark." By this time they had learned that the Comedian was but newly arrived in town; and he on the other hand was desirous of seeing what they meant to be up to. After another quart they were about to move, when, said one to the other, "As we are only going to have a stroll and a bit of fun, perhaps that there young man would like to join us."
>
> "Ah, what say you, Sir? have you any objection? but perhaps you have business on hand and are engaged—"

"No, I have nothing particular to do," was the reply. "Very well, then if you like to go with us, we shall be glad of your company."

"Well (said he,) I don't care if I do spend an hour with you." And with that they sallied forth.

After rambling about for some time in the vicinity of Tottenham Court Road, shewing him some of the Squares, &c. describing the names of streets, squares, and buildings, they approached St. Giles's, and leading him under a gateway, "Stop, (said one) we must call upon Jack, you know, for old acquaintance sake," and gave a loud knock at the door; which being opened without a word, they all walked in, and the door was instantly lock'd. He was now introduced to a man of squalid appearance, with whom they all shook hands: the mode of introduction was not however of so satis-factory a description as had been expected, being very laconic, and conveyed in the following language:—"We have got him."

"Yes, yes, it is all right—come, Jack, serve us out some grog, and then to business."

The poor Comedian in the mean time was left in the utmost anxiety and surprise to form an opinion of his situation; for as he had heard something about trepanning, pressing, &c. he could not help entertaining serious suspicion that he should either be com-pelled to serve as a soldier or a sailor; and as he had no intention "to gain a name in arms," they were neither of them suitable to his inclinations.

"Come," (said one) walk up stairs and sit down—Jack, bring the lush "—and up stairs they went.

Upon entering a gloomy room, somewhat large, with only a small candle, he had not much opportunity of discovering what sort of a place it was, though it looked wretched enough. The grog was brought—"Here's all round the gravestone, (said one)—come, drink away, my hearty—don't be alarm'd, we are rum fellows, and we'll put you up to a rig or two—we are got a rum covey in the corner there, and you must lend us a hand to get rid of him:" then, holding up the light, what was the surprise of the poor Comedian to espy a dead body of a man—"You can help us to get him away, and by G— —you shall, too, it's of no use to flinch now."

A circumstance of this kind was new to him, so that his perplexity was only increased by the discovery; but he plainly perceived by the last declaration, that having engaged in the business, it would be of no use to leave it half done: he therefore remained silent upon the subject, drank his grog, when Jack came up stairs to say the cart was ready.

"Lend a hand, (said one of them) let us get our load down stairs—come, my Master, turn to with a good heart, all's right."

With this the body was conveyed down stairs.

At the back of the house was a small yard separated from a neighbouring street by a wall—a signal was given by some one on the other side which was understood by those within— it was approaching nine o'clock, and a dark night—"Come, (said one of them,) mount you to the top of the wall, and ding the covey over to the carcass-carter." This being complied with, the dead body was handed up to him, which was no sooner done than the Carman outside, perceiving the Watchman approach—"It von't do," said he, and giving a whistle, drove his cart with an assumed air of carelessness away; while the poor Comedian, who had a new character to support, in which he did not conceive himself well up,{1} was holding the dead man on his lap with the legs projecting over the wall; it was a situation of the utmost delicacy and there was no time to recast the part, he was therefore, obliged to blunder through it as well as he could; the *perspiration of the living man fell plentifully on the features of the dead as the Charley approached in a position to pass directly under him. Those inside had sought the shelter of the house, telling him to remain quiet till the old Scout was gone by. Now although he was not fully acquainted with the consequences of discovery, he was willing and anxious to avoid them: he therefore took the advice, and scarcely moved or breathed—"Past nine o'clock," said the Watchman, as he passed under the legs of the dead body without looking up, though he was within an inch of having his castor brushed off by them. Being thus relieved, he was happy to see the cart return; he handed over the unpleasant burthen, and as quick as possible afterwards descended from his elevated situation into the street, determining at all hazards to see the result of this to him extraordinary adventure; with this view he followed the cart at a short distance, keeping his eye upon it as he went along; and in one of the streets leading to Long Acre, he perceived a man endeavouring to look into the back part of the cart, but was diverted from his object by one of the men who had introduced him to the house, while another of the confederates snatched the body from the cart, and ran with all speed down another street in an opposite direction. This movement had attracted the notice of the Watchman, who, being prompt in his movements, had sprung his rattle. Upon this, and feeling himself too heavily laden to secure his retreat, the fellow with the dead man perceiving the gate of an area open, dropped his burden down the steps, slam'd the gate after him, and continued to fly, but was stopped at the end of the street; in the mean time the Charley in pursuit had knock'd at the door of the house where the stolen goods (as he supposed) were deposited.*

1 A cant phrase for money.

It was kept by an old maiden lady, who, upon discovering the dead body of a man upon her premises, had fainted in the Watchman's arms. The detection of the running

Resurrectionist was followed by a walk to the watch-house, where his companions endeavoured to make it appear that they had all been dining at Wandsworth together, that he was not the person against whom the hue and cry had been raised. But old Snoosey{1} said it wouldn't do, and he was therefore detained to appear before the Magistrate in the morning. The Comedian, who had minutely watched their proceedings, took care to be at Bow-street in good time; where he found upon the affidavits of two of his comrades, who swore they had dined together at Wandsworth, their pal was liberated.

1 The Constable of the night.

Bob could not very well understand what was the meaning of this lingo; he was perfectly at a loss to comprehend the terms of deadbody snatching and the resurrection rig. The crowd increased as they went along; and as they did not exactly relish their company, Sparkle led. them across the way, and then proceeded to explain.

"Why," said Sparkle, "the custom of dead-body snatching has become very common in London, and in many cases appears to be winked at by the Magistrates; for although it is considered a felony in law, it is also acknowledged in some degree to be necessary for the Surgeons, in order to have an opportunity of obtaining practical information. It is however, at the same time, a source of no slight distress to the parents and friends of the parties who are dragg'd from the peaceful security of the tomb. The *Resurrection-men* are generally well rewarded for their labours by the Surgeons who employ them to procure subjects; they are for the most part fellows who never stick at trifles, but make a decent livelihood by moving off, if they can, not only the bodies, but coffins, shrouds, &c. and are always upon the look-out wherever there is a funeral—nay, there have been instances in which the bodies have been dug from their graves within a few hours after being deposited there."

"It is a shameful practice," said Bob, "and ought not to be tolerated, however; nor can I conceive how, with the apparent vigilance of the Police, it can be carried on."

"Nothing more easy," said Sparkle, "where the plan is well laid. These fellows, when they hear a passing-bell toll, skulk about the parish from ale-house to ale-house, till they can learn a proper account of what the deceased died of, what condition the body is in, &c. with which account they go to a *Resurrection Doctor*, who agrees for a price, which is mostly five guineas, for the body of a man, and then bargain with an Undertaker for the shroud, coffin, &c. which, perhaps with a little alteration, may serve to run through the whole family."

"And is it possible," said Bob, "that there are persons who will enter into such bargains?"

"No doubt of it; nay, there was an instance of a man really selling his own body to a Surgeon, to be appropriated to his own purposes when dead, for a certain weekly sum secured to him while living; but in robbing the church-yards there are always many engaged in the rig—for notice is generally given that the body will be removed in the night, to which the Sexton is made privy, and receives the information with as much ease as he did to have it brought—his price being a guinea for the use of the *grubbing irons*, adjusting the grave, &c. This system is generally carried on in little country church-yards within a few miles of London. A hackney-coach or a cart is ready to receive the stolen property, and there cannot be a doubt but many of these depredations are attended with success, the parties escaping with their prey undetected—nay, I know of an instance that occurred a short time back, of a young man who was buried at Wesley's Chapel, on which occasion one of the mourners, a little more wary than the rest, could not help observing two or three rough fellows in the ground during the ceremony, which aroused his suspicion that they intended after interment to have the body of his departed friend; this idea became so strongly rooted in his mind, that he imparted his suspicions to the remainder of those who had followed him: himself and another therefore determined if possible to satisfy themselves upon the point, by returning in the dusk of the evening to reconnoitre. They accordingly proceeded to the spot, but the gates being shut, one of them climbed to the top of the wall, where he discovered the very parties, he had before noticed, in the act of wrenching open the coffin. Here they are, said he, hard at it, as

I expected. But before he and his friend could get over the wall, the villains effected their escape, leaving behind them a capacious sack and all the implements of their infernal trade. They secured the body, had it conveyed home again, and in a few days re-buried it in a place of greater security.{1}

Bob was surprised at this description of the *Resurrection-rig*, but was quickly drawn from his contemplation of the depravity of human nature, and what he could not help thinking the dirty employments of life, by a shouting apparently from several voices as they passed the end of St. Martin's Lane: it came from about eight persons, who appeared to be journeymen mechanics, with pipes in their mouths, some of them rather *rorytorious*,{2} who, as they approached, broke altogether into the following

   SONG.{3}

"I'm a frolicsome young fellow, I live at my ease,
I work when I like, and I play when I please;
I'm frolicsome, good-natured—I'm happy and free,
And I care not a jot what the world thinks of me.

With my bottle and glass some hours I pass,
Sometimes with my friend, and sometimes with my lass:
I'm frolicsome, good-natur'd—I'm happy and free,
And I don't care one jot what the world thinks of me.

By the cares of the nation I'll ne'er be perplex'd,
I'm always good-natur'd, e'en though I am vex'd;
I'm frolicsome, good-humour'd—I'm happy and free,
And I don't care one d— —n what the world thinks of me.

1 *A circumstance very similar to the one here narrated by Sparkle actually occurred, and can be well authenticated.*

2 *Rorytorious—Noisy.*

3 *This song is not introduced for the elegance of its composition, but as the Author has actually heard it in the*

*streets at the flight of night or the peep of day, sung in
full chorus, as plain as the fumes of the pipes and the
hiccups would allow the choristers at those hours to
articulate; and as it is probably the effusion of some
Shopmate in unison with the sentiments of many, it forms
part of Real Life deserving of being recorded in this Work.*

*Particular trades have particular songs suitable to the
employment in which they are engaged, which while at work
the whole of the parties will join in. In Spitalfields,
Bethnal-green, &c. principally inhabited by weavers, it is
no uncommon thing to hear twenty or thirty girls singing,
with their shuttles going—The Death of Barbary Allen—There
was an old Astrologer—Mary's Dream, or Death and the Lady;
and we remember a Watch-maker who never objected to hear his
boys sing; but although he was himself a loyal subject, he
declared he could not bear God Save the King; and upon being
ask'd his reason—Why, said he, it is too slow—for as the
time goes, so the fingers move—Give us Drops of Brandy,
or Go to the Devil and Shake Yourself—then I shall have
some work done.*

This Song, which was repeated three or four times, was continued till their arrival at Newport-market, where the Songsters divided: our party pursued their way through Coventry-street, and arrived without further adventure or interruption safely at home. Sparkle bade them adieu, and proceeded to Bond-street; and Tom and Bob sought the repose of the pillow.

It is said that "Music hath charms to sooth the savage breast," and it cannot but be allowed that the *Yo heave ho*, of our Sailors, or the sound of a fiddle, contribute much to the speed of weighing anchor.

It is an indisputable fact that there are few causes which more decidedly form, or at least there are few evidences which more clearly indicate, the true character of a nation, than its Songs and Ballads. It has been observed by the learned Selden, that you may see which way the wind sets by throwing a straw up into the air, when you cannot make the same discovery by tossing up a stone or other weighty substance. Thus it is with Songs and Ballads, respecting the state of public feeling, when productions of a more elaborate nature fail in their elucidations: so much so that it is related of a great Statesman, who was fully convinced of the truth of the observation, that he said, "Give me the making of the national Ballads, and I care not who frames your Laws." Every day's experience tends to prove the power which the *sphere-born* Sisters of harmony, voice, and verse, have over the human mind. "I would rather," says Mr. Sheridan, "have written Glover's song of 'Hosier's Ghost' than the Annals of Tacitus."

CHAPTER XII

O what a town, what a wonderful Metropolis!
Sure such a town as this was never seen;
Mayor, common councilmen, citizens and populace,
Wand'ring from Poplar to Turnham Green.

Chapels, churches, synagogues, distilleries and county banks—
Poets, Jews and gentlemen, apothecaries, mountebanks—
There's Bethlem Hospital, and there the Picture Gallery;
And there's Sadler's Wells, and there the Court of Chancery.

O such a town, such a wonderful Metropolis,
Sure such a town as this was never seen!
O such a town, and such a heap of carriages,
Sure such a motley group was never seen;
Such a swarm of young and old, of buryings and marriages,
All the world seems occupied in ceaseless din.

There's the Bench, and there's the Bank—now only take a peep at her—
And there's Rag Fair, and there the East-London Theatre—
There's St. James's all so fine, St. Giles's all in tattery,
Where fun and frolic dance the rig from Saturday to Saturday.
O what a town, what a wonderful Metropolis,
Sure such a town as this was never seen!

A SHORT time after this day's ramble, the Hon. Tom Dash all and his friend Tallyho paid a visit to the celebrated Tattersall's.

TATTERSALS. *Tom and Bob, looking out for a good one, among the deep ones.*

"This," said Tom, "is a great scene of action at times, and you will upon some occasions find as much business done here as there is on 'Change; the dealings however are not so fair, though the profits are larger; and if you observe the characters and the visages of the visitants, it will be found it is most frequently attended by Turf-Jews and Greeks.{1} Any man indeed who dabbles in horse-dealing, must, like a gamester, be either a rook or a pigeon; {2} for horse-dealing is a species of gambling, in which as many

> 1 *Turf-Jews and Greeks—Gamblers at races, trotting-matches, &c.*
>
> 2 *Rooks and Pigeons are frequenters of gaming-houses: the former signifying the successful adventurer, and the latter the unfortunate dupe.*

depredations are committed upon the property of the unwary as in any other, and every one engaged in it thinks it a meritorious act to dupe his chapman. Even noblemen and gentlemen, who in other transactions of life are honest, will make no scruple of cheating you in horse-dealing: nor is this to be wondered at when we consider that the Lord and the Baronet take lessons from their grooms, jockeys, or coachmen, and the nearer approach they can make to the appearance and manners of their tutors, the fitter the pupils for turf-men, or gentlemen dealers; for the school in which they learn is of such a description that dereliction of principle is by no means surprising—fleecing each other is an every-day practice—every one looks upon his fellow as a bite, and young men of fashion learn how to buy and sell, from old whips, jockeys, or rum ostlers, whose practices have put them up to every thing, and by such ruffian preceptors are frequently taught to make three quarters or seventy-five per cent, profit, which is called turning an honest penny. This, though frequently practised at country fairs, &c. by horse-jobbers, &c. is here executed with all the dexterity and art imaginable: for instance, you have a distressed friend whom you know must sell; you commiserate his situation, and very kindly find all manner of faults with his horse, and buy it for half its value—you also know a Green-horn and an extravagant fellow, to whom you sell it for twice its value, and that is the neat thing. Again, if you have a horse you wish to dispose of, the same school will afford you instruction how to make the most of him, that is to say, to conceal his vices and defects, and by proper attention to put him into condition, to alter his whole appearance by hogging, cropping, and docking—by patching up his broken knees—blowing gun-powder in his dim eyes—bishoping, blistering, &c. so as to turn him out in good twig, scarcely to be known by those who have frequently seen and noticed him: besides which, at the time of sale one of these gentry will aid and assist your views by pointing out his recommendations in some such observations as the following:

'There's a horse truly good and well made.

'There's the appearance of a fine woman! broad breast, round hips, and long neck.

'There's the countenance, intrepidity, and fire of a lion.

'There's the eye, joint, and nostril of an ox.

'There's the nose, gentleness, and patience of a lamb.

'There's the strength, constancy, and foot of a mule.

'There's the hair, head, and leg of a deer.

'There's the throat, neck, and hearing of a wolf.

'There's the ear, brush, and trot of a fox.

'There's the memory, sight, and turning of a serpent.

'There's the running, suppleness, and innocence of the hare.

"And if a horse sold for sound wind, limb, and eyesight, with all the gentleness of a lamb, that a child might ride him with safety, should afterwards break the purchaser's neck, the seller has nothing to do with it, provided he has received the *bit*,{1} but laughs at the *do*.{2} Nay, they will sometimes sell a horse, warranted to go as steady as ever a horse went in harness, to a friend, assuring him at the same time that he has not a fault of any kind—that he is good as ever shoved a head through a horse-collar; and if he should afterwards rear up in the gig, and overturn the driver into a ditch, shatter the concern to pieces, spill Ma'am, and kill both her and the child of promise, the conscientious Horse-dealer has nothing to do with all this: How could he help it? he sold the horse for a good horse, and a good horse he was. This is all in the way of fair dealing. Again, if a horse is sold as sound, and he prove broken-winded, lame, or otherwise, not worth one fortieth part of the purchase-money, still it is only a piece of jockeyship—a fair manouvre, affording opportunities of merriment."

"A very laudable sort of company," said Bob.

"It is rather a mixed one," replied Tom—"it is indeed a complete mixture of all conditions, ranks, and orders of society. But let us take a peep at some of them. Do you observe that stout fellow yonder, with a stick in his hand? he has been a *Daisy-kicker*, and, by his arts and contrivances having saved a little money, is now a regular dealer, and may generally be seen here on selling days."

"Daisy-kicker," said Bob, "I don't comprehend the term."

"Then I will explain," was the reply. "Daisy-kickers are Ostlers belonging to large inns, who are known to each other by that title, and you may frequently hear them

> 1 Bit—A cant term for money.

> 2 Do—Any successful endeavour to over-reach another is by these gentlemen call'd a do, meaning—so and so has been done.

ask—When did you sell your Daisy-kicker or Grogham?—for these terms are made use of among themselves as cant for a horse. Do you also observe, he is now in close conversation with a person who he expects will become a purchaser."

"And who is he?"

"He is no other than a common informer, though in high life; keeps his carriage, horses, and servants—lives in the first style—he is shortly to be made a Consul of, and perhaps an Ambassador afterwards. The first is to all intents and purposes a Lord of Trade, and his Excellency nothing more than a titled spy, in the same way as a Bailiff is a follower of the law, and a man out of livery a Knight's companion or a Nobleman's gentleman."

Their attention was at this moment attracted by the appearance of two persons dressed in the extreme of fashion, who, upon meeting just by them, caught eagerly hold of each other's hand, and they overheard the following—'Why, Bill, how am you, my hearty?—where have you been *trotting your galloper?*—what is you arter?—how's Harry and Ben?—haven't seen you this blue moon.'{1}

'All tidy,' was the reply; 'Ben is getting better, and is going to sport a new curricle, which is now building for him in Long Acre, as soon as he is recovered.'

'Why what the devil's the matter with him, eh?'

'Nothing of any consequence, only he got mill'd a night or two ago about his blowen—he had one of his ribs broke, sprained his right wrist, and sports a *painted peeper*{2} upon the occasion, that's all.'

'Why you know he's no *bad cock* at the Fancy, and won't put up with any gammon.'

'No, but he was lushy, and so he got queer'd—But I say, have you sold your bay?'

'No, d——n me, I can't get my price.'

'Why, what is it you axes?'{3}

'Only a hundred and thirty—got by Agamemnon. Lord, it's no price at all—cheap as dirt—But I say, Bill,

    1 Blue moon—*This is usually intended to imply a long time.*

    2 Painted peeper—*A black eye.*

    3 Axes—*Among the swell lads, and those who affect the characters of knowing coveys, there is a common practice of endeavouring to coin new words and new modes of expression,*

evidently intended to be thought wit; and this affectation frequently has the effect of creating a laugh.

how do you come on with your grey, and the pie-bald poney?'

'All right and regular, my boy; matched the poney for a light curricle, and I swapped{1} the grey for an entire horse—such a rum one—when will you come and take a peep at him?—all bone, fine shape and action, figure beyond compare—I made a rare good chop of it.'

'I'm glad to hear it; I'll make a survey, and take a ride with you the first leisure day; but I'm full of business, no time to spare—I say, are, you a dealer?'

'No, no, it won't do, I lost too much at the Derby—besides, I must go and drive my Girl out—*Avait, that's the time of day,*{2} my boys—so good by—But if you should be able to pick up a brace of clever pointers, a prime spaniel, or a greyhound to match Smut, I'm your man—buy for me, and all's right—price, you know, is out of the question, I must have them if they are to be got, so look out—bid and buy; but mind, nothing but prime will do for me—that's the time of day, you know, d——n me—so good by—I'm off.' And away he went.

"Some great sporting character, I suppose," said Bob—"plenty of money."

"No such thing," said Tom, drawing him on one side—"you will hardly believe that Bill is nothing more than a Shopman to a Linen-draper, recently discharged for malpractices; and the other has been a Waiter at a Tavern, but is now out of place; and they are both upon the sharp look-out to *gammon the flats*. The former obtains his present livelihood by gambling—spends the most of his time in playing cards with *greenhorns*, always to be picked up at low flash houses, at fairs, races, milling-matches, &c. and is also in the holy keeping of the cast-off mistress of a nobleman whose family he was formerly in as a *valet-de-chambre*. The other pretends to teach sparring in the City, and occasionally has a benefit in the Minories, Duke's Place, and the Fives Court."

"They talk it well, however," said Bob.

1 Swapp'd—Exchanged.

2 That's the time of day—That's your sort—that's the barber—keep moving—what am you arter—what am you up to—there never was such times—that's the Dandy—Go along Bob, &c. are ex-pressions that are frequently made use of by the people of the Metropolis; and indeed fashion seems almost to have as much to do with our language as with our dress or manners.

"Words are but wind, many a proud word comes off a weak stomach," was the reply; "and you may almost expect not to hear a word of truth in this place, which may be termed The Sporting Repository—it is the grand mart for horses and for other fashionable animals—for expensive asses, and all sorts of sporting-dogs, town-puppies, and second-hand vehicles. Here bets are made for races and fights—matches are made up here—bargains are struck, and engagements entered into, with as much form, regularity, and importance, as the progress of parliamentary proceedings—points of doubt upon all occasions of jockeyship are decided here; and no man of fashion can be received into what is termed polished society, without a knowledge of this place and some of the visitors. The proceedings however are generally so managed, that the ostlers, the jockeys, the grooms, and the dealers, come best off, from a superiority of knowledge and presumed judgment—they have a method of patching up deep matches to *diddle the dupes*, and to introduce *throws over, doubles, double doubles*, to ease the heavy pockets of their burdens. The system of puffing is also as much in use here as among the Lottery-office Keepers, the Quack Doctors, or the_Knowing ones, by an understanding amongst each other, sell their cattle almost for what they please, if it so happens they are not immediately in want of the *ready*,{1} which, by the way, is an article too frequently in request—and here honest poverty is often obliged to sell at any rate, while the rich black-leg takes care only to sell to a good advantage, making a point at the same time not only to make the most of his cattle, but also of his friend or acquaintance."

"Liberal and patriotic-minded men!" said Bob; "it is a noble Society, and well worthy of cultivation."

"It is fashionable Society, at least," continued Tom, "and deserving of observation, for it is fraught with instruction."

"I think so, indeed," was the reply; "but I really begin to suspect that I shall scarcely have confidence to venture out alone, for there does not appear to be any part of your wonderful Metropolis but what is infested with some kind of shark or other."

"It is but too true, and it is therefore the more necessary to make yourself acquainted with them; it is rather a long lesson, but really deserving of being learnt. You

> 1 The ready—Money.

perceive what sort of company you are now in, as far as may be judged from their appearances; but they are not to be trusted, for I doubt not but you would form erroneous conclusions from such premises. The company that assembles here is generally composed of a great variety of characters—the Idler, the Swindler, the Dandy, the Exquisite, the full-pursed young Peer, the needy Sharper, the gaudy Pauper, and the aspiring School-boy, anxious to be thought a dealer and a judge of the article before him—looking at a horse with an air of importance and assumed intelligence, bidding with a trembling voice and palpitating heart, lest it should be knock'd down to him. Do you see that dashing fellow nearly opposite to us, in the green frock-coat, top-boots, and spurs?—do you mark how he nourishes his whip, and how familiar he seems to be with the knowing old covey in brown?"

"Yes; I suppose he is a dealer."

"You are right, he is a dealer, but it is in man's flesh, not horse flesh: he is a *Bum trap*{1} in search of some friend

> 1 Bum trap—A term pretty generally in use to denominate a
> Bailiff or his follower—they are also called Body-
> snatchers. The ways and means made use of by these gentry to
> make their captions are innumerable: they visit all places,

assume all characters, and try all stratagems, to secure their friends, in order that they may have an opportunity of obliging them, which they have a happy facility in doing, provided the party can bleed free.* Among others, the following are curious facts:

A Gentleman, who laboured under some peculiar difficulties, found it desirable for the sake of his health to retire into the country, where he secluded himself pretty closely from the vigilant anxieties of his friends, who were in search of him and had made several fruitless attempts to obtain an interview. The Traps having ascertained the place of his retreat, from which it appeared that nothing but stratagem could draw him, a knowing old snatch determined to effect his purpose, and succeeded in the following manner:

One day as the Gentleman came to his window, he discovered a man, seemingly in great agitation, passing and re-passing; at length, however, he stopped suddenly, and with a great deal of attention fixed his eyes upon a tree which stood nearly opposite to the window. In a few minutes he returned to it, pulled out a book, in which he read for a few minutes, and then drew forth a rope from his pocket, with which he suspended himself from the tree. The Gentleman, eager to save the life of a fellow-creature, ran out and cut him down. This was scarcely accomplished, before he found the man whom he had rescued (as he thought) from death, slapp'd him on the shoulder, informed him that he was his prisoner, and in return robbed him of his liberty!

Another of these gentry assumed the character of a poor cripple, and stationed himself as a beggar, sweeping the crossing near the habitation of his shy cock, who, conceiving himself safe after three days voluntary imprisonment, was seized by the supposed Beggar, who threw away his broom to secure his man.

Yet, notwithstanding the many artifices to which this

profession is obliged to conform itself, it must be acknowledged there are many of them who have hearts that would do honour to more exalted situations; especially when we reflect, that in general, whatever illiberality or invective may be cast upon them, they rarely if at all oppress those who are in their custody, and that they frequently endeavour to compromise for the Debtor, or at least recommend the Creditor to accept of those terms which can be complied with.

* *Bleed free—*

or other, with a writ in his pocket. These fellows have some protean qualities about them, and, as occasion requires, assume all shapes for the purpose of taking care of their customers; they are however a sort of necessary evil. The old one in brown is a well-known dealer, a deep old file, and knows every one around him—he is up to the sharps, down upon the flats, and not to be done. But in looking round you may perceive men booted and spurred, who perhaps never crossed a horse, and some with whips in their hands who deserve it on their backs—they hum lively airs, whistle and strut about with their quizzing-glasses in their hands, playing a tattoo upon their boots, and shewing themselves off with as many airs as if they were real actors engaged in the farce, that is to say, the buyers and sellers; when in truth they are nothing but loungers in search of employment, who may perhaps have to count the trees in the Park for a dinner without satisfying the cravings of nature, dining as it is termed with Duke Humphrey—others, perhaps, who have arrived in safety, are almost afraid to venture into the streets again, lest they should encounter those foes to liberty, John Doe and Richard Roe."

'If I do, may I be——' The remainder of the sentence was lost, by the speaker removing in conversation with another, when Tom turn'd round.

"O," said Tom, "I thought I knew who it was—that is one of the greatest reprobates in conversation that I ever met with."

"And who is he?"

"Why, I'll give you a brief sketch of him," continued Dashall: "It is said, and I fancy pretty well known, that he has retired upon a small property, how acquired or accumulated I cannot say; but he has married a Bar-maid of very beautiful features and elegant form: having been brought up to the bar, she is not unaccustomed to confinement; but he has made her an absolute prisoner, for he shuts her up as closely as if she were in a monastery—he never dines at home, and she is left in complete solitude. He thinks his game all safe, but she has sometimes escaped the vigilance of her gaoler, and has been seen at places distant from home.{1}

1 It is related of this gentleman, whose severity and vigilance were so harshly spoken of, that one day at table, a dashing young Military Officer, who, while he was circulating the bottle, was boasting among his dissipated friends of his dexterity in conducting the wars of Venus, that he had a short time back met one of the most lovely creatures he ever saw, in the King's Road; but he had learned that her husband so strictly confined and watched her, that there was no possibility of his being admitted to her at any hour.

"Behave handsome, and I'll put you in possession of a gun that shall bring the game down in spite of locks, bolts and bars, or even the vigilance of the eyes of Argus himself."

"How? d— —me if I don't stand a ten pound note."

"How! why easy enough; I've a plan that cannot but succeed— down with the cash, and I'll put you up to the scheme."

No sooner said than done, and he pocketed the ten pound note.

"Now," said the hoary old sinner, little suspecting that he was to be the dupe of his own artifice: "You get the husband invited out to dinner, have him well ply'd with wine by your friends: You assume the dress of a Postman—give a thundering rap at her door, which always denotes either the

arrival of some important visitor or official communication; and when you can see her, flatter, lie, and swear that her company is necessary to your existence—that life is a burden without her—tell her, you know her husband is engaged, and can't come—that he is dining out with some jolly lads, and can't possibly be home for some hours—fall at her feet, and say that, having obtained the interview, you will not leave her. Your friends in the mean time must be engaged in making him as drunk as a piper. That's the way to do it, and if you execute it as well as it is plann'd, the day's your own."

"Bravo, bravo!" echoed from every one present.

It was a high thing—the breach thus made, the horn-work was soon to be carried, and there could be no doubt of a safe lodgement in the covert-way.

The gay Militaire met his inamorata shortly afterwards in Chelsea-fields, and after obtaining from her sundry particulars of inquiry, as to the name of her husband, &c. he acquainted her with his plan. The preliminaries were agreed upon, and it was deter-mined that the maid-servant, who was stationed as a spy upon her at all times, should be dispatched to some house in the neighbour-hood to procure change, while the man of letters was to be let in and concealed; and upon her return it was to be stated that the Postman was in a hurry, could not wait, and was to call again. This done, he was to make his escape by a rope-ladder from the window as soon as the old one should be heard upon the stairs, which it of course was presumed would be at a late hour, when he was drunk.

The train having been thus laid, Old Vigilance dined out, and expected to meet the Colonel; but being disappointed, and suspicious at all times, for

   "Suspicion ever haunts the guilty mind,"

The utmost endeavours of the party to make him drunk proved ineffectual; he was restless and uncomfortable, and he could not help fancying by the visible efforts to do him up, that some mischief was brewing, or some hoax was about to be played off. He had his master-key in his pocket, and retired early.

His Lady, whose plan had succeeded admirably at home, was fearful of having the door bolted till after twelve, lest the servant's suspicions should be aroused. In the mean time, the son of Mars considered all safe, and entertained no expectation of the old Gentleman's return till a very late hour. When lo and behold, to the great surprise and annoyance of the lovers, he gently opened the street door, and fearful of awaking his faithful charmer out of her first slumber, he ascended the stairs unshod. His phosphoric matches shortly threw a light upon the subject, and he entered the apartment; when, what was the surprise and astonishment of the whole party at the discovery of their situation!

The old Gentleman swore, stormed, and bullied, declaring he would have satisfaction! that he would commence a civil suit! The Military Hero told him it would be too civil by half, and was in fact more than he expected;—reminded him of the ten pounds he had received as agency for promoting his amours;—informed him he had performed the character recommended by him most admirably. The old man was almost choked with rage; but perceiving he had spread a snare for himself, was compelled to hear and forbear, while the lover bolted, wishing him a good night, and singing, "Locks, bolts, and bars, I defy you," as an admirable lesson in return for the blustering manner in which he had received information of the success of his own scheme.

"Mr. C—— on the opposite side is a Money-procurer or lender, a very accommodating sort of person, who négociâtes meetings and engagements between young borrowers, who care not what they pay for money, and old lenders, who care not who suffers, so they can obtain enormous interest for their loans. He is a venerable looking man, and is known to most of the young Bloods who visit here. His father was a German Cook in a certain kitchen. He set up for a Gentleman at his father's death, and was taken particular notice of by Lord G——, and indeed by all the turf. He lived a gay and fashionable life, soon run out his fortune, and is now pensioned by a female whom he formerly supported. He is an excellent judge of a horse and horse-racing, upon which subjects his advice is frequently given. He is a very useful person among the generality of gentry who frequent this place of public resort. At the same time it ought to be observed, that among the various characters which infest and injure society, perhaps there are few more practised in guilt, fraud, and deceit, than the Money-lenders.

"They advertise to procure large sums of money to assist those under pecuniary embarrassment. They generally reside in obscure situations, and are to be found by anonymous signatures, such as A. B. I. R. D. V. &c. They chiefly prey upon young men of property, who have lost their money at play, horse-racing, betting, &c. or other expensive amusements, and are obliged to raise more upon any terms until their rents or incomes become payable: or such as have fortunes in prospect, as being heirs apparent to estates, but who require assistance in the mean time.

"These men avail themselves of the credit, or the ultimate responsibility of the giddy and thoughtless young spendthrift in his eager pursuit of criminal pleasures, and under the influence of those allurements, which the various places of fashionable resort hold out; and seldom fail to obtain from them securities and obligations for large sums; upon the credit of which they are enabled, perhaps at usurious interest, to borrow money or discount bills, and thus supply their unfortunate customers upon the most extravagant terms.

"There are others, who having some capital, advance money upon bonds, title-deeds, and other specialties, or tipon the bond of the parties having property in reversion. By these and other devices, large sums of money are most unwarrantably and illegally wrested from the dissipated and the thoughtless; and misery and distress are perhaps entailed upon them as long as they live, or they are driven by the prospect of utter ruin to acts of desperation or the commission of crimes.

"It generally happens upon application to the advertising party, that he, like Moses in *The School for Scandal*, is not really in possession of any money himself, but then he knows where and how to procure it from a very unconscionable dog, who may, perhaps, not be satisfied with the security ottered; yet, if you have Bills at any reasonable date, he could get them discounted. If you should suffer yourself to be trick'd out of any Bills, he will contrive, in some way or other, to negotiate them—not, as he professes, for you, but for himself and his colleagues; and, very likely, after you have been at the additional expense of commencing a suit at law against them, they have disappeared, and are in the King's Bench or the Fleet, waiting there to defraud you of every hope and expectation, by obtaining their liberty through the White-washing Act.

"These gentry are for the most part Attorneys or Pettifoggers, or closely connected with such; and notwithstanding all legal provisions to preclude them from exacting large sums, either for their agency and introduction, or for the bonds which they draw, yet they contrive to bring themselves home, and escape detection, by some such means as the following:

"They pretend that it is necessary to have a deed drawn up to explain the uses of the Annuity-bond, which the grantor of the money, who is some usurious villain, immediately acknowledges and accedes to; for

"The bond that signs the mortgage pays the shot; so that an Act which is fraught with the best purposes for the protection of the honest, but unfortunate, is in this manner subjected to the grossest chicanery of pettifoggers and pretenders, and the vilest evasions of quirking low villains of the law.

"There is also another species of money-lender, not inaptly termed the Female Banker. These accommodate Barrow-women and others, who sell fruit, vegetables, &c. in the public streets, with five shillings a day (the usual diurnal stock in such cases;) for the use of which for twelve hours they obtain the moderate premium of sixpence when the money is returned in the evening, receiving at this rate about seven pounds ten shillings per year for every five pounds they can so employ. It is however very difficult to convince the borrowers of the correctness of this calculation, and of the serious loss to which they subject themselves by a continuation of the system, since it is evident that this improvident and dissolute class of people have no other idea than that of making the day and the way alike long. Their profits (often considerably augmented by dealing in base money as well as the articles which they sell) seldom last over the day; for they never fail to have a luxurious dinner and a hot supper, with a plentiful supply of gin and porter: looking in general no farther than to keep the whole original stock with the sixpence interest, which is paid over to the female Banker in the evening, and a new loan obtained on the following morning to go to market, and to be disposed of in the same way.

"In contemplating this curious system of banking, or money lending (trifling as it may appear,) it is almost impossible not to be forcibly struck with the immense profits that are derived from it. It is only necessary for one of these sharpers to possess a capital of seventy shillings, or three pounds ten shillings, with fourteen steady and regular customers, in order to realize an income of one hundred guineas per year! So true it is, that one half of the world do not know how the other half live; for there are thousands who cannot have the least conception of the existence of such facts.

"Here comes a *Buck of the first cut*, one who pretends to know every thing and every body, but thinks of nobody but himself, and of that self in reality knows nothing.

Captain P——is acknowledged by all his acquaintance to be one of the best fellows in the world, and to beat every one at slang, but U——y and A——se. He is the terror of the Charleys, and of the poor unfortunate roofless nightly wanderers in the streets. You perceive his long white hair, and by no means engaging features. Yet he has vanity enough to think himself handsome, and that he is taken notice of on that account; when the attractions he presents are really such as excite wonder and surprise, mingled with disgust; yet he contemplates his figure in the looking-glass with self satisfaction, and asks the frail ones, with a tremulous voice, if, so help them— — he is not a good-looking fellow 1 and they, knowing their customer, of course do not fail to reply in the affirmative.

"He is a well known leg, and is no doubt present on this occasion to bet upon the ensuing Epsom races; by the bye his losses have been very considerable in that way. He has also at all times been a dupe to the sex. It is said that Susan B— —, a dashing Cyprian, eased his purse of a £500 bill, and whilst he was dancing in pursuit of her, she was dancing to the tune of a Fife; a clear proof she had an ear for music as well as an eye to business. But I believe it was played in a different Key to what he expected; whether it was a minor Key or not I cannot exactly say.

"At a ball or assembly he conceives himself quite at home, satisfied that he is the admiration of the whole of the company present; and were he to give an account of himself, it would most likely be in substance nearly as follows:

"When I enter the room, what a whisp'ring is heard; My rivals, astonish'd, scarce utter a word; "How charming! (cry all;) how enchanting a fellow! How neat are those small-clothes, how killingly yellow. Not for worlds would I honour these plebs with a smile, Tho' bursting with pride and delight all the while; So I turn to my cronies (a much honour'd few,); Crying, "S—z—m, how goes it?—Ah, Duchess, how do? Ton my life, yonder's B—uf, and Br—ke, and A— g—le, S-ff—d, W—tm—1—d, L—n, and old codger C—ri—le." Now tho', from this style of address, it appears That these folks I have known for at least fifty years, The fact is, my friends, that I scarcely know one, A mere "façon de parler," the way of the ton. What tho' they dislike it, I answer my ends, Country gentlemen stare, and suppose them my friends.

But my beautiful taste (as indeed you will guess) Is manifest most in my toilet and dress; My neckcloth of course forms my principal care, For by that we criterions of elegance swear, And costs me each morning some hours of flurry, To make it appear to be tied in a hurry. My boot-tops, those unerring marks of a blade, With Champagne are polish'd, and peach marmalade; And a violet coat, closely copied from B—ng, With a cluster of seals, and a large diamond ring; And troisièmes of buckskin, bewitchingly large, Give the finishing stroke to the *"parfait ouvrage."*

During this animated description of the gay personage alluded to, Bob had listened with the most undeviating attention, keeping his eye all the time on this extravagant piece of elegance and fashion, but could not help bursting into an immoderate fit of laughter at its conclusion. In the mean time the crowd of visitors had continued to increase; all appeared to be bustle and confusion; small parties were seen in groups communicating together in different places, and every face appeared to be animated by hopes or fears. Dashall was exchanging familiar nods and winks with those whom lie knew; but as their object was not to buy, they paid but little attention to the sales of the day, rather contenting themselves with a view of the human cattle by which they were surrounded, when they were pleasingly surprised to observe their friend Sparkle enter, booted and spurred.

"Just the thing! (said Sparkle,) I had some suspicion of finding you here. Are you buyers? Does your Cousin want a horse, an ass, or a filly?"

Tom smiled; "Always upon the ramble, eh, Sparkle. Why ask such questions? You know we are well horsed; but I suppose if the truth was known, you are *prad* sellers; if so, shew your article, and name your price."

"Apropos," said Sparkle; "Here is a friend of mine, to whom I must introduce you, so say no more about articles and prices—I have an article in view above all price—excuse me." And with this he made his way among the tribe of Jockeys, Sharpers, and Blacklegs, and in a minute returned, bringing with him a well-dressed young man, whose manners and appearance indicated the Gentleman, and whose company was considered by Tom and his Cousin as a valuable acquisition.

"Mr. Richard Mortimer," said Sparkle, as he introduced his friend— "the Hon. Mr. Dashall, and Mr. Robert Tallyho."

After the mutual interchanges of politeness which naturally succeeded this introduction—"Come," said Sparkle, "we are horsed, and our nags waiting—we are for a ride, which way do you bend your course?"

"A lucky meeting," replied Tom; "for we are upon the same scent; I expect my curricle at Hyde-Park Corner in ten minutes, and have no particular line of destination."

"Good," said Sparkle; "then we may hope to have your company; and how disposed for the evening?"

"Even as chance may direct."

"Good, again—all right—then as you are neither buyers nor sellers, let us employ the remaining ten minutes in looking around us—there is nothing to attract here—Epsom Races are all the talk, and all of business that is doing—come along, let us walk through the Park—let the horses meet us at Kensington Gate, and then for a twist among the briers and brambles."

This was readily agreed to: orders were given to the servants, and the party proceeded towards the Park.

CHAPTER XIII

What is Bon Ton? Oh d— — me (cries a Buck,
Half drunk,) ask me, my dear, and you're in luck:
Bon Ton's to swear, break windows, beat the Watch,
Pick up a wench, drink healths, and roar a catch.
Keep it up, keep it up! d— — me, take your swing—
Bon Ton is Life, my boy! Bon Ton's the thing!
"Ah, I loves Life and all the joys it yields—
(Says Madam Fussock. warm from Spitalfields;)
Bon Ton's the space 'twixt Saturday and Monday,
And riding out in one-horse shay o' Sunday;
'Tis drinking tea on summer afternoons
At Bagnigge Wells, with china and gilt spoons;
'Tis laying by our stuffs, red cloaks and pattens,
To dance cowtillions all in silks and satins."
"Vulgar! (cries Miss) observe in higher Life
The feather'd spinster and three feather'd wife;
The Club's Bon Ton—Bon Ton's a constant trade
Of rout, festino, ball and masquerade;
'Tis plays and puppet shows—'tis something new—
'Tis losing thousands every night at loo;
Nature it thwarts, and contradicts all reason;
'Tis stiff French stays, and fruit when out of season,
A rose, when half a guinea is the price;
A set of bays scarce bigger than six mice;
To visit friends you never wish to see—
Marriage 'twixt those who never can agree;
Old dowagers, dress'd, painted, patch'd and curl'd—
This is Bon Ton, and this we call the World!

AS they passed through the gate, Tom observed it was rather too early to expect much company. "Never mind," said Sparkle, "we are company enough among ourselves; the morning is fine, the curricle not arrived, and we shall find plenty of conversation, if we do not discover interesting character, to diversify our promenade.

Travelling spoils conversation, unless you are squeezed like an Egyptian mummy into a stage or a mail-coach; and perhaps in that case you may meet with animals who have voices, without possessing the power of intellect to direct them to any useful or agreeable purpose."

Tallyho, who was at all times delighted with Sparkle's descriptions of society and manners, appeared pleased with the proposition.

"Your absence from town," continued Sparkle, addressing himself to Dashall, "has prevented my introduction of Mr. Mortimer before, though you have heard me mention his Sister. They are now inhabitants of our own sphere of action, and I trust we shall all become better known to each other."

This piece of information appeared to be truly acceptable to all parties. Young Mortimer was a good-looking and well made young man; his features were animated and intelligent; his manners polished, though not quite so unrestrained as those which are to be acquired by an acquaintance with metropolitan associations.

"I am happy," said he, "to be introduced to any friends of your's, and shall be proud to number them among mine."

"You may," replied Sparkle, "with great safety place them on your list; though you know I have already made it appear to you that friendship is a term more generally made use of than understood in London—

> *"For what is Friendship but a name,*
> *A charm which lulls to sleep,*
> *A shade that follows wealth and fame,*
> *And leaves the wretch to weep?*
>
> *And Love is still an emptier sound,*
> *The modern fair one's jest;*
> *On earth unseen, or only found*
> *To warm the turtle's nest."*

"These sentiments are excellently expressed," said Tom, pinching him by the arm—"and I suppose in perfect consonance with your own?"

Sparkle felt 'the rebuke, look'd down, and seem'd confused; but in a moment recovering himself,

"Not exactly so," replied he; "but then you know, and I don't mind confessing it among friends, though you are aware it is very unfashionable to acknowledge the existence of any thing of the kind, I am a pupil of nature."

"You seem to be in a serious humour all at once," said young Mortimer.

"Can't help it," continued Sparkle—"for,

> *"Let them all say what they will,*
> *Nature will be nature still."*

"And that usurper, or I should rather say, would be usurper, Fashion, is in no way in alliance with our natures. I remember the old Duchess of Marlborough used to say 'That to love some persons very much, and to see often those we love, is the greatest happiness I can enjoy;' but it appears almost impossible for any person in London to secure such an enjoyment, and I can't help feeling it."

By the look and manner with which this last sentiment was uttered, Tom plainly discovered there was a something labouring at his heart which prompted it. "Moralizing!" said he. "Ah, Charley, you are a happy fellow. I never yet knew one who could so rapidly change *'from grave to gay, from lively to severe*; and for the benefit of our friends, I can't help thinking you could further elucidate the very subject you have so feelingly introduced."

"You are a quiz" said Sparkle; "but there is one thing to be said, I know you, and have no great objection to your hits now and then, provided they are not knock down blows."

"But," said Mortimer, "what has this to do with friendship and love? I thought you were going to give something like a London definition of the terms."

"Why," said Sparkle, "in London it is equally difficult to get to love any body very much, or often to meet those that we love. There are such numbers of acquaintances, such a constant succession of engagements of one sort or other, such a round of delights, that the town resembles Vauxhall, where the nearest and dearest friends may walk round and round all night without once meeting: for instance, at dinner you should see a person whose manners and conversation are agreeable and pleasing to you; you may wish in vain to become more intimate, for the chance is, that you will not meet so as to converse a second time for many months; for no one can tell when the dice-box of society may turn up the same numbers again. I do not mean to infer that you may not barely see the same features again; it is possible that you may catch a glimpse of them on the opposite side of Pall Mall or Bond-street, or see them near to you at a crowded rout, without a possibility of approaching.

"It is from this cause, that those who live in London are so totally indifferent to each other; the waves follow so quick, that every vacancy is immediately filled up, and the want is not perceived. The well-bred civility of modern times, and the example of some 'very popular people,' it is true, have introduced a shaking of hands, a pretended warmth, a dissembled cordiality, into the manners of the cold and warm, alike the dear friend and the acquaintance of yesterday. Consequently we continually hear such conversation as the following:—' Ah, how d'ye do? I'm delighted to see you! How is Mrs. M——?'

'She's very well, thank you.' 'Has she any increase in family?' 'Any increase! why I've only been married three months. I see you are talking of my former wife: bless you, she has been dead these three years.'—Or, 'Ah, my dear friend, how d'ye do? You have been out of town some time; where have you been? In Norfolk?' 'No, I have been two years in India.'"

This description of a friendly salutation appeared to interest and amuse both Talltho and Mortimer. Tom laughed, shrugg'd up his shoulders, acknowledged the picture was too true, and Sparkle continued.

"And thus it is, that, ignorant of one another's interests and occupations, the generality of friendships of London contain nothing more tender than a visiting card: nor are they much better, indeed they are much worse, if you renounce the world, and determine to live only with your relations and nearest connexions; for if you go to see them at one o'clock, they are not stirring; at two, the room is full of different acquaintances, who talk over the occurrences of the last night's ball, and, of course, are paid more attention to than yourself; at three, they are out shopping; at four, they are in this place dashing among the Pinks, from which they do not return till seven, then they are dressing; at eight, they are dining with two dozen friends; at nine and ten the same; at eleven, they are dressing for the ball; and at twelve, when you are retiring to rest, they are gone into society for the evening: so that you are left in solitude; you soon begin again to try the world—and we will endeavour to discover what it produces.

"The first inconvenience of a London Life is the late hour of a fashionable dinner. To pass the day in fasting, and then sit down to a great dinner at eight o'clock, is entirely against the first dictates of common sense and common stomachs. But what is to be done? he who rails against the fashion of the times will be considered a most unfashionable dog, and perhaps I have already said more than sufficient to entitle me to that appellation."

"Don't turn *King's Evidence* against yourself," said Tom; "for, if you plead guilty in this happy country, you must be tried by your Peers."

"Nay," said Mortimer, "while fashion and reason appear to be in such direct opposition to each other, I must confess their merits deserve to be impartially tried; though I cannot, for one moment, doubt but the latter must ultimately prevail with the generality, however her dictates may be disregarded by the votaries of the former."

"You are a good one at a ramble" said Tom, "and not a bad one in a spree, but I cannot help thinking you are rambling out of your road; you seem to have lost the thread of your subject, and, having been disappointed with love and friendship, you are just going to sit down to dinner."

"Pardon me," replied Sparkle, "I was proceeding naturally, and not fashionably, to my subject; but I know you are so great an admirer of the latter, that you care but little about the former."

"Hit for hit," said Tom; "but go on—you are certainly growing old, Sparkle; at all events, you appear very grave this morning, and if you continue in this humour long, I shall expect you are about taking Orders."

"There is a time for all things, but the time for that has not yet arrived."

"Well, then, proceed without sermonizing."

"I don't like to be interrupted," replied Sparkle; "and there is yet much to be said on the subject. I find there are many difficulties to encounter in contending with the fashionable customs. Some learned persons have endeavoured to support the practice of late dinners by precedent, and quoted the Roman supper; but it ought to be recollected that those suppers were at three o'clock in the afternoon, and should be a subject of contempt, instead of imitation, in Grosvenor Square. Women, however, are not quite so irrational as men, in London, for they generally sit down to a substantial lunch about three or four; if men would do the same, the meal at eight might be relieved of many of its weighty dishes, and conversation would be a gainer by it; for it must be allowed on all hands, that conversation suffers great interruption from the manner in which fashionable dinners are managed. First, the host and hostess (or her unfortunate coadjutor) are employed during three parts of the dinner in doing the work of servants, helping fish, or carving venison to twenty hungry guests, to the total loss of the host's powers of amusement, and the entire disfigurement of the fair hostess's face. Again, much time is lost by the attention every one is obliged to pay, in order to find out (which, by the way, he cannot do if he is short-sighted) what dishes are at the extreme end of the table; and if a guest is desirous of a glass of wine, he must peep through the Apollos and Cupids of the plateau, in order to find some one to take it with; otherwise he is compelled to wait till some one asks him, which will probably happen in succession; so that after having had no wine for half an hour, he will have to swallow five glasses in five minutes. Convenience teaches, that the best manner of enjoying society at dinner, is to leave every thing to the servants that servants can do; so that no farther trouble may be experienced than to accept the dishes that are presented, and to drink at your own time the wines which are handed round. A fashionable dinner, on the contrary, seems to presume beforehand on the silence, dulness, and insipidity of the guests, and to have provided little interruptions, like the jerks which the Chaplain gives to the Archbishop to prevent his going to sleep during a sermon."

"Accurate descriptions, as usual," said Tom, "and highly amusing."

Tallyho and Mortimer were intent upon hearing the remainder of Sparkle's account, though they occasionally joined in the laugh, and observed that Sparkle seemed to be in a very sentimental mood. As they continued to walk on, he resumed—

"Well then, some time after dinner comes the hour for the ball, or rout; but this is sooner said than done: it often requires as much time to go from St. James's Square to Cleveland Row, as to go from London to Hounslow.

It would require volumes to describe the disappointment which occurs on arriving in the brilliant mob of a ball-room. Sometimes, as it has been before said, a friend is seen squeezed like yourself, at the other end of the room, without a possibility of your communicating, except by signs; and as the whole arrangement of the society is regulated by mechanical pressure, you may happen to be pushed against those to whom you do not wish to speak, whether bores, slight acquaintances, or determined enemies. Confined by the crowd, stifled by the heat, dazzled by the light, all powers of intellect are obscured; wit loses its point, and sagacity its observation; indeed, the limbs are so crushed, and the tongue so parched, that, except particularly undressed ladies, all are in the case of the traveller, Mr. Clarke, when he says, that in the plains of Syria some might blame him for not making moral reflections on the state of the country; but that he must own that the heat quite deprived him of all power of thought. Hence it is, that the conversation you hear around you is generally nothing more than—"Have you been here long?—Have you been at Mrs. H——'s?—Are you going to Lady D——'s?"— Hence too,

Madam de Staël said very justly to an Englishman, "Dans vos routes le corps fait plus de frai que l'esprit." But even if there are persons of a constitution robust enough to talk, they dare not do so, when twenty heads are forced into the compass of one square foot; nay, even if, to your great delight, you see a person to whom you have much to say, and by fair means or foul, elbows and toes, knees and shoulders, have got near him, he often dismisses you with shaking you by the hand, and saying—My dear Mr.—— how do you do? and then continues a conversation with a person whose ear is three inches nearer. At one o'clock, however, the crowd diminishes; and if you are not tired by the five or six hours of playing at company, which you have already had, you may be very comfortable for the rest of the evening. This however is the round of fashionable company. But I begin to be tired even of the description."

"A very luminous and comprehensive view of fashionable society however," said Tom, "sketched by a natural hand in glowing colours, though not exactly in the usual style. I shall not venture to assert whether the subjects are well chosen, but the figures are well grouped, and display considerable ability and lively imagination in the painter, though a little confused."

"It appears to be a study from nature," said Mortimer.

"At least," continued Sparkle, "it is a study from Real Life, and delineates the London manners; for although I have been a mingler in the gaieties and varieties of a London Life, I have always held the same opinions with respect to the propriety of the manners and customs adopted, and have endeavoured to read as I ran; and it cannot be denied, that, in the eye of fashion, nothing can be more amiable than to deviate, or at least to affect a deviation, from nature, for to speak or act according to her dictates, would be considered vulgar and common-place in the last degree; to hear a story and not express an emotion you do not feel, perfectly rude and unmannerly, and among the ladies particularly. To move and think as the heart feels inclined, are offences against politeness that no person can ever in honour or delicacy forgive."

"Come, come," said Tom, "don't you be so hard on the blessings of Life—

> *"For who, that knows the thrilling touch*
> *Which Woman's love can give,*
> *Would wish to live for aught so much,*
> *As bid those beauties live?*
>
> *For what is life, which all so prize,*
> *And all who live approve,*
> *Without the fire of Woman's eyes,*
> *To bid man live and love?"*

Sparkle affected to laugh, appeared confused, and look'd down for a few moments, and they walk'd on in silence.

"I perceive," said Tom, "how the matter stands—well, I shall not be a tormentor—but remember I expect an introduction to the fair enslaver. I thought you 'defy'd the mighty conqueror of hearts,' and resolved to be free."

"Resolutions, as well as promises, are easily made," said Sparkle, "but not always so easily accomplished or performed—nor are you always accurate in your conceptions of circumstances; but no matter, your voyages are always made in search of discoveries, and, in spite of your resolutions, you may perchance be entrapp'd. But no more of this; I perceive your raillery is directed to me, and I hope you enjoy it."

"Faith," replied Tom, "you know I always enjoy your company, but I don't recollect to have found you in so prosing a humour before—Pray, which way are you directing your coursel?"

During the latter part of this conversation, Bob and young Mortimer were employed in admiring the fine piece of water which presented itself to their notice in the Serpentine River.

"Merely for a ride," was the reply; "any way you please, to pass away the time."

"Mighty cavalier, truly," said Tom; "but come, here we are at Kensington, let us mount, and away."

"Remember, I expect you and Mr. Tallyho to accompany me in the evening to a family-party. I have already stated my intention, and you are both expected."

"Upon these terms then, I am your man, and I think I may answer for my Cousin."

By this time they were at the gate, where, finding the curricle and the nags all in readiness, Sparkle and Mortimer were soon horsed, and Tom and Bob seated in the curricle. They proceeded to Richmond, taking surveys of the scenery on the road, and discoursing on the usual topics of such a journey, which being foreign to the professed intention of this work, are omitted. Suffice it to say they returned refreshed from the excursion, and parted with a promise to meet again at nine o'clock, in Grosvenor Square.

"Egad!" said Dashall, as they entered the diningroom, "there is something very mysterious in all this. Sparkle has hitherto been the life and soul of society: he seems to be deeply smitten with this young Lady, Miss Mortimer, and promises fairly, by his manner, to prove a deserter from our standard, and to inlist under the banners of Hymen."

"Not unlikely," replied Tallyho, "if what we are told be true—that it is what we must all come to."

"Be that as it may, it ought not to interfere with our pursuits, Real Life in London, though, to be sure, the Ladies, dear creatures, ought not to be forgotten: they are so nearly and dearly interwoven with our existence, that, without them, Life would be insupportable."

After dinner, they prepared for the evening party, and made their appearance in Grosvenor Squire at the appointed hour. But as this will introduce new characters to the Reader, we shall defer our account of them till the next Chapter.

CHAPTER XIV

Ye are stars of the night, ye are gems of the morn,
Ye are dew-drops whose lustre illumines the thorn;
And rayless that night is, that morning unblest,
When no beam in your eye, lights up peace in the breast;
And the sharp thorn of sorrow sinks deep in the heart,
Till the sweet lip of Woman assuages the smart;
'Tis her's o'er the couch of misfortune to bend,
In fondness a lover, in firmness a friend;
And prosperity's hour, be it ever confest,
From Woman receives both refinement and zest;
And adorn'd by the bays, or enwreath'd with the willow,
Her smile is our meed, and her bosom our pillow.

ARRIVED at Grosvenor Square, they found the party consisted of Colonel B——, his son and daughter, Miss Mortimer, and her brother, Mr. Sparkle, Mr. Merrywell, and Lady Lovelace. The first salutations of introduction being over, there was time to observe the company, among whom, Miss Mortimer appeared to be the principal magnet of attraction. The old Colonel was proud to see the friends of Mr. Sparkle, and had previously given a hearty welcome to Mr. Merrywell, as the friend of his nephew, the young Mortimer. Sparkle now appeared the gayest of the gay, and had been amusing the company with some of his liveliest descriptions of character and manners, that are to be witnessed in the metropolis. While Merrywell, who did not seem to be pleased with the particular attentions he paid to Miss Mortimer, was in close conversation with her brother.

Tom could not but acknowledge that it was scarcely possible to see Miss Mortimer, without feelings of a nature which he had scarcely experienced before. The elegant neatness of her dress was calculated to display the beauty of her form, and the vivid flashes of a dark eye were so many irresistible attacks upon the heart; a sweet voice, and smiling countenance, appeared to throw a radiance around the room, and illuminate the visages of the whole party, while Lady Lovelace and Maria B—— served as a contrast to heighten that effect which they envied and reproved. While tea was preparing, after which it was proposed to take a rubber at cards, a sort of general conversation took place: the preparations for the Coronation, the new novels of the day, and the amusements of the theatre, were canvassed in turn; and speaking of the writings of Sir Walter Scott, as the presumed author of the celebrated Scotch novels, Lady Lovelace declared she found it impossible to procure the last published from the library, notwithstanding her name has been long on the list, so much was it in request.

Sparkle replied, "That he had purchased the Novel, and would willingly lend it to the Ladies. As for the Libraries," continued he, "they are good places of accommodation, but it is impossible to please every one, either there or any where else; they are however very amusing at times, and as a proof of it, I strolled the other morning to a Circulating Library, for the express purpose of lounging away an hour in digesting the politics and news of the day; but the curious scenes to which I was witness during this short period, so distracted my attention, that, despite of the grave subjects on which I was meditating, I could not resist lending an attentive ear to all that passed around me. There was something of originality in the countenance of the Master of the Library which struck me forcibly; and the whimsical answers which he made to his numerous subscribers, and the yet more whimsical tone in which they were pronounced, more than once provoked a smile. The first person who attracted my notice was a fine showy looking woman, dressed in the extreme of fashion, with a bloom upon her cheek, which might have emulated that of the rose, with this exception, that it wanted the charm of nature. Putting a list into the hands of the Bookseller, she inquired if he had any of the productions the names of which were there transcribed. Glancing his eye over the paper, he replied (with an archness which not a little disconcerted her, and which probably occasioned her abrupt disappearance, "*The Fine Lady*, Madam, is seldom or ever at home; but *Family Secrets* we are always ready to let out." '*Characters of Eminent Men*' growled out a little vulgar consequential Citizen, whose countenance bore the stamp of that insufferable dulness that might almost tempt one to imagine him incapable of comprehending the meaning of the words which he pronounced with an air of so much self-importance; '*Characters of*

Eminent Men, 195,' repeated the Snarler, in the same tone, 'I much fear if we can boast a quarter of that number, eh! Mr. Margin?' "I fear not, Sir," replied Margin; "but such as we have are very much at your service." 'Better be in the service of the nation than in mine, by far,' said the little purse-proud gentleman, shrugging his shoulders very significantly. "Shall I send it for you, Sir?" said Margin, without noticing the last remark. 'By no means, by no means; the volume is not so large, it won't encumber me much; I believe I shall find it small enough to put in my pocket,' pursued the little great man, grinning at the shrewdness of his own observations, and stalking out with as much self-complacency as he had stalked in. I knew the man well, and could not help laughing at the lofty airs he assumed, at the manner in which he affected to decry all his countrymen without mercy, at his unwillingness to acknowledge any talent amongst them, though he himself was a man of that plodding description who neither ever had done, nor ever could do any thing to entitle him to claim distinction of any sort. The young Coxcomb who next entered, was a direct contrast to the last applicant, both in person and manner. Approaching with a fashionable contortion, he stretched out his lady-like hand, and in the most languid and affected tone imaginable, inquired for The Idler. "That, Sir," said Margin, "is amongst the works we have unhappily lost, but you will be sure to meet with it at any of the fashionable libraries in the neighbourhood of Bond Street or St. James's." The young Fop had just sense enough to perceive that the shaft was aimed at him, but not enough to relish the joke, or correct the follies which provoked it, and turned abruptly on his heel. He was met at the door by a sentimental boarding-school Miss, who came flying into the shop in defiance of her governess, and inquired, in a very pathetic tone, for *The Constant Lover*. "That, I am afraid," said Margin, "is not amongst our collection." 'Dear me,' lisped the young Lady, with an air of chagrin, 'that's very provoking, I thought that was what every one had.' "Give me leave to assure you, Ma'am, that you are quite mistaken. I fancy you will find that it is not to be met with all over London."

An old Gentleman of the old school, whose clothes were decidedly the cut of the last century, and whose stiff and formal manners were precisely of the same date with his habiliments, next came hobbling in. Poring through his spectacles over the catalogue which lay upon the counter, the first thing which caught his eye, was *An Essay upon Old Maids*. "Tom, Tom," said the complaisant Librarian, calling to a lad at the other end of the shop, "reach down the Old Maids for the gentleman. They won't appear to advantage, I'm afraid, a little dusty or damaged, with having laid so long upon the shelf," he added, with a simper, which was not lost upon any one present. A melancholy looking man, in whose countenance meekness and insipidity were alike plainly depicted, now came forward, inquiring, in an under, and what might almost be designated an alarmed tone of voice, for *The Impertinent Wife*; a female, who hung upon his arm, interrupted him by entreating, or rather insisting in no very gentle tone, 'that he would ask for something better worth having.' Margin, affecting only to hear the former speaker, immediately produced the book in question, and observed, with much naivete, "that the Impertinent Wife was sure to be in the way at all hours," at the same time not omitting to recommend Discipline as "a better work." A young man, whom I knew to be one of the greatest fortune hunters about town, with an air of consummate assurance, put out his hand for *Disinterested Marriage*. "That's a thing quite out of date—never thought of now, Sir," said Margin, who knew him as well as myself; "Allow me to recommend something of more recent date, something more sought after in the fashionable world, Splendid Misery, Sir, or—"The young man heard no more: spite of his impudence, he was so abashed by the reply, that he made a hasty retreat. The last person whom I thought it worth my while to notice, was a tall, meagre looking man, whom I recollected to have seen pointed out to me as a wit, and a genius of the first order. His wit was, however, of that dangerous sort which caused his company to be rather shunned than courted; and it was very evident, from his appearance, that he had not had the wit to work himself into the good graces of those who might have had it in their power to befriend him. Though he spoke in a very low tone, I soon found that he was inquiring for *Plain Sense*. On Margin's replying, with much nonchalance, that *Plain Sense* had of late become very rare, finding himself disappointed in his first application, his next aim was *Patronage*. "That, Sir, (said the wary bookseller) is so much sought after, that I really cannot promise it to you at present; but if, as I conclude, you merely want something to beguile a leisure hour or two, probably *The Discontented Man* will answer the purpose very well."

To this description of Sparkle, the whole company listened with attention and delight, frequently interrupting him with bursts of laughter. Tea was handed round, and then cards introduced. Young Mortimer and Merrywell seemed to take but little interest in the play, and evidently discovered their anxiety to be liberated, having some other object in view. Mortimer felt no great portion of pleasure in passing his time with his uncle, the Colonel, nor with his sister, Lady Lovelace, who was a perfect model of London affectation; besides, his friend Mr. Merrywell, who was to him what Tom Dashall and Sparkle had been to Tallyho, had made an engagement to introduce him to some of his dashing acquaintances in the West. Nods and winks were interchanged between them, and could not but be noticed by Tom and Bob, though Sparkle was so intent upon the amusements of the moment, and the company of the lovely Caroline, as to appear immoveable.

Mr. Merrywell at length stated that he must be compelled to quit the party. Young Mortimer also apologized; for as he and his friend were engaged for an early excursion in the morning, he should take a bed at his habitation, in order to be fully prepared. This was the first step to breaking up the party.

Merrywell called Sparkle on one side, saying he had something of importance to communicate. It was twelve o'clock, and the gentlemen, after taking a formal leave of the ladies and the Colonel, and a promise on the part of Sparkle to meet them again the next morning at twelve, to escort them to the Exhibition, left the house.

"I am really happy," said Merrywell to Sparkle as they passed the door, "to have had the honour of this introduction, and shall have much pleasure in becoming better acquainted with Mr. Sparkle, who, though personally unknown to me, his name and fame are familiar.

Mr. Mortimer and myself are going to take a review of the neighbourhood of St. James's, probably to shake an elbow."

"Excellent," said Tom; "here is a fine opportunity for Mr. Tallyho to take a like survey, and, if agreeable, we will join the party. Though I am by no means a friend to gaming, I conceive it necessary that every person should see the haunts of its votaries, and the arts they make use of, in order to avoid them."

"You are right, and therefore let us have a peep at them." With this they 'walk'd on, listening with attention to the following lines, which were recited by Sparkle:

> *"Behold yon group, fast fix'd at break of day,*
> *Whose haggard looks a sleepless night betray,*
> *With stern attention, silent and profound,*
> *The mystic table closely they surround;*
> *Their eager eyes with eager motions join,*
> *As men who meditate some vast design:*
> *Sure, these are Statesmen, met for public good,*
> *For some among them boast of noble blood:*
> *Or are they traitors, holding close debate*
> *On desp'rate means to overthrow the State?*
> *For there are men among them whose domains*
> *And goods and chattels lie within their brains.*
> *No, these are students of the blackest art*
> *That can corrupt the morals or the heart;*
> *Yet are they oft in fashion's ranks preferred,*
> *And men of honour, if you take their word.*
> *But they can plunder, pillage, and devour,*
> *More than poor robbers, at the midnight hour;*
> *Lay deeper schemes to manage lucky hits,*
> *Than artful swindlers, living by their wits.*
> *Like cunning fowlers, spread th' alluring snare,*
> *And glory when they pluck a pigeon bare.*
> *These are our gamesters, who have basely made*
> *The cards and dice their study and their trade."*{1}

1 *Gaming is generally understood to have been invented by the Lydians, when they were under the pressure of a great famine. To divert themselves from dwelling on their sufferings, they contrived the balls, tables, &c. and, in*

order to bear their calamity the better, were accustomed to play for the whole day together, without interruption, that they might not be rack'd with the thought of food, which they could not obtain. It is not a little extraordinary that this invention, which was originally intended as a remedy for hunger, is now a very common cause of that very evil.

"True," said Merrywell, as Sparkle concluded, though he did not like the satire upon his own favourite pursuit; "those delineations are correct, and the versification good, as far as it applies to the worst species of the gaminghouse."

"O," said Tom, "then pray, Sir, which is the worst?"

"Nonsense," said Sparkle, "there is neither worse nor best; these Hells are all alike. *Sharks, Greeks, Gamblers, Knowing Ones, Black-legs, and Levanters*, are to be met with at them all, and *they meet to bite one another's heads off.*"

"An admirable description, truly, of the company you are about to introduce us to, Gentlemen," said Tallyho.

"I don't understand Greeks, Hells, and Black-legs," said Mortimer, "and should like an explanation."

"With all my heart," replied Sparkle—"*Hell* is the general title now given to any well-known gaming-house, and really appears to be well chosen; for all the miseries that can fall to the lot of human nature, are to be found in those receptacles of idleness, duplicity, and villany. Gaming is an estate to which all the world has a pretence, though few espouse it who are willing to secure either their estates or reputations: and these Hells may fairly be considered as so many half-way houses to the Fleet or King's Bench Prisons, or some more desperate end. The love of play is the most incurable of insanities: robbery, suicide, and the extensive ruin of whole families, have been known to proceed from this unfortunate and fatal propensity.

"*Greeks, Gamblers, Knowing Ones, and Black-legs*, are synonimous terms, applied to the frequenters of the modern Hells, or Gaming-houses, and may be distinguished from the rest of society by the following peculiarities in pursuits and manners.

"The *Greeks* of the present day, though they may not lay claim to, or boast of all the attributes of the *Greeks* of antiquity, must certainly be allowed to possess that quality for which the latter were ever so celebrated, namely, *cunning and wariness*: for although no modern Greek can be said to have any resemblance to Achilles, Ajax, Patroclus, or Nestor, in point of courage, strength, fidelity, or wisdom, he may nevertheless boast of being a close copier of the equally renowned chief of Ithaca. You will find him in most societies, habited like a gentleman; his clothes are of the newest fashion, and his manners of the highest polish, with every appearance of candour and honour; while he subsists by unfair play at dice, cards, and billiards, deceiving and defrauding all those with whom he may engage; disregarding the professions of friendship and intimacy, which are continually falling from his lips.

"To become a good *Greek* (which, by the way, is a contradiction) it will be found necessary to follow these instructions:

"In the first place, lie should be able to command his temper; he should speak but little, and when he does mingle in conversation, he should most decidedly deprecate play, as a source of the greatest evil that can prey upon society, and elucidate its tendencies by striking examples which are well known to himself, and which are so forcibly impressed upon his recollection, that he is determined never to play deep again, but has no objection to a sociable and friendly game now and then, just to pass the time away a little agreeably. By this means he may readily mark down his man, and the game once in view, he should not appear too eager in the pursuit of it, but take good care, as the proverb says, to give a sprat, in order to catch a herring. This should be done by allowing some temporary success, before he make a final hit.

"There is perhaps no art which requires so much of continual practice as that of *Greekery*. It is therefore necessary, that the professor should frequently exercise himself in private with cards and dice, in order that his digits may be trained to a proper degree of agility, upon which the success of his art principally depends. He should also be accustomed to work with some younger man than himself, who, having once been a pigeon, is become a naute, that is enlightened and will not peach—consequently, he serves as an excellent decoy to others.

"To ascertain the property of the pigeon he intends to pluck, is another essential requisite; and when this important information is obtained, (which should be before he commences operations) he should affect the utmost liberality as to time, &c. and make a show of extending every honourable facility to his opponent, even by offers of pecuniary assistance; by which means, (if he should be fortunate enough to have it accepted) he may probably, by good management, obtain a legal security from him, and thus be enabled to fasten on his prey whenever he pleases.

"The title of a military man, such as Captain, is very useful to the Greek, as it introduces him well to society, and if he has once held a commission in the army, so much the better. If not, it can be assumed, so that if any unpleasant regimental peculation should be introduced, he may place his hand on the left side of his breast, declare he is astonished and alarmed at the calumnious spirit of the times, shake his head, and interlard his conversation with commonplace ejaculations; such as the following—Indeed—No—Why I know Harry very well—he's a bit of a blood—can it be possible—I should not have thought it—bless my heart—exactly so—good God—a devilish good joke tho'—that's very true, says I—so says he, &c. &c.

"A Greek should be a man of some personal courage, never shrink from a row, nor be afraid to' fight a duel. He should be able to bully, bluster, swagger and swear, as occasion may require; nay, in desperate cases, such us peaching, &c. he should not object even to assassination. He should invite large parties to dine with him frequently, and have a particular sort of wine for particular companies. He should likewise be able to swallow a tolerable quantity of the juice of the grape himself, as well as know how to appear as if he were drinking, when he is merely passing the bottle, and so manage it passing, as to seem drunk at proper times. When good opportunities present themselves for the exercise of his art, and when a hit is really to be made, he should positively refuse to suffer play of any kind in his house, alleging that he has seen enough of it, and cut the concern. This serves to increase the desire for it in others. On any decisive occasion, when a train is known to be well laid, he should appear to be drunk before any one of the party; in which case he should take care beforehand to instruct his decoy to pluck the pigeon, while he, as a supposed observer, is betting with some one in the company, (of course an accomplice) and is also a loser.

"Greeks, who know each other, are enabled to convey information by means of private signals, without uttering a word, and consequently without detection. At whist, or other games on the cards, fingers are admirable conveyancers of intelligence, and by dexterous performers are so managed, as to defy the closest scrutiny, so as to have the natural appearance of pliancy, while, among the *knowing ones*, their movements are actually deciding the fate of a rubber."

"Egad!" said Mortimer, "you seem to understand the business so well, I wonder you don't open shop."

"My knowledge," continued Sparkle, "is but theoretical. I cannot boast of much practical information, for it is long since I shook the lucky castor."

"O, then, you are discontented because you have no luck."

"Not so," said Sparkle, "for I never play very deep, so that, win or lose, I can never suffer much; but I am willing to give information to others, and with that view I have detailed the nature of the houses and the general character of their frequenters, according to my own conception of them. The *Levanter* is a *Black-leg*, who lives by the *broads*{1} and the *turf*,{2} and is accustomed to work as it were by *telegraph*{3} with his pal; and if you take the broads in hand in their company, you are sure to be work'd, either by glazing, that is, putting you in the front of a looking-glass, by which means your hand is discovered by your antagonist, or by private signals from the pal. On the turf he will pick up some nobleman or gentleman, who he knows is not *up to the rig*—bet him fifty or a hundred on a horse—pull out his pocket-book—set down the name, and promise to be at the stand when the race is over; but takes care to be seen no more, unless he is the winner, which he easily ascertains by the direction his pal takes immediately on the arrival of the horses. But hold, we must dismiss the present subject of contemplation, for here we are at the very scene of action, and now for ocular demonstration."

No. 40, now 32, Pall Mall, was the place of destination, a house well known, said, in Koubel's time, to be more *à la Française,* and of course more of a gambling-house, than any other of the same description in London. The former were good judges of their business, and did things in prime order; but, if report say true, the new Establishment

1 Broads—*A cant term for cards.*

2 Turf—*A cant term for horse-racing.*

3 Telegraph—*To work the telegraph, is to impart information by secret signs and motions, previously concerted between the parties.*

has completely eclipsed their precursors: it is now conducted wholly by aliens—by Frenchmen!!! who are said to have realized 80,000L. within a very short space of time; and that a certain nobleman, whose name is not Dormouse, has serious reason to remember that he has been a visitor.

These concerns are considered of so much importance, and are found to be so very productive, that regular co-partnerships are entered into, the business is conducted almost with the precision of a mercantile establishment; all kinds of characters embark in these speculations, and rapid fortunes are to be made by them; this alone ought to deter young men from play, since it sufficiently indicates how much the chances are in favour of the tables. But many high and noble names resort to them.

"There's N—g—nts proud Lord, who, to angle for pelf,
Will soon find the secret of diddling himself;
There's Herbert, who lately, as knowing one's tell,
Won a tight seven hundred at a House in Pall Mall.

Captain D—v—s, who now is a chick of the game,
For altho' in high feather, the odds will soon tame;
And the Marquis of Bl—ndf—rd, who touch'd 'em up rare

For a thousand in Bennet Street (all on the square);
There's Li—d and C—m—ck, who'd a marine to be,
For none drills a guinea more ably than he;
There's a certain rum Baronet, every one knows,
Who on Saturday nights to the Two Sevens{1} goes,

With J— — and Cl— —, Billy W— — and two more,
So drunk, that they keep merry hell in a roar.
Long D—ll—n, their C—rt—r, a son of a gun;
Bill B— —, the Doctor, that figure of fun;

Bankers, Dealers and Demireps, Cuckolds in droves,
A T—l—r, a T—nf—ld, a Cr—kf—ld, and Cl—ves;
A H—rtf—rd, a Y—rm—th, of frail ones ten score;
X—ft—e, S—br—gt and E—ll—s, and still many more."

"Come along," said Merrywell, "let us see what they are made of; are either of you known? for Cerberus, who keeps the door, is d— —d particular, in consequence of some rows they have recently had, and the devil is careful to pick his customers."

"To pluck them, you mean," said Tom; "but perhaps you are in possession of the pass-word—if so, lead on."

1 *The Two Sevens*—A nick-name for the well-known house, No. 77, Jermyn Street.

Tallyho had already heard so much about Hells, Gambling-houses, and Subscription-houses, that he was all anxiety for an interior view, and the same feeling animated Mortimer. As they were about to enter, they were not a little surprised to find that houses which are spoken of so publicly, have in general the appearance of private dwellings, with the exception that the hall-door is left ajar during the hours usually devoted to play, like those of trap-cages, to catch the passing pigeons, and to obviate the delay which might be occasioned by the necessity of knocking—a delay which might expose the customers to the glances of an unsuspecting creditor—a confiding father, or a starving wife; and, as Merrywell observed, "It was to be understood that the entrance was well guarded, and that no gentleman could be permitted to risk or lose his money, without an introduction." A very necessary precaution to obviate the danger of being surprised by the officers of the law; but that rule is too easily to be broken, for any gentleman whom the door-keeper has sufficient reason to think is not an Officer of Justice, finds the avenues to these labyrinths too ready for his admission.

On passing the outer-door, they found themselves impeded by a second, and a third, and each door constructed with a small spy-hole, exhibiting the ball of a ruffian's eye, intently gazing on and examining their figures. It is necessary to observe, that if the visitor is known to be a fair pigeon, or an old crow, he is at once admitted by these gentlemen, and politely bowed up stairs; and as Merrywell appeared to be well known, no obstruction was offered, and they proceeded through the last, which was an iron door, and were shewn directly into the room, which presented a scene of dazzling astonishment.

On entering, they discovered the votaries of gaming around an oblong table, covered with green cloth, and the priests of the ceremony in the centre, one to deal cards and decide events, and another to assist him in collecting the plunder which should follow such decisions. Being engaged in the play, but little notice was taken of the arrival of the party, except by two or three eagle-eyed gentlemen, who, perceiving there were some *New-comes*{1}

> 1. Newcomes—The name given to any new faces discovered among the usual visitants.

and always keeping business in view, made up to Merrywell, began to be very talkative—was happy to see him—hoped he had been well—and congratulated him on the introduction of his friends—took snuff, and handed the box round with all the appearance of unaffected friendship.

Real Life in London - Volume I

EASTER HUNT.

"These," said Tom Dashall to his Cousin, drawing him on one side, "are the Proprietors{1} of this concern;

> 1 In order that the class of men by whom houses of this description are generally kept, and to shew the certainty they have of accumulating riches, as well as to guard the young and inexperienced against being decoyed, it may not be amiss to animadvert upon a few of the most prominent and well known.
>
> No. 7, Pall Mall, is kept by B——l, who has been a public and noted gambler for these forty years, and is generally termed the Father of the Houses. He was at one time a poor man, but now, by his honest earnings, is in possession of some tens of thousands. It is said that he was originally a stable-boy, and, in process of time, arose to be a jobber in horse-flesh, but has at length feathered his nest with pigeons down.
>
> No. 77, St. James's Street, nick-named the Two Sevens, kept by Messrs. T. C. C. T. is a well-known House, where things are conducted with great civility and attention, and the best possible treatment may generally be relied upon, though they are rather sparing of refreshments, and apt to grumble if a customer has a run of good luck. A Prussian Officer, however, not long ago, kick'd up a devil of a row about losing a very large sum of money; but it is scarcely necessary to add it was all in vain, for there was no redress.
>
> The produce of this Bank, (which Paddy B—— calls the Devil's Exchequer, whence you can draw neither principal nor interest,) furnishes elegant houses and equipages, both in town and country, and, it is possible, may one day or other send a Member to Parliament, or a General to the field.
>
> No. 10, King Street, St. James's, is conducted by old and young D——s L——r; the father is too old in iniquity to remember his progress from poverty to affluence.

*No. 5, King-street, is kept by Mr. A— —l; the former
residing at No. 3, Leicester-place, the latter No. 3, — —
Street; and both live in prime style. The former, in his
youth, was an errand boy, and he became so willing in doing
little jobs, that his employers have paid him most
handsomely. The latter gentleman, who may be seen frequently
driving a dennet, and looking both sides of the road at
once, is a chip of the old block: but as it is not our
intention to visit the sins of the sou upon the father, we
shall not enter into a minute examination of him.*

*No. 6, in Bury-street, is only about a year's standing.
This table was set up by a broken adventurer, Capt. B— —,
with Mr. — —, a jeweller, and a man whose agents keep a
house of ill fame, no way inferior in attribute to his
house in Bury-street. They commenced with narrow funds,
and now, thank the gulls, are independent.*

*The next door, No. 7, is held by M— —g, a map-seller,
living at Charing Cross; Carl—s, formerly an under-
strapper at Ben—t's, living at King's Road, Chelsea; H— —ll,
a tallow-chandler, living at No. 8, Bury-street; and
his brother, a brick-layer, residing somewhere off Grosvenor
Place. These fellows have carried on their depredations for
some time, but now have closed for awhile, being one of the
houses against whom a Jew, named Portugal John, and another
named the Young Black Diamond, have commenced proceedings,
for sums had and received, and by indictment.*

*No. 28, in the same street, is the property of one O— —
d, formerly a menial servant, and not long ago a porter to
B— —l.*

*These examples shew by incontestible inference, that the
keepers of those tables have an advantage, which renders
their success certain, while it fleeces the men who attend
them. We always have seen these Proprietors in the same
unchangeable affluence, driving their equipages, keeping*

their country houses, &c. &c. while those who play invariably sink into poverty. It has been often—very often remarked, that young men who commence this career of folly and vice, by degrees lose that freshness and fashionable appearance which they at first possessed, and at last are seen wandering about St. James's Park counting the trees, and dining on a gravel hash, for want of more genial fare, in a threadbare coat, half-polished boots, a greasy hat, and a dirty cravat; while the plunderers of their happiness and property are driving by them in luxury, enjoying their pleasure by contrast with their victim, and sneering at his miseries.

Of all the vices which deform this Metropolis (and there are not a few) the most ruinous is that of Rouge et Noir gambling, for that is practised in the day time, and it is a matter of astonishment to think that it has remained undisturbed by the law, and hitherto unnoticed by the Press. At this moment no less than twelve of these Hells are open to the public in the noon-day; and no less than five or six profane the Sabbath by their sinful practices. Although London has been, time out of mind, infested with the imps of play, yet it was not until within these last ten or fifteen years that they dared open their dens to the honest light of day. About that period, or a very short time before, Rouge et Noir was imported, amongst other fashionable things, from France; and to this game we are indebted for the practice of gambling in the day-light.

It is impossible to put down the vice of Gaming wholly, and not all the various enactments of the legislature against it have succeeded; but that the ruinous and infamous practice of indulging that vice in the midst of crowded day should be suffered, for upwards of sixteen years, in the centre of British society, when it can easily be suppressed, calls forth our wonder, and gives a stronger proof to us that our Societies for the Suppression of Vice, &c. &c. are shadows with a name. When the Hazard tables open, it is at an hour when the respectable and controlled youths of London are within the walls of their homes; few are abroad except the modern man of ton, the rake, the sot, the robber, and the vagabond; and the dangers of gaming on these orders of society is little indeed, when compared with the baneful effects of that vice upon the mercantile youth of London. It is to this class, and to the youth of the middling orders of society, that gaming is destructive, and it is upon these that the Rouge et Noir tables cast the most fatal influence. Young men of this order cannot in general be absent from their families after midnight, the hour when the nocturnal Hells formerly yawned upon their victims; but now the introduction of Rouge et Noir has rendered the abominable track of play a morning and evening's lounge, set forth in all the false glare which the artful proprietors can invent to deceive the thoughtless; and thus it affords opportunities and temptations to such youth almost irresistible.

When the glittering of London pleasures first meets the eye of a young man placed upon the road of a mercantile life, or when he enters any of the multifarious departments in the machine of society which always lead the industrious and prudent to honourable emolument, he too frequently misconceives the fashionable gamester's character, and confounds his crimes with elegant accomplishments. The road to pleasure is broad, and the gates of these Hells are open to him at hours when he can be absent, and can indulge his whim without suspicion—for at first he looks upon his new enjoyment but a mere whim, which he can abandon at any moment. But how different is the proof! He goes on—his new made wings carry him through a region of delight, and he believes himself to possess the powers of the eagle—still lighter he ascends, and the solid earth on which he formerly trod in safety, recedes immeasurably from his giddy eye—at length his wings prove wax, they melt before the sun, and the victim of his own folly tumbles into the abyss of destruction.

It is no uncommon thing, nay, we will positively declare it to be a very frequent practice of these misled young men, when they have been initiated, and have the temporary command of money belonging to their employers, to go to the Rouge et Noir tables, armed (as they think) with impenetrable armour—a large sum; and, in the hope of profiting to a certain amount, risk that property, the loss of which would be the loss of every thing dear to them in society. They believe, from the greatness of the amount they possess, that they can command a small gain, and not for a moment doubt they will be able to replace or return the money entrusted to their care; but little do they know the fickleness of luck, and less do they suspect the odds and imposing roguery arrayed against them. Their first loss is trifling, but they have to win that back iu addition to their expected profits; for this purpose they stake a larger sum, which, if they lose, increases their task, and so on, until the half-frantic victims see no hope but desperation, and their remaining stock is placed upon the chance of a single card. The event closes, and the man who yesterday enjoyed the good opinion of the world, and the esteem and confidence of his friends, to-day becomes the veriest outcast of society! These are common cases, one of which, for example, we will describe as the facts occurred:—In the year 1816, a Clerk, possessing the highest reputation, became a frequenter of a Rouge et Noir table. From the nature of his employment, he had daily the command of large sums, which, for a short time, he risked at play successfully. One day, however, he brought with him his employer's money, to the amount of 1700L. the whole of which, in two days, he lost. We may judge of the unhappy young man's feelings by his subsequent conduct. He wrote a confession of the affair to the man he wronged, retired to a tavern, and blew his brains out!

These gaming-tables open at half-past twelve o'clock, continue their orgies until five, and recommence at seven in the evening. How many young men are passing their doors at

*these hours with the property of others in their pockets! —
and what a temptation to risk it! It would seem as if these
places were set up as shops designed chiefly for the
accommodation of mid-day dealers in ill-fortune, as if
levelled directly at those men who cannot or will not spend
their nights in gambling; and how the proprietors contrive
to escape detection and punishment is surprising,
considering that the law affords ample means to put them
down.*

they know their customers, and place themselves here to watch the progress of their gains. Their attentions are always directed to the new-comers. Remorseless, avaricious, and happy—unmarked with the lines of care, which contract and deform the faces of their victims, "They smile and smile, and murder while they smile." They will explain the fairness of the game, and tell you of the great losses they have sustained; but as this is no place for explanation, we must look on and say nothing."

By this time, Merrywell and Mortimer were mingled in the throng at the table. Sparkle was engaged in conversation with an old acquaintance, a profusion of money was flying about, and a large heap or bank was placed in the centre. All was anxiety, and, for a few moments, no sound was heard, but the awful numbers of the eventful dealer; every countenance was hushed in expectation, and every eye was fixed upon the coming card, which should decide the fate of hundreds. It was an awful moment to every one engaged in the play; but the pause was succeeded with a sort of harlequinade movement, to a scene of confusion and uproar scarcely to be conceived.

The appearance at the door of half a dozen persons armed with pistols, rushing past the guardians, and bearing away all before them, had such an instantaneous effect upon the company, that they all arose, as it were, to receive them, and the leader of the party threw himself suddenly upon the pile of Bank-notes in the centre of the table, with intent to seize the whole bank.

Confusion and dismay were now visibly depicted on every countenance, for some, actuated by desperation at the prospect of ruin, and others by the urgings of avarice, determined to have a scramble for the notes, which they commenced most furiously, each one securing as much as he could to himself. There was tumbling and tossing, and pulling and shoving, mouths stuffed with hundreds, hundreds of mouths that were supperless, and likely to continue so, unless they could now make sure of something. Bank paper was literally going for nothing. However, the pistols being the most powerful, the armed forces succeeded in seizing the greatest share of the stock, and a negative sort of silence was at length restored. The party was materially decreased; for, seeing they were betrayed, every one, after an endeavour to secure a share of the spoil, deemed it necessary to make good his retreat; and among the rest, our party, who had not interfered with the play, or assisted in the entertainment, soon found themselves in the street.

"Egad," said Sparkle, "I think we are in luck to escape so easily; we might have been compelled to make our appearance at Bow Street to-morrow, an occurrence I would studiously avoid."

"Well done, old steady," said Tom; "it is not long, you know, since you was there, after a night's lodging in the neighbourhood."

"That was under very different circumstances," continued Sparkle; "in defence of a woman I would risk my life at any time, but I would by no means incur the imputation of being a gambler—it is a character I abhor. I have before said I would never venture into those dens again, to herd with swindlers of all descriptions."

"They all seem gay fellows, too," said Bob.

"Yes," replied Sparkle; "but the character and conduct of a young man has ere now been altered in one night: the evil effects produced by initiation to those Hells are incalculable."

"Moralizing at midnight," said Tom; "an excellent title for a volume *sparkling* contemplations."

"To be written by the Hon. Tom Dashall, or the Merry Devil of Piccadilly," was the reply.

"Huzza!" said Merrywell, "if this is the case, our time will not be lost in this excursion. Did you hear that Lord —— has been compelled to put down his establishment in consequence of his losses at play? pray don't forget to mention that in the work."

"Tis no new thing," continued Sparkle, "for Lords of the present day, since I believe there are few of the nobility who are not either Greeks or Pigeons; indeed, the list of visitors to these places contains names of many persons who should set better examples to the humbler classes of the community; for the unfortunate results of this too fatal propensity to parents and society have been severely felt. Among many instances on record, a very interesting one is related of a young Subaltern in a regiment of cavalry, who, by successive losses, was reduced to such a state of distress, as to form the desperate resolution of trying the road. In a moment of agony, he accidentally met with an opportunity which seemed to favour his design, having learned that a certain Baronet, recently returned from India with abundance of wealth, had laid it out on landed estates in England, and that he would on a certain day cross the country with a large sum of money, after collecting his rents.

"He laid his plan for a meeting on a retired spot, and succeeded in stopping the carriage—' Your money or your life,' said he, presenting his pistol with a trembling hand. The Baronet, perceiving there was a sort of gentlemanly air about him which indicated something more than might be calculated on in the character of a highwayman, presented him with his purse, a watch, and a valuable diamond ring, remarking, he could not help conceiving that he was unaccustomed to the trade, and that it was most desirable he should abandon it for ever. The young Officer, though considerably confused and embarrassed by this observation, was not to be disappointed of his booty, returned this property, and demanded the larger sum, which for safety had been concealed in the bottom of the carriage. The manner however in which this was done, only served to confirm the suspicions of the Baronet, which he could not help expressing, as he acknowledged the accuracy of the Highwayman's information, and produced the property, observing, he was sure that circumstances of no common kind could have impelled him to this flagrant breach of the laws. He asked as a favour, that he would grant him an interview at some future period, pledging his honour that he should have no occasion to repent such a singular mark of confidence.

"The Officer replied that he had, and he felt he could with safety trust both his life and his honour in the veracity of Sir ——, and appointed a meeting at the London Coffee House, Ludgate Hill, only stipulating, that at such meeting both parties were to be unattended. As the day of meeting approached, the Baronet thought seriously of the solicited rencontre, and after enjoining perfect secresy on the part of his friend, Col. ——, entreated him to be his companion. The Colonel laughed at the idea, that any man who had robbed another should so indiscreetly place his life in his hands, had no conception of his keeping his appointment, and solemnly assured the Baronet that he would in no case divulge who or what he was, that he might become acquainted with.

"The Colonel ridiculed his friend's credulity as they entered the house, and were shewn to a private room. The appointed hour was eight in the evening, and, as the clock of St. Paul's struck, a Gentleman inquiring for Sir —— was shewn into the room—wine was ordered, and for an hour a general conversation on the popular topics of the day ensued, when the Gentleman, evidently under deeply impressed feelings of embarrassment and disappointment, in which the Colonel seemed to partake, arose, and politely took his leave.

"' Well,' said the Baronet, 'what think you of my Highwayman now 1—am I not right?—is he not a gentleman?'

"' And this is the robber, is it, Sir?' said the Colonel—'Be assured he shall swing for it—why, Sir, I know him well, he is a —— in my own regiment.'

"'Hold,' said the Baronet, 'don't be rash, remember the solemn promise you have given, and do not deceive me—I hold you bound to me, and will not permit you to break your engagement—I have better objects in view than the death of a fellow-creature.'

"He then requested to be informed of the general tenor of the young man's conduct, which he found to be excellent, and that he was an indefatigable officer—'Indeed,' said the Colonel, 'it would give me the greatest pain to lose him—an incomparably affectionate husband and father. He has but one vice, to which may be attributed his destruction, viz. his inordinate passion for gaming; but I cannot feel justified in screening so flagrant an offender—the law must take its course.'

"'Moderate your indignation,' said the worthy Baronet, assuming a more serious tone, 'and remember you must be personalty answerable to me for any disclosure you may think proper to make; and that inasmuch as you injure him, you must injure me. You have already given him so high a character in every respect but one, that I must interest you further in his behalf, and beg you to assist me in my endeavours to reclaim, instead of punishing him.'

"The Colonel was surprised; but the Baronet was inflexible. In vain he urged that the magnitude of the crime utterly precluded such a proceeding.

"' It must be done,' said the Baronet, 'it shall be done. Leave all the consequences to me; he has now left us in extreme, though suppressed agitation—There is no time to lose—fly to save him.'

"The Colonel expressed his readiness to try the experiment.

"' Then,' said the Baronet, 'follow him immediately, assure him of my forgiveness, and that if he will pledge his word to forsake this dangerous vice, what he has already obtained he may hold as a gift, and I will add whatever may be necessary to extricate him from any temporary embarrassment.'

"It was an important embassy—life or death was to be decided by it. The Colonel took his departure, certain of finding him at home taking leave of his family, and, reaching his habitation a short time after his arrival, witnessed a scene of misery which, although he had partly anticipated, he could not have conceived. He found him, surrounded by his wife and children, in an agony of desperation and despair.

"When he entered the apartment, the poor culprit, convinced by the presence of his Colonel that all was lost, fell on his knees, and supplicated if possible that his fame, not his life, might be spared for the sake of his afflicted but innocent and injured family. Language has no power to describe the surprise and consternation with which, after a severe lecture, he received the joyful intelligence of which his Colonel was the bearer. He returned with his Commanding Officer to — — Square, where he was received by the Baronet as a repentant friend; and has lived to repair his error, and become deservedly distinguished as an ornament to society, civil and religious as well as military."

"That must be truly gratifying to the worthy Baronet,{1}' said Tom.

"No doubt of it," continued Sparkle, "it must be a source of continued pleasure to find his labours have had so beneficial a result, having in all probability saved a whole family from destruction. Surely it may be said, that

> *"Among the idiot pranks of Wealth's abuse,*
> *None seem so monstrous, none have less excuse,*
> *Than those which throw an heritage away*
> *Upon the lawless chance of desperate play;*
> *Nor is there among knaves a wretch more base*
> *Than he who steals it with a smiling face,*
> *Who makes diversion to destruction tend,*
> *And thrives upon the ruin of a friend."*

—"Yet the Greek, like the swindler{l} and the horse jockey,

> *1 Swindler—Is a term originally derived from the German, Schwindel, which signifies merely to cheat. It was first introduced as a cant term, and used to signify obtaining of goods, credit, or money, under false pretences. It has since had a legislative adoption, being parliamentary recognised by an Act for the prevention of it. The artifices, schemes, and crimes, resorted to by these gentry, are so numerous, that it would be impossible to describe them all. One mode of practice, however, is not uncommon in London.*

Three or four swell Jews contrive to hire a large house with some spare rooms, in the City, that are turned into warehouses, in which are a number of casks, boxes, &e. filled with sand; and also a quantity of large sugar-loaves in appearance, which are only clay done up in blue paper, but corded and made up with great nicety.

An elegant Counting-house is likewise furnished with books and other apparatus, to deceive the eye and give the appearance of extensive business, great regularity, and large property. The Clerks in attendance are a set of Jews, who are privy to the scheme, and equally ready at fraud as those who profess to be the Principals.

A Dining-room elegantly furnished upon the mace,* receives you

> ** The Mace—Is a person who carries all the appearance of a great and rich man, with servants, carriages, &c. for the purpose of defrauding tradesmen and others, by all manner of plans most calculated to entrap the parties they intend to dupe.*

whenever it is necessary to admit of your visits; a Black Servant opens the street-door, and the foot of the staircase presents surtouts, boots, livery-cloths, a large blue coat with a yellow cape, and habiliments in which the opulent! array their servants. With these and similar merchant-like appearances Trade is commenced, and persons dispatched to provincial manufacturing towns, to buy various articles; for the amount of the first purchases, bills are drawn upon the Firm, and even before the goods are pack'd up, and sent according to order, the acceptances are paid, and, by this means, credit is partly established, which, once accomplished, they are in want of large assortments for exportation upon credit, at one, two, and three months. The goods are accordingly chosen and forwarded to their associates in London, where they are immediately disposed of at 20 or 30 per cent, cheaper than the prime cost, and the money realised. The first bills become due, are noted, and protested. The second are presented, but the House has stopped payment, and the Owners are bankrupts. By the time the third month's bills become due, the docket is struck, the Assignees chosen, and there is not sixpence in the pound left for the Creditors. Petitions are ineffectually presented to the Chancellor, for a number of fictitious Creditors, of the same profession and persuasion, over-swear the just ones, and by exceeding them in number and value, the House obtains its certificate, and has again the power of committing similar depredations.

Perhaps the most daring and systematic proceeding of this kind was that lately detected in the conspiracy of Mosely Wolfe and his confederates, for which he is now suffering the sentence of the law.

prides himself on his success, boasts of his being *down as a nail*, and—"

"*Down as a nail!*" said Bob, "I don't remember hearing that expression before."

"*Down as a hammer, or Down as a nail*" continued Sparkle, "are cant or slang terms made use of among gamblers, and are synonimous with being up; and it must be confessed that there are many ups and downs amongst them. These flash words are well understood by many a young Greek, who perhaps knows nothing of the Greek Testament, although the use of them has proved in some cases beyond the comprehension of a Judge. Hence the necessity of knowing Life; for if a man gets familiarized with low life, he will necessarily be up, and consequently stand a great chance of being a rising genius. How proper it must be to know how to get a rise upon a fellow, or, in other words, to get him in a line!

"A learned Judge once, examining a queer covy, a flash customer, or a rum fellow, asked him his reason for suspecting the prisoner at the bar of stealing a watch, (which among the lads is scientifically termed nimming a toiler, or nabbing a clicker,) replied as follows:—

'Why, your honour, only because you see as how I was up to him.'—'How do you mean, what is being up to him?'—'Why, bless your heart, I was down upon him, and had him bang.' But still perceiving the learned Gentleman's want of nous, he endeavoured to explain by saying, That he was *up to his gossip*,—that he stagged him, for he was not to be done—that he knew the trick, and was up the moment the chap came into the Cock and Hen Club, where he was tucking in his grub and bub.—Had the learned Judge been up himself, much time and trouble might have been saved; and indeed the importance of being down as a nail, to a man of fashion, is almost incalculable; for this reason it is, that men of high spirit think it no derogation from their dignity or rank, to be well acquainted with all the slang of the coachman and stable-boy, all the glossary of the Fancy, and all the mysterious language of the scamps, the pads, the divers, and all upon the lay, which, by an attentive and apt scholar, may easily be procured at a Gaming-house.

"Of Hells in general, it may fairly be asserted, that they are infernally productive; no other line of business can be compared to these money mills, since they are all thriving concerns, the proprietors of which keep their country houses, extensive establishments, dashing equipages; and

> *"While they have money they ride it in chaises.*
> *And look very big upon those that have none."*

"It certainly is a pity that men do not keep constantly in their recollection, that no calculation of chances can avail them, and that between the après, the limitation of stakes, and other manouvres, the table must eventually be an immense winner.

"For Greeks stick at nothing to gain their own ends, And they sacrifice all their acquaintance and friends;

> *And thus luckless P'— —n, to gain what he'd lost,*

Put his faith in a Greek, which he knows to his cost; Join'd a bank, as he thought, when the sly Greeking elf Of a friend soon contriv'd for to break it himself. You credulous pigeons! I would have you beware, Of falling yourselves in a similar snare."

"We ought to consider ourselves greatly obliged," said Merry well, "for the accurate description of characters you have given. But have you heard the report that is now in circulation, that a certain Marquis of high military celebrity, and whose property is, or was, very considerable, has lost almost his last shilling?"

"I," said Sparkle, "am seldom surprised at such rumours, particularly of persons who are known to be players, for they are rich and poor in rapid succession; but if there be any truth in the report, there is a fine example of perseverance before him—for Lord — —, after a long run of ill-luck, being refused the loan of an additional rouleau,{1} on account of his score being rather long, left the company in dudgeon, and determining on revenge, actually opened another Hell in opposition to the one he had left, and by that means recovered all his money."

"That was well done," rejoined Tallyho.

"It was rather too much of a trading concern for a Lord," said Tom.

"Not for a gambling Lord," replied Merry well; "for there is in fact nothing beneath a Greek, in the way of play: besides, it was a trying situation, and required some desperate attempt—they care not who they associate with, so they do but bring grist to the mill."

"The confusion of persons and characters at a Gaming-house," said Sparkle, "are almost incredible, all ranks and descriptions are mingled together.

"What confusion of titles and persons we see Amongst Gamesters, who spring out of every degree, From the prince to the pauper; all panting for play, Their fortune, their time, and their life pass away; Just as mingled are Pigeons, for 'tis no rebuke For a Greek to pluck all, from a Groom to a Duke."

"It is too true," said Dashall, "and equally as certain, that there are continually new comers ready and willing to be duped, or at least ready to risk their property, notwithstanding the warnings they have from their more experienced friends."

"And is there no possibility of obtaining fair play?" inquired Bob, "or redress for being pigeon'd, as you term it?"

> 1 A Rouleau—Is a packet containing one hundred guineas; but as guineas are not quite so fashionable in the present day as they formerly were, some of these Houses, for the accommodation of their customers, circulate guinea-notes upon their bankers.

"None," said Sparkle; "for if men will play at bowls, they must expect rubbers; and the system of confederacy is carried on every where, though perhaps with most success in those professed Gambling-houses, which young men of property ought carefully to avoid."

By this time they had reached the end of St. James's Street; it was therefore proposed by Sparkle that they should separate, particularly as it was growing late, or rather early in the morning; and, as they had been in some degree baffled in their attempt to take a minute survey of the proceedings in Pall Mall, they had no decided object in view. Accordingly they parted, Tom and Bob pursuing their way along Piccadilly, while Sparkle, Merrywell, and Mortimer, proceeded down Bond Street.

"I am by no means satisfied," said Tom, "with this evening's ramble, nor exactly pleased to find our friend Sparkle is getting so sentimental."

"He is, at least," said Tallyho, "very communicative and instructive—I should feel less embarrassment at a future visit to one of those places, though, I can assure you, I should carefully avoid the chance of becoming a pigeon; but to know these things is certainly useful."

"We must lay our plans better for the future," said Tom—"example is better than precept; and, as for Sparkle, I strongly suspect he is studying a part in All for Love, or the World well lost. That kind of study is too laborious for me, I can't bear to be fettered; or if it be true that it is what we must all come to, my time is not yet arrived. Though I confess Miss Mortimer has many attractions not to be overlooked by an attentive observer; at the same time I perceive this Mr. Merrywell is equally assiduous to obtain the young lady's favours."

By this time they had arrived at home, where, after partaking of refreshment, they retired to rest.

CHAPTER XV

> *"Cataracts of declamation thunder here,*
> *There, forests of no meaning spread the page,*
> *In which all comprehension wanders, lost,*
> *While fields of pleasantry amuse us there*
> *With many descants on a nation's woes.*
> *The rest appears a wilderness of strange,*
> *But gay confusion — roses for the cheeks,*
> *And lilies for the brows of faded age;*
> *Teeth for the toothless, ringlets for the bald,*
> *Heav'n, earth, and ocean, plunder'd of their sweets;*
> *Nectareous essences, Olympian dews,*
> *Sermons and City feasts, and fav'rite airs,*
> *Ethereal journeys, submarine exploits,*
> *And Katerfelto with his hair on end,*
> *At his own wonders wond'ring for his bread."*

"WELL," said Tom, "it must be confessed that a Newspaper is a most convenient and agreeable companion to the breakfast-table," laying down the *Times* as he spoke: "it is a sort of literary hotch-potch, calculated to afford amusement suited to all tastes, rank-, and degrees; it contains

> *"Tales of love and maids mistaken,*
> *Of battles fought, and captives taken."*

"Then, I presume," said Bob, "you have been gratified and interested in the perusal?"

"It is impossible to look down the columns of a newspaper," replied Tom, "without finding subjects to impart light; and of all the journals of the present day, the *Times* appears to me the best in point of information and conduct; but I spoke of newspapers generally, there is such a mixture of the *utile et dulce*, that the Merchant and the Mechanic, the Peer, the Poet, the Prelate, and the Peasant, are all deeply concerned in its contents. In truth, a newspaper is so true a mark of the caprice of Englishmen, that it may justly be styled their coat of arms. The Turkish Koran is not near so sacred to a rigid Mahometan—a parish-dinner to an Overseer—a turtle-feast to an Alderman, or an election to a Freeholder, as a Gazette or Newspaper to an Englishman: by it the motions of the world are watched, and in some degree governed—the arts and sciences protected and promoted—the virtuous supported and stimulated—the vicious reproved and corrected—and all informed."

"Consequently," said Bob, "a good Newspaper is really a valuable article."

"Doubtless," continued Tom; "and John Bull—mistake me not, I don't mean the paper which bears that title—I mean the population of England, enjoy a Newspaper, and there are some who could not relish their breakfasts without one; it is a sort of general sauce to every thing, and to the *quid nunc* is indispensable—for if one informs him of a naval armament, he will not fail to toast the Admirals all round in pint bumpers to each, wishes them success, gets drunk with excessive loyalty, and goes with his head full of seventy-fours, sixty-fours, frigates, transports, fire-ships, &c. In its diversified pages, persons of every rank, denomination, and pursuit, may be informed—the Philosopher, the Politician, the Citizen, the Handicraftsman, and the Gossip, are regaled by the novelty of its contents, the minuteness of its details, and the refreshing arrivals of transactions which occupy the attention of human beings at the greatest or nearest distances from us—

> "— —*a messenger of grief*
> *Perhaps to thousands, and of joy to some:*
> *What is it but a map of life,*
> *Its fluctuations and its vast concerns?"*

It may with propriety be compared to the planetary system: the light which it diffuses round the mental hemisphere, operates according as it is seen, felt, understood, or enjoyed: for instance, the Miser is gladdened by an account of the rise of the stocks—the Mariner is rejoiced, at the safety of his vessel after a thunder-storm—the Manufacturer, to hear of the revival of foreign markets—the Merchant, that his cargo is safely arrived—the Member, that his election is secured—the Father, that his son is walling to return home—the Poet, that his production has been favourably received by the public—the Physician, that a difficult cure is transmitting his fame to posterity—the Actor, that his talents are duly appreciated—the Agriculturist, that grain fetches a good price—the upright man, that his character is defended—the poor man, that beer, meat, bread, and vegetables, are so within his reach that he can assure himself of being able to obtain a good Sunday's dinner.

"Tho' they differ in narrie, all alike, just the same, Morning Chronicle, Times, Advertiser, British Press, Morning Post, of News—what a host We read every day, and grow wiser; The Examiner, Whig—all alive to the gig, While each one his favourite chooses; Star, Traveller, and Sun, to keep up the fun, And tell all the world what the news is."

"Well done," said Bob, "you seem to have them all at your tongue's end, and their general contents in your head; but, for my part, I am struck with surprise to know how it is they find interesting matter enough at all times to fill their columns."

"Nothing more easy," continued Dashall, "especially for a newspaper whose contents are not sanctioned by authority; in which case they are so much the more the receptacle of invention—thence—We hear—it is said—a correspondent remarks—whereas, &c—all which serve to please, surprise, and inform. We hear, can alter a man's face as the weather would a barometer—It is said, can distort another like a fit of the spasm—If, can make some cry—while Suppose, can make others laugh—but a Whereas operates like an electric shock; and though it often runs the extremity of the kingdom in unison with the rest, they altogether form a very agreeable mixture, occasionally interspersed, as opportunity offers, with long extracts from the last published novel, and an account of the prevailing fashions. But domestic occurrences form a very essential part of this folio: thus, a marriage hurts an old maid and mortifies a young one, while it consoles many a poor dejected husband, who is secretly pleased to find another fallen into his case—a death, if of a wife, makes husbands envy the widower, while, perhaps, some one of the women who censure his alleged want of decent sorrow, marry him within a month after—in fact, every person is put in motion by a Newspaper.

> *"Here various news is found, of love and strife;*
> *Of peace and war, health, sickness, death, and life;*
> *Of loss and gain, of famine and of store;*
> *Of storms at sea, and travels on the shore;*
> *Of prodigies and portents seen in air;*
> *Of fires and plagues, and stars with blazing hair;*
> *Of turns of fortune, changes in the state,*
> *The falls of favourites, projects of the great."*

"It is a bill of fare, containing all the luxuries as well as necessaries, of life. Politics, for instance, are the roast beef of the times; essays, the plum pudding; and poetry the fritters, confections, custards, and all the *et cotera* of the table, usually denominated trifles. Yet the four winds are not liable to more mutability than the vehicles of these entertainments; for instance, on Monday, it is whispered—on Tuesday, it is rumoured—on Wednesday, it is conjectured—on Thursday, it is probable—on Friday, it is positively asserted—and, on Saturday, it is premature. But notwithstanding this, some how or other, all are eventually pleased; for, as the affections of all are divided among wit, anecdote, poetry, prices of stocks, the arrival of ships, &c. a Newspaper is a repository where every one has his hobby-horse; without it, coffee-houses, &c. would be depopulated, and the country squire, the curate, the exciseman, and the barber, and many others, would lose those golden opportunities of appearing so very wise as they do.

A Newspaper may also be compared to the Seasons. Its information varies on the roll of Time, and much of it passes away as a Winter, giving many a bitter pang of the death of a relative or hopeful lover; it is as a Spring, for, in the time of war and civil commotion, its luminary, the editor, like the morning sun, leads Hope forward to milder days and happier prospects—the smiles of peace; it is the heart's Summer calendar, giving news of marriages and births for heirs and patrons; it is the Autumn of joy, giving accounts of plenty, and guarding the avaricious against the snares of self-love, and offering arguments in favour of humanity. It is more; a Newspaper is one of the most faithful lessons that can be represented to our reflections, for, while it is the interpreter of the general economy of nature, it is a most kind and able instructress to improve ourselves.

What are our lives but as the ephemeral appearance of an advertisement? Our actions but as the actions of a popular contest? Our hopes, fears, exultations, but as the cross readings of diurnal events? And although grief is felt at the perusal of accidents, offences, and crimes, which are necessarily and judiciously given, there is in every good Newspaper an impartial record, an abstract of the times, a vast fund of useful knowledge; and, finally, no person has reason, after perusing it, to rise without being thankful that so useful a medium is offered to his understanding; at least, this is my opinion."

"And now you have favoured me with this opinion," rejoined Tallyho, "will you be kind enough to inform me to what fortunate circumstance I am indebted for it?"

"The question comes very apropos," continued Tom—"for I had nearly forgotten that circumstance, so that you may perhaps be inclined to compare my head to a newspaper, constantly varying from subject to subject; but no matter, a novelty has just struck my eye, which I think will afford us much gratification: it is the announcement of an exhibition of engravings by living artists, under the immediate patronage of his Majesty, recently opened in Soho Square, through the public spirited exertions of Mr. Cooke, a celebrated engraver—And now I think of it, Mortimer and his Sister intend visiting Somerset House—egad! we will make a morning of it in reviewing the Arts—what say you?"

"With all my heart," returned Bob.

"Be it so, then," said Tom—"So-ho, my boy—perhaps we may meet the love-sick youth, poor Sparkle; he has certainly received the wound of the blind urchin—I believe we must pity him—but come, let us prepare, we will lounge away an hour in walking down Bond Street—peep at the wags and the wag-tails, and take Soho Square in our way to Somerset House. I feel myself just in the humour for a bit of gig, and 1 promise you we will make a night of it."

The preliminaries of their route being thus arranged, in half an hour they were on their road down Bond Street, marking and remarking upon circumstances and subjects as they arose.

"Who is that Lady?" said Bob, seeing Tom bow as a dashing carriage passed them.

"That is a Lady Townley, according to the generally

received term."

"A lady of title, as I suspected," said Bob.

"Yes, yes," replied Tom Dashall, "a distinguished personage, I can assure you—one of the most dashing demireps of the present day, basking at this moment in the plenitude of her good fortune. She is however deserving of a better fate: well educated and brought up, she was early initiated into the mysteries and miseries of high life. You seem to wonder at the title I have given her."

"I am astonished again, I confess," replied Bob; "but it appears there is no end to wonders in London—nor can I guess how you so accurately know them."

"Along residence in London affords opportunities for

discovery.

"As the French very justly say, that *Il n'y a que le premier pas qui coûte*, and just as, with all the sapience of medicine, there is but a degree betwixt the Doctor and the Student, so, after the first step, there is but a degree betwixt the Demirep and the gazetted Cyprian, who is known by head-mark to every insipid Amateur and Fancier in the town.

"The number of these frail ones is so great, that, if I were to attempt to go through the shades and gradations, the distinctions and titles, from the promiscuous Duchess to the interested Marchande de mode, and from her down to the Wood Nymphs of the English Opera, there would be such a longo ordine génies, that although it is a very interesting subject, well worthy of investigation, it would occupy a considerable portion of time; however, I will give you a

slight sketch of some well known and very topping articles. Mrs. B—
—m, commonly called B——g, Mrs. P——n, and Mrs. H——d, of
various life. "The modern Pyrrha, B——g, has a train as long as an
eastern monarch, but it is a train of lovers. The Honourable B——
C——n, that famous gentleman miller, had the honour at one time
(like Cromwell,) of being the Protector of the Republic. The infamous
Greek, bully, informer and reprobate W——ce, was her accomplice
and paramour at another. Lord V——l boasted her favours at a third
period; and she wished to look upon him in a fatherly light; but it
would not do. Mr. C. T. S. the nephew of a great naval character, is
supposed to have a greater or prior claim there; but the piebald
harlequin is owned not by "Light horse, but by heavy."

"Mr. P——y, however, was so struck with the increased

attractions of this Cyprian, that he offered to be her protector during
a confinement which may be alarming to many, but interesting to a
few. This was being doubly diligent, and accordingly as it was two
to one in his favour, no wonder he succeeded in his suit. The
difficulties which Madame laboured under were sufficient to decide
her in this youth's favour; and the preference, upon such an
occasion, must have been highly flattering to him. On the score of
difficulties, Cyprians are quite in fashion; for executions and arrests
are very usual in their mansions, and the last comer has the exquisite
felicity of relieving them.

"Although this dashing Lady was the daughter of a bathing woman
at Brighton, she was not enabled to keep her head above water.

"I must not forget Poll P——n, whose select friends have such cause
to be proud of lier election. This Diana is not descended from a
member of the Rump Parliament, nor from a bum bailiff; but was the
daughter of a bumboat woman at Plymouth. She has, however, since
that period, commenced business for herself; and that in such a
respectable and extensive line, that she counts exactly seven
thousand customers! all regularly booked. What a delectable
amusement to keep such a register! *Neanmoins*, or *nean plus*, if you
like. It is reported that the noble Y—— was so delighted with her at
the Venetian fête given by Messrs. W—ll—ms and D—h—r—ty, that
he gave the Virgin Unmasked several very valuable presents, item, a

shawl value one hundred guineas, &c. and was honoured by being put on this Prime Minister of the Court of Love's list—number Seven thousand and one! What a fortunate man!

"Mrs. H——d is lineally descended, not from William the Conqueror, but from W——s the coachman. She lived, for a considerable time, in a mews, and it was thought that it was his love for the *Muses* which attached C—— L—— so closely to her. She was seduced at a most indelicately juvenile age by a Major M——l, who protected her but a short time, and then deserted her. Then she became what the Cyprians term Lady Townly, till Mr. H——d, a youth with considerable West India property in expectation, married her.

"On this happy occasion, her hymeneal flame burned with so much warmth and purity, that she shared it with a linen-draper, and the circumstance became almost immediately known to the husband! This was a happy presage of future connubial felicity! The very day before this domestic exposure, and the happy vigil of Mr. H——d's happier "*jour des noces,*" the darling of the Muses or Mewses, Mr. L—— procured Lady H——d's private box for her at one of the theatres, whither she and Mrs. CI——y, the mistress of an officer of that name, repaired in the carriage of the Mews lover, which has become completely "the Demirep or Cyprian's Diligence," and these patterns for the fair sex had poured out such plentiful libations to Bacchus, that her ladyship's box exhibited the effects of their devotions! What a regale for the Princess of Madagascar!

"The guardians, or trustees, of Mr. H——d now withheld his property, and Madame assisted him into the King's Bench, during which time she kept terms with Mr. L—— at Oxford. On her return, she got acquainted with a Capt. Cr——ks, whom she contrived soon afterwards to lodge, in the next room to her husband, in the Bench; but to whom she kindly gave the preference in her visits.

"Whether C—— L——, W—lk—s the linen-draper, or Capt. C——k, be the most favoured swain, or swine, I venture not to say; but the former has devoted his time, his chariot, and his female acquaintances' boxes in public to her. As a pledge of his love, she helped herself to a loose picture of great value belonging to him, which very nearly fell into the hands of John Doe or Richard Roe, on her husband's account, afterwards. The palm should, however, certainly be given to Mr. L——, as he courted her classically, moralized to her sentimentally, sung psalms and prayed with her fervently, and, on all occasions, treated her like a lady."

"Ha," said a fashionably dressed young man, who approached towards Dashall, "Ha, my dear fellow, how goes it with you? Haven't seen you this month; d——d unlucky circumstance—wanted you very much indeed—glorious sport—*all jolly and bang up.*" "Glad to hear it," said Tom,—"sorry you should have experienced any wants on my account."

"Which way are you going? Come along, I'll tell you of such a spree—regular, and nothing but—You must know, a few days ago, sauntering down Bond-street, I overtook Sir G. W. 'Ha! my gay fellow,' said he, 'I thought you were at Bibury; you're the very man I want. My brother Jack has lost a rump and dozen to a young one, and we want to make up a select party, a set of real hardheaded fellows, to share the feast. I have already recruited Sir M. M., the buck Parson, Lord Lavender, and Tom Shuffleton. Then there's yourself, I hope, my brother and I, the young one, and A——'s deputy, the reprobate Curate, whom we will have to make fun of. We dine at half-past seven, at Long's, and there will be some sport, I assure you.'

"I accepted the invitation, and met the company before mentioned. A rump and dozen is always a nominal thing. There was no rump, except Lavender's, which projects like a female's from the bottom of a tight-laced pair of stays; and as for the dozen, I believe we drank nearer three dozen of different expensive wines, which were tasted one after the other with a quickness of succession, which at last left no taste, but a taste for more drink, and for all sorts of wickedness.

"This tasting plan is a very successful trick of tavern keepers, which enables them to carry off half bottles of wine, to swell the reckoning most amazingly, and so to bewilder people as to the qualities of the wine, that any thing, provided it be strong and not acid, will go down at the heel of the evening. It is also a grand manouvre; to intoxicate a Johnny Raw, and to astonish his weak mind with admiration for the founder of the feast. Therefore, the old trick of 'I have got some particularly high-flavoured Burgundy, which Lord Lavender very much approved t'other day;' and, 'Might I, Sir, ask your opinion of a new importation of Sillery?' or, 'My Lord, 1 have bought all the Nabob's East India Madeira,' &c. was successfully practised.

"Through the first course we were stag-hunting, to a man, and killed the stag just as the second course came on the table. This course was occupied by a great number of long shots of Sir M. M., and by Lavender offering to back himself and the buck Parson against any other two men in England, as to the number of head of game which they would bag from sun-rise to sun-set upon the moors. A foot race, and a dispute as to the odds betted on the second October Meeting, occupied the third course. The desert was enlivened by a list of ladies of all descriptions, whose characters were cut up full as ably as the haunch of venison was carved; and here boasting of success in love was as general as the custom is base. One man of fashion goes by the name of Kiss and tell.

"After an hour of hard drinking, as though it had been for a wager, a number of very manly, nice little innocent and instructive amusements were resorted to. We had a most excellent maggot race for a hundred; and then a handycap for a future poney race. We had pitching a guinea into a decanter, at which the young one lost considerably. We had a raffle for a gold snuff box, a challenge of fifty against Lord Lavender's Dusseldorf Pipe, and five hundred betted upon the number of shot to be put into a Joe Manton Rifle. We played at *te-to-tum*; and the young one leaped over a handkerchief six feet high for a wager: he performed extremely well at first, but at last Lavender, who betted against him, kept plying him so with wine, and daring him to an inch higher and higher, until at last the young one broke his nose, and lost five hundred guineas by his boyish diversion.

Now we had a fulminating letter introduced as a hoax upon Shuffleton; next, devils and broiled bones; then some blasphemous songs from the Curate, who afterwards fell asleep, and thus furnished an opportunity for having his face blacked. We then got in a band of itinerant musicians; put crackers in their pockets; cut off one fellow's tail; and had a milling match betwixt the baronet in the chair and the stoutest of them, who, having had spirits of wine poured over his head, refused to let the candle be put to it!

Peace being restored, a regular supper appeared; and then a regular set-to at play, where I perceived divers signals thrown out, such as rubbing of foreheads and chins, taking two pinches of snuff and other private telegraphic communications, the result of which was, the young one, just of age, being greeked to a very great amount.

We now sallied forth, like a pack in full cry, with all the loud expression of mirth and riot, and proceeded to old 77, which, being shut up, we swore like troopers, and broke the parlour windows in a rage. We next cut the traces of a hackney coach, and led the horses into a mews, ?where we tied them up; coachee being asleep inside the whole time. We then proceeded to old *Ham-a-dry-ed*, the bacon man's, called out Fire, and got the old man down to the door in his shirt, when Lavender ran away with his night-cap, and threw it into the water in St. James's Square, whilst the Baronet put it in right and left at his sconce, and told him to hide his d——d ugly masard. This induced him to come out and call the Watch, during which time the buck Parson got into his house, and was very snug with the cook wench until the next evening, when *old fusty mug* went out upon business.

After giving a view holloa! we ran off, with the Charleys in full cry after us, when Sir G. W., who had purposely provided himself with a long cord, gave me one end, and ran to the opposite side of Jermyn Street with the other in his hand, holding it about two feet from the pavement. The old Scouts came up in droves, and we had 'em down in a moment, for every mother's son of the guardians were caught in the trap, and rolled over each other slap into the kennel. Never was such a prime bit of gig! They lay stunn'd with the fall—broken lanterns, staves, rattles, Welsh wigs, night-caps and old hats, were scattered about in abundance, while grunting, growling, and swearing was heard in all directions. One old buck got his jaw-bone broken; another staved in two of his crazy timbers, that is to say, broke a couple of ribs; a third bled from the nose like a pig; a fourth squinted admirably from a pair of painted peepers; their numbers however increasing, we divided our forces and marched in opposite directions; one party sallied along Bond Street, nailed up a snoosy Charley in his box, and bolted with his lantern: the others were not so fortunate, for A——'s deputy cushion thumper, the young one, and the Baronet's brother, got safely lodged in St. James's Watch-house.

"Broad daylight now glar'd upon us—Lavender retired comfortably upon Madame la Comtesse in the Bench; Sir M. M. was found chanting Cannons with some Wood nymphs not an hundred and fifty miles off from Leicester Square; I had the President to carry home on my shoulders, bundled to bed, and there I lay sick for four and twenty hours, when a little inspiring Coniac brought me to my senses again, and now I am ready and ripe for another spree. Stap my vitals if there isn't Lavender—my dear fellow, adieu—remember me to Charley Sparkle when you see him—by, by." And with this he sprung across the road, leaving Bob and his Cousin to comment at leisure upon his folly.

They were however soon aroused from their reflections by perceiving a Groom in livery advancing rapidly towards them, followed by a curricle, moving at the rate of full nine miles per hour.

"Who have we here?" said Bob.

"A character well known," said Tom; "that is Lady L——, a dashing female whip of the first order—mark how she manages her tits—take a peep at her costume and learn while you look."

"More than one steed must Delia's empire feel Who sits triumphant o'er the flying wheel; And as she guides it through th' admiring throng, With what an air she smacks the silken thong!"

The Lady had a small round riding-hat, of black beaver, and sat in the true attitude of a coachman—wrists pliant, elbows square, she handled her whip in a scientific manner; and had not Tom declared her sex, Bob would hardly have discovered it from her outward appearance. She was approaching them at a brisk trot, greeting her numerous acquaintance as she passed with familiar nods, at each giving her horses an additional touch, and pursing up her lips to accelerate their speed; indeed, she was so intent upon the management of her reins, and her eyes so fixed upon her cattle, that there was no time for more than a sort of sidelong glance of recognition; and every additional smack of the whip seem'd to say, *"Here I come—that's your sort."* Her whole manner indeed was very similar to what may be witnessed in Stage-coachmen, Hackneymen, and fashionable Ruffians, who appear to think that all merit consists in copying them when they tip a brother whip the go-by, or almost graze the wheel of a Johnny-raw, and turn round with a grin of self-approbation, as much as to say—*"What d'ye think of that now, eh f— there's a touch for you—lord, what a flat you must be!"*

Bob gazed with wonder and astonishment as she passed.

"How?" said he, "do the ladies of London frequently take the whip?—"

"—Hand of their husbands as well as their horses," replied Tom—"often enough, be assured."

"But how, in the name of wonder, do they learn to drive in this style?"

"Easily enough; inclination and determination will accomplish their objects. Why, among the softer sex, we have female Anatomists—female Students in Natural History—Sculptors, and Mechanics of all descriptions—Shoe-makers and Match-makers—and why not Charioteers?"

"Nay, I am not asking why; but as it appears rather out of the common way, I confess my ignorance has excited my curiosity on a subject which seems somewhat out of nature."

"I have before told you, Nature has nothing to do with Real Life in London."

"And yet," continued Bob, "we are told, and I cannot help confessing the truth of the assertion, with respect to the ladies, that

"— —*Loveliness*

*Needs not the foreign aid of ornament,
But is, when unadorned, adorn'd the most,"
This certainly implies a natural or native grace."*

"Pshaw," said Dashall, "that was according to the Old school; such doctrines are completely exploded now-a-days, for Fashion is at variance with Nature in all her walks; hence, driving is considered one of the accomplishments necessary to be acquired by the female sex in high life, by which an estimate of character may be formed: for instance—if a lady take the reins of her husband, her brother, or a lover, it is strongly indicative of assuming the mastery; but should she have no courage or muscular strength, and pays no attention to the art of governing and guiding her cattle, it is plain that she will become no driver, no whip, and may daily run the risk of breaking the necks of herself and friends. If however she should excel in this study, she immediately becomes masculine and severe, and she punishes, when occasion requires, every animal within the reach of her lash—acquires an ungraceful attitude and manner—heats her complexion by over exertion—sacrifices her softness to accomplish her intentions—runs a risk of having hard hands, and perhaps a hard heart: at all events she gains unfeminine habits, and such as are found very difficult to get rid of, and prides herself on being the go, the gaze, the gape, the stare of all who see her."

"A very admirable, and no doubt equally happy state," quoth Bob, half interrupting him.

"If she learn the art of driving from the family coachman, it cannot be doubted but such tuition is more than likely to give her additional grace, and to teach her all that is polite; and then the pleasure of such company whilst superintending her studies, must tend to improve her mind; the freedom of these teachers of coachmanship, and the language peculiar to themselves, at first perhaps not altogether agreeable, is gradually worn away by the pride of becoming an accomplished whip—to know how to *turn a corner in style—tickle Snarler in the ear—cut up the yelper—take out a fly's eye in bang-up twig.*"

"Excellent! indeed," cried Bob, charmed with Dashall's irony, and willing to provoke it farther; "and pray, when this art of driving is thoroughly learned, what does it tend to but a waste of time, a masculine enjoyment, and a loss of feminine character—of that sweet, soft and overpowering submission to and reliance on the other sex, which, whilst it demands our protection and assistance, arouses our dearest sympathies—our best interests—attaches, enraptures, and subdues us?"

"Nonsense," continued Tom, "you might ask such questions for a month—who cares about these submissions and reliances—protections and sympathies—they are not known, at least it is very unfashionable to acknowledge their existence. Why I have known ladies so infatuated and affected by an inordinate love of charioteering, that it has completely altered them, not only as to dress, but manners and feeling, till at length they have become more at home in the stable than the drawing-room; and some, that are so different when dressed for dinner, that the driving habiliments appear like complete masquerade disguises. Indeed, any thing that is natural is considered quite out of nature; and this affectation is not wholly confined to the higher circles, for in the City even the men and the women seem to have changed places.

> *"Man-milliners and mantua-makers swarm*
> *With clumsy hands to deck the female form—*
> *With brawny limbs to fit fine ladies' shapes,*
> *Or measure out their ribbons, lace and tapes;*
> *Or their rude eye the bosom's swell surveys,*
> *To cut out corsets or to stitch their stays;*
> *Or making essences and soft perfume,*
> *Or paint, to give the pallid cheek fresh bloom;*
> *Or with hot irons, combs, and frizzling skill,*
> *On ladies' heads their daily task fulfil;*
> *Or, deeply versed in culinary arts,*
> *Are kneading pasty, making pies and tarts;*
> *Or, clad in motley coat, the footman neat*
> *Is dangling after Miss with shuffling feet,*
> *Bearing in state to church her book of pray'r,*
> *Or the light pocket she disdains to wear;{1}*
> *Or in a parlour snug, 'the powdered lout*
> *The tea and bread and butter hands about.*

Where are the women, whose less nervous hands
Might fit these lighter tasks, which pride demands?
Some feel the scorn that poverty attends,
Or pine in meek dépendance on their friends;
Some patient ply the needle day by day,
Poor half-paid seamsters, wasting life away;
Some drudge in menial, dirty, ceaseless toil,
Bear market loads, or grovelling weed the soil;
Some walk abroad, a nuisance where they go,
And snatch from infamy the bread of woe."

"It is a strange sort of infatuation, this fashion," said Bob, "and it is much to be regretted it should operate so much to the injury of the fair—"

"Do you see that young man on the opposite side of the way," inquired Dashall, (stopping him short) "in nankin breeches and jockey-boots?"

"I do," replied Tallyho; "and pray who is he?"

"The son of a wealthy Baronet who, with an eye to the main chance in early life, engaged in some mercantile speculations, which proving productive concerns, have elevated him to his present dignity, beyond which it is said he cannot go on account of his having once kept a shop. This son is one of what may be termed the *Ciphers of society*, a sort of useful article, like an 0 in arithmetic, to denominate numbers; one of those characters, if character it may be termed, of which this Metropolis and its vicinity would furnish us with regiments. Indeed, the

1 It is related that a young lady of *haut ton* in Paris was observed to have a tall fellow always following her wherever she went. Her grandmother one day asked her what occasion there was for that man to be always following her; to which she replied—"I must blow my nose, must not I, when I want?" This great genius was actually employed to carry her pocket-handkerchief. general run of Fashionables are little better than Ciphers,—very necessary at times in the House of Commons, to suit the purposes and forward the intentions of the Ministers, by which they obtain *titles* to which they

are not *entitled,* and transmit to posterity a race of ennobled boobies. What company, what society does not abound with Ciphers, and oftentimes in such plenty that they are even serviceable to make the society considerable? What could we do to express on paper five hundred without the two ciphers, or being compelled to write eleven letters to explain what is equally well done in three figures? These Ciphers are useful at general meetings upon public questions, though, if they were all collected together in point of intellectual value, they would amount to nought. They are equally important as counters at a card-table, they tell for more than they are worth. Among the City Companies there are many of them to be found: and the Army is not deficient, though great care is generally taken to send the most conspicuous Ciphers on foreign service. Public offices under Government swarm with them; and how many round O's or ciphers may be found among the gentlemen of the long robe, who, as Hudibras observes,

"— —*never ope*
Their mouths, but out there flies a trope."

In the twelve Judges it must be allowed there is no cipher, because they have two figures to support them; but take these two figures away, and the whole wit of mankind may be defied to patch up or recruit the number without having recourse to the race of Ciphers.

"I have known a Cipher make a profound Statesman and a Secretary—nay, an Ambassador; but then it must be confess'd it has been by the timely and prudent application of proper supporters; and it is certain, that Ciphers have more than once shewn themselves significant in high posts and stations, and in more reigns than one. Bounteous nature indulges mankind in a boundless variety of characters as well as features, and has given Ciphers to make up numbers, and very often by such additions renders the few much more significant and conspicuous. The Church has its Ciphers—for a mitre looks as well on a round 0 as on any letter in the alphabet, and the expense to the nation is equally the same; consequently, John Bull has no right to complain.

"*See in Pomposo a polite divine,*
More gay than grave, not half so sound as fine;

The ladies' parson, proudly skill'd is he,
To 'tend their toilet and pour out their tea;
Foremost to lead the dance, or patient sit
To deal the cards out, or deal out small wit;
Then oh! in public, what a perfect beau,
So powder'd and so trimm'd for pulpit show;
So well equipp'd to tickle ears polite
With pretty little subjects, short and trite.
Well cull'd and garbled from the good old store
Of polish'd sermons often preached before;
With precious scraps from moral Shakespeare brought.
To fill up awkward vacancies of thought,
Or shew how he the orator can play
Whene'er he meets with some good thing to say,
Or prove his taste correct, his memory strong,
Nor let his fifteen minutes seem too long:
His slumbering mind no knotty point pursues,
Save when contending for his tithes or dues."

Thus far, although it must be allowed that ciphers are of use, it is not every cipher that is truly useful. There are Ciphers of indolence, to which some mistaken men give the title of men of fine parts—there are Ciphers of Self-interest, to which others more wrongfully give the name of Patriots—there are Bacchanalian Ciphers, who will not leave the bottle to save the nation, but will continue to guzzle till no one figure in Arithmetic is sufficient to support them—then there are Ciphers of Venus, who will abandon all state affairs to follow a Cyprian, even at the risk of injuring a deserving wife—Military Ciphers, who forsake the pursuit of glory, and distrustful of their own merit or courage, affirm their distrust by a sedulous attendance at the levees of men of power. In short, every man, in my humble opinion, is no other than a Cipher who does not apply his talents to the care of his morals and the benefit of his country."

"You have been ciphering for some time," said Boh, "and I suppose you have now finished your sum."

"I confess," continued Tom, "it has been a puzzling one—for, to make something out of nothing is impossible."

"Not in all cases," said Bob.

"How so?—why you have proved it by your own shewing, that these nothings are to be made something of."

"I perceive," replied Tom, "that your acquaintance with Sparkle is not thrown away upon you; and it argues well, for if you are so ready a pupil at imbibing his lessons, you will soon become a proficient in London manners and conversation; but a Cipher is like a *round robin*,{1} it has neither beginning nor end: its centre is vacancy, its circle ambiguity, and it stands for nothing, unless in certain connections."

They were now proceeding gently along Oxford Street, in pursuit of their way to Soho Square, and met with little worthy of note or remark until they arrived near the end of Newman Street, where a number of workmen were digging up the earth for the purpose of making new-drains. The pathway was railed from the road by scaffolding poles strongly driven into the ground, and securely tied together to prevent interruption from the passengers.—Tom was remarking upon the hardihood and utility of the labourers at the moment when a fountain of water was issuing from a broken pipe, which arose as high as a two pair of stairs window, a circumstance which quickly drew a number of spectators around, and, among the rest, Tom and his Cousin could not resist an inclination to spend a few minutes in viewing the proceedings.

The Irish *jontlemen*, who made two or three ineffectual attempts to stop the breach, alternately got soused by the increased violence of the water, and at every attempt were saluted by the loud laughter of the surrounding multitude.

To feelings naturally warm and irritable, these vociferations of amusement and delight at their defeat, served but to exasperate and enrage; and the Irishmen in strong terms expressed their indignation at the merriment which their abortive attempts appeared to excite: at length, one of the *Paddies* having cut a piece of wood, as he conceived, sufficient to stop the effusion of water, with some degree of adroitness thrust his arm into the foaming fluid, and for a moment appeared to have arrested its progress.

"*Blood-an-owns!* Murphy," cried he, "scoop away the water, and be after handing over the mallet this way." In a moment the spades of his comrades were seen in

> 1 Round Rubin—*A Letter or Billet, so composed as to have the signatures of many persons in a circle, in order that the reader may not be able to discover which of the party signed first or last.*

action to accomplish his instructions, while one, who was not in a humour to hear the taunts of the crowd, very politely scoop'd the water with his hands among the spectators, which created a general desire to avoid his liberal and plentiful besprinklings, and at the same time considerable confusion among men, women, and children, who, in effecting their escape, were seen tumbling and rolling over each other in all directions.

"Be off wid you all, and be d— —d to you," said the Hibernian; while those who were fortunate enough to escape the cooling fluid he was so indifferently dispensing, laughed heartily at their less favoured companions.

Bob was for moving onward.

"Hold," said Dash all, "it is two to one but you will see some fun here."

He had scarcely said the word, when a brawny Porter in a fustian jacket, with his knot slung across his shoulder, manifested dislike to the manner in which the Irish *jontleman* was pursuing his amusement.

"D— —n your Irish eyes," said he, "don't throw your water here, or I'll lend you my *bunch of fives*." {1}

"Be after being off, there," replied Pat; and, without hesitation, continued his employment.

The Porter was resolute, and upon receiving an additional salute, jumped over the railings, and re-saluted poor Pat with a *muzzier*,{2} which drew his claret in a moment. The Irishman endeavoured to rally, while the crowd cheered the Porter and hooted the Labourer. This was the signal for hostilities. The man who had plugg'd up the broken pipe let go his hold, and the fountain was playing away as briskly as ever—all was confusion, and the neighbourhood in alarm. The workmen, with spades and pick-axes, gathered round their comrade, and there was reason to apprehend serious mischief would occur; one of them hit the Porter with his spade, and several others were prepared to follow his example; while a second, who seem'd a little more blood-thirsty than the rest, raised his pickaxe in a menacing attitude; upon perceiving which, Dashall jump'd over the rail and

> 1 Bunch of fives—A flash term for the fist, frequently made use of among the lads of the Fancy, who address each other some-times in a friendly way, with—Ha, Bill, how goes it?—tip us your bunch of fives, my boy.

> 2 Muzzier—A blow on the mouth.

arrested his arm, or, if the blow had been struck, murder must have ensued. In the mean time, several other persons, following Tom's example, had disarmed the remainder. A fellow-labourer, who had been engaged at a short distance, from the immediate scene of action, attacked the man who had raised the pickaxe, between whom a pugilistic encounter took place, the former swearing, 'By Jasus, they were a set of cowardly rascals, and deserved *quilting.*'{1} The water was flowing copiously—shovels, pickaxes, barrows, lanterns and other implements were strewed around them—the crowd increased—Tom left the combatants (when he conceived no real danger of unfair advantage being taken was to be apprehended) to enjoy their rolling in the mud; while the Porter, who had escaped the vengeance of his opponents, was explaining to those around him, and expostulating with the first aggressor, upon the impropriety of his conduct. The shouts of the multitude at the courageous proceedings of the Porter, and the hootings at the shameful and cowardly manner of defence pursued by the Labourers, roused the blood of the Irishmen, and one again seized a spade to attack a Coal-heaver who espoused the cause of the Porter—a disposition was again manifested to cut down any one who dared to entertain opinions opposite to their own—immediately a shower of mud and stones was directed towards him—the spade was taken away, and the Irishmen armed themselves in a similar way with the largest stones they could find suitable for throwing. In this state of things, the houses and the windows in the neighbourhood were threatened with serious damage. The crowd retreated hallooing, shouting, hissing, and groaning; and in this part of the affray Bob got himself well bespattered with mud. Tom again interfered, and after a few minutes, persuaded the multitude to desist, and the Irishmen to drop their weapons. The Porter made his escape, and the men resumed their work; but, upon Dashall's return to the

> 1 Quilting—To quilt a person among the knowing Covies, is to give another a good thrashing; probably, this originated in the idea of warming—as a quilt is a warm companion, so a set-to is equally productive of heat; whether the allusion holds good with respect to comfort, must be left to the decision of those who try it on, (which is to make any attempt or essay where success is doubtful.)

spot where he had left Tallyho, the latter was not to be found; he was however quickly relieved from suspense.

"Sir," said a stout man, "the neighbourhood is greatly indebted to your exertions in suppressing a riot from which much mischief was to be apprehended—your friend is close at hand, if you will step this way, you will find him—he is getting his coat brushed at my house, and has sustained no injury."

"It is a lucky circumstance for him," said Tom: "and I think myself fortunate upon the same account, for I assure you I was very apprehensive of some serious mischief resulting from the disturbance."

CHAPTER XVI

"Blest be the pencil which from death can save
The semblance of the virtuous, wise and brave,
That youth and emulation still may gaze
On those inspiring forms of ancient days,
And, from the force of bright example bold,
Rival their worth, and be what they behold."

".....I admire,
None more admires the painter's magic skill,
Who shews me that which I shall never see,
Conveys a distant country into mine,
And throws Italian light on British walls."

AS they entered the house, a few doors up Newman Street, Tallyho met them, having divested himself of the mud which had been thrown upon his garments by the indiscriminating hand of an enraged multitude; and after politely thanking the gentleman for his friendly accommodation, they were about to proceed to the place of their original destination; when Dashall, perceiving an elegantly dressed lady on the opposite side of the way, felt, instinctively as it were, for the usual appendage of a modern fashionable, the quizzing-glass; in the performance of this he was subjected to a double disappointment, for his rencontre with the Hibernians had shivered the fragile ornament to atoms in his pocket, and before he could draw forth the useless fragments, the more important object of his attention was beyond the power of his visual orbs.

"It might have been worse," said he, as he survey'd the broken bauble: "it is a loss which can easily be repaired, and if in losing that, I have prevented more serious mischief, there is at least some consolation. Apropos, here is the very place for supplying the defect without loss of time. Dixon," {1} continued he, looking at

> 1 *This gentleman, whose persevering endeavours in his*
> *profession entitle him to the patronage of the public,*
> *without pretending to second sight, or the powers that are*

so frequently attributed to the seventh son of a seventh son, has thrown some new lights upon the world. Although he does not pretend to make "Helps to Read," his establishment at No. 93, Newman Street, Oxford Road, of upwards of thirty years' standing, is deservedly celebrated for glasses suited to all sights, manufactured upon principles derived from long study and practical experience. Indeed, if we are to place any reliance on his Advertisements, he has brought them to a state of perfection never before attained, and not to be surpassed.

the name over the door—"aye, I remember to have seen his advertisements in the papers, and have no doubt I may be suited here to a *shaving*"

Upon saying this, they entered the house, and found the improver of spectacles and eye-glasses surrounded with the articles of his trade, who, in a moment, recognized Tom as the chief instrument in quelling the tumult, and added his acknowledgments to what had already been offered for his successful exertions, assuring him at the same time, that as he considered sight to be one of the most invaluable blessings "bestowed on mankind, he had for many years devoted the whole of his time and attention to the improvement of glasses—put into his hand a short treatise on the subject, and on the important assistance which may be afforded by a judicious selection of spectacles to naturally imperfect or overstrained eyes. Bob, in the mean time, was amusing himself with reading bills, pamphlets, and newspapers, which lay upon the counter.

Dashall listened with attention to his dissertation on sight, spectacles, focusses, lens, reflection, refraction, &c.; but, as he was not defective in the particular organs alluded to, felt but little interested on the subject; selected what he really wanted, or rather what etiquette required, when, to their great gratification, in came Sparkle. After the first salutations were over, the latter purchased an opera-glass; then, in company with Tom and Bob, proceeded to Oxford Street, and upon learning their destination, determined also to take a peep at the Exhibition.

"Come along," said Tom, catching hold of his arm, and directing him towards Soho Square. But Sparkle recollecting that he had appointed to meet Miss Mortimer, her Brother, and Merry well, to accompany them to Somerset House, and finding time had escaped with more rapidity than he expected, wished them a good morning, hoped they should meet again in the course of the day, and departed.

"You see," said Tom, "Sparkle is fully engaged in the business of love; Miss Mortimer claims all his attention for the present."

"You appear to be very envious of his enjoyments," replied Bob.

"Not so, indeed," continued Tom; "I am only regretting that other pursuits have estranged him from our company."

On entering the Exhibition at Soho, Tom, whose well-known taste for science and art, and particularly for the productions of the pencil and graver, had already rendered him conspicuous among those who knew him, made the following remarks: "I am really glad," said he, "to find that the eminent engravers of our country have at length adopted a method of bringing at one view before the public, a delineation of the progress made by our artists in a branch so essentially connected with the performance and durability of the Fine Arts. An Exhibition of this kind is well calculated to dispel the vulgar error, that engraving is a servile art in the scale of works of the mind, and mostly consigned to the copyist. An Establishment of this kind has long been wanted, and is deserving of extensive patronage."

Having secured Catalogues, they proceeded immediately to the gratifying scene.{1} The disposition and arrangement

> 1 *The major part of the 405 subjects and sets of subjects, consisting of about 800 prints, are of moderate size, or small engravings for descriptive or literary publications, &e. They are the lesser diamonds in a valuable collection of jewellery, where there are but few that are not of lucid excellence, and worthy of glistening in the diadem of Apollo, or the cestus of Venus. So indeed they have, for here are many subjects from ancient and modern poetry, and*

other literature, and from portraits of beautiful women. Among the first class, the exquisitely finishing graver of Mr. Warren gives us many after the designs of Messrs. Westall, Wilkie, Smirke, Cooke, Uwins, and Corbould; as do the lucid gravers of Messrs. Englehart and Rhodes, the nicely executing hands of Messrs. Mitan, Romney, Finden, Robinson, &c. Among the latter class, are Anna Boleyn, &c. by Mr. Scriven, who marks so accurately the character of the objects, and of the Painter he works from, in his well blended dot and stroke; Mrs. Hope, by Dawe; many lovely women, by Mr. Reynolds; a Courtship, by Mr. Warren, from Terburg, in the Marquis of Stafford's Collection; two Mary Queen of Scots, by Messrs. Warren and Cooper.— —From pictures of the old and modern Masters, are capital Portraits of celebrated characters of former and present times; of Mrs. Siddons, of Cicero, M. Angelo, Parmigiano, Fenelon, Raleigh, A. Durer, Erasmus, Cromwell, Ben Jonson, Selden, Swift, Gay, Sterne, Garrick, &c. of Byron, Bonaparte, West, Kenible, young Napoleon, of nearly all the English Royal Family, and many of the Nobility.

— —Of all the charmingly engraved Landscapes of foreign and home Views, and of the Animal pieces, are many from Messrs. W. B. and G. Cooke's recent publications of The Coast of England, &c. of Mr. Hakewell's Italy, Mr. Nash's Paris, Captain Batty's France, &c. Mr. Neale's Vieios, many of Mr. Scott's and Mr. Milton's fine Animal Prints; exquisitely engraved Architecture by Mr. Le Keaux, Mr. Lowry, Mr. G. Cooke, &c. Among the large Prints are the two last of Mr. Holloway's noble set from Raffaelle's Cartoons; the Battle of Leipzig, finely executed by Mr. Scott, and containing Portraits of those monstrous assailers of Italy and of the common rights of mankind, the Emperors of Austria and Russia; Jaques from Shakspeare, by Mr. Middiman, Reynolds' Infant Hercules by Mr. Ward, The Bard, by J. Bromley, jun. possessing the energy of the original by the late President Mr. West, and The Poacher detected, by Mr. Lupton, from Mr. Kidd's beautiful picture.

of the plates, and the company dispersed in various parts of the rooms, were the first objects of attention, and the whole appearance was truly pleasing. At one end was to be seen an old Connoisseur examining a most beautiful engraving from an excellent drawing by Clennell{1}—-another contemplating the brilliance of Goodall in his beautiful print of the Fountains of Neptune in the Gardens of Versailles. Dash all, who generally took care to see all before him, animate and inanimate, was occasionally

> 1 Luke Clennell—This unfortunate artist, a native of Morpeth, in Northumberland, and known to the world as an eminent engraver on wood, as well as a painter of no ordinary talent, has furnished one of those cases of human distress and misery which calls for the sympathy and aid of every friend to forlorn genius. In the midst of a prosperous career, with fortune "both hands full," smiling on every side, munificently treated by the British Institution, employed on an important work by the Earl of Bridgewater (a picture of the Fête given by the City of London to the Allied Sovereigns,) and with no prospect but that delightful one of fame and independence, earned by his own exertions, the most dreadful affliction of life befel him, and insanity rooted where taste and judgment so conspicuously shone. The wretched artist was of necessity separated from his family; his young wife, the mother of his three infants, descended to the grave a broken-hearted victim, leaving the poor orphans destitute. The Print alluded to in this case, representing the Charge of the Life Guards at Waterloo in 1816, was published by subscription for their benefit.

casting glimpses at the pictures and the sprightly females by which they were surrounded, and drawing his Cousin to such subjects as appeared to be most deserving of attention; among which, the fine effect produced by Mr. W. B. Cooke stood high in his estimation, particularly in his View of Edinburgh from Calton Hill, and Brightling Observatory in Rose Hill—Le Keux, in his Monument, also partook of his encomiums—T. Woolroth's Portraits, particularly that of the Duchess of Kent, claimed attention, and was deservedly admired, as well as a smaller one of Mr. Shalis by the same artist; indeed, the whole appeared to be selected, combined and arranged under the direction of a master, and calculated at once to surprise and delight. After enjoying an hour's lounge in this agreeable company,

"Come," said Dashall, "we will repair to Somerset House, and amuse ourselves with colours.

"Halloo!" said a smart looking young man behind them—*"what am you arter?—where is you going to?"*

Upon turning round, Dashall discovered it to be the exquisite Mr. Mincingait, who, having just caught a glimpse of him, and not knowing what to do with himself, hung as it were upon the company of Tom and his friend, by way of killing a little time; and was displaying his person and apparel to the greatest advantage as he pick'd his way along the pavement, alternately picking his teeth and twirling his watch-chain. Passing the end of Greek Street, some conversation having taken place upon the dashing Society in which he had spent the previous evening, Tom indulged himself in the following description of *How to Cut a Dash.*

"Dashing society," said he, "is almost every where to be found in London: it is indeed of so much importance among the generality of town residents, that a sacrifice of every thing that is dear and valuable is frequently made to appearance."

"You are a quiz," said Mincingait; "but I don't mind you, so go your length."

"Very well," continued Tom; "then by way of instruction to my friend, I will give my ideas upon the subject, and if perchance you should find any resemblance to yourself in the picture I am about to draw, don't let all the world know it. If you have an inclination to cut a dash, situation and circumstances in life have nothing to do with it; a good bold face and a stock of assurance, are the most essential requisites. With these, you must in the first place fall upon some method to trick a tailor (provided you have not certain qualms that will prevent you) by getting into his debt, for much depends upon exteriors. There is no crime in this, for you pay him if you are able—and good clothes are very necessary for a dash; having them cut after the newest fashion, is also very essential. Sally forth, if on a sunday morning in quest of a companion with whom you have the night previous (at a tavern or confectioner's) engaged to meet at the corner. After having passed the usual compliments of the morning with him, place yourself in a fashionable attitude, your thumbs thrust in your pantaloon's pockets—the right foot thrown carelessly across the left, resting on the toe, exhibits your line turned ancle, or new boot, and is certainly a very modest attitude—your cravat finically adjusted, and tied sufficiently tight to produce a fine full-blooming countenance: corsets and bag pantaloons are indispensably necessary to accoutre you for the stand. When in this trim, dilate upon the events of the times—know but very little of domestic affairs—expatiate and criticise upon the imperfections or charms of the passing multitude—tell a fine story to some acquaintance who knows but little about you, and, by this means, borrow as much money as will furnish you with a very small bamboo, or very large cudgel; extremes are very indispensable for a good dash.

"It is extremely unbecoming for a gentleman of fashion to pay any regard to that old superstitious ceremony of what is commonly called *'going to church'*—or, at most, of attending more than half a day in the week. To attend public worship more than one hour in seven days must be very fatiguing to a person of genteel habits—besides it would be countenancing an old established custom. In former times, a serious and devout attention to divine service was not thought improper; but should a gentleman of modern manners attend public worship, to discover, according to the law of the polite, what new face of fashion appears, I need not mention the absurdity of decent behaviour.

'What go to meeting, say?—why this the vulgar do, Yes, and it is a custom old as Homer too! Sure, then, we folks of fashion must with this dispense, Or differ in some way from folks of common sense.'

"Melodious, indeed, are the voices of ladies and gentlemen whispering across the pews, politely inquiring after each other's health—the hour at which they got home from their Saturday evening's party—what gallants attended them; and what lasses they saw safe home. How engaging the polite posture of looking on the person next you, or in sound sleep, instead of sacred music, playing loud bass through the nose! But to have proceeded methodically in enumerating the improvements in manners, I ought, first, to have mentioned some of the important advantages of staying from church until the service is half finished. Should you attend at the usual hour of commencing service, you might be supposed guilty of rising in the morning as early as nine or ten o'clock, and by that means be thought shockingly ungenteel—and if seated quietly in the pew, you might possibly remain unnoticed; but, by thundering along the aisle in the midst of prayer or sermon, you are pretty sure to command the attention of the audience, and obtain the honour of being thought by some, to have been engaged in some genteel affair the night before! Besides, it is well known that it is only the vulgar that attend church in proper time.

"When you parade the streets, take off your hat to every gentleman's carriage that passes; you may do the same to any pretty woman—for if she is well bred, (you being smartly dressed) she will return the compliment before she be able to recollect whether your's be a face she has seen somewhere or not; those who see it, will call you a dashing fellow. When a beggar stops you, put your hand in your pocket, and tell him you are very sorry you have no change; this, you know, will be strictly true, and speaking truth is always a commendable quality;—or, if it suits you better, bid him go to the churchwarden—this you may easily do in a dashing way. Never think of following any business or profession,—such conduct is unworthy of a dasher. In the evening, never walk straight along the foot-way, but go in a zigzag direction—this will make some people believe you have been dashing down your bottle of wine after dinner. No dasher goes home sober.

"On making your appearance in the ball-room, put your hat under your arm: you will find an advantage in this, as it will make a stir in the room to make way for you and your hat, and apprize them of your entrance.

After one or two turns around the room, if the sets are all made up, make a stand before one of the mirrors, to adjust your cravat, hair, &c. Be sure to have your hair brushed all over the forehead, which will give you a very ferocious appearance. If you catch a strange damsel's eyes fixed upon you, take it for granted that you are a fascinating fellow, and cut a prodigious dash. As soon as the first set have finished.dancing, fix your thumbs as before-mentioned, and make a dash through the gaping crowd in pursuit of a partner; if you are likely to be disappointed in obtaining one with whom you are acquainted, select the smallest child in the room; by that means, you will attract the attention of the ladies, and secure to you the hand of a charming Miss for the next dance. When on the floor with one of those dashing belles, commence a *tête-a-tête* with her, and pay no attention whatever to the figure or steps, but walk as deliberately as the music will admit (not dropping your little chit chat) through the dance, which is considered, undoubtedly, very graceful, and less like a mechanic or dancing-master. The dance finished, march into the bar, and call for a glass of blue-ruin, white-tape, or stark-naked, which is a very fashionable liquor among the 'ton,' and if called on to pay for it, tell the landlord you have left your purse in one of your blues at home; and that you will recollect it at the next ball—this, you know, can be done in a genteel way, and you will be 'all the go.' Return into the room, and either tread upon some gentleman's toes, or give him a slight touch with your elbow: which, if he be inclined to resent, tell him, 'pon lionour,' you did not observe him, or, if inclined to suffer it with impunity—' Get out of the way, fellow, d——n you.'

On your way home, after escorting your fair inamorata to her peaceful abode, make a few calls for the purpose of taking a little more stimulus with some particular friends, and then return home for the night to 'steep your senses in forgetfulness.'"

"A very amusing and useful account, truly," said Bob, as his Cousin closed his chapter of instructions How to Cut a Dash.

"It is, at least, a just and true delineation of living character."

"Not without a good portion of caricature," said Mincingait. "You are downright scurrilous, and ought not to be tolerated in civilized society. Sink me, if you are not quite a bore, and not fit company for a Gentleman. so I shall wish you a good morning."

Tom and Bob laughed heartily at this declaration of the Dashing Blade, and, wishing him a pleasant walk and a safe return, they separated.

By this time they had arrived at Somerset House: it was near three o'clock, and the Rooms exhibited a brilliant crowd of rank and fashion, which considerably enhanced the value of its other decorations.

"I have already," said Dashall, "given you a general description of this building, and shall therefore confine my present observations wholly to the establishment of the Royal Academy for the encouragement of the Fine Arts, for the cultivation of which London is now much and deservedly distinguished; and to the progressive improvement in which we are indebted to that Exhibition we have already witnessed. This Academy was opened by Royal Charter in 1768; and it consists of forty members, called Royal Academicians, twenty Associates, and six Associate Engravers. The first President was the justly celebrated Sir Joshua Reynolds; the second, the highly respected Benjamin West; and the present, is Sir Thomas Lawrence.

"The Academy possesses a fine collection of casts and models, from antique statues, &c. a School of colouring, from pictures of the best masters. Lectures are delivered by the stated Professors in their various branches, to the Students during the winter season; prize medals are given annually for the best academy figures and drawings of buildings; and gold medals for historical composition in painting, sculpture, and designs in Architecture, once in two years; which latter are presented to the successful Artists in full assembly, accompanied with a discourse from the President, calculated to stimulate perseverance and exertion. Students have at all times, (except during the regular vacations,) an opportunity of studying nature from well chosen models, and of drawing from the antique casts.

"This Exhibition is generally opened on the first of May. The number of works of art, consisting of paintings, sculptures, models, proof engravings and drawings, generally exhibited, are upwards of one thousand; and are usually visited by all the gaiety and fashion of the Metropolis, between the hours of two and five o'clock in the day. The rooms are elegant and spacious; and I consider it at all times a place where a shilling may be well spent, and an hour or two well enjoyed.

> "Some spend a life in classing grubs, and try,
> New methods to impale a butterfly;
> Or, bottled up in spirits, keep with care
> A crowd of reptiles—hideously rare;
> While others search the mouldering wrecks of time,
> And drag their stores from dust and rust and slime;
> Coins eat with canker, medals half defac'd,
> And broken tablets, never to be trac'd;
> Worm-eaten trinkets worn away of old,
> And broken pipkins form'd in antique mould;
> Huge limbless statues, busts of heads forgot,
> And paintings representing none knows what;
> Strange legends that to monstrous fables lead,
> And manuscripts that nobody can read;
> The shapeless forms from savage hands that sprung,
> And fragments of rude art, when Art was young.
> This precious lumber, labell'd, shelv'd, and cas'd,
> And with a title of Museum grac'd,
> Shews how a man may time and fortune waste,
> And die a mummy'd connoisseur of taste."

EXHIBITION SOMERSET HOUSE, Tom & Bob among the Connoiseurs.

On entering the rooms, Bob was bewildered with delight; the elegance of the company, the number and excellence of the paintings, were attractions so numerous and splendid, as to leave him no opportunity of decidedly fixing his attention. He was surrounded by all that could enchant the eye and enrapture the imagination. Moving groups of interesting females were parading the rooms with dashing partners at their elbows, pointing out the most beautiful paintings from the catalogues, giving the names of the artists, or describing the subjects. Seated on one of the benches was to be seen the tired Dandy, whose principal inducement to be present at this display of the Arts, was to exhibit his own pretty person, and attract a little of the public gaze by his preposterous habiliments and unmeaning countenance; to fasten upon the first person who came within the sound of his scarcely articulate voice with observing, "It is d——d hot, 'pon honour—can't stand it—very fatiguing—I wonder so many persons are let in at once—there's no such thing as seeing, I declare, where there is such a crowd: I must come again, that's the end of it." On another, was the full-dressed Elegante, with her bonnet in one hand, and her catalogue in the other, apparently intent upon examining the pictures before her, while, in fact, her grand aim was to discover whether she herself was observed. The lounging Blood, who had left his horses at the door, was bustling among the company with his quizzing-glass in his hand, determined, if possible, to have a peep at every female he met, caring as much for the Exhibition itself, as the generality of the visitors cared for him. The Connoisseur was placing his eye occasionally close to the paintings, or removing to short distances, right and left, to catch them in the most judicious lights, and making remarks on his catalogue with a pencil; and Mrs. Roundabout, from Leadenhall, who had brought her son Dicky to see the show, as she called it, declared it was the '*most finest* sight she ever seed, lifting up her hand and eyes at the same time as Dicky read over the list, and charmed her by reciting the various scraps of poetry inserted in the catalogue to elucidate the subjects. It was altogether a source of inexpressible delight and amusement. Tom, whose taste for the arts qualified him well for the office of guide upon such an occasion, directed the eye of his Cousin to the best and most masterly productions in the collection, and whose attention was more particularly drawn to the pictures (though occasionally devoted to the inspection of a set of well-formed features, or a delicately turned ancle,) was much pleased to find Bob so busy in enquiry and observation.

"We have here," said Tom, "a combination of the finest specimens in the art of painting laid open annually for public inspection. Music, Poetry, and Painting, have always been held in high estimation by those who make any pretensions to an improved mind and a refined taste. In this Exhibition the talents of the Artists in their various lines may be fairly estimated, and the two former may almost be said to give life to the latter, in which the three are combined. The Historian, the Poet, and the Philosopher, have their thoughts embodied by the Painter; and the tale so glowingly described in language by the one, is brought full before the eye by the other; while the Portrait-painter hands down, by the vivid touches of his pencil, the features and character of those who by their talents have deservedly signalized themselves in society. The face of nature is displayed in the landscape, and the force of imagination by the judicious selector of scenes from actual life. Hence painting is the fascinating region of enchantment. The pencil is a magic wand; it calls up to view the most extensive and variegated scenery calculated to wake the slumbering mind to thought.

> "— — To mark the mighty hand
> That, ever busy, wheels the silent spheres,
> Works in the secret deep; shoots steaming thence
> The fair profusion that o'erspreads the Spring;
> Flings from the sun direct the naming day;
> Feeds every creature; hurls the tempest forth;
> And as on earth this grateful change revolves.
> With transport touches all the springs of life."

"Upon my life!" cried Bob, "we seem to have no need of Sparkle now, for you are endeavouring to imitate him."

"Your observations maybe just, in part," replied Tom; "but I can assure you I have no inclination to continue in the same strain. At the same time, grave subjects, or subjects of the pencil and graver, are deserving of serious consideration, except where the latter are engaged in caricature."

"And that has its utility," said Bob.

"To be sure it has," continued Tom—"over the human mind, wit, humour and ridicule maintain authoritative influence. The ludicrous images which flit before the fancy, aided by eccentric combinations, awaken the risible powers, and throw the soul into irresistible tumults of laughter. Who can refrain from experiencing risible emotions when he beholds a lively representation of Don Quixote and Sancho Pança—Hudibras and his Ralpho—merry old Falstaff shaking his fat sides, gabbling with Mrs. Quickly, and other grotesque figures to be found in the vast variety of human character? To lash the vices and expose the follies of mankind, is the professed end of this species of painting.

> "*Satire has always shone among the rest;*
> *And is the boldest way, if not the best,*
> *To tell men freely of their foulest faults.*"

Objects well worthy of attention—like comedy—may degenerate, and become subservient to licentiousness and profligacy; yet the shafts of ridicule judiciously aimed, like a well-directed artillery, do much execution. With what becoming severity does the bold Caricature lay open to public censure the intrigues of subtle Politicians, the chicanery of corrupted Courts, and the flattery of cringing Parasites! Hence satirical books and prints, under temperate regulations, check the dissoluteness of the great. Hogarth's Harlot's and Rake's Progress have contributed to reform the different classes of society—nay, it has even been doubted by some, whether the Sermons of a Tillotson ever dissuaded so efficaciously from lust, cruelty, and intemperance, as the Prints of an Hogarth. Indeed it may with truth be observed, that the art of Painting is one of those innocent and delightful means of pleasure which Providence has kindly offered to brighten the prospects of life: under due restriction, and with proper direction, it may be rendered something more than an elegant mode of pleasing the eye and the imagination; it may become a very powerful auxiliary to virtue."

"I like your remarks very well," said Bob; "but there is no such thing as paying proper attention to them at present; besides, you are moralizing again."

"True," said Tom, "the subjects involuntarily lead me to moral conclusions—there is a fine picture—Nature blowing Bubbles for her Children, from the pencil of Hilton; in which is united the simplicity of art with allegory, the seriousness of moral instruction and satire with the charms of female and infantine beauty; the graces of form, action, colour and beauty of parts, with those of collective groups; and the propriety and beauty of——"

He was proceeding in this strain, when, turning suddenly as he supposed to Tallyho, he was not a little surprised and confused to find, instead of his Cousin, the beautiful and interesting Miss Mortimer, at his elbow, listening with close attention to his description.

"Miss Mortimer," continued he—which following immediately in connection with his last sentence, created a buz of laughter from Sparkle, Merrywell, and Mortimer, who were in conversation at a short distance, and considerably increased his confusion.

"Very gallant, indeed," said Miss Mortimer, "and truly edifying. These studies from nature appear to have peculiar charms for you, but I apprehend your observations were not meant for my ear."

"I was certainly not aware," continued he, "how much I was honoured; but perceiving the company you are in, I am not much astonished at the trick, and undoubtedly have a right to feel proud of the attentions that have been paid to my observations."

By this time the party was increased by the arrival of Col. B——, his daughter Maria, and Lady Lovelace, who, with Sparkle's opera glass in her hand, was alternately looking at the paintings, and gazing at the company. Sparkle, in the mean time, was assiduous in his attentions to Miss Mortimer, whose lively remarks and elegant person excited general admiration.

The first greetings of such an unexpected meeting were followed by an invitation on the part of the Colonel to Tom and Bob to dine with them at half past six.

Tallyho excused himself upon the score of a previous engagement; and a wink conveyed to Tom was instantly understood; he politely declined the honour upon the same ground, evidently perceiving there was more meant than said; and after a few more turns among the company, and a survey of the Pictures, during which they lost the company of young Mortimer and his friend Merry well, (at which the Ladies expressed themselves disappointed) they, with Sparkle, assisted the females into the Colonel's carriage, wished them a good morning, and took their way towards Temple Bar.

"I am at a loss," said Dashall, "to guess what you meant by a prior engagement; for my part, I confess I had engaged myself with you, and never felt a greater inclination for a ramble in my life."

"Then," said Bob, "I'll tell you—Merry well and Mortimer had determined to give the old Colonel and his company the slip; and I have engaged, provided you have no objection, to dine with them at the Globe in Fleet Street, at half past four. They are in high glee, ready and ripe for fun, determined to beat up the eastern quarters of the town."

"An excellent intention," continued Tom, "and exactly agreeable to my own inclinations—we'll meet them, and my life on't we shall have a merry evening. It is now four—we will take a walk through the temple, and then to dinner with what appetite we may—so come along. You have heard of the Temple, situated close to the Bar, which takes its name. It is principally occupied by Lawyers, and Law-officers, a useful and important body of men, whose lives are devoted to the study and practice of the law of the land, to keep peace and harmony among the individuals of society, though there are, unfortunately, too many pretenders to legal knowledge, who prey upon the ignorant and live by litigation{1}—such as persons who have

> 1 *In a recent meeting at the Egyptian Hall, a celebrated Irish Barrister is reported to have said, that 'blasphemy*

was the only trade that prospered.' The assertion, like many others in the same speech, was certainly a bold one, and one which the gentleman would have found some difficulty in establishing. If, however, the learned gentleman had substituted the word law for blasphemy, he would have been much nearer the truth.

Of all the evils with which this country is afflicted, that of an excessive passion for law is the greatest. The sum paid annually in taxes is nothing to that which is spent in litigation. Go into our courts of justice, and you will often see sixty or seventy lawyers at a time; follow them home, and you will find that they are residing in the fashionable parts of the town, and living in the most expensive manner. Look at the lists of the two houses of parliament, and you will find lawyers predominate in the House of Commons; and, in the upper house, more peers who owe their origin to the law, than have sprung from the army and navy united. There is scarcely a street of any respectability without an attorney, not to mention the numbers that are congregated in the inns of court. In London alone, we are told, there are nearly three thousand certificated attornies, and in the country they are numerous in proportion.

While on the subject of lawyers, we shall add a few unconnected anecdotes, which will exhibit the difference between times past and present.

In the Rolls of Parliament for the year 1445, there is a petition from two counties in England, stating that the number of attornies had lately increased from sixteen to twenty-four, whereby the peace of those counties had been greatly interrupted by suits. And it was prayed that it might be ordained, that there should only be six attornies for the county of Norfolk, the same number for Suffolk, and two for the city of Norwich.

The profits of the law have also increased in proportion. We now frequently hear of gentlemen at the bar making ten or fifteen thousand pounds a year by their practice; and a solicitor in one single suit, (the trial of Warren Hastings) is said to have gained no less than thirty-five thousand pounds! How different three centuries ago, when Roper, in his life of Sir Thomas More, informs us, that though he was an advocate of the greatest eminence, and in full business, yet he did not by his profession make above four hundred pounds per annum. There is, however, a common tradition on the other hand, that Sir Edward Coke's gains, at the latter end of this century, equalled those of a modern attorney general; and, by Lord Bacon's works, it appears that he made 6000L. per annum whilst in this office. Brownlow's profits, likewise, one of the prothonotaries during the reign of Queen Elizabeth, were 6000L. per annum; and he used to close the profits of the year with a laus deo; and when they happened to be extraordinary,—maxima laus deo.

There is no person, we believe, who is acquainted with the important duties of the Judges, or the laborious nature of their office, will think that they are too amply remunerated; and it is not a little remarkable, that when law and lawyers have increased so prodigiously, the number of the Judges is still the same. Fortescue, in the dedication of his work, De Laudibus Legum Anglise, to Prince Edward, says that the Judges were not accustomed to sit more than three hours in a day; that is, from eight o'clock in the morning until eleven; they passed the remainder of the day in studying the laws, and reading the Holy Scriptures.

Carte supposes, that the great reason for the lawyers pushing in shoals to become members of Parliament, arose from their desire to receive the wages then paid them by their constituents. By an act of the 5th of Henry IV. lawyers were excluded from Parliament, not from a contempt of the common law itself, but the professors of it, who, at this time, being auditors to men of property, received an annual stipend, pro connlio impenso et impendendo, and were treated as retainers. In Madox's Form. Anglican, there is a form of a retainer during his life, of John de Thorp, as counsel to the Earl of Westmoreland; and it appears by the Household Book of Algernon, fifth Earl of Northumberland, that, in the beginning of the reign of Henry the Eighth, there was, in that family, a regular establishment for two counsellors and their servants.

A proclamation was issued on the 6th of November, in the twentieth year of the reign of James I. in which the voters for members of Parliament are directed, "not to choose curious and wrangling lawyers, who may seek reputation by stirring needless questions."

A strong prejudice was at this time excited against lawyers. In Aleyn's Henry VIII. (London, 1638,) we have the following philippic against them:—

> *"A prating lawyer, (one of those which cloud*
> *That honour'd science,) did their conduct take;*
> *He talk'd all law, and the tumultuous crowd*
> *Thought it had been all gospel that he spake.*
> *At length, these fools their common error saw,*
> *A lawyer on their side, but not the law."*

Pride the drayman used to say, that it would never be well till the lawyers' gowns, like the Scottish colours, were hung up in Westminster Hall.

From Chaucer's character of the Temple Manciple, it would appear that the great preferment which advocates in this time chiefly aspired to, was to become steward to some great man: he says,—"

> *"Of masters he had mo than thryis ten,*
> *That were of law expert and curious,*
> *Of which there were a dozen in that house,*

Worthy to ben stuards of house and londe,
Of any lord that is in Englonde."

been employed as clerks to Pettifoggers, who obtain permission to sue in their names; and persons who know no more of law than what they have learned in Abbot's Park,{1} or on board the Fleet,{2} who assume the title of Law Agents or Accountants, and are admirably fitted for Agents in the Insolvent Debtor's Court under the Insolvent Act, to make out Schedules, &c. Being up to all the arts and manouvres practised with success for the liberation of themselves, they are well calculated to become tutors of others, though they generally take care to be well paid for it."

By this time they were entering the Temple. "This," continued Tom, "is an immense range of buildings, stretching from Fleet-street to the river, north and south; and from Lombard-street, Whitefriars, to Essex-street in the Strand, east and west.

"It takes its name from its being founded by the Knights Templars in England. The Templars were crusaders, who, about the year 1118, formed themselves into a military body at Jerusalem, and guarded the roads for the safety of pilgrims. In time the order became very powerful. The Templars in Fleet-street, in the thirteenth century, frequently entertained the King, the Pope's nuncio, foreign ambassadors, and other great personages.

"It is now divided into two societies of students, called the Inner and Middle Temple, and having the name of Inns of Court.

"These societies consist of Benchers, Barristers, Students, and Members. The government is vested in the Benchers. In term time they dine in the hall of the society, which is called keeping commons. To dine a fortnight in each term, is deemed keeping the term; and twelve of these terms qualify a student to be called to year of Henry the Sixth, when Sir Walter Beauchamp, as counsel, supported the claim of precedence of the Earl of Warwick, against the then Earl Marshal, at the bar of the House of Lords. Mr. Roger Hunt appeared in the same capacity for the Earl Marshal, and both advocates, in their exordium, made most humble protestations, entreating the lord against whom they were retained, not to take amiss what they should advance on the part of their own client.

Another point on which the lawyers of the present age differ from their ancestors, is in their prolixity. It was reserved for modern invention to make a trial for high treason last eight days, or to extend a speech to nine hours duration.

> 1 *Abbot's Park—The King's Bench.*

> 2 *On board the Fleet—The Fleet Prison.*

"These societies have the following officers and servants: a treasurer, sub-treasurer, steward, chief butler, three under-butlers, upper and under cook, a pannierman, a gardener, two porters, two wash-pots, and watchmen.

"The Benchers assume and exercise a power that can scarcely be reconciled to the reason of the thing. They examine students as to their proficiency in the knowledge of the law, and call candidates to the bar, or reject them at pleasure, and without appeal. It is pretty well known that students in some cases eat their way to the bar; in which there can be no great harm, because their clients will take the liberty afterwards of judging how far they have otherwise qualified themselves. But every man that eats in those societies should be called, or the rejection should be founded solely on his ignorance of the law, and should be subject to an appeal to a higher jurisdiction; otherwise the power of the Benchers may be exercised on private or party motives.

"The expence of going through the course of these Societies is not great. In the Inner Temple, a student pays on admission, for the fees of the society, 3L. 6s. 8d. which, with other customary charges, amounts to 4L 2s. A duty is also paid to the King, which is high. Terms may be kept for about 10s. per week, and, in fact, students may dine at a cheaper rate here than any where beside. The expences in the principal societies of like nature are something more.

"Their kitchens, and dinner-rooms, merit the inspection of strangers, and may be seen on applying to the porter, or cooks, without fee or introduction. Our time is short now, or we would take a peep; you must therefore content yourself with my description.

"The Temple is an irregular building. In Fleet-street are two entrances, one to the Inner, and the other to the Middle Temple. The latter has a front in the manner of Inigo Jones, of brick, ornamented with four large stone pilastres, of the Ionic order, with a pediment. It is too narrow, and being lofty, wants proportion. The passage to which it leads, although designed for carriages, is narrow, inconvenient, and mean.

"The garden of the Inner Temple is not only a most happy situation, but is laid out with great taste, and kept in perfect order. It is chiefly covered with green sward,, which is pleasing to the eye, especially in a city, and is most agreeable to walk on. It lies, as you perceive, along the river, is of great extent, and has a spacious gravel walk, or terrace, on the bank of the Thames. It forms a crowded promenade in summer, and at such times is an interesting spot.

"The Middle Temple has a garden, but much smaller,, and not so advantageously situated.

"The hall of the Middle Temple is a spacious and elegant room in its style. Many great feasts have been given in it in old times. It is well worth a visit.

"The Inner Temple hall is comparatively small, but is a fine room. It is ornamented with the portraits of several of the Judges. Before this hall is a broad paved terrace, forming an excellent promenade, when the gardens are not sufficiently dry.

"There are two good libraries belonging to these societies, open to students, and to others on application to the librarian, from ten in the morning till one, and in the afternoon from two till six.

"The Temple church belongs in common to the two societies. The Knights Templars built their church on this site, which was destroyed, and the present edifice was erected by the Knights Hospitallers. It is in the Norman style of architecture, and has three aisles, running east and west, and two cross aisles. At the western end is a spacious round tower, the inside of which forms an elegant and singular entrance into the church, from which it is not separated by close walls, but merely by arches. The whole edifice within has an uncommon and noble aspect. The roof of the church is supported by slight pillars of Sussex marble, and there are three windows at each side, adorned with small pillars of the same marble. The entire floor is of flags of black and white marble; the roof of the tower is supported with six pillars, having an upper and lower range of small arches, except on the eastern side, opening into the church: The length of the church is eighty-three feet; the breadth sixty; and the height thirty-four; the height of the inside of the tower is forty-eight feet, and its diameter on the floor fifty-one.

"In the porch or tower are the tombs of eleven Knights Templars; eight of them have the figures of armed knights on them, three of them being the tombs of so many Earls of Pembroke. The organ of this church is one of the finest in the world.

"The Temple church is open for divine service every day, at eleven o'clock in the morning, and at four in the afternoon. There are four entrances into the Temple, besides those in Fleet-street; and it is a thoroughfare during the day, but the gates are shut at night. The gardens are open to the public in summer. It is a place of much business and constant traffic, I assure you."

"I perceive it," said Bob, "by the number of persons passing and repassing, every one apparently animated and impelled by some business of importance."

"Yes, it is something like a steam-boiler, by which a considerable portion of the engines of the Law are kept in motion. They can alarm and allay according to the pockets of their customers, or the sagacity which they are able to discover in their heads. There are perhaps as many Quacks in this profession as in any other," continued Tom, as they regained Fleet-street; when, perceiving it was half past four o'clock by St. Dunstan's—"But we must now make the best of our way, or we may be cut out of the good things of this *Globe*."

"What are so many persons collected together here for?" enquired Bob.

"Merely to witness a little of ingenious machinery. Keep your eye on the two figures in the front of the church with clubs in their hands."

"I do," said Bob; "but there does not appear to me to be any thing very remarkable about them."

He scarcely uttered the words, when he observed that these figures struck their clubs upon the bells which hung between them to denote the time of day.

"These figures," said Tom, "and the circumstance of giving them motion every fifteen minutes by the movements of the clock, have attracted a great deal of notice, particularly among persons from the country, and at almost every quarter of an hour throughout the day they are honoured with spectators. The church itself is very ancient, and has been recently beautified. The *Bell thumpers,* whose abilities you have just had a specimen of, have been standing there ever since the year 1671."

"It is hard service," said Bob, "and they must certainly deserve a pension from Government more than many of the automatons who are now in the enjoyment of the national bounties."

"You are right enough," said a Translator of Soles,{1} who had overheard Bob's last remark, with a pair of old shoes under his arm; "and d— —n me if I would give a pair of *crazy crabshells*{2} without *vamp or whelt for the whole boiling of 'em*{3}-there is not one on 'em worth a bloody jemmy."{4}

Upon hearing this from the political Cobbler, a disturbed sort of shout was uttered by the surrounding spectators, who had rather increased than diminished in number, to hear the observations of the leathern-lung'd Orator; when Tom, giving his Cousin a significant pinch of the arm, impelled him forward, and left them to the enjoyment of their humour.

"Political observations are always bad in the street," said Tom; "it is a subject upon which scarcely any two persons agree distinctly-*Old Wax and Bristles* is about *three sheets in the wind,*{5} and no doubt there are enough to take advantage of any persons stopping at this time of the day."{6}

"What have we here?" said Bob, who observed a concourse of people surrounding the end of Fetter Lane.

"Only a couple more of striking figures," replied Tom, "almost as intelligent as those we have just seen."

> 1 Translator of Soles—A disciple of St. Crispin, alias a cobbler, who can botch up old shoes, so as to have the appearance of being almost new, and who is principally engaged in his laudable occupation by the second-hand shoe-sellers of Field Lane, Turn Stile, &c. for the purpose of turning an honest penny, i.e. to deceive poor purchasers.
>
> 2 Crab-shells—A cant term for shoes.
>
> 3 Whole boding of 'em—The whole kit of 'em, &c. means the whole party.
>
> 4 Bloody Jemmy—A cant term for a sheep's head.
>
> 5 Three sheets in the wind—A cant phrase intending to explain that a person is more than half drunk.
>
> 6 This was a hint well given by Dashall; for, in the present times, it is scarcely possible to be aware of the numerous depredations that are committed in the streets of the Metropolis in open day-light; and it is a well-known fact, that Fleet Street, being one of the leading thoroughfares, is at almost all times infested with loose characters of every description, from the well-dressed Sharpers, who hover round the entrances to billiard-tables to mark new comers, and give information to the pals in waiting, somewhere within call, and who are called Macers-to the wily Duffers or Buffers, willing to sell extraordinary bargains, and the Cly-faker, or Pickpocket.

Bob bustled forward, and looking down the lane, perceived two Watchmen, one on each side the street, bearing poles with black boards inscribed in white letters, "Beware of bad houses," and a lantern hanging to each.

"These," said Tom, "are not decoy ducks, but scare crows, at least they are intended for such; whether their appearance does not operate as much one way as it does the other, is, I believe, a matter of doubt."

"Beware of bad houses," said Bob—"I don't exactlY see the object."

"No, perhaps not," continued his Cousin; "but I will tell you: this is a method which the Churchwardens of parishes sometimes take of shaming the *pa-pa* or *fie fie* ladies from their residences, or at least of discovering their visitors; but I am half inclined to think, that nine times out of ten the contrary effect is produced; for these men who are stationed as warnings to avoid, are easily to be blinded by the gay and gallant youths, who have" an inclination to obtain an admission to the fair cyprians; besides which, if the first inhabitants are really induced to quit, the house is quickly occupied by similar game, and the circumstance of the burning out, as it is termed, serves as a direction-post to new visitors; so that no real good is eventually effected-Come, we had better move on—there is nothing more extraordinary here."

"This is Peele's Coffee House," continued he—"a house celebrated for its general good accommodations. Here, as well as at the Chapter Coffee House, in Paternoster Row, all the newspapers are kept filed annually, and may be referred to by application to the Waiters, at the very trifling expense of a cup of coffee or a glass of wine. The Monthly and Quarterly Reviews, and the provincial papers, are also kept for the accommodation of the customers, and constitute an extensive and valuable library; it is the frequent resort of Authors and Critics, who meet to pore over the news of the day, or search the records of past times."

"An excellent way of passing an hour," said Bob, "and a proof of the studied attention which is paid not only to the comforts and convenience of their customers, but also to their instruction."

"You are right," replied Tom; "in London every man has an opportunity of living according to his wishes and the powers of his pocket; he may dive, like Roderick Random, into a cellar, and fill his belly for four pence, or regale himself with the more exquisite delicacies of the London Tavern at a guinea; while the moderate tradesman can be supplied at a chop-house for a couple of shillings; and the mechanic by a call at the shop over the way at the corner of Water Lane,{1} may purchase his half pound of ham or beef, and retire to a public-house to eat it; where he obtains his pint of porter, and in turn has an opportunity of reading the *Morning Advertiser*, the *Times*, or the *Chronicle*. Up this court is a well-known house, the sign of the Old Cheshire Cheese; it has long been established as a chop-house, and provides daily for a considerable number of persons; but similar accommodations are to be found in almost every street in London. Then again, there are cook-shops of a still humbler description where a dinner may be procured at a still more moderate price; so that in this great Metropolis there is accommodation for all ranks and descriptions of persons, who may be served according to the delicacy of their appetites and the state of their finances.

"A Chop-house is productive of all the pleasures in life; it is a combination of the most agreeable and satisfactory amusements: indeed, those who have never had an opportunity of experiencing the true happiness therein to be found, have a large portion of delight and gratification to discover: the heart, the mind and the constitution are to be mended upon crossing its threshold; and description must fall short in its efforts to pourtray its enlivening and invigorating influence; it is, in a word, a little world within itself, absolutely a universe in miniature, possessing a system peculiar to itself, of planets and satellites,

> 1 This allusion was made by the Hon. Tom Dashall to the Shop of Mr. Cantis, who was formerly in the employ of Mr. Epps, and whose appearance in opposition to him at Temple Bar a few years back excited a great deal of public attention, and had the effect of reducing the prices of their ham and beef. Mr. Epps generally has from fourteen to twenty Shops, and sometimes more, situated in different parts of the Metropolis, and there is scarcely a street in London where

there is not some similar place of accommodation; but Mr. Epps is the most extensive purveyor for the public appetite. At these shops, families may be supplied with any quantity, from an ounce to a pound, of hot boiled beef and ham at moderate prices; while the poor are regaled with a plate of cuttings at a penny or twopence each.

and fixed stars and revolutions, and its motions are annual, rotatory and diurnal, in all its extensive diversity of waiters, cooks, saucepans, fryingpans, gridirons, salamanders, stoves and smoke-jacks; so that if you wish to know true and uncloying delight, you are now acquainted with where it is to be found. Not all the sages of the ancient or the modern world ever dreamed of a theory half so exquisite, or calculated to afford man a treat so truly delicious.

"Within the doors of a Chop-house are to be found food for both body and soul-mortal and mental appetites-feasting for corporeal cravings and cravings intellectual-nourishment at once for the faculties both of mind and body: there, in fact, the brain may be invigorated, and the mind fed with good things; while the palate is satisfied by devouring a mutton chop, a veal cutlet, or a beef steak; and huge draughts of wisdom may be imbibed while drinking a bottle of soda or a pint of humble porter.

"In this delightful place of amusement and convenience, there is provender for philosophers or fools, stoics or epicureans; contemplation for genius of all denominations; and it embraces every species of science and of art, (having an especial eye to the important art of Cookery;) it encompasses all that is worthy of the sublimest faculties and capacities of the soul; it is the resort of all that is truly good and glorious on earth, the needy and the noble, the wealthy and the wise. Its high estimation is universally acknowledged; it has the suffrage of the whole world, so much so, that at all times and in all seasons its supremacy is admitted and its influence recognized. The name, the very name alone, is sufficient to excite all that is pleasant to our senses (five or seven, how many soever there may be.) A Chop-house! at that word what delightful prospects are presented to the mind's eye-what a clashing of knives and forks and plates and pewter pots, and rushing of footsteps and murmurings of expectant hosts enter into our delighted ears—what gay scenes of varied beauty, and many natured viands and viscous soups, tarts, puddings and pies, rise before our visual nerves-what fragrant perfumes, sweet scented odours, and grateful gales of delicate dainties stream into our olfactory perceptions,

> ". . . Like the sweet south
> Upon a bank-a hank of violets, giving
> And taking odour."

Its powers are as vast as wonderful and goodly, and extend over all animal and animated nature, biped and quadruped, the earth, the air, and all that therein is. By its high decree, the beast may no longer bask in the noon tide of its nature, the birds must forsake their pure ether, and the piscatory dwellers in the vasty deep may spread no more their finny sails towards their caves of coral. The fruits, the herbs, and the other upgrowings of the habitable world, and all created things, by one wave of the mighty wand are brought together into this their common tomb. It is creative also of the lordliest independence of spirit. It excites the best passions of the heart—it calls into action every kind and generous feeling of our nature—it begets fraternal affection and unanimity and cordiality of soul, and excellent neighbourhood among men-it will correct antipodes, for its ministerial effects will produce a Radical advantage-its component parts go down with the world, and are well digested."

"Your description," said Bob, "has already had the effect of awakening appetite, and I feel almost as hungry as if I were just returning from a fox-chace."

"Then," continued the Hon. Tom Dashall, "it is not only admirable as a whole, its constituent and individual beauties are as provocative of respect as the mass is of our veneration. From among its innumerable excellencies—I will mention one which deserves to be held in recollection and kept in our contemplation-what is more delightful than a fine beef-steak?-spite of Lexicographers, there is something of harmony even in its name, it seems to be the key-note of our best constructed organs, (organs differing from all others, only because they have no stops,) it circles all that is full, rich and sonorous—I do not mean in its articulated enunciation, but in its internal acceptation—there—there we feel all its strength and diapas, or force and quantity."

"Admirable arrangements, indeed," said Bob. "True," continued Tom; "and all of them comparatively comfortable, according to their gradations ana the rank or circumstances of their customers. The Tavern furnishes wines, &c.; the Pot-house, porter, ale, and liquors suitable to the high or low. The sturdy Porter, sweating beneath his load, may here refresh himself with heavy wet;{l} the Dustman, or the Chimney-sweep, may sluice

1 Heavy wet-A well-known appellation for beer, porter, or ale.

Am ivory{1} with the Elixir of Life, now fashionably termed Daffy's."

"Daffy's," said Tallyho-"that is somewhat new to me, I don't recollect hearing it before?"

"Daffy's Elixir," replied Dashall, "was a celebrated quack medicine, formerly sold by a celebrated Doctor of that name, and recommended by him as a cure for all diseases incident to the human frame. This Gin, Old Tom, and Blue Ruin, are equally recommended in the present day; in consequence of which, some of the learned gentlemen of the sporting' world have given it the title of Daffy's, though this excellent beverage is known by many other names.

"For instance, the Lady of refined sentiments and delicate nerves, feels the necessity of a little cordial refreshment, to brighten the one and enliven the other, and therefore takes it on the sly, under the polite appellation of white wine. The knowing Kids and dashing Swells are for a drap of blue ruin, to keep all things in good twig. The Laundress, who disdains to be termed a dry washer,—dearly loves a dollop {2} of Old Tom, because, while she is up to her elbows in suds, and surrounded with steam, she thinks a drap of the old gemman (having no pretensions to a young one) would comfort and strengthen her inside, and consequently swallows the inspiring dram. The travelling Gat-gut Scraper, and the Hurdy-Grinder, think there is music in the sound of max, and can toss off their kevartern to any tune in good time. The Painter considers it desirable to produce effect by mingling his dead white with a little sky blue. The Donkey driver and the Fish-fag are bang-up for a flash of lightning, to illumine their ideas. The Cyprian, whose marchings and counter marchings in search of custom are productive of extreme fatigue, may, in some degree, be said to owe her existence to Jockey; at least she considers him a dear boy, and deserving her best attentions, so long as she has any power. The Link-boys, the Mud-larks, and the Watermen, who hang round public-house doors to feed horses, &c. club up their brads for a kevartern of Stark-naked in three outs. The Sempstress and Straw Bonnet-maker are for a yard of White Tape; and

> 1 Sluice the ivory—Is originally derived from sluicery, and means washing, or passing over the teeth.
>
> 2 Dollop—Is a large or good quantity of any thing: the whole dollop means the whole quantity.

the Swell Covies and Out and Outers, find nothing so refreshing after a night's spree, when the victualling-office is out of order, as a little Fuller's-earth, or a dose of Daffy's; so that it may fairly be presumed it is a universal beverage—nay, so much so, that a certain gentleman of City notoriety, though he has not yet obtained a seat in St. Stephen's Chapel, with an ingenuity equal to that of the *Bug-destroyer to the King*,{1} has latterly decorated his house, not a hundred miles from Cripplegate, with the words Wine and Brandy Merchant to her Majesty, in large letters, from which circumstance his depository of the refreshing and invigorating articles of life has obtained the appellation of the Queen's Gin Shop."

Bob laughed heartily at his Cousin's interpretation of Daffy's.

While Tom humm'd, in an under tone, the fag end of a song, by way of conclusion—

> "Why, there's old Mother Jones, of St. Thomas's Street,
> If a jovial companion she chances to meet,
> Away to the gin-shop they fly for some max,
> And for it they'd pawn the last smock from their backs;

For the juniper berry,
It makes their hearts merry,
With a hey down, down deny,
Geneva's the liquor of life."

By this time they were at the Globe; upon entering which, they were greeted by Mortimer and Merry well, who had arrived before them; and dinner being served almost immediately, they were as quickly seated at the table, to partake of an excellent repast.

1 It is a well-known fact, that a person of the name of
Tiffin announced himself to the world under this very
seductive title, which, doubtless, had the effect of
bringing him considerable custom from the loyal subjects of
his great patron.

CHAPTER XVII

"Here fashion and folly still go hand in hand,
With the Blades of the East, and the Bucks of the Strand;
The Bloods of the Park, and paraders so gay,
Who are lounging in Bond Street the most of the day—
Who are foremost in all that is formed for delight,
At greeking, or wenching, or drinking all night;
For London is circled with unceasing joys:
Then, East, West, North and South, let us hunt them, my boys."

THE entrance to the house had attracted Tallyho's admiration as they proceeded; but the taste and elegance of the Coffee-room, fitted up with brilliant chandeliers, and presenting amidst a blaze of splendour every comfort and accommodation for its visitors, struck him with surprise; in which however he was not suffered to remain long, for Merrywell and Mortimer had laid their plans with some degree of depth and determination to carry into execution the proposed ramble of the evening, and had ordered a private room for the party; besides which, they had invited a friend to join them, who was introduced to Tom and Bob, under the title of Frank Harry. Frank Harry was a humorous sort of fellow, who could tell a tough story, sing a merry song, and was up to snuff, though he frequently got snuffy, singing,

"The bottle's the Sun of our table,

His beams are rosy wine:
We, planets never are able

Without his beams to shine.
Let mirth and glee abound,

You'll soon grow bright

With borrow'd light,
And shine as he goes round."

He was also a bit of a dabbler at Poetry, a writer of Songs, Epigrams, Epitaphs, &c.; and having been a long resident in the East, was thought to be a very useful guide on such an excursion, and proved himself a very pleasant sort of companion: he had a dawning pleasantry in his countenance, eradiated by an eye of vivacity, which seemed to indicate there was nothing which gave him so much gratification as a mirth-moving jest.

"What spirits were his, what wit and what whim, Now cracking a joke, and now breaking a limb."

Give him but food for laughter, and he would almost consider himself furnished with food and raiment. There was however a pedantic manner with him at times; an affectation of the clerical in his dress, which, upon the whole, did not appear to be of the newest fashion, or improved by wearing; yet he would not barter one wakeful jest for a hundred sleepy sermons, or one laugh for a thousand sighs. If he ever sigh'd at all, it was because he had been serious where he might have laugh'd; if he had ever wept, it was because mankind had not laugh'd more and mourn'd less. He appeared almost to be made up of contrarieties, turning at times the most serious subjects into ridicule, and moralizing upon the most ludicrous occurrences of life, never failing to conclude his observations with some quaint or witty sentiment to excite risibility; seeming at the same time to say,

> "How I love to laugh;
> Never was a weeper;
> Care's a silly calf,
> Joy's my casket keeper."

During dinner time he kept the table in a roar of laughter, by declaring it was his opinion there was a kind of puppyism in pigs that they should wear tails—calling a great coat, a spencer folio edition with tail-pieces—Hercules, a man-midwife in a small way of business, because he had but twelve labours—assured them he had seen a woman that morning who had swallowed an almanac, which he explained by adding, that her features were so carbuncled, that the red lettered days were visible on her face—that Horace ran away from the battle of Philippi, merely to prove that he was no lame poet—he described Critics as the door-porters to the Temple of Fame, whose business was to see that no persons slipped in with holes in their stockings, or paste buckles for diamond ones, but was much in doubt whether they always performed their duty honestly—he called the Sun the *Yellow-hair'd Laddie* —and the Prince of Darkness, the *Black Prince*—ask'd what was the difference between a sigh-heaver and a coal-heaver; but obtaining no answer, I will tell you, said he—The coal-heaver has a load at his back, which he can carry—but a sigh-heaver has one at his heart, which he can not carry. He had a whimsical knack of quoting old proverbs, and instead of saying, the Cobbler should stick to his last, he conceived it ought to be, the Cobbler should stick to his wax, because he thought that the more practicable—What is bred in the bone, said he, will not come out with the skewer; and justified his alteration by asserting it must be plain enough to the fat-headed comprehensions of those epicurean persons who have the magpie-propensity of prying into marrow-bones.

Dashall having remarked, in the course of conversation, that *necessity has no law.*

He declared he was sorry for it—it was surely a pity, considering the number of learned Clerks she might give employ to if she had—her Chancellor (continued he) would have no sinecure of it, I judge: hearing the petitions of her poor, broken-fortuned and bankrupt, subjects would take up all his terms, though every term were a year, and every year a term. Thus he united humour with seriousness, and seriousness with humour, to the infinite amusement of those around him.

Merrywell, who was well acquainted with, and knew his humour, took every opportunity of what is called drawing him out, and encouraging his propensity to punning, a species of wit at which he was particularly happy, for puns fell as thick from him as leaves from autumn bowers; and he further entertained them with an account of the intention he had some short time back of petitioning for the office of pun-purveyor to his late Majesty; but that before he could write the last line—"And your petitioner will ever pun" it was bestowed upon a Yeoman of the Guard. Still, however, said he, I have an idea of opening business as a pun-wright in general to his Majesty's subjects, for the sale and diffusion of all that is valuable in that small ware of wit, and intend to advertise—Puns upon all subjects, wholesale, retail, and for exportation. N B. 1. An allowance will be made to Captains and Gentlemen going to the East and West Indies—Hooks, Peakes, Pococks,{1} supplied on

1 Well-known dramatic authors.

moderate terms—worn out sentiments and *clap-traps* will be taken in exchange. N B. 2. May be had in a large quantity, in a great deal box, price five acts of sterling comedy per packet, or in small quantities, in court-plaster sized boxes, price one melodrama and an interlude per box. N B. 3. The genuine puns are sealed with a true Munden grin—all others are counterfeits—Long live Apollo, &c. &c.

The cloth being removed, the wine was introduced, and

"*As wine whets the wit, improves its native force,
And gives a pleasant flavour to discourse,*"

Frank Harry became more lively at each glass—"Egad!" said he, "my intention of petitioning to be the king's punster, puts me in mind of a story."

"Can't you sing it?" enquired Merrywell.

"The pipes want clearing out first," was the reply, "and that is a sign I can't sing at present; but signal as it may appear, and I see some telegraphic motions are exchanging, my intention is to shew to you all the doubtful interpretation of signs in general."

"Let's have it then," said Tom; "but, Mr. Chairman, I remember an old Song which concludes with this sentiment—

"*Tis hell upon earth to be wanting of wine.*"

"The bottle is out, we must replenish."

The hint was no sooner given, than the defect was remedied; and after another glass,

"King James VI. on his arrival in London, (said he) was waited on by a Spanish Ambassador, a man of some erudition, but who had strangely incorporated with his learning, a whimsical notion, that every country ought to have a school, in which a certain order of men should be taught to interpret signs; and that the most expert in this department ought to be dignified with the title of Professor of Signs. If this plan were adopted, he contended, that most of the difficulties arising from the ambiguity of language, and the imperfect acquaintance which people of one nation had with the tongue of another, would be done away. Signs, he argued, arose from the dictates of nature; and, as they were the same in every country, there could be no danger of their being misunderstood. Full of this project, the Ambassador was lamenting one day before the King, that the nations of Europe were wholly destitute of this grand desideratum; and he strongly recommended the establishment of a college founded upon the simple principles he had suggested. The king, either to humour this Quixotic foible, or to gratify his own ambition at the expense of truth, observed, in reply, 'Why, Sir, I have a Professor of Signs in one of the northernmost colleges in my dominions; but the distance is, perhaps, six hundred miles, so that it will be impracticable for you to have an interview with him.' Pleased with this unexpected information, the Ambassador exclaimed—'If it had been six hundred leagues, I would go to see him; and I am determined to set out in the course of three or four days.' The King, who now perceived that he had committed himself, endeavoured to divert him from his purpose; but, finding this impossible, he immediately caused letters to be written to the college, stating the case as it really stood, and desired the Professors to get rid of the Ambassador in the best manner they were able, without exposing their Sovereign. Disconcerted at this strange and unexpected message, the Professors scarcely knew how to proceed. They, however, at length, thought to put off their august visitant, by saying, that the Professor of Signs was not at home, and that his return would be very uncertain. Having thus fabricated the story, they made preparations to receive the illustrious stranger, who, keeping his word, in due time reached their abode. On his arrival, being introduced with becoming solemnity, he began to enquire, who among them had the honour of being Professor of Signs? He was told in reply, that neither of them had that exalted honour; but the learned gentleman, after whom he enquired, was gone into the Highlands, that they conceived his stay would be considerable; but that no one among them could even conjecture the period of his return. 'I will wait his coming,' replied the Ambassador, 'if it be twelve months.'

"Finding him thus determined, and fearing, from the journey he had already undertaken that he might be as good as his word, the learned Professors had recourse to another stratagem. To this they found themselves driven, by the apprehension that they must entertain him as long as he chose to tarry; and in case he should unfortunately weary out their patience, the whole affair must terminate in a discovery of the fraud. They knew a Butcher, who had been in the habit of serving the colleges occasionally with meat. This man, they thought, with a little instruction might serve their purpose; he was, however, blind with one eye, but he had much drollery and impudence about him, and very well knew how to conduct any farce to which his abilities were competent.

"On sending for Geordy, (for that was the butcher's name) they communicated to him the tale, and instructing him in the part he was to act, he readily undertook to become Professor of Signs, especially as he was not to speak one word in the Ambassador's presence, on any pretence whatever. Having made these arrangements, it was formally announced to the Ambassador, that the Professor would be in town in the course of a few days, when he might expect a silent interview. Pleased with this information, the learned foreigner thought that he would put his abilities at once to the test, by introducing into his dumb language some subject that should be at once difficult, interesting, and important. When the day of interview arrived, Geordy was cleaned up, decorated with a large bushy wig, and covered over with a singular gown, in every respect becoming his station. He was then seated in a chair of state, in one of their large rooms, while the Ambassador and the trembling Professors waited in an adjoining apartment.

"It was at length announced, that the learned Professor of Signs was ready to receive his Excellency, who, on entering the room, was struck with astonishment at his venerable and dignified appearance. As none of the Professors would presume to enter, to witness the interview, under a pretence of delicacy, (but, in reality, for fear that their presence might have some effect upon the risible muscles of Geordy's countenance) they waited with inconceivable anxiety, the result of this strange adventure, upon which depended their own credit, that of the King, and, in some degree, the honour of the nation.

"As this was an interview of signs, the Ambassador began with Geordy, by holding up one of his fingers; Geordy replied, by holding up two. The Ambassador then held up three; Geordy answered, by clenching his fist, and looking sternly. The Ambassador then took an orange from his pocket, and held it up; Geordy returned the compliment, by taking from his pocket a piece of a barley cake, which he exhibited in a similar manner. The ambassador, satisfied with the vast attainments of the learned Professor, then bowed before him with profound reverence, and retired. On rejoining the agitated Professors, they fearfully began to enquire what his Excellency thought of their learned brother? 'He is a perfect miracle,' replied the Ambassador, 'his worth is not to be purchased by the wealth of half the Indies.' 'May we presume to descend to particulars?' returned the Professors, who now began to think themselves somewhat out of danger. 'Gentlemen,' said the Ambassador, 'when I first entered into his presence, I held up one finger, to denote that there is one God. He then held up two, signifying that the Father should not be divided from the Son. I then held up three, intimating, that I believed in Father, Son, and Holy Ghost. He then clenched his fist, and, looking sternly at me, signified, that these three are one; and that he would defy me, either to separate them, or to make additions. I then took out an orange from my pocket, and held it up, to show the goodness of God, and to signify that he gives to his creatures not only the necessaries, but even the luxuries of life. Then, to my utter astonishment, this wonderful man took from his pocket a piece of bread, thus assuring me, that this was the staff of life, and was to be preferred to all the luxuries in the world. Being thus satisfied with his proficiency and great attainments in this science, I silently withdrew, to reflect upon what I had witnessed.' "Diverted with the success of their stratagem, the Professors continued to entertain their visitor, until he thought prudent to withdraw. No sooner had he retired, than the opportunity was seized to learn from Geordy, in what manner he had proceeded to give the Ambassador such wonderful satisfaction; they being at a loss to conceive how he could have caught his ideas with so much promptitude, and have replied to them with proportionable readiness. But, that one story might not borrow any features from the other, they concealed from Geordy all they had learned from the Ambassador; and desiring him to begin with his relation, he proceeded in the following manner:—'When the rascal came into the room, after gazing at me a little, what do you think, gentlemen, that he did? He held up one finger, as much as to say, you have only one eye. I then held up two, to let him know that my one eye was as good as both of his. He then held up three, as much as to say, we have only three eyes between us. This was so provoking, that I bent my fist at the scoundrel, and had it not been for your sakes, I should certainly have risen from the chair, pulled off my wig and gown, and taught him how to insult a man, because he had the misfortune to lose one eye. The impudence of the fellow, however, did not stop here; for he then pulled out an orange from his pocket, and held it up, as much as to say, Your poor beggarly country cannot produce this. I then pulled out a piece of good cake, and held it up, giving him to understand, that I did not care a farthing for his trash. Neither do I; and I only regret, that I did not thrash the scoundrel's hide, that he might remember how he insulted me, and abused my country.' We may learn from hence, that if there are not two ways of telling a story, there are at least two ways of understanding Signs, and also of interpreting them."

This story, which was told with considerable effect by their merry companion, alternately called forth loud bursts of laughter, induced profound silence, and particularly interested and delighted young Mortimer and Tallyho; while Merrywell kept the glass in circulation, insisting on *no day-light*{1} nor *heel-taps,*{2} and the lads began to feel themselves all in high feather. Time was passing in fearless enjoyment, and Frank Harry being called on by Merrywell for a song, declared he had no objection to tip 'em a rum chant, provided it was agreed that it should go round.

This proposal was instantly acceded to, a promise made that he should not be at a loss for a good *coal-box*;{3} and after a little more rosin, without which, he said, he could not pitch the key-note, he sung the following

    SONG.

Oh, London! dear London! magnanimous City,
Say where is thy likeness again to be found?

Here pleasures abundant, delightful and pretty,
All whisk us and frisk us in magical round;

1 No day-light—That is to leave no space in the glass; or, in other words, to take a bumper.

2 Heel-taps—To leave no wine at the bottom.

3 Coal-box—A very common corruption of chorus.

Here we have all that in life can merry be,
Looking and laughing with friends Hob and Nob,

More frolic and fun than there's bloom on the cherry-tree,
While we can muster a Sovereign Bob.

(Spoken)—Yes, yes, London is the large world in a small compass: it contains all the comforts and pleasures of human life—"Aye aye, (says a Bumpkin to his more accomplished Kinsman) Ye mun brag o' yer Lunnun fare; if smoak, smother, mud, and makeshift be the comforts and pleasures, gie me free air, health and a cottage."—Ha, ha, ha, Hark at the just-catch'd Johnny Rata, (says a bang-up Lad in a lily-shallow and upper toggery) where the devil did you come from? who let you loose upon society? d————e, you ought to be coop'd up at Exeter 'Change among the wild beasts, the Kangaroos and Catabaws, and shewn as the eighth wonder of the world! Shew 'em in! Shew 'em in! stir him up with a long pole; the like never seen before; here's the head of an owl with the tail of an ass—all alive, alive O! D———me how the fellow stares; what a marvellous piece of a mop-stick without thrums.—"By gum (says the Bumpkin) you looks more like an ape, and Ise a great mind to gie thee a douse o' the chops."—You'd soon find yourself chop-fallen there, my nabs, (replies his antagonist)—you are not up to the gammon—you must go to College and learn to sing

Oh, London! dear London! &c.

Here the streets are so gay, and the features so smiling,

With uproar and noise, bustle, bother, and gig;
The lasses (dear creatures!) each sorrow beguiling,

The Duke and the Dustman, the Peer and the Prig;
Here is his Lordship from gay Piccadilly,

There an ould Clothesman from Rosemary Lane;
Here is a Dandy in search of a filly,

And there is a Blood, ripe for milling a pane.

(Spoken)—All higgledy-piggledy, pigs in the straw—Lawyers, Lapidaries, Lamplighters, and Lap-dogs—Men-milliners, Money-lenders, and Fancy Millers, Mouse-trap Mongers, and Matchmen, in one eternal round of variety! Paradise is a pail of cold water in comparison with its unparalleled pleasures—and the wishing cap of Fortunatus could not produce a greater abundance of delight—Cat's Meat—Dog's Meat—Here they are all four a penny, hot hot hot, smoking hot, piping hot hot Chelsea Buns—Clothes sale, clothes—Sweep, sweep—while a poor bare-footed Ballad Singer with a hoarse discordant voice at intervals chimes in with

"*They led me like a pilgrim thro' the labyrinth of care,*
You may know me by my sign and the robe that I wear;"

so that the concatenation of sounds mingling all at once into one undistinguished concert of harmony, induces me to add mine to the number, by singing—

Oh, London! dear London! &c.

The Butcher, whose tray meets the dough of the Baker,

And bundles his bread-basket out of his hand;
The Exquisite Lad, and the dingy Flue Faker,{1}

And coaches to go that are all on the stand:
Here you may see the lean sons of Parnassus,

The puffing Perfumer, so spruce and so neat;
While Ladies, who flock to the fam'd Bonassus,

Are boning our hearts as we walk thro' the street.

(Spoken)—"In gude truth," says a brawney Scotchman, "I'se ne'er see'd sic bonny work in a' my liefe—there's nae walking up the streets without being knock'd doon, and nae walking doon the streets without being tripp'd up."—"Blood-an-oons, (says an Irishman) don't be after blowing away your breath in blarney, my dear, when you'll want it presently to cool your barley broth."—"By a leaf," cries a Porter with a chest of drawers on his knot, and, passing between them, capsizes both at once, then makes the best of his way on a jog-trot, humming to himself, Ally Croaker, or Hey diddle Ho diddle de; and leaving the fallen heroes to console themselves with broken heads, while some officious friends are carefully placing them on their legs, and genteelly easing their pockets of the possibles; after which they toddle off at leisure, to sing

Oh, London! dear London! &c.

Then for buildings so various, ah, who would conceive it,

Unless up to London they'd certainly been?
'Tis a truth, I aver, tho' you'd scarcely believe it,

That at the Court end not a Court's to be seen;
Then for grandeur or style, pray where is the nation

For fashion or folly can equal our own?
Or fit out a fête like the grand Coronation?

I defy the whole world, there is certainly none.

(Spoken)—Talk of sights and sounds—is not there the Parliament House, the King's Palace, and the Regent's Bomb—The Horse-guards, the Body-guards, and the Black-guards—The Black-legs, and the Bluestockings—The Horn-blower, and the Flying Pie-man—The Indian Juggler—Punch and Judy—(imitating the well-known Showman)—The young and the old, the grave and the gay—The modest Maid and the willing Cyprian—The Theatres—The Fives Court and the Court of Chancery—

1 Flue Faker—A cant term for Chimney-sweep.

The Giants in Guildhall, to be seen by great and small, and,
what's more than all, the Coronation Ball—

Mirth, fun, frolic, and frivolity,
To please the folks of quality:

For all that can please the eye, the ear, the taste, the touch,
the smell,

Whether bang-up in life, unfriended or undone,

No place has such charms as the gay town of London.

Oh, Loudon! dear London! &c.

The quaint peculiarities of the Singer gave indescribable interest to this song, as he altered his voice to give effect to the various cries of the inhabitants, and it was knock'd down with three times three rounds of applause; when Merrywell, being named for the next, sung, accompanied with Dashall and Frank Harry, the following

GLEE.

"Wine, bring me wine—come fill the sparkling glass,
Brisk let the bottle circulate;
Name, quickly name each one his fav'rite lass,
Drive from your brows the clouds of fate:

Fill the sparkling bumper high,
Let us drain the bottom dry.

Come, thou grape-encircled Boy!
From thy blissful seats above,
Crown the present hours with joy,
Bring me wine and bring me love:
Fill the sparkling bumper high,
Let us drain the bottom dry.

Bacchus, o'er my yielding lip
Spread the produce of thy vine;
Love, thy arrows gently dip,
Temp'ring them with generous wine:
Fill the sparkling bumper high,
Let us drain the bottom dry."

In the mean time, the enemy of life was making rapid strides upon them unheeded, till Dashall reminded Merrywell of their intended visit to the East; and that as he expected a large portion of amusement in that quarter, he proposed a move.

They were by this time all well primed—ripe for a rumpus—bang-up for a lark or spree, any where, any how, or with any body; they therefore took leave of their present scene of gaiety.

CHAPTER XVIII

"Wand'ring with listless gait and spirits gay,
They Eastward next pursued their jocund way;
With story, joke, smart repartee and pun,
Their business pleasure, and their object fun."

IT was a fine moonlight evening, and upon leaving the Globe, they again found themselves in the hurry, bustle, and noise of the world. The glare of the gas-lights, and the rattling of coaches, carts and vehicles of various-descriptions, mingled with

"The busy hum of men,"

attracted the attention of their eyes and ears, while the exhilarating juice of the bottle had given a circulation to the blood which enlivened imagination and invigorated fancy. Bob conceived himself in Elysium, and Frank Harry was as frisky as a kitten. The first object that arrested their progress was the house of Mr. Hone, whose political Parodies, and whose trials on their account, have given him so much celebrity. His window at the moment exhibited his recent satirical publication entitled a Slap at Slop and the Bridge Street Gang.{1}

> 1 *The great wit and humour displayed in this publication have deservedly entitled it to rank high among the jeu desprit productions of this lively age—to describe it were impossible—to enjoy it must be to possess it; but for the information of such of our readers as are remote from the Metropolis, it may perhaps be necessary to give something like a key of explanation to its title. A certain learned Gentleman, formerly the Editor of the Times, said now to be the Conductor of the New Times, who has by his writings rendered himself obnoxious to a numerous class of readers, has been long known by the title of Dr. Slop; in his publication, denominated the mock Times, and the Slop Pail, he has been strenuous in his endeavours to support and*

uphold a Society said to mis-call themselves The Constitutional Society, but now denominated The Bridge Street Gang; and the publication alluded to, contains humorous and satirical parodies, and sketches of the usual contents of his Slop Pail; with a Life of the learned Doctor, and an account of the origin of the Gang.

"Here," said Tom, "we are introduced at once into a fine field of observation. The inhabitant of this house defended himself in three different trials for the publication of alleged impious, profane, and scandalous libels on the Catechism, the Litany, and the Creed of St. Athanasius, with a boldness, intrepidity, and perseverance, almost unparalleled, as they followed in immediate succession, without even an allowance of time for bodily rest or mental refreshment."

"Yes," continued Frank Harry, "and gained a verdict on each occasion, notwithstanding the combined efforts of men in power, and those whose constant practice in our Courts of Law, with learning and information at their fingers ends, rendered his enemies fearful antagonists."

"It was a noble struggle," said Tallyho; "I remember we had accounts of it in the country, and we did not fail to express our opinions by subscriptions to remunerate the dauntless defender of the rights and privileges of the British subject."

"*Tip us your flipper*"{1} said Harry—-"then I see you are a true bit of the bull breed—one of us, as I may say. Well, now you see the spot of earth he inhabits—zounds, man, in his shop you will find amusement for a month—see here is The House that Jack Built—there is the Queen's Matrimonial Ladder, do you mark?—What think you of these qualifications for a Gentleman?

"In love, and in liquor, and o'ertoppled with debt, With women, with wine, and with duns on the fret."

There you have the Nondescript—

>"A something, a nothing—what none understand,
>Be-mitred, be-crowned, but without heart or hand;
>There's Jack in the Green too, and Noodles, alas!

"Who doodle John Bull of gold, silver, and brass.

"Come," said Dashall, "you must cut your story short; I know if you begin to preach, we shall have a sermon as long as from here to South America, so allons;" and with this impelling his Cousin forward, they

> 1 Tip us your Flipper—your mawley—your daddle, or your thieving hook; are terms made use of as occasions may suit the company in which they are introduced, to signify a desire to shake hands.

approached towards Saint Paul's, chiefly occupied in conversation on the great merit displayed in the excellent designs of Mr. Cruikshank, which embellish the work they had just been viewing; nor did they discover any thing further worthy of notice, till Bob's ears were suddenly attracted by a noise somewhat like that of a rattle, and turning sharply round to discover from whence it came, was amused with the sight of several small busts of great men, apparently dancing to the music of a weaver's shuttle.{1}

"What the devil do you call this?" said he—"is it an exhibition of wax-work, or a model academy?"

"Neither," replied Dashall; "this is no other than the shop of a well-known dealer in stockings and nightcaps, who takes this ingenious mode of making himself popular, and informing the passengers that

> "Here you may be served with all patterns and sizes,
> From the foot to the head, at moderate prices;"

with woolens for winter, and cottons for summer—Let us move on, for there generally is a crowd at the door, and there is little doubt but he profits by those who are induced to gaze, as most people do in London, if they can but entrap attention. Romanis is one of those gentlemen who has contrived to make some noise in the world by puffing advertisements, and the circulation of poetical handbills. He formerly kept a very small shop for the sale of hosiery nearly opposite the East-India House, where he supplied the Sailors after receiving their pay for a long voyage, as well as their Doxies, with the articles in which he deals, by obtaining permission to style himself "Hosier to the Rt. Hon. East India Company." Since which, finding his trade increase and his purse extended, he has extended his patriotic views of clothing the whole population of London by opening shops in various parts, and has at almost all times two or three depositories for

1 Romanis, the eccentric Hosier, generally places a loom near the door of his shops decorated with small busts; some of which being attached to the upper movements of the machinery, and grotesquely attired in patchwork and feathers, bend backwards and forwards with the motion of the works, apparently to salute the spectators, and present to the idea persons dancing; while every passing of the shuttle produces a noise which may be assimilated to that of the Rattlesnake, accompanied with sounds something like those of a dancing-master beating time to his scholars. his stock. At this moment, besides what we have just seen, there is one in Gracechurch Street, and another in Shoreditch, where the passengers are constantly assailed by a little boy, who stands at the door with some bills in his hand, vociferating—Cheap, cheap."

"Then," said Bob, "wherever he resides I suppose may really be called Cheapside?"

"With quite as much propriety," continued Ton, "as the place we are now in; for, as the Irishman says in his song,

> "At a place called Cheapside they sell every thing dear."

During this conversation, Mortimer, Merrywell, and Harry were amusing themselves by occasionally addressing the numerous Ladies who were passing, and taking a peep at the shops—giggling with girls, or admiring the taste and elegance displayed in the sale of fashionable and useful articles—justled and impeded every now and then by the throng. Approaching Bow Church, they made a dead stop for a moment.

"What a beautiful steeple!" exclaimed Bob; "I should, though no architect, prefer this to any I have yet seen in London."

"Your remark," replied Dashall, "does credit to your taste; it is considered the finest in the Metropolis. St. Paul's displays the grand effort of Sir Christopher Wren; but there are many other fine specimens of his genius to be seen in the City. His Latin Epitaph in St. Paul's may be translated thus: 'If you seek his monument, look around you;' and we may say of this steeple, 'If you wish a pillar to his fame, look up.' The interior of the little church, Walbrook,{1} (St. Stephen's) is likewise considered a

> 1 *This church is perhaps unrivalled, for the beauty of the architecture of its interior. For harmony of proportion, grace, airiness, variety, and elegance, it is not to be surpassed. It is a small church, built in the form of a cross. The roof is supported by Corinthian columns, so disposed as to raise an idea of grandeur, which the dimensions of the structure do not seem to promise. Over the centre, at which the principal aisles cross, is a dome divided into compartments, the roof being partitioned in a similar manner, and the whole finely decorated. The effect of this build-ing is inexpressibly delightful; the eye at one glance embracing a plan full and distinct, and afterwards are seen a greater number of parts than the spectator was prepared to expect. It is known and admired on the Continent, as a master-piece of art. Over the altar is a fine painting of the martyrdom of St. Stephen, by West.*

chef d'ouvre of the same artist, and serves to display the versatility of his genius."

Instead however of looking up, Bob was looking over the way, where a number of people, collected round a bookseller's window, had attracted his attention.

"Apropos," cried Dashall,—"The Temple of Apollo—we should have overlook'd a fine subject, but for your remark—yonder is Tegg's Evening Book Auction, let us cross and see what's going on. He is a fellow of 'infinite mirth and good humour,' and many an evening have I passed at his Auction, better amused than by a farce at the Theatre."

They now attempted to cross, but the intervening crowd of carriages, three or four deep, and in a line as far as the eye could reach, for the present opposed an obstacle.

"If I could think of it," said Sparkle, "I'd give you the Ode on his Birth-day, which I once saw in MS.—it is the *jeu d'esprit* of a very clever young Poet, and who perhaps one of these days may be better known; but poets, like anatomical subjects, are worth but little till dead."

"And for this reason, I suppose," says Tom, "their friends and patrons are anxious they should rather be starved than die a natural death."

"Oh! now I have it—let us remain in the Church-yard a few minutes, while the carriages pass, and you shall hear it."

> *"Ye hackney-coaches, and ye carts,*
> *That oft so well perform your parts*
> *For those who choose to ride,*
> *Now louder let your music grow—*
> *Your heated axles fiery glow—*
> *Whether you travel quick or slow-*
> *In Cheapside.*
>
> *For know, "ye ragged rascals all,"*
> *(As H——- would in his pulpit bawl*
> *With cheeks extended wide)*
> *Know, as you pass the crowded way,*
> *This is the happy natal day*
> *Of Him whose books demand your stay*
> *In Cheapside.*
>
> *'Twas on the bright propitious morn*
> *When the facetious Tegcy was born,*
> *Of mirth and fun the pride,*
> *That Nature said "good Fortune follow,*
> *Bear him thro' life o'er hill and hollow,*
> *Give him the Temple of Apollo*
> *In Cheapside."*

Then, O ye sons of Literature!
Shew your regard for Mother Nature,
Nor let her be denied:
Hail! hail the man whose happy birth
May tell the world of mental worth;
They'll find the best books on the earth
In Cheapside.

"Good!" exclaimed Bob; "but we will now endeavour to make our way across, and take a peep at the subject of the Ode."

Finding the auction had not yet commenced, Sparkle proposed adjourning to the Burton Coffee House in the adjacent passage, taking a nip of ale by way of refreshment and exhilaration, and returning in half an hour. This proposition was cordially agreed to by all, except Tallyho, whose attention was engrossed by a large collection of Caricatures which lay exposed in a portfolio on the table beneath the rostrum. The irresistible broad humour of the subjects had taken fast hold of his risible muscles, and in turning them over one after the other, he found it difficult to part with such a rich fund of humour, and still more so to stifle the violent emotion it excited. At length, clapping his hands to his sides, he gave full vent to the impulse in a horse-laugh from a pair of truly Stentorian lungs, and was by main force dragged out by his companions.

While seated in the comfortable enjoyment of their nips of ale, Sparkle, with his usual vivacity, began an elucidation of the subjects they had just left. "The collection of Caricatures," said he, "which is considered the largest in London, are mostly from the pencil of that self-taught artist, the late George Woodward, and display not only a genuine and original style of humour in the design, but a corresponding and appropriate character in the dialogue, or speeches connected with the figures. Like his contemporary in another branch of the art, George Morland, he possessed all the eccentricity and thoughtless improvidence so common and frequently so fatal to genius; and had not his good fortune led him towards Bow Church, he must have suffered severe privations, and perhaps eventually have perished of want. Here, he always found a ready market, and a liberal price for his productions, however rude or hasty the sketch, or whatever might be the subject of them."

"As to books," continued he, "all ages, classes, and appetites, may be here suited. The superficial dabbler in, and pretender to every thing, will find collections, selections, beauties, flowers, gems, &c. The man of real knowledge may here purchase the elements, theory, and practice of every art and science, in all the various forms and dimensions, from a single volume, to the Encyclopedia at large. The dandy may meet with plenty of pretty little foolscap volumes, delightfully hot-pressed, and exquisitely embellished; the contents of which will neither fatigue by the quantity, nor require the laborious effort of thought to comprehend. The jolly *bon-vivant* and Bacchanal will find abundance of the latest songs, toasts, and sentiments; and the Would-be-Wit will meet with Joe Miller in such an endless variety of new dresses, shapes, and sizes, that he may fancy he possesses all the collected wit of ages brought down to the present moment. The young Clerical will find sermons adapted to every local circumstance, every rank and situation in society, and may furnish himself with a complete stock in trade of sound orthodox divinity; while the City Epicure may store himself with a complete library on the arts of confectionary, cookery, &c, from Apicius, to the "Glutton's Almanack." The Demagogue may furnish himself with flaming patriotic speeches, ready cut and dried, which he has only to learn by heart against the next Political Dinner, and if he should not 'let the cat out,' by omitting to substitute the name of Londonderry for Cæsar, he may pass off for a second Brutus, and establish an equal claim to oratory with Burke, Pitt, and Fox. The——"

"Auction will be over," interrupted Bob, "before you get half through your descriptive Catalogue of the Books, so finish your nip, and let us be off."

They entered, and found the Orator hard at it, knocking down with all the energy of a Crib, and the sprightly wit of a Sheridan. Puns, bon mots, and repartees, flew about like crackers.

"The next lot, Gentlemen, is the Picture of London,—impossible to possess a more useful book—impossible to say what trouble and expence may be avoided by the possession of this little volume.

When your Country Cousins pay you a visit, what a bore, what an expence, to be day after day leading them about—taking them up the Monument—down the Adelphi—round St. Paul's—across the Parks, through the new Streets—along the Strand, or over the Docks, the whole of which may be avoided at the expence of a few shillings. You have only to clap into their pocket in the morning this invaluable little article, turn them out for the day, and, if by good luck they should not fall into the hands of sharpers and swindlers, your dear Coz will return safe home at night, with his head full of wonders, and his pockets empty of cash!"

"The d——l," whispered Bob, "he seems to know me, and what scent we are upon."

"Aye," replied his Cousin, "he not only knows you, but he knows that some of your cash will soon be in his pockets, and has therefore made a dead set at you."

"Next lot, Gentlemen, is a work to which my last observation bore some allusion; should your friends, as I then observed, fortunately escape the snares and dangers laid by sharpers and swindlers to entrap the unwary, you may, perchance, see them safe after their day's ramble; but should—aye, Gentlemen, there's the rub—should they be caught by the numerous traps and snares laid for the Johnny Raw and Greenhorn in this great and wicked metropolis, God knows what may become of them. Now, Gentlemen, we have a remedy for every disease—here is the London Spy or Stranger's Guide through the Metropolis; here all the arts, frauds, delusions, &c. are exposed, and—Tom, give that Gentleman change for his half crown, and deliver Lot 3.—As I was before observing, Gentlemen—Turn out that young rascal who is making such a noise, cracking nuts, that I can't hear the bidding.—Gentlemen, as I before observed, if you will do me the favour of bidding me—"

"Good night, Sir," cried a younker, who had just exploded a detonating cracker, and was making his escape through the crowd.

"The next lot, gentlemen, is the Young Man's best Companion, and as your humble Servant is the author, he begs to decline any panegyric—modesty forbids it—but leaves it entirely with you to appreciate its merits—two shillings—two and six—three shillings—three and six—four, going for four—for you, Sir, at four."

"Me, Sir! Lord bless you, I never opened my mouth!"

"Perfectly aware of that, Sir, it was quite unnecessary—I could read your intention in your eye—and observed the muscle of the mouth, call'd by anatomists the

zygomaticus major, in the act of moving. I should have been dull not to have noticed it—and rude not to have saved you the trouble of speaking: Tom, deliver the Gentleman the lot, and take four shillings."

"Well, Sir, I certainly feel flattered with your acute and polite attention, and can do no less than profit by it—so hand up the lot—cheap enough, God knows."

"And pray," said Dashall to his Cousin as they quitted, "what do you intend doing with all your purchases? why it will require a waggon to remove them."

"O, I shall send the whole down to Belville Hall: our friends there will be furnished with a rare stock of entertainment during the long winter evenings, and no present I could offer would be half so acceptable."

"Well," remarked Mortimer, "you bid away bravely, and frequently in your eagerness advanced on yourself: at some sales you would have paid dearly for this; but here no advantage was taken, the mistake was explained, and the bidding declined in the most fair and honourable manner. I have often made considerable purchases, and never yet had reason to repent, which is saying much; for if I inadvertently bid for, and had a lot knocked down to me, which I afterwards disliked, I always found an acquaintance glad to take it off my hands at the cost, and in several instances have sold or exchanged to considerable advantage. One thing I am sorry we overlooked: a paper entitled, "Seven Reasons," is generally distributed during the Sale, and more cogent reasons I assure you could not be assigned, both for purchasing and reading in general, had the seven wise men of Greece drawn them up. You may at any time procure a copy, and it will furnish you with an apology for the manner in which you have spent your time and money, for at least one hour, during your abode in London."

Please, Sir, to buy a ha'porth of matches, said a poor, squalid little child without a shoe to her foot, who was running by the side of Bob—it's the last ha'porth, Sir, and I must sell them before I go home.

This address was uttered in so piteous a tone, that it could not well be passed unheeded.

"Why," said Tallyho, "as well as Bibles and Schools for all, London seems to have a match for every body."

"Forty a penny, Spring-radishes," said a lusty bawling fellow as he passed, in a voice so loud and strong, as to form a complete contrast to the little ragged Petitioner, 'who held out her handful of matches continuing her solicitations. Bob put his hand in his pocket, and gave her sixpence.

"We shall never get on at this rate," said Tom; "and I find I must again advise you not to believe all you hear and see. These little ragged run-abouts are taught by their Parents a species of imposition or deception of which you are not aware, and while perhaps you congratulate yourself with 'the thought of having done a good act, you are only contributing to the idleness and dissipation of a set of hardened beings, who are laughing at your credulity; and I suspect this is a case in point—do you see that woman on the opposite side of the way, and the child giving her the money?"

"I do," said Tallyho; "that, I suppose, is her mother?"

"Probably," continued Dashall—"now mark what will follow."

They stopped a short time, and observed that the Child very soon disposed of her last bunch of matches, as she had termed them, gave the money to the woman, who supplied her in return with another last bunch, to be disposed of in a similar way.

"Is it possible?" said Bob.

"Not only possible, but you see it is actual; it is not however the only species of deceit practised with success in London in a similar way; indeed the trade of match-making has latterly been a good one among those who have been willing to engage in it. Many persons of decent appearance, representing themselves to be tradesmen and mechanics out of employ, have placed themselves at the corners of our streets, and canvassed the outskirts of the town, with green bags, carrying matches, which, by telling a pityful tale, they induce housekeepers and others, who commiserate their situation, to purchase; and, in the evening, are able to figure away in silk stockings with the produce of their labours. There is one man, well known in town, who makes a very good livelihood by bawling in a stentorian voice,

> "Whow whow, will you buy my good matches,
> Whow whow, will you buy my good matches,
> Buy my good matches, come buy 'em of me."

He is usually dressed in something like an old military great coat, wears spectacles, and walks with a stick."

"And is a match for any body, match him who can,", cried Frank Harry; "But, bless your heart, that's nothing to another set of gentry, who have infested our streets in clean apparel, with a broom in their hands, holding at the same time a hat to receive the contributions of the passengers, whose benevolent donations are drawn forth without inquiry by the appearance of the applicant."

"It must," said Tallyho, "arise from the distresses of the times."

"There may be something in that," said Tom; "but in many instances it has arisen from the depravity of the times—to work upon the well-known benevolent feelings of John Bull; for those who ambulate the public streets of this overgrown and still increasing Metropolis and its principal avenues, are continually pestered with impudent impostors, of both sexes, soliciting charity—men and women, young and old, who get more by their pretended distresses in one day than many industrious and painstaking tradesmen or mechanics do in a week. All the miseries, all the pains of life, with tears that ought to be their honest and invariable signals, can be and are counterfeited—

limbs, which enjoy the fair proportion of nature, are distorted, to work upon humanity—fits are feigned and wounds manufactured—rags, and other appearances of the most squalid and abject poverty, are assumed, as the best engines of deceit, to procure riches to the idle and debaucheries to the infamous. Ideal objects of commiseration are undoubtedly to be met with, though rarely to be found. It requires a being hackneyed in the ways of men, or having at least some knowledge of the town, to be able to discriminate the party deserving of benevolence; but

> *"A begging they will go will go,*
> *And a begging they will go."*

The chief cause assigned by some for the innumerable classes of mendicants that infest our streets, is a sort of innate principle of independence and love of liberty. However, it must be apparent that they do not like to work, and to beg they are not ashamed; they are, with very few exceptions, lazy and impudent. And then what is collected from the humane but deluded passengers is of course expended at their festivals in Broad Street, St. Giles's, or some other equally elegant and appropriate part of the town, to which we shall at an early period pay a visit. Their impudence is intolerable; for, if refused a contribution, they frequently follow up the denial with the vilest execrations.

> *"To make the wretched blest,*
> *Private charity is best."*

"The common beggar spurns at your laws; indeed many of their arts are so difficult of detection, that they are enabled to escape the vigilance of the police, and with impunity insult those who do not comply with their wishes, seeming almost to say,

> *"While I am a beggar I will rail,*
> *And say there is no sin but to be rich;*
> *And being rich, my virtue then shall be,*
> *To say there is no vice but beggary."*

"Begging has become so much a sort of trade, that parents have been known to give their daughters or sons the begging of certain streets in the metropolis as marriage portions; and some years ago some scoundrels were in the practice of visiting the outskirts of the town in sailors' dresses, pretending to be dumb, and producing written papers stating that their tongues had been cut out by the Algerines, by which means they excited compassion, and were enabled to live well."

"No doubt it is a good trade," said Merry well, "and I expected we should have been made better acquainted with its real advantages by Capt. Barclay, of walking and sporting celebrity, who, it was said, had laid a wager of 1000L. that he would walk from London to Edinburgh in the assumed character of a beggar, pay all his expences of living well on the road, and save out of his gains fifty pounds."

"True," said Tom, "but according to the best account that can be obtained, that report is without foundation. The establishment, however, of the Mendicity Society{1}

> 1 The frauds and impositions practised upon the public are so numerous, that volumes might be filled by detailing the arts that have been and are resorted to by mendicants; and the records of the Society alluded to would furnish instances that might almost stagger the belief of the most credulous. The life of the infamous Vaux exhibits numerous instances in which he obtained money under genteel professions, by going about with a petition soliciting the aid and assistance of the charitable and humane; and therefore are continually cheats who go from door to door collecting money for distressed families, or for charitable purposes. It is, however, a subject so abundant, and increasing by every day's observation, that we shall for the present dismiss it, as there will be other opportunities in the course of the work for going more copiously into it.

is calculated to discover much on this subject, and has already brought to light many instances of depravity and deception, well deserving the serious consideration of the public."

As they approached the end of the Poultry,—"This," said Dashall, "is the heart of the first commercial city in the known world. On the right is the Mansion House, the residence of the Lord Mayor for the time being."

The moon had by this time almost withdrawn her cheering beams, and there was every appearance, from the gathering clouds, of a shower of rain.

"It is rather a heavy looking building, from what I can see at present," replied Tallyho.

"Egad!" said Tom, "the appearance of every thing at this moment is gloomy, let us cross."

With this, they crossed the road to Debatt's the Pastry Cook's Shop.

"Zounds!" said Tom, casting his eye upon the clock, "it is after ten; I begin to suspect we must alter our course, and defer a view of the east to a more favourable opportunity, and particularly as we are likely to have an accompaniment of water."

"Never mind," said Merrywell, "we can very soon be in very comfortable quarters; besides, a rattler is always to be had or a comfortable lodging to be procured with an obliging bed-fellow—don't you begin to croak before there is any occasion for it—what has time to do with us?"

"Aye aye," said Frank Harry, "don't be after damping us before we get wet; this is the land of plenty, and there is no fear of being lost—come along."

"On the opposite side," said Tom, addressing his Cousin, "is the Bank of England; it is a building of large extent and immense business; you can now only discern its exterior by the light of the lamps; it is however a place to which we must pay a visit, and take a complete survey upon some future occasion. In the front is the Royal Exchange, the daily resort of the Merchants and Traders of the Metropolis, to transact their various business."

"Come," said Merry well, "I find we are all upon the right scent—Frank Harry has promised to introduce us to a house of well known resort in this neighbourhood—we will shelter ourselves under the staple commodity of the country—for the Woolsack and the Woolpack, I apprehend, are synonymous."

"Well thought of, indeed," said Dashall; "it is a house where you may at all times be certain of good accommodation and respectable society—besides, I have some acquaintance there of long standing, and may probably meet with them; so have with you, my boys. The Woolpack in Cornhill," continued he, addressing himself more particularly to Tallyho, "is a house that has been long established, and deservedly celebrated for its general accommodations, partaking as it does of the triple qualifications of tavern, chop-house, and public-house. Below stairs is a commodious room for smoking parties, and is the constant resort of foreigners,{1}

> 1 There is an anecdote related, which strongly induces a belief that Christian VII. while in London, visited this house in company with his dissipated companion, Count Holcke, which, as it led to the dismissal of Holcke, and the promotion of the afterwards unfortunate Struensée, and is perhaps not very generally known, we shall give here.
>
> One day while in London, Count Holcke and Christian vir. went to a well-known public-house not far from the Bank, which was much frequented by Dutch and Swedish Captains: Here they listened to the conversation of the company, which, as might be expected, was full of expressions of admiration and astonishment at the splendid festivities daily given in honour of Christian VII. Count Holcke, who spoke German in its purity, asked an old Captain what he thought of his King, and if he were not proud of the honours paid to him by the English?—"I think (said the old man dryly) that with such counsellors as Count Holcke, if he escapes destruction it will be a miracle."—' Do you know Count Holcke, my friend, (said the disguised courtier) as you speak of him thus familiarly?'—"Only by report (replied the Dane); but every person in Copenhagen pities the young Queen, attributing the coolness which the King shewed towards her, ere he set out on his voyage, to the malicious advice of Holcke." The confusion of this minion may be

easier conceived than described; whilst the King, giving the Skipper a handful of ducats, bade him speak the truth and shame the devil. As soon, however, as the King spoke in Danish, the Skipper knew him, and looking at him with love and reverence, said in a low, subdued tone of voice—" Forgive me, Sire, but I cannot forbear my tears to see you exposed to the temptations of this extensive and wicked Metropolis, under the pilotage of the most dissolute nobleman of Denmark." Upon which he retired, bowing profoundly to his Sovereign, and casting at Count Holcke a look full of defiance and reproach. Holcke's embarrassment was considerably increased by this, and he was visibly hurt, seeing the King in a manner countenanced the rudeness of the Skipper.

This King, who it should seem determined to see Real Life in London, mingled in all societies, participating in their gaieties and follies, and by practices alike injurious to body and soul, abandoned himself to destructive habits, whose rapid progress within a couple of years left nothing but a shattered and debilitated hulk afflicted in the morning of life with all the imbecility of body and mind incidental to extreme old age.

who are particularly partial to the brown stout, which they can obtain there in higher perfection than in any other house in London. Brokers and others, whose business calls them to the Royal Exchange, are also pretty constant visitors, to meet captains and traders—dispose of different articles of merchandise—engage shipping and bind bargains—it is a sort of under Exchange, where business and refreshment go hand in hand with the news of the day, and the clamour of the moment; beside which, the respectable tradesmen of the neighbourhood meet in an evening to drive dull care away, and converse on promiscuous subjects; it is generally a mixed company, but, being intimately connected with our object of seeing *Real Life in London*, deserves a visit. On the first floor is a good room for dining, where sometimes eighty persons in a day are provided with that necessary meal in a genteel style, and at a moderate price—besides other rooms for private parties. Above these is perhaps one of the handsomest rooms in London, of its size, capable of dining from eighty to a hundred persons. But you will now partake of its accommodations, and mingle with some of its company."

By this time they had passed the Royal Exchange, and Tom was enlarging upon the new erections lately completed; when all at once,

"Hallo," said Bob, "what is become of our party?" "All right," replied his Cousin; "they have given us the slip without slipping from us—I know their movements to a moment, we shall very soon be with them—this way—this way," said he, drawing Bob into the narrow passage which leads to the back of St. Peter's Church, Cornhill—"this is the track we must follow."

Tallyho followed in silence till they entered the house, and were greeted by the Landlord at the bar with a bow of welcome; passing quickly to the right, they were saluted with immoderate volumes of smoke, conveying to their olfactory nerves the refreshing fumes of tobacco, and almost taking from them the power of sight, except to observe a bright flame burning in the middle of the room. Tom darted forward, and knowing his way well, was quickly seated by the side of Merrywell, Mortimer, and Harry; while Tallyho was seen by those who were invisible to him', groping his way in the same direction, amidst the laughter of the company, occasionally interlarded with scraps which caught his ear from a gentleman who was at the moment reading some of the comments from the columns of the Courier, in which he made frequent pauses and observations.

"Why, you can't see yourself for smoke," said one; "D———n it how hard you tread," said another. And then a line from the Reader came as follows—"The worthy Alderman fought his battles o'er again—Ha, ha, ha—Who comes here 1 upon my word, Sir, I thought you had lost your way, and tumbled into the Woolpack instead of the Skin-market.—' It is a friend of mine, Sir.'—That's a good joke, upon my soul; not arrived yet, why St. Martin's bells have been ringing all day; perhaps he is only half-seas over—Don't tell me, I know better than that—D———n that paper, it ought to be burnt by—The fish are all poison'd by the Gas-light Company—Six weeks imprisonment for stealing two dogs!—Hides and bark—How's sugars to-day?—Stocks down indeed—Yes, Sir, and bread up—Presto, be gone—What d'ye think of that now, eh?—Gammon, nothing but gammon—On table at four o'clock ready dressed and—Well done, my boy, that's prime."

These sentences were uttered from different parts of the room in almost as great a variety of voices as there must have been subjects of conversation; but as they fell upon the ear of Tallyho without connection, he almost fancied himself transported to the tower of Babel amidst the confusion of tongues.

"Beg pardon," said Tallyho, who by this time had gained a seat by his Cousin, and was gasping like a turtle for air—"I am not used to this travelling in the dark; but I shall be able to see presently."

"See," said Frank Harry, "who the devil wants to see more than their friends around them? and here we are *at home to a peg*."

"I shall have finished in two minutes, Gentlemen," said the Reader,{1} cocking up a red nose, that shone with resplendent lustre between his spectacles, and then continuing to read on, only listened to by a few of those around him, while a sort of general buz of conversation was indistinctly heard from all quarters.

They were quickly supplied with grog and segars, and Bob, finding himself a little better able to make use of his eyes, was throwing his glances to every part of the room, in order to take a view of the company: and while Tom was congratulated by those who knew him at the *Round Table*—Merrywell and Harry were in close conversation with Mortimer.

At a distant part of the room, one could perceive boxes containing small parties of convivials, smoking and drinking, every one seeming to have some business of importance to claim occasional attention, or engaged in,

"The loud laugh that speaks the vacant mind." In one corner was a stout swarthy-looking man, with large whiskers and of ferocious appearance, amusing those around him with conjuring tricks, to their great satisfaction and delight; nearly opposite the Reader of the Courier, sat an elderly Gentleman{2} with grey hair, who heard

1 To those who are in the habit of visiting this room in an evening, the character alluded to here will immediately be familiar. He is a gentleman well known in the neighbourhood as an Auctioneer, and he has a peculiar manner of reading with strong emphasis certain passages, at the end of which he makes long pauses, laughs with inward satisfaction, and not infrequently infuses a degree of pleasantry in others. The Courier is his favourite paper, and if drawn into an argument, he is not to be easily subdued.

"At arguing too each person own'd his skill,
For e'en tho' vanquish'd, he can argue still."

2 This gentleman, who is also well known in the room, where he generally smokes his pipe of an evening, is plain and blunt, but affable and communicative in his manners—bold in his assertions, and has proved himself courageous in defending them—asthmatic, and by some termed phlegmatic; but an intelligent and agreeable companion, unless thwarted in his argument—a stanch friend to the late Queen and the constitution of his country, with a desire to have the Constitution, the whole Constitution, and nothing but the Constitution.

what was passing, but said nothing; he however puffed away large quantities of smoke at every pause of the Reader, and occasionally grinn'd at the contents of the paper, from which. Tallyho readily concluded that he was in direct political opposition to its sentiments.

The acquisition of new company was not lost upon to those who were seated at the round table, and it was not long before the Hon. Tom Dashall was informed that they hoped to have the honour of his Cousin's name as a member; nor were they backward in conveying a similar hint to Frank Harry, who immediately proposed his two friends, Mortimer and Merry well; an example which was followed by Tom's proposing his Cousin.

ROAD TO A FIGHT. Plate I.

Such respectable introductions could not fail to meet the approbation of the Gentlemen present,—consequently they were unanimously elected Knights of the Round Table, which was almost as quickly supplied by the Waiter with a capacious bowl of punch, and the healths of the newmade Members drank with three times three; when their attention was suddenly drawn to a distant part of the room, where a sprightly Stripling, who was seated by the swarthy Conjuror before mentioned, was singing the following Song:

>   THE JOYS OF A MILL,
>   OR
>   A TODDLE TO A FIGHT.

"Now's the time for milling, boys, since all the world's agog for it,
Away to Copthorne, Moulsey Hurst, or Slipperton they go;
Or grave or gay, they post away, nay pawn their very togs for it,
And determined to be up to all, go down to see the show:
Giddy pated, hearts elated, cash and courage all to view it,
Ev'ry one to learn a bit, and tell his neighbours how to do it;
E'en little Sprites in lily whites, are fibbing it and rushing it,
Your dashing Swells from Bagnigge Wells, are flooring it and flushing it:

Oh! 'tis a sight so gay and so uproarious,
That all the world is up in arms, and ready for a fight.
The roads are so clogg'd, that they beggar all description now,
With lads and lasses, prim'd and grogg'd for bang-up fun and glee;
Here's carts and gigs, and knowing prigs all ready to kick up a row,
And ev'ry one is anxious to obtain a place to see;
Here's a noted sprig of life, who sports his tits and clumner too,
And there is Cribb and Gully, Belcher, Oliver, and H armer too,
With Shelton, Bitton, Turner, Hales, and all the lads to go it well,
Who now and then, to please the Fancy, make opponents know it well:

Oh! 'tis a sight, &c.
But now the fight's begun, and the Combatants are setting to,

Silence is aloud proclaim'd by voices base and shrill;
Facing, stopping—-fibbing, dropping—claret tapping—betting too—
Reeling, rapping—physic napping, all to grace the mill;
Losing, winning—horse-laugh, grinning—mind you do not glance away,
Or somebody may mill your mug, and of your nob in Chancery;
For nobs and bobs, and empty fobs, the like no tongue could ever tell—
See, here's the heavy-handed Gas, and there's the mighty Nonpareil:

Oh! 'tis a sight, &c.
Thus milling is the fashion grown, and ev'ry one a closer is;
With lessons from the lads of fist to turn out quite the thing;
True science may be learn'd where'er the fam'd Mendoza is,
And gallantry and bottom too from Scroggins, Martin, Spring;
For sparring now is all the rage in town, and country places too,
And collar-bones and claret-mugs are often seen at races too;
While counter-hits, and give and take, as long as strength can hold her seat,
Afford the best amusement in a bit of pugilistic treat:

Oh! 'tis a sight, &c.

While this song was singing, universal silence prevailed, but an uproar of approbation followed, which lasted for some minutes, with a general call of encore, which however soon subsided, and the company was again restored to their former state of conversation; each party appearing distinct, indulged in such observations and remarks as were most suitable or agreeable to themselves.

Bob was highly pleased with this description of a milling match; and as the Singer was sitting near the person who had excited a considerable portion of his attention at intervals in watching his tricks, in some of which great ingenuity was displayed, he asked his Cousin if he knew him.

"Know him," replied Tom, "to be sure I do; that is no other than Bitton, a well-known pugilist, who frequently exhibits at the Fives-Court; he is a Jew, and employs his time in giving lessons."

"Zounds!" said Mortimer, "he seems to have studied the art of Legerdemain as well as the science of Milling."

"He is an old customer here," said a little Gentleman at the opposite side of the table, drawing from his pocket a box of segars{1}—"Now, Sir," continued he, "if you wish for a treat," addressing himself to Tallyho, "allow me to select you one—there, Sir, is asgar like a nosegay—I had it from a friend of mine who only arrived yesterday—you don't often meet with such, I assure you."

Bob accepted the offer, and was in the act of lighting it, when Bitton approached toward their end of the room with some cards in his hand, from which Bob began to anticipate he would shew some tricks upon them.

As soon as he came near the table, he had his eye upon the Hon. Tom Dashall, to whom he introduced 'himself by the presentation of a card, which announced his benefit for the next week at the Fives-Court, when all the prime lads of the ring had promised to exhibit.

"Egad!" said Dashall, "it will be an excellent opportunity—what, will you take a trip that way and see the mighty men of fist?"

"With all my heart," said Tallyho.

"And mine too," exclaimed Mortimer.

It was therefore quickly determined, and each of the party being supplied with a ticket, Bitton canvassed the room for other customers, after which he again retired to his seat.

"Come," said a smartly dressed Gentleman in a white hat, "we have heard a song from the other end of the room, I hope we shall be able to muster one here."

> 1 *This gentleman, whose dress and appearance indicate something of the Dandy, is a resident in Mark Lane, and usually spends his evening at the Round Table, where he*

appears to pride himself upon producing the finest segars that can be procured, and generally affords some of his friends an opportunity of proving them deserving the recommendations with which he never fails to present them.

This proposition was received with applause, and, upon Tom's giving a hint, Frank Harry was called upon—the glasses were filled, a toast was given, and the bowl was dispatched for a replenish; he then sung the following Song, accompanied with voice, manner, and action, well calculated to rivet attention and obtain applause:

PIGGISH PROPENSITIES,

THE BUMPKIN IN TOWN.

*"A Bumpkin to London one morning in Spring,
Hey derry, ho derry, fal de rai la,
Took a fat pig to market, his leg in a string,
Hey derry, ho derry, fal de rai la;
The clown drove him forward, while piggy, good lack!
Lik'd his old home so well, he still tried to run back—*

(Spoken)—Coome, coome (said the Bumpkin to himself,) Lunnun is the grand mart for every thing; there they have their Auction Marts, their Coffee Marts, and their Linen Marts: and as they are fond of a tid-bit of country pork, I see no reason why they should not have" a Pork and Bacon Mart—so get on (pig grunts,) I am glad to hear you have a voice on the subject, though it seems not quite in tune with my

Hey derry, ho derry, fal de ral la.

*It chanc'd on the road they'd a dreadful disaster,
Hey derry, ho derry, fal de rai la;
The grunter ran back 'twixt the legs of his master,
Hey derry, ho derry, fal de rai la;
The Bumpkin he came to the ground in a crack,
And the pig, getting loose, he ran all the way back!*

(Spoken)—Hallo, (said the clown, scrambling up again, and scratching his broken head,) to be sure I have heard of sleight-of-hand, hocus-pocus and sich like; but by gum this here be a new manouvre called sleight of legs; however as no boanes be broken between us, I'll endeavour to make use on 'em once more in following the game in view: so here goes, with a

Hey derry, ho derry, &c.

He set off again with his pig in a rope,

Hey derry, ho derry, fal de rai la,
Reach'd London, and now for good sale 'gan to hope
Hey derry, ho derry, fal de rai la;
But the pig, being beat 'till his bones were quite sore.
Turning restive, rush'd in at a brandy-shop door.

(Spoken)—The genteeler and politer part of the world might feel a little inclined to call this piggish behaviour; but certainly after a long and fatiguing journey, nothing can be more refreshing than a *drap of the cratur*; and deeming this the regular mart for the good stuff, in he bolts, leaving his master to sing as long as he pleased—Hey derry, he deny, &c.

Here three snuffy Tabbies he put to the rout,

Hey derry, ho derry, fal de rai lft,
With three drams to the quartern, that moment serv'd out,
Hey derry, ho derry, fal de rai la;
The pig gave a grunt, and the clown gave a roar,
When the whole of the party lay flat on the floor!

(Spoken)—Yes, there they lay all of a lump; and a precious group there was of them: The old women, well prun'd with snuff and twopenny, and bang-up with gin and bitters—the fair ones squalled; the clown growled like a bear with a broken head; the landlord, seeing all that could be seen as they roll'd over each other, stared, like a stuck pig! while this grand chorus of soft and sweet voices from the swinish multitude was accompanied by the pig with his usual grunt, and a

Hey derry, ho derry, &o.

The pig soon arose, and the door open flew,

Hey derry, ho derry, fal de ral la,
When this scrambling group was expos'd to my view,
Hey deny, ho derry, fal de ral la;
He set off again, without waiting for Jack,
And not liking London, ran all the way back!

(Spoken)—The devil take the pig! (said the Bumpkin) he is more trouble than enough. "The devil take you (said Miss Sukey Snuffle) for you are the greatest hog of the two; I dare say, if the truth was known, you are brothers."—"I declare I never was so exposed in all my life (said Miss Delia Doldrum.) There's my beautiful bloom petticoat, that never was rumpled before in all my life—I'm quite shock'd!"—"Never mind, (said the landlord) nobody cares about it; tho' I confess it was a shocking affair."—'I wish he and his pigs were in the horse-pond (continued she, endeavouring to hide her blushes with her hand)—Oh my—oh my!'—"What?" (said Boniface)—'Oh, my elbow! (squall'd out Miss Emilia Mumble) I am sure I shall never get over it.'—"Oh yes you will (continued he) rise again, cheer your spirits with another drop of old Tom, and you'll soon be able to sing

Hey derry, ho derry, &c.

By mutual consent the old women all swore,

Hey derry, ho derry, fal de rai la,
That the clown was a brute, and his pig was a boar,
Hey derry, ho derry, fal de rai la;
He paid for their liquor, but grumbled, good lack,
Without money or pig to gang all the way back.

(Spoken)—By gum (said he to himself, as he turn'd from the door) if the Lunneners likes country pork, country pork doant seem to like they; and if this be the success I'm to expect in this mighty great town in search of the Grand Mart, I'll come no more, for I thinks as how its all a flax; therefore I'll make myself contented to set at home in my own chimney corner in the country, and sing

Hey derry, ho derry, &c.

This song had attracted the attention of almost every one in the room; there was a spirit and vivacity in the singer, combined with a power of abruptly changing his voice, to give effect to the different passages, and a knowledge of music as well as of character, which gave it an irresistible charm; and the company, who had assembled round him, at the close signified their approbation by a universal shout of applause.

All went on well—songs, toasts and sentiments—punch, puns and witticisms, were handed about in abundance; in the mean time, the room began to wear an appearance of thinness, many of the boxes were completely deserted, and the Knights of the Bound Table were no longer surrounded by their Esquires—still the joys of the bowl were exhilarating, and the conversation agreeable, though at times a little more in a strain of vociferation than had been manifested at the entrance of our party. It was no time to ask questions as to the names and occupations of the persons by whom he was surrounded; and Bob, plainly perceiving Frank Harry was getting into Queer Street, very prudently declined all interrogatories for the present, making, however, a determination within himself to know more of the house and the company.

Mortimer also discovered symptoms of lush-logic, for though he had an inclination to keep up the chaff, his dictionary appeared to be new modelled, and his lingo abridged by repeated clips at his mother tongue, by which he afforded considerable food for laughter.

Perceiving this, Tallyho thought it prudent to give his Cousin a hint, which was immediately taken, and the party broke up.

CHAPTER XIX

"O there are swilling wights in London town
Term'd jolly dogs—choice spirits—alias swine,
Who pour, in midnight revel, bumpers down,
Making their throats a thoroughfare for wine.

These spendthrifts, who life's pleasures thus outrun,
Dosing with head-aches till the afternoon,
Lose half men's regular estate of Sun,
By borrowing too largely of the Moon:

And being Bacchi plenus—full of wine—
Although they have a tolerable notion
Of aiming at progressive motion,
Tis not direct, 'tis rather serpentine."

UPON leaving the house, it was quickly discovered that Mortimer was at sea without a rudder or compass, but was still enabled to preserve the true line of beauty, which is said to be in a flowing curve; Merrywell was magnanimous, Frank Harry moppy, and all of them rather muggy. Harry was going Eastward, and the remainder of the party Westward; it was half-past one in the morning—the weather had cleared up as their brains had been getting foggy.

Tom proposed a rattler.

Frank Harry swore by the Bacchanalian divinity they might ride in the rumble-tumble if they liked, but none of it for him, and began to stammer out

How sweet in—the—wood-lands
Wi—ith ii—eet hound—and horn—
To awaken—shrill—hiccup)—echo,
And taste the—(hiccup)—fresh morn.

During this time, having turned to the right on leaving the Woolpack, instead of the left, they were pursuing their way down

Gracechurch Street, in a line with London Bridge, without discovering their mistake; nor were they aware of the situation they were in till they reached the Monument.

"Zounds!" said Tom, "we are all wrong here."

"All right," said Merrywell—"all right, my boys—go it, my kidwhys."

Bob hearing his Cousin's exclamation, began to make enquiries.

"Never mind," said Tom, "we shall get housed presently—I have it—I know the shop—it is but seldom I get out of the way, so come along—I dare say we shall see some more fun yet."

Saying this, he led the way down Thames street and in a short time introduced them to the celebrated house in Dark-House Lane, kept open at all hours of the night for the accommodation of persons coming to market, and going off by the Gravesend boats and packets early in the morning.

On entering this house of nocturnal convenience, a wide field for observation was immediately opened to the mind of Dashall: he was no novice to the varieties of character generally to be found within its walls; and he anticipated an opportunity of imparting considerable information to his Cousin, though somewhat clogg'd by his companions; being known however at the bar, he found no difficulty in providing them with beds: which being accomplished,

"Now," said Tom, "for a new scene in Real Life. Here we are situated at Billingsgate, on the banks of the Thames; in another hour it will be all alive—we will refresh ourselves with coffee, and then look around us; but while it is preparing, we will take a survey of the interior—button up—tie a silk handkerchief round your neck, and we may perhaps escape suspicion of being mere lookers on; by which means we shall be enabled to mingle with the customers in the tap-room, and no doubt you will see some rum ones."

They now entered the tap or general room, which exhibited an appearance beyond the powers of description.

In one corner lay a Sailor fast asleep, having taken so much ballast on board as to prevent the possibility of any longer attending to the log, but with due precaution resting his head on a bundle which he intended to take on board his ship with him in the morning, and apparently well guarded by a female on each side; in another was a weather-beaten Fisherman in a Guernsey frock and a thick woollen night-cap, who, having just arrived with a cargo of fish, was toiling away time till the commencement of the market with a pipe and a pint, by whose side was seated a large Newfoundland dog, whose gravity of countenance formed an excellent contrast with that of a man who was entertaining the Fisherman with a history of his adventures through the day, and who in return was allowed to participate in the repeatedly filled pint—a Waterman in his coat and badge ready for a customer—and two women, each having a shallow basket for the purpose of supplying themselves with fish at the first market for the next day's sale.

'Going to Gravesend, Gentlemen?' enquired the Waterman, as Tom and Bob took their seats near him.

"No," was the reply.

"Beg pardon, Sir; thought as how you was going down, and mought want a boat, that's all; hope no offence."

"I vas down at the Frying Pan in Brick Lane yesterday, (said the communicative adventurer;) Snivelling Bill and Carrotty Poll was there in rum order—you know Carrotty? Poll? so Poll, (Good health to you) you knows how gallows lushy she gets—veil, as I vas saying, she had had a good day vith her fish, and bang she comes back to Bill—you knows she's rather nutty upon Bill, and according to my thinking they manages things pretty veil together, only you see as how she is too many for him: so, when she comes back, b———tme if Bill vasn't a playing at skittles, and hadn't sold a dab all day; howsomdever he was a vinning the lush, so you know Bill didn't care—but, my eyes! how she did blow him up vhen she com'd in and see'd him just a going to bowl and tip, she tipp'd him a vollopper right across the snout vhat made the skittles dance again, and bang goes the bowl at her sconce instead of the skittles: it vas lucky for her it did not hit her, for if it had, I'll be d———d if ever she'd a cried

Buy my live flounders any more—he vas at play vith Sam Stripe the tailor; so the flea-catcher he jumps in between 'em, and being a piece-botcher, he thought he could be peace-maker, but it voudn't do, tho' he jump'd about like a parch'd pea in a frying-pan—Poll called him Stitch louse, bid him pick up his needles and be off—Bill vanted to get at Poll, Poll vanted to get at Bill—and between them the poor Tailor got more stripes upon his jacket than there is colours in a harlequin's breeches at Bartlemy Fair—Here's good health to you—it was a bodkin to a but of brandy poor Snip didn't skip out of this here vorld into that 'are?"

"And how did they settle it?" enquired the Fisherman.

'I'll tell you all about it: I never see'd such a b———dy lark in all my life; poor Sam is at all times as thin as a thread-paper, and being but the ninth part of a man, he stood no chance between a man and a voman—Bill vas bleeding at the konk like a half-killed hog, and Carrotty Moll, full of fire and fury, vas defending herself vith her fish-basket—Billy vas a snivelling, Poll a stoearing, and the poor Tailor in a funk—thinks I to myself, this here vont never do—so up I goes to Poll—Poll, says I———' To the devil I pitch you,' says she—only you know I knows Poll veil enough—she tried to sneak it over me, but she found as how I know'd better—Poll, says I, hold your luff—give us no more patter about this here rum rig—I'll give cost price for the fish, and you shall have the money; and while I was bargaining with her, d———n me if Bill and the Tailor vasn't a milling avay in good style, till Stripe's wife comes in, gives Snivelling Billy a cross-buttock and bolted off with her fancy, like as the song says, The devil took the tailor

"Vith the broad cloth under his arm."

I never laugh'd so in all my life; I thought I should———'

At this moment a nod from the Landlord informed Tom his coffee was ready, when they were ushered into the parlour.

Bob, who had during the conversation in the other room, (which had occasionally been interrupted by the snores of the sleepy Sailor, the giggling of the Girls who appeared to have him in charge, and a growl from the dog,) been particularly attentive to the narration of this adventure, remarked that there was a peculiarity of dialect introduced, which, to a person coming out of the country, would have been wholly unintelligible.

"Yes," replied Tom, "almost every trade and every calling of which the numerous inhabitants of this overgrown town is composed, has a language of its own, differing as widely from each other as those of provincials. Nor is this less observable in high life, where every one seems at times to aim at rendering himself conspicuous for some extraordinary mode of expression. But come, I perceive the morning is shedding its rays upon us, and we shall be able to take a survey of the more general visitors to this place of extensive utility and resort—already you may hear the rumbling of carts in Thames Street, and the shrill voice of the Fishwives, who are preparing for a day's work, which they will nearly finish before two-thirds of the population leave their pillows. This market, which is principally supplied by fishing smacks and boats coming from the sea up the river Thames, and partly by land carriage from every distance within the limits of England, and part of Wales, is open every morning at day-light, and supplies the retailers for some miles round the Metropolis. The regular shop-keepers come here in carts, to purchase of what is called the Fish Salesman, who stands as it were between the Fisherman who brings his cargo to market and the Retailer; but there are innumerable hawkers of fish through the streets, who come and purchase for themselves at first hand, particularly of mackarel, herrings, sprats, lobsters, shrimps, flounders, soles, &c. and also of cod and salmon when in season, and at a moderate rate, composing an heterogeneous group of persons and characters, not easily to be met with elsewhere." "Then," said Bob, "there is a certainty of high and exalted entertainment;—I should suppose the supply of fish is very considerable."

"The quantity of fish consumed," replied Tom, "in London is comparatively small, fish being excessively dear in general: and this is perhaps the most culpable defect in the supply of the capital, considering that the rivers of Great Britain and the seas round her coast teem with that food.—There are on an average about 2500 cargoes of fish, of 40 tons each, brought to Billingsgate, and about

20,000 tons by land carriage, making a total of about 120,000 tons; and the street venders form a sample of low life in all its situations.

> "————In such indexes, although small
> To their subsequent volumes, there is seen
> The baby figure of the giant mass
> Of things to come at large."

And the language you have already heard forms a part of what may be termed Cockneyism."

"Cockneyism," said Bob, with an inquisitiveness in his countenance.

"Yes," continued Tom, "Cockney is universally known to be the contemptuous appellation given to an uneducated native of London, brought into life within the sound of Bow bell—pert and conceited, yet truly ignorant, they generally discover themselves by their mode of speech, notwithstanding they have frequent opportunities of hearing the best language; the cause, I apprehend, is a carelessness of every thing but the accumulation of money, which is considered so important with them—that they seem at all times to be in eager pursuit of it.

> "O Plutus, god of gold! thine aid impart,
> Teach me to catch the money-catching art;
> Or, sly Mercurius! pilfering god of old,
> Thy lesser mysteries at least unfold."

You will hear these gentry frequently deliver themselves in something like the following manner:

"My eyes, Jim, vat slippy valking 'tis this here morning—I should ave fell'd right down if so be as how I adn't cotch'd ould of a postis—vere does you thinks I ave been? vy all the vay to Vapping Vail, an a top o Tower Hill—I seed a voman pillar'd—such scrouging and squeeging, and peltin vith heggs—ow funny!

"A female Fruit-seller will say to a Lady Oyster-dealer—Law, my dear Mrs. Melton, how ar you this cowld morning, Mem.?—the streets vil be nice and dirty—vel, for my part, I always likes dry vether—do your usband vork at Foxall still?—I likes to warm my cowld nose vith a pinch of your snuff—ow wery obliging—But come, I hear the bustle of Billingsgate, and you shall have a peep at the people. By this time they are all alive."

Bob laughed at his Cousin's specimens of cockney language, and they sallied forth, to make further observations.

It was now a fine morning, the Sun shone with resplendent lustre upon all around them, and danced in playful dimples on the sportive Thames; there was however but little opportunity at the moment for them to contemplate subjects of this sort, their eyes and ears being wholly attracted by the passing and repassing of the persons desirous to sell or supply themselves with fish; Thames Street was almost blocked up with carts, and the hallooing and bawling of the different drivers, loading or unloading, formed an occasional symphony to the continual hum of those who were moving in all directions to and from the market.

"By yer leaf" said a sturdy built fellow, sweating under a load of fish which appeared to press him almost down—"what the devil do you stand in the way for?"

Bob, in stepping on one side to make room for this man to pass, unfortunately trod upon the toe of an Hibernian lady, who was bearing away a large basket of shrimps alive, and at the same time gave her arm so forcible a jerk with his elbow, as disengaged her hand from the load; by which means the whole cargo was overturned smack into the bosom of a smartly dressed youth in white ducks, who was conducting some Ladies on board one of the Gravesend boats. The confusion that followed is scarcely to be conceived—the agitation of Talt who at hearing the vociferated lamentations of the Irish woman—the spluttering of the disconcerted Dandy—the declaration of the owner of the shrimps, "that so help her God he should pay for her property"—the loud laughter of those around them, who appeared to enjoy the embarrassment of the whole party—and the shrimps hopping and jumping about amid the dirt and slush of the pavement, while the Ladies were hunting those which had fallen into the bosom of their conductor—formed a scene altogether, which, in spite of the confusion of his Cousin, almost convulsed the Hon. Tom Dashall with laughter, and which served but to increase the rancour of the owner of the shrimps, and the poor toe-suffering Irishwoman, the execrations of the Dandy Gentleman and his Ladies, and the miseries of poor Bob; to escape from which, he gave the Hibernian and her employer enough to purchase plaster for the one, and a fresh cargo for the other, and seizing Tom by the arm, dragged him away from the scene of his misfortunes in fishery.

Their progress however was presently impeded by a sudden scream, which appeared to come from a female, and .drew together almost all the people on the spot, it seemed as if it had been a preconcerted signal for a general muster, and it was quickly ascertained that fisty-cuffs were the order of the day, by the vociferations of the spectators, and the loud acclamations of "Go it, Poll—pitch it into her—mill her snitcher—veil done, Sail—all pluck—game to the back-bone—peppermint her upper-story, and grapple her knowledge-box—D———n my eyes, but that vas a good one, it has altered her weather-cock and shifted her wind—There's your dairies—stand out of the way—Upon my sole you have overturned all my flounders—D———n you and your dabbs too."

Tom and Bob took up a favourable position for observation at the corner of a fish-stall, where they could quietly witness the combatants, and take a general survey of the proceedings.

"Now," said Tom, "here is a lark for you, a female fight."

"Fine salmon, or cod, Gentlemen," said an elderly woman—"I wish I could tempt you to be customers."

"Well," said Bob, "they are at it in good earnest."

BILLINGSGATE. Tom & Bob taking a Survey after a Night Spree.

"O yes," said the woman, "we always have it in real earnest, no sham—I wish Poll may sarve her out, for Sall is a d————d saucy b———h at all times."

"And what have they quarrelled about?" inquired Dashall.

"Jealousy, Sir, nothing else; that there man in the night-cap, with the red ruff round his neck, is Sail's fancy man, and he sometimes lets her have a cargo of fish for services done and performed, you understand—and so Sail she comes down this morning, and she finds Poll having a phililoo with him, that's all; but I wish they would go and have it out somewhere else, for it spoils all business—Nance, go and get us a quartern of Jacky, that I may ax these Gentlemen to drink, for its a cold morning, and perhaps they are not used to be up so early."

Tom saw the drift of this in a moment, and taking the hint, supplied the needful to Nance, who was dispatched for the heart-cheering beverage, which they could perceive was in high reputation by those around them. The effluvia of the fish, the fumes of tobacco, and the reviving scent of the gin-bottle, rendered their olfactory salutations truly delightful. Nor could they escape the Fish-wife without becoming participators in the half pint of blue ruin.

"Come," said Tom, "we will now stroll a little further, and take a survey of the street; but first we will give a look here.

"This," said he, "is the Custom House, a splendid building recently erected, in consequence of the old one being demolished by fire in 1814." "It is, indeed," replied Bob, admiring the south front, which is executed in Portland stone.

"Do you observe," continued Tom, "the central compartment, which comprises what is called the Long Room, and which we will visit presently, is quite plain, except the attic, which is elegantly ornamented?—that alto-relievo contains allegorical representations of the arts and sciences, as connected with and promoting the commerce and industry of the nation—that to the west, a representation of the costume and character of the various nations with whom we hold intercourse in our commercial relations—in the centre, under the large massive dial-plate, are inscribed in large bronze letters the names of the founders and the date of its erection—the figures which support the dial in a recumbent position are emblematical of industry and plenty—that bold projection in the centre, gives a suitable character to the King's warehouse, and forms an appropriate support to the imperial arms upheld by the attributes of Ocean and Commerce."

Bob gazed with admiration and delight on this truly admirable and extensive pile of national architecture; the gentle breeze from the river, the occasional dash of the oar, and the activity which appeared on board the different vessels; together with the view of London Bridge on one side, over which he could perceive pedestrians and vehicles of various kinds passing and repassing, and the Tower on the other, conspired to heighten and give a most imposing effect to the scene.

"The designs," said Tallyho, "are truly creditable to the taste and science of the architect."

"And this Quay in front, is intended to be enlarged by filling up a part of the river; besides which, a new wall and quay are to be formed from the Tower to Billingsgate, and numerous other improvements are projected in the contiguous streets and lanes." "Not before it is necessary," was the reply. "It would be impossible," continued Dashall, "to visit all the apartments this building contains; we will however have a look at the Long Room, and as we proceed I will endeavour to give you some further information. We are now entering the East wing, which is a counterpart of that on the West, having like this a grand stair-case with a double flight of steps, which conduct to a lobby at each end of the long room, lighted by these vertical lantern-lights, the ceilings being perforated in square compartments, and glazed. These lobbies serve to check the great draughts of air which would otherwise flow through the room if it opened directly from the stair-case."

They now entered the Long Room, the imposing appearance of which had its due effect upon Tallyho.

"Bless me!" cried he in a state of ecstasy, "this is a room to boast of indeed."

"Yes," replied his Cousin, "there is not such another room in Europe; it is 190 feet long by 66 wide, and proportionably high, divided into three compartments by these eight massive pillars, from which, as you perceive, spring the three domes, which are so richly ornamented, and ventilated through the centre of each."

"And all of stone?" inquired Bob.

"Not exactly so," was the reply; "the floor (excepting the situation of the officers and clerks) is of stone, but the walls and ceilings are drawn out and tinted in imitation."

"And what are these antique pedestals for, merely ornaments?"

Tom was pleased at this inquiry, and with a smile of satisfaction replied—"No, these pedestals do double duty, and are something like what the rural poet, Goldsmith, describes in his *Deserted Village*—

> "The chest contriv'd a double debt to pay,
> A bed by night, a chest of drawers by day."

These are ornamental during the summer, but useful in the winter; they contain fire-places completely hid from view."

"Fire-places," re-echoed Bob.

"Yes," continued his Cousin; "the smoke, descending, passes through the piers on each side, and by their means a sufficient warmth is at all times kept up in the room."

"That is a capital contrivance," said Tallyho.

"Then, to prevent the possibility of sustaining any serious injury from fire, on the ground, one and two pair stories, the communication is cut off by means of iron doors, which run on wheels in chase in the centre of the walls, and are moved backward and forward by a windlass; which doors are closed every evening, and would effectually prevent a communication beyond their boundaries. Fire-proof rooms also, as repositories for valuable books and papers, are provided on each floor, where the important documents of the establishment are deposited every evening, and removed in trunks to the respective offices. There are in all 121 rooms devoted to various offices. This however is the principal: here the general business is transacted, particularly for all foreign concerns, both inwards and outwards. The Ship Master first makes the report of the cargo here; the entries of which, either for payment of duties, warehousing, or subsequent exportation, are all passed with the respective officers in this room. The business of the customs is managed by nine Commissioners, whose jurisdiction extends over all parts of England. We will now pass out at the west wing, adjourn to yon Tavern, refresh and refit, and after which a further walk."

"With all my heart," said Tallyho.

"What ho, Master B———," said Dashall, saluting the Landlord as he entered the Tavern—"How does the world wag with you?—send us some soda water—the newspaper—let somebody clean our boots—give us pen, ink and paper, and prepare us some breakfast with all speed, but no fish, mind that."

The Landlord bowed assent to his honourable customer; and by the time they were ready, their orders were complied with.

"Pray," inquired Dashall of the obliging Landlord, who came in to ask if they were supplied with all they wished for, "did you ever recover any thing from that dashing Blade that so obligingly ordered his dinner here?"

"Never got a halfpenny—no no, he was not one of those sort of gentry—nor do I ever wish to see such again in my house."

This was uttered in a tone of discontent, which evidently shewed he had no relish for the conversation.

Dashall could not refrain from laughter; upon perceiving which, the Landlord withdrew with a loud slam of the door, and left his customers to enjoy their mirth.

"What are you laughing at?" cried Bob.

"Why," continued his Cousin,

> *"There was, as fame reports, in days of yore,*
> *At least some fifty years ago, or more,*
> *A pleasant wight on town — — "*

And there are many pleasant fellows now to be met with; but you shall have the tale as I had it: This house has been celebrated for furnishing excellent dinners, and the cookery of fish in particular; consequently it has been the resort of the Bucks, the Bloods, and the dashing Swells of the town, and I myself have been well entertained here. It will therefore not be wondered at that its accommodations should attract the notice of a Sharper whose name and character were well known, but who was in person a total stranger to the unsuspecting Landlord, whom however he did not fail to visit.

Calling one afternoon for the purpose of seeing how the land lay, in high twig, and fashionably dressed, he was supplied with a bottle of sherry, and requested the landlord to take a part with him—praised the wine, talked of the celebrity of his house for fish, and gave an order for a dinner for sixteen friends during the following week. The bait was swallowed,

"For a little flattery is sometimes well."

'But are your wines of the first quality? (inquired the visitor;) for good eating, you know, deserves good drinking, and without that we shall be like fishes out of water.'—' Oh, Sir, no man in London can supply you better than myself (was the reply;) but, if you please, you shall select which you may like best, my stock is extensive and good.' He was consequently invited into the cellar, and tasted from several binns, particularly marking what he chose to conceive the best. Upon returning to the parlour again—' Bless me, (cried he) I have had my pocket pick'd this morning, and lost my handkerchief—can you oblige me with the loan of one for present use? and I will send it back by one of my servants.'

'Certainly, Sir,' was the reply; and the best pocket-handkerchief was quickly produced, with another bottle of wine, the flavour of which he had approved while below. He then wrote a letter, which he said must be dispatched immediately by a Ticket-porter to Albemarle Street, where he must wait for an answer. This being done, lie desired a coach to be called—asked the Landlord if he had any silver he could accommodate him with, as he had occasion to go a little further, but would soon return. This being complied with, by the Landlord giving him twenty shillings with the expectation of receiving a pound note in return, he threw himself into the coach, wished his accommodating Host good afternoon, promised to return in less than an hour, but has never shewn his face here since. Poor B———don't like to hear the circumstance mentioned."

"Zounds!" said Tallyho, "somebody was green upon the occasion; I thought people in London were more guarded, and not so easily to be done. And who did he prove to be after all?"

"No other than the well-known Major Semple, whose depredations of this sort upon the public rendered him so notorious."

Having finished their repast, Tom was for a move; and they took their way along Thames Street in the direction for Tower Hill.

CHAPTER XX

"This life is all chequer'd with pleasures and woes
That chase one another like waves of the deep,
Each billow, as brightly or darkly it flows,
Reflecting our eyes as they sparkle or weep;
So closely our whims on our miseries tread,
That the laugh is awak'd ere the tear can be dried;
And as fast as the rain-drop of pity is shed,
The goose-plumage of folly can turn it aside;
But, pledge me the cup! if existence can cloy
With hearts ever light and heads ever wise,
Be ours the light grief that is sister to joy,
And the short brilliant folly that flashes and dies."

"THE building before us," said Tom, "is the Tower of London, which was formerly a palace inhabited by the various Sovereigns of this country till the reign of Queen Elizabeth. Fitzstephens says, it was originally built by Julius Cæsar; but I believe there is no proof of the truth of this assertion, except that one of the towers is to this day called Cæsar's Tower."

"It seems a place of great security," said Bob.

"Yes—William the Conqueror erected a fortress on part of its present site, to overawe the inhabitants of London on his gaining possession of the City, and about twelve years afterwards, in 1078, he erected a larger building than the first, either on the site of the former or near it. This building, repaired or rebuilt by succeeding Princes, is that which is now called the White Tower."

"It appears altogether to be a very extensive building," said Tallyho; "and what have we here? (turning his eyes to the left)—the modern style of those form a curious contrast to that we are now viewing."

"That is called Trinity Square, and the beautiful edifice in the centre is the Trinity House; it is a new building, of stone, having the advantage of rising ground for its site, and of a fine area in the front." "The Trinity House," reiterated Bob, "some ecclesiastical establishment, I presume, from its title?"

"There you are wrong," continued Dashall; "it is a Corporation, which was founded in the year 1515 by Henry VIII. and consists of a Master, four Wardens, eighteen Elder Brothers, in whom is vested the direction of the Company, and an indefinite number of younger Brothers; for any sea-faring man may be admitted into the Society by that name, but without any part of the controul of its concerns. The elder Brethren are usually selected from the most experienced commanders in the navy and the merchants' service, with a few principal persons of his Majesty's Government."

"But what, in the name of wonder," inquired Bob, "have Sailors to do with the Trinity?"

"As much as other persons," was the reply; "if it is the anchor of hope, as we are taught, they have as great a right to rely upon it as any body else—besides, the names given to houses and places in London have nothing to do with their occupations or situations, any more than the common language of life has to do with nature; else why have we a Waterloo House in the vicinity of St. Giles's for the sale of threads, laces, and tapes—a Fleet for the confinement of prisoners, or the King's Bench devoted to the same purposes, unless it is,

> *"That when we have no chairs at home,*
> *The King (God bless him) grants us then a bench."*

Though London contains a round of delights and conveniences scarcely to be equalled, it is at the same time a combination of incongruities as difficult to be conceived. The denomination of this House has therefore nothing to do with the business to which it is devoted. The body which transacts its concerns is called The Master, Wardens and Assistants, of the Guild, or Fraternity of the most glorious and undivided Trinity, and of St. Clement, in the parish of Deptford, Stroud, in the county of Kent."

"An admirable illustration of your assertion," replied Bob; "and pray may I be allowed, without appearing romantic or unnecessarily inquisitive, to ask what are the objects of the Institution?"

"Certainly. The use of this Corporation is to superintend the general interests of the British shipping, military and commercial. To this end, the powers of the Corporation are very extensive; the principal of which are, to examine the children educated in mathematics in Christ's Hospital—examine the masters of the King's ships—appoint pilots for the Thames—erect light-houses and sea-marks—grant licenses to poor seamen, not free of the City, to row on the Thames—and superintend the deepening and cleansing of the river; they have power to receive donations for charitable purposes, and annually relieve great numbers of poor seamen and seamen's widows and orphans; and as they alone supply outward-bound ships with ballast, on notice of any shoal or obstruction arising in the river Thames, they immediately direct their men and lighters to work on it till it is removed. The profits arising to the Corporation by this useful regulation is very considerable."

During this conversation they had continued to walk towards the Trinity House, and were now close to it.

"Come," continued Dashall, "the interior is worth seeing: there are some fine paintings in it, and the fitting up is altogether of an elegant description."

Upon making application at the door, and the customary payment of a shilling each, they were admitted. The appearance of the Hall, which is grand, though light and elegant, particularly attracted the attention of Tallyho. The double stair-case, which leads to the court-room, was an object of peculiar delight. The beautiful model of the Royal William in the Secretary's Office was much admired; but the Court-room was abundant in gratification. Here they were ushered into a spacious apartment,*particularly elegant, being unincumbered; the ceiling finished in a superior style, and decorated with paintings of the late King and Queen—James the Second—Lord Sandwich—Lord Howe, and Mr. Pitt. Here Bob wandered from portrait to portrait, examining the features and character of each, and admiring the skill and ability of the artists. At the upper end of the room he was additionally pleased to find a large painting containing a group of about twenty-four of the elder Brethren, representing them at full length, attended by their Secretary, the late Mr. Court. Many of the persons being well remembered by Dashall, were pointed out by him to his Cousin, and brought to his recollection names deservedly celebrated, though now no more. This picture was the gift of the Merchant Brethren in 1794.

Tallyho was much delighted with his survey of this truly elegant building, and the luminous account given by his Cousin of the various persons whose portraits met his eye, or whose names and characters, connected with the establishment, had become celebrated for scientific research or indefatigable industry.

"It will occupy too much time this morning," said Dashall, "to visit the interior of the Tower, as I have dispatched a Ticket-porter to Piccadilly, ordering my curricle to be at Tom's Coffee-house at one; we will therefore defer that pleasure to the next opportunity of being this way. We will however take a look at the Bank and the Exchange, then a trundle into the fresh air for an hour, and return home to dinner; so come along, but we will vary our walk by taking another road back."

With this intention, they now crossed Tower Hill, and turned to the left, along the Minories.

"Here is a place," said Dashall, "well known, and no doubt you have often heard of—Sparrow Corner and Rosemary Lane are better known by the appellation of Rag Fair. It is a general mart for the sale of second-hand clothes, and many a well-looking man in London is indebted to his occasional rambles in this quarter for his appearance. The business of this place is conducted with great regularity, and the dealers and collectors of old clothes meet at a certain hour of the afternoon to make sales and exchanges, so that it is managed almost upon the same plan as the Royal Exchange, only that the dealers here come loaded with their goods, which must undergo inspection before sales can be effected: while the Merchant carries with him merely a sample, or directs his Purchaser to the warehouse where his cargo is deposited. The principal inhabitants of this place are Jews, and they obtain supplies from the numerous itinerant collectors from all quarters of London and its suburbs, whom you must have observed parading the streets from the earliest hour of the morning, crying *Ould clothes—Clothes sale."*

"It surely can hardly be a trade worth following," said Talltho.

"There are many hundreds daily wandering the streets, however," replied Tom, "in pursuit of cast-off apparel, rags, and metals of different sorts, or at least pretend so. The Jews are altogether a set of traders. I do not mean to confine my observations to them only, because there are persons of other sects employed in the same kind of business; and perhaps a more dangerous set of cheats could scarcely be pointed at, as their chief business really is to prowl about the houses and stables of people of rank and fortune, in order to hold out temptations to their servants, to pilfer and steal small articles not likely to be missed, which these fellows are willing to purchase at about one-third of their real value. It is supposed that upwards of 15,000 of these depraved itinerants among the Jews are daily employed in journeys of this kind; by which means, through the medium of base money and other fraudulent dealings, many of them acquire property with which they open shops, and then become receivers of stolen property; the losses thus sustained by the public being almost incalculable—

> *"For wid coot gould rings of copper gilt—'tis so he gets his bread,*
> *Wit his sealing-vax of brick-dust, and his pencils without lead."*

It is estimated that there are from fifteen to twenty thousand Jews in the Metropolis, and about five or six thousand more stationed in the great provincial and seaport towns. In London they have six Synagogues, and in the country places there are at least twenty more. Most of the lower classes of those distinguished by name of German or Dutch Jews, live principally by their wits, and establish a system of mischievous intercourse all over the country, the better to enable them to carry on then-fraudulent designs in every way. The pliability of their consciences is truly wonderful—

> *"For they never stick at trifles, if there's monies in the way."*

Nay, I remember the time when they used to perambulate our streets openly, professing to purchase base coin, by bawling—"Any bad shilling, any bad shilling." The interference of the Police however has prevented the calling, though perhaps it is impossible to prevent a continuance of the practice any more than they can that of utterance. These men hesitate not to purchase stolen property, or metals of various kinds, as well as other articles pilfered from the Dock-yards, and stolen in the provincial towns, which are brought to the Metropolis to elude detection, and vice versa; in some cases there are contrivances that the buyer and seller shall not even see each other, in order that no advantage may be taken by giving information as to the parties." "Upon my life, the contrivances of London are almost incomprehensible," said Bob, "and might deter many from venturing into it; but this surprises me beyond any thing."

"It is however too lamentably true," continued Tom; "for these people, educated in idleness from the earliest infancy, acquire every debauched and vicious principle which can fit them for the most complicated arts of fraud and deception, to which they seldom fail to add the crime of perjury, whenever it can be useful to shield themselves or their friends from the punishment of the law. Totally without moral education, and very seldom trained to any trade or occupation by which they can earn an honest livelihood by manual labour—their youths excluded from becoming apprentices, and their females from engaging themselves generally as servants, on account of the superstitious adherence to the mere ceremonial of their persuasion, as it respects meat not killed by Jews—nothing can exceed their melancholy condition, both as it regards themselves and society. Thus excluded from the resources which other classes of the community possess, they seem to have no alternative but to resort to those tricks and devices which ingenuity suggests, to enable persons without an honest means of subsistence to live in idleness.

"The richer Jews are in the practice of lending small sums to the poorer classes of their community, in order that they may support themselves by a species of petty traffic; but even this system contributes in no small degree to the commission of crimes, since, in order to render it productive to an extent equal to the wants of families who do not acquire any material aid by manual labour, they are induced to resort to unlawful means of increasing it, by which they become public nuisances. From the orange-boy and the retailer of seals, razors, glass and other wares, in the public streets, or the collector of

> "Old rags, old jags, old bonnets, old bags,"

to the shop-keeper, dealer in wearing apparel, or in silver and gold, the same principles of conduct too generally prevail.

"The itinerants utter base money, to enable them by selling cheap, to dispose of their goods; while those who are stationary, with very few exceptions, receive and purchase at an under price whatever is brought them, without asking questions; and yet most of their concerns are managed with so much art, that we seldom hear of a Jew being hanged; and it is also a fact, that during the holidays (of which they have many in the course of a year,) or at one of their weddings, you may see the barrow-woman of yesterday decked out in gay and gaudy attire of an expensive nature."

By this time they had reached the top of the minories, and were turning down Houndsditch. "We are now," said Dashall, "close to another place chiefly inhabited by Jews, called Duke's Place, where they have a very elegant Synagogue, which has been visited by Royalty, the present King having, during his Regency, honoured them with a visit, through the introduction of the late Mr. Goldsmid. If it should be a holiday, we will be present at the religious ceremonies of the morning." With this they entered Duke's Place, and were soon within the walls of this Temple of Judaism. In taking a view of it, Bob was much gratified with its splendid decorations, and without being acquainted with their forms, had *doff'd his castor*,{1} but was presently informed by his Cousin that he must keep his hat on. The readers appeared to him to be singers; but the whole of the service being Hebrew, it was of little consequence to him, whether read or sung. He perceived, during the performances of these prayers, which were every now and then joined in by almost every one present, that many of the congregation appeared to be in close conversation, which, however, was taken no notice of by the persons officiating. He was well pleased with the singing of a youth and the accompaniment of a gentleman in a cock'd hat; for although he could not discover that he actually produced words, he produced sounds in many instances bearing a strong similarity to those of a bassoon. The venerable appearance and devotion of the High Priest, who was habited in a robe of white, also attracted his attention; while the frequent bursts of the congregation, joining in the exercises of the morning, in some instances almost provoked his risibility.

"The religious ceremonies of these people," said Tom, as they left the synagogue, "though somewhat imposing as to form and appearance, do not seem to be strongly interesting, for many of them are engaged during the whole of the service in some species of traffic; buying and

1 Doff'd his castor—Taken off his hat.

selling, or estimating the value of goods for sale. They are such determined merchants and dealers, that they cannot forget business even in the house of prayer. We have two sets of them. This is the Dutch Synagogue; but the most ancient is that of the Portuguese, having been established in England ever since the Usurpation. The members of it being mostly wealthy, are extremely attentive to their poor, among whom there is said not to be a single beggar or itinerant; while the Dutch or German. Jews get no education at all: even the most affluent of them are said to be generally unable either to read or write the language of the country that gave them birth. They confine themselves to a bastard or vulgar Hebrew, which has little analogy to the original. They observe the particular ritual of the German Synagogue, and also include the Polish, Russian, and Turkish Jews established in London. With the exception of a few wealthy individuals, and as many families who are in trade on the Royal Exchange, they are in general a very indigent class of people. Their community being too poor to afford them adequate relief, they have resorted to the expedient of lending them small sums of money at interest, to trade upon, which is required to be repaid monthly or weekly, as the case may be, otherwise they forfeit all claim to this aid.

"The Portuguese Jews are generally opulent and respectable, and hold no community with the others. They use a different liturgy, and their language is even different. They never intermarry with the Jews of the Dutch Synagogue. They pride themselves on their ancestry, and give their children the best education which can be obtained where they reside. The Brokers upon the Exchange, of the Jewish persuasion, are all or chiefly of the Portuguese Synagogue. Their number is limited to twelve by Act of Parliament, and they pay 1000 guineas each for this privilege."

They had now reached the end of Houndsditch, when, passing through Bishopsgate Church Yard and Broad Street, they were soon at the Bank.

"This building," said Dashall, "covers an extent of several acres of ground, and is completely isolated."

"Its exterior," replied Bob, "is not unsuited to the nature of the establishment, as it certainly conveys an idea of strength and security."

"That's true," continued Tom; "but you may observe a want of uniformity of design and proportion, arising from its having been erected piece-meal, at different periods, and according to different plans, by several architects. This is the principal entrance; and opposite to it is the shortest street in the Metropolis, called Bank Street; it contains but one house. Now we will take a survey of the interior."

They entered the Hall, where Tallyho was much pleased to be instructed as to the methodical way they have of examining notes for a re-issuing or exchanging into coin.

"Here," said Dashall, "are the Drawing-offices for public and private accounts. This room is seventy-nine feet long by forty; and, at the further end, you observe a very fine piece of sculpture: that is a marble Statue of King William III. the founder of the Bank. Thi national establishment was first incorporated by act of Parliament in 1694. The projector of the scheme was a Mr. James Paterson, a native of Scotland; and the direction of its concerns is vested in a Governor, Deputy-Governor, and twenty-four Directors, elected annually at a general Court of the Proprietors. Thirteen of the Directors, with the Governor, form a Court for the transaction of business. The Bank is open every day from nine in the morning till five in the afternoon, holidays excepted. It is like a little town. The Clerks at present are about 1000 in number, but a reduction is intended. The Rotunda is the most interesting apartment—we will go and have a look at the Money-dealers.

"Here," continued he, as they entered the Rotunda, and mingled among the various persons and sounds that are so well known in that seat of traffic, "from the hours of eleven to three a crowd of eager Money-dealers assemble, and avidity of gain displays itself in ever-varying shapes, at times truly ludicrous to the disinterested observer. You will presently perceive that the justling and crowding of the Jobbers to catch a bargain, frequently exceed in disorder the scrambling at the doors of our theatres for an early admission: and sa loud and clamorous at times are the mingled noises of the buyers and sellers, that all distinction of sound is lost in a general uproar."

Of this description, Tallyho had an absolute proof in a few minutes, for the mingling variety of voices appeared to leave no space in time for distinguishing either the sense or the sound of the individual speakers; though it was evident that, notwithstanding the continual hubbub, there was a perfect understanding effected between parties for the sale and transfer of Stock, according to the stipulations bargained for.

"Ha, Mr. M———," said the Hon. Tom Dashall, "how do you do?"

"Happy to say well, Sir, thank you," was the reply. "Any commands?—markets are pretty brisk this morning, and we are all alive."

"Pray," said Tallyho, "who is that extraordinary looking Lady with such red lips and cheeks, beneath the garb of sadness?"

"A constant visitor here," replied Mr. M. "I may say a day scarcely passes without her being present."

"She has a curious appearance," said Bob; "her dress is all black from head to foot, and yet her cheeks disclose the ruddy glow of uninterrupted health. Is it that her looks belie her garb, or that her garb belies her looks?"

"Hush," said Mr. M. "let her pass, and I will give you some information relative to her, which, if it does not gratify you, will at least satisfy some of your inquiries. I am half inclined to believe that all is not right in the seat of government with her, (pointing his finger to his head;) and she is therefore rather deserving of pity than an object of censure or ridicule; though I have reason to believe she frequently meets with attacks of the latter, when in search of the sympathy and benefit to be derived from a proper exercise of the former. Her name is Miss W———. Her father was formerly a two-penny postman, who resided at Rockingham Row, Walworth, and was himself somewhat eccentric in his dress and manners, and it was not at all unusual to meet him in the morning in the garb of his office, though decidedly against his inclination, and to see him on 'Change during 'Change hours, in silk stockings, and in every other way dressed as a Merchant, attending there according to custom and practice; and he managed, by some means or other, to keep up a character of respectability, and to give an accomplished education to the younger branches of this family; so that this lady, though unfortunate in her present circumstances, has been well brought up, and mingled in polished society; and, if you were to enter into conversation with her now, you would find her intelligent in the selection of her words and the combination of sentences, to explain to you the most improbable events, and the most unheard of claims that she has upon all the Governments in the known world. This, however, would be done with good temper, unless any thing like an insulting observation should be conceived, or intended to be conveyed."

"And, pray, what is supposed to be the cause of her present manners and appearance?" inquired Bob.

"It is principally attributed," replied Mr M. "to the circumstance of losing a beloved brother, who she now continually declares is only kept from her by the persons who daily visit the Rotunda, with a view to prevent the recovery of the property she lays claim to, and the particulars of which she generally carries in her pocket. That brother however suffered the penalty of the law for a forgery;{1} but this she cannot be induced to believe.

*1 The lamentable effusion of blood which has taken place
within the last twenty years, in consequence of forgeries on
the Bank of England, has already excited a very considerable
portion of public interest and indignation; and it is much
to be feared that notwithstanding the very serious expence
the Corporation have incurred, with a view to remedy the
evil, by rendering the imitation more difficult, the
anticipated result is not likely to be obtained. It will
hardly be conceived that the Governors have expended as much
as one hundred thousand pounds in this laudable undertaking,
and, upon producing an impression, we are told it can be
imitated by one, who, within three weeks produced a fac-
simile, and puzzled the makers of the original note to
discover which was the work-manship of their own hands. Nay,
even an engraver on wood is said to have produced an
excellent imitation in a few hours. It is however sincerely
to be hoped that an effectual stop will be eventually put to
the possibility of committing this crime, which, we
apprehend, nine times out of ten brings the poor, needy,
half-starved retailer of paper to the gallows, while the
more un-principled wholesale dealer escapes detection.*

*While on the subject of forged notes, we cannot help
deprecating the circulation of what are termed flash
notes, which, if not originally intended to deceive and
defraud, are calculated to accomplish these objects, when in
the hands of the artful and designing. We think there is a
tradesman in the vicinity of the Bank who presents such of
his customers as visits his repository to have their hair
cut, &c. with a Hash note, purporting to be for 50l.; and we
have also reason to believe that more than one attempt has
been detected, where the parties have really endeavoured to
pass them as valid Bank of England paper.   The danger
therefore must be evident.*

We have reason to think she is frequently much straitened for want of the necessary supplies for sustenance, and she has temporary relief occasionally from those who knew her family and her former circumstances in life, while she boldly perseveres in the pursuit of fancied property, and the restoration of her brother.

"I have heard her make heavy complaints of the difficulties she has had to encounter, and the privations she has been subjected to; but her own language will best speak the impressions on her mind. Here is a printed letter which was circulated by her some time ago:—

To the worthy Inhabitants of the Parish of St. Mary, Newington, Surrey.

It is with feelings of deep regret I have to deplore the necessity that compels me to adopt a public measure, for the purpose of obtaining my property from those gentlemen that hold it in trust. For a period of ten years I have endured the most cruel and unjustifiable persecution, which has occasioned the premature death of my mother; a considerable loss of property; all my personal effects of apparel and valuables; has exposed me to the most wanton and barbarous attacks, the greatest insults, and the severe and continual deprivation of every common necessary. Having made every appeal for my right, or even a maintenance, without effect, I now take the liberty of adopting the advice of some opulent friends in the parish, and solicit general favour in a loan by subscription for a given time, not doubting the liberal commiseration of many ladies and gentlemen, towards so great a sufferer. As it is not possible to describe the wrongs I have endured, the misery that has been heaped upon me, in so limited a space, I shall be happy to give every explanation upon calling for the result of this entreaty and to those ladies and gentlemen that condescend to favour

S. WHITEHEAD

With their presence, at

The White Hart Inn, Borough.

Besides Bills to an immense amount, accepted by the Dey of Algiers, and payable by his Grand Plenipotentiary.

Various sums in the English and Irish Funds, in the names of various Trustees: in the 3 per cent. Consols—3 per cent. 1726—3 per cent.

South Sea Annuities—3 per cent. Old South Sea Annuities—4 per cent. 3 per cent. 5 per cent. Long Annuities.

Besides various Freehold, Copyhold, and Leasehold Estates, Reversions and Annuities, of incalculable value.

One of the Freehold Estates is that known by the name of Ireland's Row, and the Brewhouse adjacent, Mile End; the Muswell Hill Estate; a large House in Russell Square, tenanted at present by Mr. B———dd!!!

"For the truth of this statement, or the real existence of any property belonging to her, I am not able to vouch. She is well known in all the offices of this great Establishment, is generally peaceable in her conduct, and communicative in her conversation, which at times distinguishes her as a person of good education."

"Hard is the fortune which your Sex attends, Women, like princes, find few real friends; All who approach them their own ends pursue, Lovers and ministers are seldom true. Hence oft from reason heedless beauty strays, And the most trusted guide the most betrays."

The conversation was here interrupted by the arrival of a Gentleman, who, taking Mr. M. on one side, Tom and Bob wished him a good morning. They proceeded to view the various offices which branch out from the Rotunda, and which are appropriated to the management of each particular stock, in each of which Bob could not help admiring the happy disposition of every department to facilitate business. The arrangement of the books, and the clerks, under the several letters of the alphabet, he conceived was truly excellent.

"The Corporation of the Bank," said Dashall, "are prohibited from trading in any sort of goods or merchandize whatsoever; but are to confine the use of their capital to discounting Bills of Exchange, and to the buying and selling of gold and silver bullion; with a permission however to sell such goods as are mortgaged or pawned to them and not redeemed within three months after the expiration of the time for their redemption. Their profits arise from their traffic in bullion; the discounting of Bills of Exchange for Bankers, Merchants, Factors, and Speculators; and the remuneration they receive from Government, for managing the public funds, and for receiving the subscriptions on loans and lotteries. But we may ramble about in these places for a month, and still have novelty in store; and there is a little world underneath the greater part of this extensive building devoted to printing-offices, ware-rooms, &c."

They had now reached the door which leads into Bartholomew Lane, and, upon descending the steps, and turning to the left, Bob's eyes soon discovered the Auction Mart, "What have we here?" inquired he.

"That," replied his Cousin, "is a building which may deservedly be rank'd as one of the ornaments of the City; and its arrangements and economy, as well as the beauty of its interior, are well deserving the notice of every stranger. This fine establishment, which serves as a focus for the sale of estates and other property by public auction, is both useful and ornamental; it was built about the time when the spirit of combination was so strong in London. You must know, some years back, every kind of business and trade appeared likely to be carried on by Joint Stock Companies, and the profits divided upon small shares. Many Fire-offices have to date their origin from this source—the Hope, the Eagle, the Atlas, and others. The Golden Lane Brewery was opened upon this principle; some Water Companies were established; till neighbourhood and partnership almost became synonimous; and, I believe, among many other institutions of that kind, the Building before us is one. It contains many handsome rooms and commodious offices; but, as for offices, every street and every alley abounds with them, and, now-a-days, if you want to hire a Cook or a Scullion, you have nothing to do but to send a letter to a Register-office, and you are suited in a twinkling. It was an excellent idea, and I remember the old Buck who used to call himself the founder of establishments of that nature, or rather the first introducer of them to the notice of Englishmen, poor old Courtois."

John Courtois is said to have been a native of Picardy, where he was born about the year 1737 or 1738. He repaired to this country while yet young, in the character of *valet de chambre* to a gentleman who had picked him up in his travels; and, as he came from one of the poorest of the French provinces, he "took root," and throve wonderfully on his transplantation to a richer soil.

On the death of his master, he removed to the neighbourhood of the Strand; and St. Martin's Street,. Leicester Square, became the scene of his industry and success. At a time when wigs were worn by boys, and a Frenchman was supposed the only person capable of making one fit "for the grande monarque," he commenced business as a perruquier, and soon acquired both wealth and celebrity. To this he joined another employment, which proved equally lucrative and appropriate, as it subjected both masters and servants to his influence. This was the keeping of a register-office, one of the first known in the Metropolis, whence he drew incalculable advantages. He is also said to have been a dealer in hair, which he imported largely from the continent. And yet,, after all, it is difficult to conceive how he could have realized a fortune exceeding 200,000L.! But what may not be achieved by a man who despised no gains, however small, and in his own expressive language, considered farthings as "the seeds of guineas!"

The following appears to be a true description of this very extraordinary man, whom we ourselves have seen more than once:— "Old Courtois was well known for more than half a century in the purlieus of St. Martin's and the Haymarket. His appearance was meagre and squalid, and his clothes, such as they were, were pertinaciously got up in exactly the same cut and fashion, and the colour always either fawn or marone. For the last thirty years, the venerable chapeau was uniformly of the same cock. The principal feat, however, in which this fervent votary of Plutus appeared before the public, was his nearly fatal affair with Mary Benson, otherwise Mrs. Maria Theresa Phepoe. In April 1795, this ill-fated-woman projected a rather bungling scheme, in order to frighten her old acquaintance and visitor, Courtois, out of a considerable sum of money. One evening, when she was certain of his calling, she had her apartment prepared for his reception in a species of funereal style—a bier, a black velvet pall, black wax candles lighted, &c. No sooner had the friend entered the room, than the lady, assisted by her maid, pounced on him, forced him into an arm chair, in which he was forcibly held down by the woman, while the hostess, brandishing a case-knife or razor, swore with some violent imprecations, that instant should be his last, if he did not give her an order on his "banker for a large sum of money. The venerable visitor, alarmed at the gloomy preparations and dire threats of the desperate female, asked for pen, ink, and paper; which being immediately produced, he wrote a check on his banker for two thousand pounds. He immediately retired with precipitation, happy to escape without personal injury. The next morning, before its opening, he attended at the Banker's, with some Police-officers; and on Mrs. Phepoe's making her appearance with the check, she was arrested, and subsequently tried at the Old Bailey, on a capital charge, grounded on the above proceedings. However, through the able defence made by her counsel (the late Mr. Fielding) who took a legal objection to the case as proved, and contended that she never had or obtained any property of Mr. Courtois, on the principle that possession constituted the first badge of ownership, she was only sentenced to twelve months' imprisonment."

"Some years since, the late Lord Gage met Courtois, at the court-room of the East India House, on an election business. "Ah, Courtois!" said his Lordship, "what brings you here?"—'To give my votes, my Lord,' was the answer.—"What! are you a proprietor?—'Most certainly.'—"And of more votes than one?"—'Yes, my Lord, I have four!'—"Aye, indeed! why then, before you take the book, pray be kind enough to pin up my curls!" With which modest request the proprietor of four votes, equal to ten thousand pounds, immediately complied!

"M. Courtois married a few years since, and has left several children. On reflecting that his widow's thirds would amount to an immense sum, with his usual prudence he made a handsome settlement on her during his lifetime. As his sons were not of very economical habits, he has bequeathed them small annuities only; and vested the bulk of his fortune in trustees on behalf of his daughters, who are infants.

"Until his death, he invariably adhered to the costume of the age in which he was born. A three-cocked hat, and a plum-coloured coat, both rather the worse for wear, in which we have seen him frequently, invariably designated his person and habits; while a penurious economy, that bid defiance to all vulgar imitation, accompanied him to his grave. His death occurred in 1819, in the 80th or 81st year of his age."

"Such characters," observed Tallyho, "notwithstanding their eccentricity, afford useful lessons to those who, in this giddy and dissipated age, devote a part of their time to thinking."

"No doubt of it," replied Dashall; "they furnish examples of what may be done by perseverance and determination, and almost seem to verify the assertion, that every one may become rich if he pleases. But come, we must move towards Tom's Coffee House, in our way to which we will pass through the Royal Exchange, which lies directly before us. It was originally a brick building, erected by Sir Thomas Gresham in the year 1567, but being destroyed by the fire of London in 1666, the present building of Portland stone was raised in its place, the first stone of which was laid by Charles II. in 1667; in consequence of which his statue has been placed in the centre of its quadrangle, around which the Merchants assemble daily to transact their commercial business.{1}

> 1 *The merry Monarch was fond of the Citizens, and frequently honoured the Lord Mayor's table with his presence. It is said of him, that, on retiring to his carriage one day after dining with the civic Sovereign, he was followed by the latter, who, with a freedom inspired by the roseate Deity, laid hold of His Majesty by the arm, and insisted that he should not go until he had drunk t'other bottle. The Monarch turned round, and good-humouredly repeating a line from an old song—"The man that is drunk is as great as a king," went back to the company, and doubtless complied with the Lord Mayor's request.*

"It has two principal fronts, one in Cornhill, and the other, which you now see, is at the end of Threadneedle Street; each of which has a piazza, affording a convenient shelter from the sun and rain. It is open as a thoroughfare from eight in the morning till six in the evening; but the hours in which business is chiefly transacted, are from two to five. Its extent is 203 feet by 171."

By this time they had passed the gate, and Bob found himself in a handsome area with a fine piazza carried entirely round, and furnished with seats along the four walks, for Merchants of different nations, who meet, each at their different stations, and was immediately attracted by the appearance of the numerous specimens of art with which it was adorned.

"Do you observe," said his Cousin, "within these piazzas are twenty-eight niches; all vacant but that in which is placed a statue of Sir Thomas Gresham, in the north-west angle; and that in the south-west, which presents a statue of Sir John Barnard, Magistrate of the City, and one of its Representatives in Parliament. Those smaller statues in the niches of the wall of the Quadrangle, in the upper story, are the Kings and Queens of England, beginning with Edward I. on the North side, and ending with his late Majesty on the East. As far as Charles I. they were executed by Gabriel Cibber. The various frames which are placed around under the piazza, contain the names, residences and occupations of Tradesmen, Mechanics and others. The grand front in Cornhill has been under repair lately, and in its appearance, no doubt, is greatly improved. The steeple which is just raised, is a handsome dome, surmounted by the original grasshopper, rendered somewhat celebrated by a prophecy, that certain alterations would take place in men, manners, and times, when the grasshopper on the top of the Exchange should meet the dragon at the top of Bow Church; and strange and extraordinary as it may appear, this very circumstance is said to have taken place, as they have both been seen in the warehouse of some manufacturer, to whom they were consigned for repair; in addition to which, if Crockery's{1} relation of the transmogrifications of England is to be believed, the prophecy is in a considerable degree a whimsical and laughable Burletta, in one act, has recently been produced at the Royal Coburg Theatre, in which Mr. Sloman sings, with admirable comicality, the following Song, alluded to by the Hon. Tom Dashall, to the tune of O, The Roast Beef of Old England.

"From Hingy I came with my Master, O dear,
But Lunnun is not like the same place, that's clear;
It has nigh broke my heart since I have been here!
O, the old times of Old England,
O dear, the good English old times.

The town is so changed, that I don't know a spot;
The times are so hard, there's no vork to be got;
And for porter they charges you tip-pence a pot!
O, the old times, &c.

Then the sides of the houses are stuck full of bills
About Blacking, Mock-Auctions, and vonderful Fills;
But for von vot they cures, a hundred they kills!
O, the old times, &c.

There's the names are all halter'd verewer I goes,
And the people all laughs at the cut of my close;
The men are turn'd vomen, the belles are turn'd beaux!
O, the old times, &c.

Ven I vent out to Hingy, if any von died,
A good vooden coffin they used to prowide,
But hiron vons now keeps the poor vorms houtside!
O, the old times, &c.

There's the Lancaster schools now all over the land,
Vot teaches the children to scribble on sand—
And a hugly Bonassus vot lives in the Strand!
O, the new times, &c.

There's a new Life-preserver, vith vich you cant drown;
And a new kind of Sov'reigns just com'd into town,
Von is vorth a pound note, and the other a crown!
O, the new times, &c.

The Play-bills have hard vords, vot I cannot speak;
And the horgans plays nothing but Latin and Greek;

*And it's rain'd every day now for more than a veek!
O, the new times, &c.*

*There's a man valks on vater and don't vet his feet;
And a patent steam-kitchen, vot cooks all your meat;
And Epp's ham and beef shop in every street!
O, the new times, &c.*

*I valks up and down vith the tears in my hye;
Vot they vonce call'd a vaggon is now call'd a fly;
And the boys points their fingers, and calls I—a"Guy!
O, the old times of Old England,
O dear, the good English old times."*

There is a stair-case in each front, and one on each side, which lead to a gallery above, running round the whole building, containing the offices of various establishments; but I believe, in the original plan, shops were intended to fill the building to the top. At present, the upper rooms are occupied by Lloyd's celebrated Subscription Coffee-house, for the use of Under-writers and Merchants—by the Royal Exchange Insurance Company, and various offices of individuals. There are also the Gresham Lecture—Rooms, where lectures are read pursuant to the will of the late Sir Thomas Gresham, who bequeathed to the City of London and the Mercers' Company, all the profits arising from these and other premises in Cornhill, in trust to pay salaries to four lecturers in divinity, astronomy, music, and geometry; and three readers in civil law, physic, and rhetoric, who read lectures daily in term time.

"This we may consider the grand mart of the universe! where congregate those sons of Commerce the British Merchants, who, in dauntless extent of enterprise, hold such distinguished pre-eminence!"

Tallyho viewed the scene before him with an inquisitive eye, and was evidently wrapped in surprise at the "busy hum of men," all actuated by one universal object, the acquisition of wealth. The spacious area exhibited a mass of mercantile speculators, numerously grouped, in conversation; under the piazzas appeared a moving multitude in like manner engaged, while the surrounding seats were in similar occupation; Dashall and Bob, of the many hundreds of individuals present, were perhaps the only two led to the place by curiosity alone.

Tallyho, who, on every occasion of "doubtful dilemma," looked to his cousin Dashall for extrication, expressed his surprise at the appearance of a squalid figure, whose lank form, patched habiliments, and unshorn beard, indicated extreme penury; in familiar converse with a gentleman fashionably attired, and of demeanour to infer unquestionable respectability.

"Interest," said Tallyho, "supersedes every other consideration, else these two opposites would not meet."

"Your observation is just," replied his cousin; "the tatterdemallion to whom you allude, is probably less impoverished than penurious; perhaps of miserly habits, and in other respects disqualified for polite society. What then, he is doubtless in ample possession of the essential requisite; and here a monied man only is a good man, and without money no man can be respectable."{1}

Here the continued and deafening noise of a hand-bell, rung by one of the Exchange-keepers underlings, perched on the balcony over the southern gate, interrupted Mr. Dashall's remarks; it was the signal for locking up the gates, and inferring at the same time obedience to the summons with due promptitude and submission, on pain of being detained two hours "in duresse vile."

Sufficient alacrity of egression not having been shown, the Keepers closed the two gates, and at the same time locked the east and western avenues; thus interdicting from egress above three hundred contumacious individuals, including the Hon. Tom Dashall and his Cousin.

A considerable time having now elapsed without any prospect of enlargement, dissatisfaction gained ground apace, and shortly ripened into actual mutiny. The disaffected now proceeded to hold a council of war, and after a few moments deliberation, it was resolved unanimously to storm the avenues! Dashall and

1 Some years ago, a gentleman of extensive property, residing in the country, was desirous of raising, by way of loan on the security of landed estates, the sum of 30,000L. His Solicitor in London, with whom he had corresponded on the subject, summoned him at last to town; a lender was found, who was to meet the Solicitor at a certain time and place appointed, in the neighbourhood of the Exchange. The borrower, on the day and near the hour fixed upon, was in the area of the Royal Exchange, when there crossed over a wretched looking being, the very personification of misery. The gentleman, unsolicited, gave the poor object a shilling. On going to the appointed rendezvous, how great was his astonishment to find in the person of the wealthy monied man the identical receiver of his bounty!—"Ha, ha," cried he, "you shall not fare the worse for your generosity!" and actually advanced the money on terms much easier than expected. This personage was the celebrated Daniel Dancer.

Tallyho declined taking any part in the enterprise; they took a right view of the affair; they were mere casual visitants, not likely ever again to suffer a similar restraint, while the others were in the daily practice of transacting business on the spot: to them therefore the frequent recurrence of the present disaster might happen—theirs then was the cause, as being most particularly interested.

An attack was made by the prisoners upon the portals opening into Bank Buildings and Sweeting's Kents; but the former having been shattered sometime since on a similar occasion, and subsequently very strongly repaired, it was found impregnable, at least to any immediate exertion of force, and being neither furnished with a park of artillery, nor with the battering ram of the ancients, the little army faced to the right about, enfiladed the area, and took up a new position, in due order of assault, against the door of the avenue leading into Sweeting's Rents. The affair was decided, and without bloodshed; the bars soon bent before the vigour of the assailants; one of these was taken into custody by a Beadle, but rescued, and the attack recommenced with success; when the opposite door was also opened by the Shop-keeper living in that avenue, and the Exchange was finally cleared at four minutes past five o'clock, after above an hour's detention, including the time occupied in storming the avenues.

The triumph of liberty was now complete; the intrepid phalanx disbanded itself; and our Heroes having made the farewell conge to their victorious compeers, proceeded into Cornhill, where, Dashall espying his curricle at the door of Tom's Coffee House, they, after refreshing themselves, took a cheerful country drive over London Bridge, Clapham Common, Wandsworth, &c. from which they returned at six o'clock to dinner, determined to have a night's rest before they proceeded in search of further adventures.

CHAPTER XXI

"Happy the man, who void of cares and strife,
In silken or in leathern purse retains
A SPLENDID shilling! he nor hears with pain
New oysters cried, nor sighs for cheerful ale;

But I, whom griping penury surrounds,
And hunger, sure attendant upon want,
With scanty offal and small acid tiff,
Wretched repast, my meagre corse sustain!
Or solitary walk, or doze at home
In garret vile!"

TALKING over, at the breakfast-table, the occurrences of the preceding day—"On my conscience!" exclaimed Tallyho, "were the antediluvian age restored, and we daily perambulated the streets of this immense Metropolis during a hundred years to come, I firmly believe that every hour would bring a fresh accession of incident."

"Ad infinitum," answered Dashall; "where happiness is the goal in view, and fifteen hundred thousand competitors start for the prize, the manouvres of all in pursuit of the grand ultimatum must ever exhibit an interesting and boundless variety. London,

> *". . . the needy villain's general home,*
> *The common sewer of Paris and of Rome!"*

where ingenious vice too frequently triumphs over talented worth—where folly riots in the glare of luxury, and merit pines in indigent obscurity.—Allons donc!—another ramble, and chance may probably illustrate my observation."

"Take notice," said the discriminating Dashall to his friend, as they reached the Mall in St. James's Park, "of that solitary knight of the woeful countenance; his thread-bare raiment and dejected aspect, denote disappointment and privation;—ten imperial sovereigns to a plebeian shilling, he is either a retired veteran or a distressed poet."

The object of curiosity, who had now seated himself, appeared to have attained the age of fifty, or more—a bat that had once been black—a scant-skirted blue coat, much the worse for wear—a striped waistcoat—his lank legs and thighs wrapt in a pair of something resembling trowsers, but "a world too wide for his shrunk shanks"—short gaiters—shoes in the last stage of consumption—whiskers of full dimensions—his head encumbered with an unadjusted redundancy-of grey hair: such were the habiliments and figure of this son of adversity!

The two friends now seated themselves on the same bench with the stranger, who, absorbed in reflection, observed not their approach.

The silence of the triumvirate was broken in upon by Tom, who, with his usual suavity of manners, politely addressed himself to the unknown, on the common topic of weather, *et cetera*, without eliciting in reply more than an assenting or dissenting monosyllable, "You have seen some service, Sir?"

"Yes."

"In the army, I presume?"

"No."

"Under Government?"

"Yes."

"In the navy, probably?"

"No."

"I beg your pardon," continued Dashall—"my motives originate not in idle inquisitiveness; if I can be of any service———"

The stranger turned towards him an eye of inquiry. "I ask not from impertinent curiosity," resumed Dashall, "neither would I wish indelicately to obtrude an offer of assistance, perhaps equally unnecessary as unacceptable; yet there are certain mutabilities of life wherein sympathy may be allowed to participate."

"Sir," said the other, with an immediate grateful expansion of mind, and freedom of communication—"I am inexpressibly indebted for the honour of your solicitude, and feel no hesitation in acknowledging that I am a literary writer; but so seldom employed, and, when employed, so inadequately requited, that to me the necessaries of life are frequently inaccessible."

Here Tallyho interrupted the narrator by asking—whence it was that he had adopted a profession so irksome, precarious, and unproductive?

"Necessity," was the reply. "During a period of eight years, I performed the duties as senior Clerk of an office under Government; four years ago the establishment was broken up, without any provision made for its subordinate dependents; and thus I became one of the twenty thousand distressed beings in London, who rise from bed in the morning, unknowing where to repose at night, and are indebted to chance for a lodging or a dinner!"{1}   1 The following calculation, which is curious in all its parts, cannot fail to interest the reader:—

The aggregate Population on the surface of the known habitable Globe is estimated at 1000,000,000 souls. If therefore we reckon with the Ancients, that a generation lasts 30 years, then in that space 1000,000,000 human beings will be born and die; consequently, 91,314 must be dropping into eternity every day, 3800 every hour, or about 63 every minute, and more than one every second. Of these 1000,000,000 souls, 656,000,000 are supposed to be Pagans, 160,000,000 Mahomedans, 9,000,000 Jews, only 175,000,000 are called Christians, and of these only 50,000,000 are Protestants.

There are in London 502 places of Worship—one Cathedral, one Abbey, 114 Churches, 132 Chapels and Chapels of Ease, 220 Meet-ings and Chapels for Dissenters, 43 Chapels for Foreigners, and 6 Synagogues for Jews. About 4050 public and private Schools, including Inns of Courts, Colleges, &c. About 8 Societies for Morals; 10 Societies for Learning and Arts; 112 Asylums for Sick and Lame; 13 Dispensaries, and

704 Friendly Societies. Charity distributed £800,000 per annum.

There are about 2500 persons committed for trial in one year: The annual depredations amount to about £2,100,000. There are 19 Prisons, and 5204 Alehouses within the bills of Mortality. The amount of Coin counterfeited is £200,000 per annum. Forgeries on the Bank of England in the year £150,000. About 3000 Receivers of Stolen Goods. About 10,000 Servants at all times out of place. Above 20,000 miserable individuals rise every morning without knowing how or by what means they are to be supported during the passing day, or where, in many instances, they are to lodge on the succeeding night.

London consumes annually 112,000 bullocks; 800,000 sheep and lambs; 212,000 calves; 210,000 hogs; 60,000 sucking pigs; 7,000,000 gallons of milk, the produce of 9000 cows; 10,000 acres of ground cultivated for vegetables; 4000 acres for fruit; 75,000 quarters of wheat; 700,000 chaldrons of coals; 1,200,500 barrels of ale and porter; 12,146,782 gallons of spirituous liquors and compounds; 35,500 tons of wine; 17,000,000 pounds of butter, 22,100,000 pounds of cheese; 14,500 boat loads of cod.

"May I ask," said Mr. Dashall, "from what species of literary composition you chiefly derive your subsistence?"

"From puffing—writing rhyming advertisements for certain speculative and successful candidates for public favour, in various avocations; for instance, eulogizing the resplendent brilliancy of Jet or Japan Blacking—the wonderful effects of Tyrian-Dye and Macassar Oil in producing a luxuriant growth and changing the colour of the hair, transforming the thinly scattered and hoary fragments of age to the redundant and auburn tresses of youth—shewing forth that the "Riding Master to his late Majesty upwards of thirty years, and Professor of the Royal Menage of Hanover, sets competition at defiance, and that all who dare presume to rival the late Professor of the Royal Menage of Hanover, are vile unskilful pretenders, ci-devant stable-boys, and totally undeserving the notice of an enlightened and discerning public! In fact, Sir, I am reduced to this occasional humiliating employment, derogatory certainly to the dignity of literature, as averting the approach of famine. I write, for various adventurers, poetical panegyric, and illustrate each subject by incontrovertible facts, with appropriate incident and interesting anecdote."

"And these facts," observed Bob Tallyho, "respectably authenticated?"

"By no means," answered the Poet; "nor is it necessary, nobody takes the trouble of inquiry, and all is left to the discretion of the writer and the fertility of his invention."

"On the same theme, does not there exist," asked Dashall, "a difficulty in giving it the appearance of variety?"

"Certainly; and that difficulty would seem quite insurmountable when I assure you, that I have written for a certain Blacking Manufacturer above two hundred different productions on the subject of his unparalleled Jet, each containing fresh incident, and very probably fresh incident must yet be found for two hundred productions more! But the misfortune is, that every thing is left to my invention, and the remuneration is of a very trifling nature for such mental labour: besides, it has frequently happened that the toil has proved unavailing—the production is rejected—the anticipated half-crown remains in the accumulating coffers of the Blacking-manufacturer, and the Author returns, pennyless and despondingly, to his attic, where, if fortune at last befriends him, he probably may breakfast dine and sup, tria juncta in uno, at a late hour in the evening!" "And," exclaimed the feeling Dashall, "this is real Life in London!"

"With me actually so," answered the Poet.

The Blacking-maker's Laureat now offered to the perusal of his sympathising friends the following specimen of his ability in this mode of composition:—

PUG IN ARMOUR;
OR,
THE GARRISON ALARMED.

"Whoe'er on the rock of Gibraltar has been,
A frequent assemblage of monkeys has seen
Assailing each stranger with volleys of stones,
As if pre-determin'd to fracture his bones!

A Monkey one day took his turn as a scout,
And gazing his secret position about,
A boot caught his eye, near the spot that was plac'd,
By w * * * *n's jet; Blacking transcendently grac'd;
And, viewing his shade in its brilliant reflection,
He cautiously ventured on closer inspection.

The gloss on its surface return'd grin for grin,
Thence seeking his new-found acquaintance within,
He pok'd in the boot his inquisitive snout,
Head and shoulders so far, that he could not get out;
And thus he seem'd cas'd—from his head to his tail,
In suit of high-burnish'd impregnable mail!

Erect on two legs then, with retrograde motion,
It stalk'd; on the Sentry impressing a notion
That this hostile figure, of non-descript form,
The fortress might take by manoeuvre or storm!

Now fixing his piece, in wild terror he bawls—
"A legion of devils are scaling the walls!"
The guards sallied forth 'mid portentous alarms,
Signal-guns were discharged, and the drums beat to arms;
And Governor then, and whole garrison, ran
To meet the dread foe in this minikin man!

"A man—'tis a monkey!" Mirth loudly exclaim'd,
And peace o'er the garrison then was proclaim'd;
And Pug was released, the strange incident backing

The merits, so various, of W* * * *n's Jet Blacking."

This trifle, well enough for the purpose, was honoured with approbation.

The two friends, unwilling to offend the delicacy of the Poet by a premature pecuniary compliment at this early stage of acquaintance, took his address and departed, professing an intention of calling upon him at his lodgings in the evening.

"I would not, were I a bricklayer's labourer," exclaimed Bob, "exchange situations with this unfortunate literary hack—this poor devil of mental toil and precarious result, who depends for scanty subsistence on the caprice of his more fortunate inferiors, whose minds, unexpanded by liberal feeling, and absorbed in the love of self, and the sordid consideration of interest, are callous to the impression of benevolence!—But let us hope that few such cases of genius in adversity occur, even in this widely extended and varied scene of human vicissitude."

"That hope," replied his Cousin, "is founded on

"The baseless fabric of a vision!"

There are, at this moment, thousands in London of literary merit, of whom we may truly say,

*"Chill penury repress their noble rage,
And freeze the genial current of the soul!"*

Men unsustained by the hand of friendship, who pine in unheeded obscurity, suffering the daily privations of life's indispensable requisites, or obtaining a scanty pittance at the will of opulent ignorance, and under the humiliating contumely, as we have just been informed, even of Blacking Manufacturers!

"But here is a man, who, during a period of eight years, held a public situation, the duties of which he performed satisfactorily to the last; and yet, on the abolition of the establishment, while the Principal retires in the full enjoyment of his ample salary, this senior Clerk and his fellows in calamity are cast adrift upon the world, to live or starve, and in the dearth of employment suitable to their habits and education, the unfortunate outcasts are left to perish, perhaps by the hand of famine in the streets, or that of despondency in a garret; or, what is worse than either, consigned to linger out their remaining wretched days under the "cold reluctant charity" of a parish workhouse.{1}

"When the principal of a Public-office has battened for many years on his liberal salary, and the sole duties required of him have been those of occasionally signing a few official papers, why not discontinue his salary on the abolition of the establishment, and partition it out in pensions to those disbanded Clerks by whose indefatigable exertions the business of the public has been satisfactorily conducted? These allowances, however inadequate to the purpose of substantiating all the comforts, might yet realise the necessaries of life, and, at least, would avert the dread of absolute destitution."

A pause ensued—Dashall continued in silent rumination—a few moments brought our Heroes to the Horse Guards; and as the acquirement "devoutly to be wished" was a general knowledge of metropolitan manners, they proceeded to the observance of Real Life in a Suttling House.

Child's Suttling House at the Horse Guards is the almost exclusive resort of military men, who, availing themselves of the intervals between duty, drop in to enjoy a pipe and pint.

> "To fight their battles o'er again,
> Thrice to conquer all their foes,
> And thrice to slay the slain."

In the entrance on the left is a small apartment, bearing the dignified inscription, in legible characters on the door, of "The Non-Commissioned Officers' Room." In front of the bar is a larger space, boxed off, and appropriated to the use of the more humble heroical aspirants, the private men; and passing through the bar, looking into Whitehall, is the *Sanctum Sanctorum*, for the reception of the more exalted rank, the golden-laced, three-striped, subordinate commandants, Serjeant-Majors and Serjeants, with the colour-clothed regimental appendants of Paymasters and Adjutants' Clerks, *et cetera*. Into this latter apartment our accomplished friends were ushered with becoming

> 1 "Swells then thy feeling heart, and streams thine eye
> O'er the deserted being, poor and old,
>
> Whom cold reluctant parish-charity
> Consigns to mingle with his kindred mold."
> —Charlotte Smith.

respect to their superior appearance, at the moment when a warm debate was carrying on as to the respective merits of the deceased Napoleon and the hero of Waterloo.

The advocate of the former seemed unconnected with the army: the adherent to the latter appeared in the gaudy array of a Colour-Serjeant of the Foot Guards, and was decorated with a Waterloo medal, conspicuously suspended by a blue ribbon to the upper button of his jacket; and of this honourable badge the possessor seemed not less vain than if he had been adorned with the insignia of the most noble order of the Garter.

"I contend, and I defy the universe to prove the contrary," exclaimed the pertinacious Serjeant in a tone of authoritative assertion, "that the Duke of Wellington is a greater man than ever did, does, or hereafter may exist!"

"By no means," answered the Civilian. "I admit, so far as a thorough knowledge of military tactics, and a brilliant career of victory constitutes greatness, his grace of Wellington to be a great hero, but certainly not the greatest 'inan that ever did, does, or hereafter may exist!" "Is there a greater man? Did there ever exist a greater?—when and where?" the Serjeant impatiently demanded.

"Buonaparte was a greater," answered the opposing disputant; "because to military renown unparalleled in the annals of ancient or modern history, he added the most consummate knowledge of government; and although his actions might frequently partake of arbitrary sway, (and who is the human being exempted from human frailty) yet he certainly created and sustained, in her most elevated zenith, the splendour of France, till crushed by the union of nations in arms; and if power is the criterion of greatness, who was, is, or ever can be greater than the man, who, emerging from obscurity, raised himself solely by his mental energies to the highest elevation of human glory; and who, this Island excepted, commanded the destinies of all Europe! The most determined of his enemies will not deny, calmly and duly appreciating his merits, that he possessed unrivalled talent; and this fact the hero, whose cause you so vehemently espouse, would, I have no doubt, be the foremost in acknowledging."

In deficiency of argument, the Serjeant resorted to invective; the vociferous disputation reached the next room, and was taken up by the rank and file in a manner not less tumultuous; when an honest native of the "Emerald Isle" good-humouredly terminated the war of words, calling for half a quartern of gin, with which to qualify a pint of Whitbread's entire.

"To the immortal memory of St. Patrick, and long life to him!" exclaimed Patrick O'Shaughnessy. "If there did not exist but them two selves, bad luck to the spalpeen who will say that the Duke and my Lord Londondery would not be the greatest men in the universe!"

This sally led to a cessation of hostilities, which might have been followed by a definitive treaty of peace, but the dæmon of discord again made its appearance in the tangible shape of a diminutive personage, who, hitherto silently occupying a snug out-of-the-way corner by the fireplace, had escaped observation.

Dashall and his Cousin emerging from the Sanctum Sanctorum, where their presence seemed to have operated as a check on the freedom of discussion, had just seated themselves in the room allotted to the private soldiers, when, in a broad northern accent, the aforesaid taciturn gentleman, selecting the two strangers, who, of all the company, seemed alone worthy the honour of his notice, thus addressed them:

"I crave your pardon, Sirs—but I guess frae your manner that ye are no unacquainted wi' the movements o' high life—do you ken how lang the King means to prolong his abode amang our neebors owre the water, his hair-brain'd Irish subjects, whase notions o' loyalty hae excited sae mony preposterously antic exhibitions by that volatile race O' people?"

"I am not in possession," answered Dashall, "of any information on the subject."

"By the manes of the Priest," exclaimed Mr. O'Shaughnessy, "but the King (God bless him) has visited the land of green Erin, accompanied by the spirit of harmony, and praties without the sauce of butter-milk be his portion, who does not give them both a hearty welcome!—Arrah, what mane you by a preposterous exhibition? By hecky, the warm hearts of the sons and daughters of St. Patrick have exhibited an unsophisticated feeling of loyalty, very opposite indeed to the chilling indifference, not to say worse of it, of those his subjects at home; and as Sir William, the big Baronet of the City, said in the House that gives laws to the land, Why should not his Majesty be cheered up a little?"

This effusion of loyalty was well received, and Dashall and his Cousin cordially united in the general expression of approbation.

"This is a' vera weel," said the Northern; "but an overstrained civility wears ay the semblance o' suspicion, and fulsome adulation canna be vera acceptable to the mind o' delicate feeling: for instance, there is my ain country, and a mair ancient or a mair loyal to its legitimate Sovereign there disna exist on the face o' the whole earth; wad the King condescend to honor wi' his presence the palace o' Holyrod House, he wad experience as ardent a manifestation o' fidelity to his person and government in Auld Reekie as that shown him in Dublin, though aiblins no quite sae tumultuous; forbye, it wadna hae been amiss to hae gaen the preference to a nation whare his ancestors held sway during sae mony centuries, and whare, in the castle of Edinburgh, is still preserved the sacred regalia, with which it migh no hae been unapropos to hae graced his royal head and hand amidst the gratifying pageantry o' a Scotch coronation. Sure I am that North Britain has never been honored publicly wi' a royal visit.—Whether ony branch o' the present reigning family hae been there incognita they best ken themselves."

"You seem to have forgot," observed Tallyho, "the visit of the Duke of Cumberland to Scotland in the year 1745."

"Begging your pardon for setting you right in that particular," answered the cynic, with a most significant expression of countenance, "that, Sir, was not a visit, but a visitation!"

"Appropriate enough," whispered Dashall to Tallyho.

"Augh, boderation to nice distinctions!" exclaimed O'Shaughnessy; "here, Mister Suttler be after tipping over anoder half quartern of the cratur, wid which to drink success to the royal visitant."

"And that the company may participate in the gratifying expression of attachment to their Sovereign, Landlord," said Dashall, "let the glass go round."

"Testifying our regard for the Sovereign," resumed the Northern, "it canna be understood that we include a' the underlings o' Government. We ought, as in duty bound, to venerate and obey the maister o' the house; bat it is by no means necessary that we should pay a similar respect to his ox and his ass, his man-servant and his maid-servant. May be, had he been at hame on a late occasion o' melancholy solemnity, blood wadna hae been spilt, and mickle dool and sorrow wad hae been avoided."

"We perfectly understand your allusion," said one from the group of Life-guardsmen: "Of us now present there were none implicated in the unfortunate occurrences either of that day or a subsequent one: yet we must not silently hear our comrades traduced—perhaps then it may be as well to drop the subject."

"I canna think o' relinquishing a topic 0' discourse," answered the Northern, "replete wi' mickle interest, merely at your suggestion; it may be ye did your duty in obeying the commands, on that lamentable occasion, O' your superior officers, and it is to be hoped that the duty O' the country, towards those with whom originated the mischief, will not be forgotten; there is already on record against the honour 0' your corps a vera serious verdict."

Here the Life-guardsmen spontaneously started up; but the immediate interposition of Dashall averted me impending storm; while Tallyho, imitating the generosity of his Cousin, ordered the circulation once more of the bottle, to Unanimity betwixt the military and the people. Harmony thus restored, the two friends took their leave, amidst the grateful acknowledgments of the company, O'Shaughnessy swearing on their departure, that doubtless the two strangers were begot in Ireland, although they might have come over to England to be born! While the pertinacious Northern observed, that appearances were aften deceitful, although, to be sure, the twa friends had vera mickle the manners 0' perfectly well-bred gentlemen, and seem'd, forbye, to hae a proper sense o' national honor.

Proceeding into Whitehall, Tallyho much admired the statue-like figures of the mounted sentries in the recesses by the gate of the Horse-guards; the relief had just approached; the precision of retirement of the one party, and advance to its post of the other: the interesting appearance of the appropriately caparisoned and steady demeanour of the horses, and their instinctive knowledge of military duty, excited deservedly prolonged attention,

"One would think," said Tallyho, "that these noble animals are really actuated by reasoning faculties."

"Hereafter," replied Dashall, "you will still more incline to this opinion, when we have an opportunity of being present on a cavalry field-day in Hyde Park, where manoeuvre will appear to have attained its acme of perfection, as much from the wonderful docility of the horse as the discipline of the rider."{l}

"But hold, who have we here?—Our friend Sparkle, gazing about him with an eye of inquisitive incertitude, as if in search of lost property."

As his two friends approached, he seemed bewildered in the labyrinth of conjecture.—"I have lost my horse!" he exclaimed, in answer to the inquiry of Dashall. "Having occasion to stop half an hour at Drummond's, I gave the animal in charge of an Israelite urchin, and now neither are to be seen."

Casting a look down the street, they at last discerned the Jew lad, quickly, yet carefully leading the horse along, with two boys mounted on its back. Thoroughly instructed in the maxim—Get money, honestly if you can, but get it by any means! young Moses had made the most of the present opportunity, by letting out the horse, at a penny a ride, from Charing Cross to the Horse Guards; this, by his own confession, was the fifteenth trip! Sparkle, highly exasperated, was about to apply the discipline of the whip to the shoulders of the thrifty speculator, when Tallyho, interceding in his behalf, he was released, with a suitable admonition.

> 1 Not long since some cavalry horses, deemed "unfit for further service," were sold at Tattersal's. Of one of these a Miller happened to be the purchaser. Subservient now to the ignoble purposes of burthen, the horse one day was led,'with a sack of flour on his back, to the next market-town; there while the Miller entered a house for a few moments, and the animal quietly waited at the door, a squadron of dragoons drew up in an adjacent street, forming by sound of trumpet; the instant that the Miller's horse heard the well-known signal, it started off with as much celerity as its burthen admitted, and, to the great amusement of the troop, and astonishment of the spectators, took its station in the ranks, dressing in line, with the accustomed precision of an experienced veteran in the service; and it was with considerable difficulty that the Miller, who had now hastened to the spot, could induce the animal to relinquish its military ardour, to which it still appeared to cling with renewed and fond pertinacity!

Sparkle, mounting his recovered charger, left his pedestrian friends for the present, to continue their excursion; who, proceeding up St. Martin's Lane, and admiring that noble edifice, the Church, reached, without other remarkable occurrence, the quietude of Leicester Square.

Close by is Barker's Panorama, an object of attraction too prominent to be passed without inspection. They now entered, and Tallyho stood mute with delight at the astonishing effect of the perspective; while, as if by the powers of enchantment, he seemed to have been transported into other regions. Amidst scenes of rich sublimity, in the centre of a vast amphitheatre, bounded only by the distant horizon, far remote from the noisy bustle of the Metropolis, he gave full scope to his imagination; and after an hour of pleasing reverie, left the fascinating delusion with evident reluctance.

Emerging once more into the gay world, the two associates, in search of Real Life in London, proceeded through Covent Garden Market, where fruit, flowers, and exotics in profusion, invite alike the eye and the appetite.

Onwards they reached the classic ground of Drury, "Where Catherine Street descends into the Strand."

"I never," said the Hon. Tom Dashall, "pass this spot without a feeling of veneration—the scenes of "olden times" rise on my view, and the shades of Garrick, and our late loss, and not less illustrious Sheridan, flit before me! This was then, as now, the seat of Cyprian indulgence—the magnet of sensual attraction, where feminine youth and beauty in their most fascinating and voluptuous forms were let out by the unprincipled procuress, and the shrines of Venus and Apollo invited the votaries of each to nocturnal sacrifice.{1}

> 1 *The avenue to the boxes of Drury Lane Theatre was, in the time of Garrick, through Vinegar Yard. In this passage an old spider, better known, perhaps, by the name of a Procuress, had spread her web, alias, opened a Bagnio, and obtained a plentiful living by preying on those who unfortunately or imprudently fell into her clutches. Those who are not unacquainted with haddocks, will understand the loose fish alluded to, who beset her doors, and accosted with smiles or insults every one that passed. It happened that a noble Lord, in his way to the theatre, with his two daughters under his arm, was most grossly attacked by this band of "flaming ministers." He immediately went behind the scenes, and insisted on seeing Mr. Garrick, to whom he*

represented his case, and so roused the vengeance of the little Manager, that he instantly, full of wrath, betook himself to this unholy Sybil: —

"Twin-child of Cacus; Vulcan was their sire, Full offspring both of healthless fume and fire!"
Finding her at the mouth of her cavern, he quickly gave veut to his rage in the most buskin'd strain, and concluded by swearing that he would have her ousted. To this assault she was not backward in reply, but soon convinced him that she was much more powerful in abusive language than our Roscius, though he had recourse in his speech to Milton's "hell-born bitch," and other phrases of similar celebrity, whilst she entirely depended on her own natural resources. Those to whom this oratory is not new, have no need of our reporting any of it; and those to whom it is a perfect mystery, boast a "state the more gracious," and are the more happy in their ignorance. None of this rhapsody, however, although teeming with blasphemy and abuse, had any effect on Garrick, and he would have remained unmoved had she not terminated in the following manner, which so excited the laughter of the collected mob, and disconcerted "the soul of Richard," that, without another word to say, he hastily took shelter in the theatre. Putting her arms akimbo, and letting down each side of her mouth with wonderful expression of contempt, she exclaimed—"You whipper snapper! you oust me! You be d— —-d! My house is as good as your's—aye, and better too. I can come into your's whenever I like, and see the best that you can do for a shilling; but d— —-me if you, or any body else, shall come into mine for less than a fifteen-penny negus."

"This street and neighbourhood was wont to exhibit, nightly, a melancholy proof of early infamy. Here might be seen a prolonged succession of juvenile voluptuaries, females, many of them under fourteen years of age, offering themselves to indiscriminate prostitution, in a state verging on absolute nudity, alluring the passengers, by every seductive wile, to the haunts of depravity, from which retreat was seldom effected without pecuniary exaction, and frequently accompanied by personal violence. The nuisance has been partly abated, but entirely to remove it would be a task of more difficult accomplishment than that of cleansing the Augean stable, and would baffle all the labours of Hercules!"

"This fact," observed Tallyho, "throws an indelible stain on metropolitan police."

"Not so," answered his companion, "scarce a day passes without groups of these unfortunates being held before a magistrate, and humanely disposed of in various ways, with the view of preventing a recurrence to vicious habits,—but in vain;—the stain is more attributed to the depraved nature of man, who first seduces, and then casts off to infamy and indigence the unhappy victim of credulity. Many of these wretched girls would, in all probability, gladly have abstained from the career of vice, if, on their first fall, they had experienced the consoling protection of parents or friends;—but, shut out from home,—exiled from humanity,—divested of character, and without resources,—no choice is left, other than mendicity or prostitution!"{1}

The sombre reflections occasioned by these remarks gradually gave way to those of a more enlivening hue, as the two friends proceeded along the Strand. The various display, at the tradesmen's shop windows, of useful and ornamental articles,—the continued bustle of the street,—the throng of passengers of every description, hurrying on in the activity of business, or more leisurely lounging their way under the impulse of curiosity,—the endless succession of new faces, and frequent occurrence of interesting incident;—these united in forming an inexhaustible fund of amusement and admiration.

> 1 *"Hatton Garden.—On Saturday, no less than fifteen unfortunate girls, all elegantly attired, were placed at the bar, charged by Cadby, the street-keeper on the Foundling Estate, with loitering about the neighbourhood for their nocturnal purposes. The constable stated, that repeated complaints had been made to him by many of the inhabitants, of the disgraceful practice of vast numbers of frail ones, who resort every night to Brunswick Square. He had been therefore instructed to endeavour to suppress the nuisance.*

About twelve o'clock on Friday night, while perambulating the district, he found the fifteen prisoners at the bar in Brunswick Square, at their usual pursuits, and all of them were in the act of picking up gentlemen. He procured assistance, and they were taken into custody, and conveyed to the watch-house.

None of the prisoners could deny the charge, but expressed great contrition at being under the painful necessity of procuring their subsistence in so disgraceful a manner. They were examined individually, by the magistrates, as to the origin that brought them to disgrace. Some, from their admission, were farmers' daughters, and had been decoyed from their relatives, and brought to London, and subsequently deserted by their seducers. Some were nursery-maids—others, girls seduced from boarding schools. Their tales were truly distressing—some had only been six months in such infamy, others twelve months, and some two years and upwards.

The worthy magistrate, with much feeling, admonished them on the evil course they were following, and pointed out the means still left for them to return to the paths of virtue; and on their severally promising never to appear again in that quarter, they were discharged."

Passing through Temple Bar, "Once more," said Dashall, "we enter the dominions of another Sovereign,—the Monarch of the City,—than whom there is none more tenacious of the rights and immunities of his subjects. Professing a strictly civil government, and consequent hostility to military interference, it does not always happen that the regal sway of the East harmonizes with that of the West, and the limited reign of the former is generally most popular when most in opposition to that of the latter. Several important events have occurred wherein a late patriotic Right Honourable Chief Magistrate has had the opportunity of manifesting a zealous, firm, and determined attachment to the privileges of the community: the good wishes of his fellow-citizens have accompanied his retirement, and his private and public worth will be long held in deserved estimation."

Turning up the Old Bailey, and passing, with no pleasing sensations, that structure in front of which so many human beings expiate their offences with their lives, without, in any degree, the frequency of the dreadful example lessening the perpetration of crime,—"The crowd thickens," exclaimed the 'Squire; and advancing into Smithfield, a new scene opened on the view of the astonished Tallyho. An immense and motley crowd was wedged together in the open space of the market, which was surrounded by booths and shows of every description, while the pavement was rendered nearly impassable by a congregated multitude, attracted by the long line of stalls, exhibiting, in ample redundancy, the gorgeously gilt array of gingerbread monarchs, savory spice-nuts, toys for children and those of elder growth, and the numerous other *et cetera* of Bartholomew Fair, which at that moment the Lord Mayor of London, with accustomed state and formality, was in the act of proclaiming.

A more dissonant uproar now astounded the ears of Bob than ever issued from the hounds at falt in the field or at variance in the kennel! The prolonged stunning and vociferous acclamation of the mob, accompanied by the deeply sonorous clangor of the gong—the shrill blast of the trumpet—the hoarse-resounding voices of the mountebanks, straining their lungs to the pitch of extremity, through speaking tubes—the screams of women and children, and the universal combination of discord, announced the termination of the Civic Sovereign's performance in the drama; "the revelry now had began," and all was obstreperous uproar, and "confusion worse confounded."

In the vortex of the vast assemblage, the Hon. Tom Dashall and his Cousin were more closely hemmed in than they probably would have been at the rout of female distinction, where inconvenience is the order of the night, and pressure, to the dread of suffocation, the criterion of rank and fashion. Borne on the confluent tide, retreat was impracticable; alternately then, stationary and advancing with the multitude, as it urged its slow and undulating progress; or paused at the attractions of Wombwell and Gillman's rival menageries—the equestrian shows of Clark and Astley—the theatres of Richardson and Gyngell, graced by the promenade of the *dramatis personæ* and lure of female nudity—the young giantess—the dwarfs—and the accomplished lady, who, born without arms, cuts out watch-papers with her toes, and takes your likeness with her teeth!—Amidst these and numerous other seductive impediments to their progress, our pedestrians, resisting alike temptation and invitation, penetrated the mass of spectators, and gained an egress at Long Lane, uninjured in person, and undamaged in property, "save and except" the loss, by Bob, of a shoe, and the rent frock of his honourable Cousin. To repair the one and replace the other was now the predominant consideration. By fortunate proximity to a descendant of St. Crispin, the latter object was speedily effected; but the difficulty of finding, in that neighbourhood, a knight of the thimble, appearing insurmountable, the two friends pursued their course, Dashall drawing under his arm the shattered skirts of his garment, until they reached Playhouse Yard, in Upper Whitecross Street, St. Luke's, to which they had been previously directed, the epitome of Monmouth Street, chiefly inhabited by tailors and old clothes retailers, where purchase and repair are equally available.

Entering a shop occupied by an intelligent Scotch tailor, who, with his son, was busily employed in making up black cloth and kerseymere waistcoats, his spouse, a native of Edinburgh, with a smile of complacency and avidity of utterance that strongly indicated a view to the main chance, put her usual inquiry:

"What is your wull, Gentlemen—what wad you please to want?"

"My good lady," answered Dashall, "we would be glad to accept the services of your husband," exhibiting at same time the rent skirts of his frock. "This accident was sustained in passing, or rather in being squeezed through the Fair; my friend too, experienced a trifling loss; but, as it has been replaced, I believe that he does not require present amendment."

The materials destined to form the black waistcoats were then put aside, while the northern adept in the exercise of the needle proceeded to operate on the fractured garment; and a coat being supplied, *ad interim*, Tom and his friend accepted the "hospitable invitation of the guid wife, and seated themselves with unhesitating sociability.

"And sae ye hae been to the Fair, gentlemen?" "We have, madam," said Dashall, "and unintentionally so; we were not, until on the spot, aware of any such exhibition, and got within its vortex just as the Lord Mayor had licensed, by proclamation, the commencement of this annual scene of idleness, riot and dissipation!"

"Hoot awa, Sir, ye wadna wish to deprive us o' our amusements; poor folks dinna often enjoy pleasure, and why should na they hae a wee bit o' it now and then, as weel as the rich?"

"I know not, my good lady," exclaimed Bon, "that I can altogether assimilate with your's my ideas of pleasure; if it consists in being pressed nearly to death by a promiscuous rabble, in attempts on your pocket, shoes trod off your feet by the formidable iron-cased soles of a drayman's ponderous sandals, to say nothing of the pleasing effect thus produced upon your toes, and in having the coat torn off from your back, I would freely resign to the admirers of such pleasure the full benefit of its enjoyment."

"Accidents wull happen ony where and in ony situation," replied the garrulous wife; "ye may be thankfu', gentlemen, that its nae waur,— and, for the matter o' the rent frock, my guid man wull repair it in sic a way that the disaster wull no be seen, and the coat wull look as weel as ever."

The promise was verified; the reparation was made with equal neatness and celerity; something beyond the required remuneration was given; and Dashall inquiring if the worthy dame of *Auld Reekie* would take a drop of cordial, the friendly offer was accepted, and the glass of good fellowship having been drank, and civilities interchanged, the strangers departed.

They were now in Whitecross Street, where sojourned their acquaintance of the morning, the distressed Poet; and, from the accuracy of description, had no difficulty in ascertaining his place of residence.

It was in a public-house; a convenient lodging for the forlorn being, who, exiled from friendship, and unconnected by any ties of consanguinity, can dress his scanty meal by a gratuitous fire, and where casual generosity may sometimes supply him with a draught of Hanbury's exhilarating beverage.

At the bar, directly facing the street door, the strangers, on inquiring for the Poet by name, were directed by the landlord, with a sarcastical expression of countenance, to "the first floor *down the chimney!*" while the Hostess, whose demeanour perfectly accorded with that of the well-manner'd gentlewoman, politely interfered, and, shewing the parlour, sent a domestic to acquaint her lodger that he was wanted below stairs.

The summons was instantaneously obeyed; but as the parlour precluded the opportunity of private conversation, being partly occupied by clamorous butchers, with whom this street abounds to redundancy, the Poet had no other alternative than that of inviting the respectable visitants to his attic, or, as the Landlord facetiously named the lofty domicile, his first floor down the chimney!

Real Life in London must be seen, to be believed. The Hon. Tom Dashall and his friend Tallyho were reared in the lap of luxury, and never until now formed an adequate conception of the distressing privations attendant on suffering humanity.

With a dejection of spirits evidently occasioned by the humiliating necessity of ushering his polished friends into the wretched asylum of penury, the Poet led the way with tardy reluctancy, while his visitors regretted every step of ascent, under the appalling circumstance of giving pain to adversity; yet they felt that to recede would be more indelicate than to advance.

The apartment which they now entered seemed a lumber room, for the reception of superfluous or unserviceable furniture, containing not fewer than eleven decayed and mutilated chairs of varied description; and the limited space, to make the most of it in a pecuniary point of view, was encroached upon by three uncurtained beds, of most impoverished appearance,—while, exhibiting the ravages of time in divers fractures, the dingy walls and ceiling, retouched by the trowel in many places with a lighter shade of repairing material, bore no unapt resemblance to the Pye-bald Horse in Chiswell-street! Calculating on its utility and probable future use, the builder of the mansion had given to this room the appendage of a chimney, but evidently it had for many years been unconscious of its usual accompaniment, fire. Two windows had originally admitted the light of heaven, but to reduce the duty, one was internally blocked up, while externally uniformity was preserved. A demolished pane of glass in the remaining window, close to which stood a small dilapidated table, gave ingress to a current of air; the convenient household article denominated a clothes-horse, stood against the wall; and several parallel lines of cord were stretched across the room, on which to hang wet linen, a garret being considered of free access to all the house, and the comfort or health of its occupant held in utter derision and contempt!

Here then,—

> "In the worst Inn's worst room, with cobwebs hung,
> The walls of plaster and the floors of dung,"

entered Dashall and his Cousin Tallyho. The latter familiarly seating himself on the ricketty remains of what had once been an arm-chair, but now a cripple, having lost one of its legs, the precarious equilibrium gave way under the unaccustomed shock of the contact, and the 'Squire came to the ground, to his no small surprise, the confusion of the poet, and amusement of Dashall!

With many apologies for the awkwardness of their very humble accommodation, and grateful expression of thanks for the honour conferred upon him, the Poet replaced Tallyho in a firmer seat, and a silence of some few moments ensued, the two friends being at a loss in what manner to explain, and the Poet unwilling to inquire the object of their visit.

Dashall began at last, by observing that in pursuit of the knowledge of Real Life in London, he and his accompanying friend had met with many incidents both ludicrous and interesting; but that in the present instance their visit was rather influenced by sympathy than curiosity, and that where they could be serviceable to the interest of merit in obscurity, they always should be happy in the exercise of a duty so perfectly congenial with their feelings.

Many years had elapsed since the person, to whom these remarks were addressed, had heard the voice of consolation, and its effect was instantaneous; his usual sombre cast of countenance became brightened by the glow of cheerful animation, and he even dwelt on the subject of his unfortunate circumstances with jocularity:

"The elevated proximity of a garret," he observed, "to the sublimer regions, has often been resorted to as the *roost of genius*; and why should I, of the most slender, if any, literary pretensions, complain? And yet my writings, scattered amongst the various fugitive periodical publications of this and our sister island, if collected together, would form a very voluminous compilation."

"I have always understood," said Bob, "that the quality, not the quantum, constituted the fame of an author's productions."

"True, Sir," answered the Poet; "and I meant not the vanity of arrogating to myself any merit from my writings, with reference either to quantum or quality. I alluded to the former, as merely proving the inefficacy of mental labour in realizing the necessaries of life to an author whom celebrity declines acknowledging. Similarly situated, it would appear was the Dutchman mentioned by the late Doctor Walcot,

> *"My Broder is te poet, look,*
> *As all te world must please,*
> *For he heb wrote, py Got, a book*
> *So big as all this cheese!"*

"On the other hand, Collins, Hammond, and Gray, wrote each of them but little, yet their names will descend to posterity!—And had Gray, of his poems the *Bard*, and the *Elegy in a Country Church Yard*, written only one, and written nothing else, he had required no other or better passport to immortality!"{1}

> 1 *Of that great and multitudinous writer, Doctor Samuel*
> *Johnson, the following anecdote is told: "Being one morning*
> *in the library at Buckingham House honoured with the*

presence of Royalty, the King, his late Majesty, inquired why he, (Mr. Johnson) did not continue to write. "May it please your Majesty," answered the Doctor, "I think I have written enough." — "I should have thought so too," his Majesty replied, "if, Doctor Johnson, you had not written so well."

In this opinion the visitants, who were both well conversant with our native literature, readily acquiesced.

"Have you never," asked Dashall, "thought of publishing a volume by subscription?"

"I meditated such intention," answered the Poet, "not long ago; drew up the necessary Prospectus, with a specimen of the Poetry, and perambulated the Metropolis in search of patronage. In some few instances I was successful, and, though limited the number, yet the high respectability of my few Subscribers gave me inexpressible satisfaction; several of our nobility honoured me with their names, and others, my patrons, were of the very first class of literature. Nevertheless, I encountered much contumelious reception; and after an irksome and unavailing perseverance of a month's continuance, I was at last compelled to relinquish all hope of success.

"Having then on my list the name of a very worthy Alderman who lately filled the Civic Chair with honour to himself and advantage to his fellow-citizens, I submitted my prospectus in an evil hour to another Alderman, a baronet, of this here and that there notoriety!

"Waiting in his Banking-house the result of my application, he condescended to stalk forth from the holy of holies, his inner room, with the lofty demeanour of conscious importance, when, in the presence of his Clerks and others, doubtless to their great edification and amusement, the following colloquy ensued, bearing in his hand my unlucky Prospectus, with a respectful epistle which had accompanied it:—

"Are you the writer," he asked in a majesterial tone, "of this here letter?"

"I am, Sir W*****m, unfortunately!"

"Then," he continued, "you may take them there papers back again, I have no time to read Prospectuses, and so Mister Poet my compliments, and good morning to you!!!"

"These literally were his words; and such was the astounding effect they produced on my mind, that, although I had meant to have passed through the Royal Exchange, I yet, in the depth of my reverie, wandered I knew not where, and, before recovering my recollection, found myself in the centre of London Bridge!"

The detail of this fact, so characteristic of rude, ungentlemanly manners, and the barbarian ignorance of this great man of little soul, excited against him, with Dashall and his friend, a mingled feeling of ridicule, contempt and reprobation!

"Real Life in London still!" exclaimed Talltho; "intellect and indigence in a garret, and wealth and ignorance in a banking-house!—I would at least have given him, in deficiency of other means, the wholesome castigation of reproof."

"I did," said the Poet, "stung to the quick by such unmerited contumely, I retired to my attic, and produced a philippic named the Recantation: I cannot accommodate you at present with a copy of the Poem, but the concluding stanzas I can repeat from memory:—

> *"C****s, thy house in Lombard Street*
> *Affords thee still employment meet,*
> *Thy consequence retaining;*
> *For there thy Partners and thy Clerks*
> *Must listen to thy sage remarks,*
> *Subservient, uncomplaining.*
>
> *And rob'd in Aldermanic gown,*
> *With look and language all thy own,*
> *Thou mak'st thy hearers stare,*
> *When this here cause, so wisely tried,*
> *Thou put'st with self-applause aside,*
> *To wisely try that there.*
>
> *Nor can thy brother Cits forget*

When thou at civic banquet sate,
And ask'd of Heaven a boon,
A toast is call'd, on thee all eyes
Intent, when peals of laughter rise—
A speedy peace and soon!

Nor yet orthography nor grammar,
Vain effort on thy pate to hammer,
Impregnable that fort is!
Witness thy toast again,—Three Cs;
For who would think that thou by these
Meant Cox, and King, and Curtis
*C****s, though scant thy sense, yet Heaven*
To thee the better boon hast given
Or wealth—then sense despise,
And deem not Fate's decrees amiss,
For still "where ignorance is bliss
'Tis folly to be wise!"

"Bravo!" exclaimed Dashall; "re-issue your Prospectus, my friend, and we will accelerate, with our best interest and influence, the publication of your volume. Let it be dedicated to the Hon. Tom Dashall and his Cousin Bob Tallyho. In the meanwhile, accept this trifle, as a complimentary *douceur* uniformly given on such occasions; and, amidst the varied scenes of Real Life in London, I shall frequently recur to the present as the most gratifying to my feelings."

"By this the sun was out of sight,
And darker gloamin brought the night."

The benevolent associates now departed, pleased with the occurrences of the day, and, more than all, with the last, wherein the opportunity was afforded them of extending consolation and relief to genius in adversity!

CHAPTER XXII

........*"Mark!*
He who would cut the knot that does entwine
And link two loving hearts in unison,
May have man's form; but at his birth, be sure on't,
Some devil thrust sweet nature's hand aside
Ere she had pour'd her balm within his breast,
To warm his gross and earthly mould with pity.

.......I know what 'tis
When worldly knaves step in with silver beards,
To poison bliss, and pluck young souls asunder."

TOM and his Cousin were surprised the next morning by a visit from Mr. Mortimer and his friend Merrywell, whose dismal features and long visages plainly indicated some unpleasant disaster, and Tom began to fear blame would be attached to them for leaving his party at Darkhouse Lane.

"Pray," said Merrywell, "can you tell me where to find your friend Sparkle?"

"Indeed," replied Dashall, a little relieved by this question, "I am not Sparkle's keeper; but pray be seated—what is the matter, is it a duel, do you want a second?—I know he is a good shot."

"This levity, Sir," said Mortimer, "is not to be borne. The honour of a respectable family is at stake, and must be satisfied. No doubt you, as his very oldest friend, know where he is; and I desire you will immediately inform me, or————"

"Sir," said Dashall, who was as averse as unused to be desired by any person—"do you know whom you address, and that I am in my own house? if you do, you have certainly discarded all propriety of conduct and language before you cross'd the threshold."

"Gentlemen," said Merrywell, "perhaps some explanation is really necessary here. My friend Mortimer speaks under agonized feelings, for which, I am sure, your good sense will make every allowance. Miss Mortimer———"

"Miss Mortimer," exclaimed Dashall, rising from his seat, "you interest me strongly, say, what of Miss Mortimer?"

"Alas," said Mortimer, evidently endeavouring to suppress emotions which appeared to agitate his whole frame, and absorb every mental faculty, "we are unable to account for her absence, and strongly suspect she is in company with your friend Sparkle—can you give us any information relative to either of them?"

Dashall assured them he knew nothing of the fugitives, but that he would certainly make every inquiry in his power, if possible to find out Sparkle. Upon which they departed, though not without hinting they expected Tom had the power of making a search more effectually than either Mortimer or Merrywell.

"Egad!" said Tom to Tallyho, "this absence of Sparkle means something more than I can at present conceive; and it appears that we must now venture forth in search of our guide. I hope he has taken a good direction himself."

"Mortimer appears hurt," continued Bob, "and I can scarcely wonder at it."

"It is a trifle in high life now-a-days," replied Dashall, "and my life for it we shall obtain some clue to his mode of operation before the day is out. Love is a species of madness, and oftentimes induces extraordinary movements. I have discovered its existence in his breast for some time past, and if he is really with the lady, I wonder myself that he has not given some sort of intimation; though I know he is very cautious in laying his plans, and very tenacious of admitting too many persons to know his intentions, for fear of some indiscreet friend unintentionally frustrating his designs."

"I apprehend we shall have a wild-goose chase of it," rejoined Bob.

"It serves however," continued Tom, "to diversify our peregrinations; and if it is his pleasure to be in love, we will endeavour to chase pleasure in pursuit of the Lover, and if guided by honourable motives, which I cannot doubt, we will wish him all the success he can wish himself, only regretting that we are deprived of his agreeable company.

> *"Still free as air the active mind will rove,*
> *And search out proper objects for its love;*
> *But that once fix'd, 'tis past the pow'r of art*
> *To chase the dear idea from the heart.*
> *'Tis liberty of choice that sweetens life,*
> *Makes the glad husband and the happy wife."*

"But come, let us forth and see how the land lies; many persons obtain all their notoriety from an elopement; it makes a noise in the world, and even though frequently announced in our newspapers under fictitious titles, the parties soon become known and are recollected ever after; and some even acquire fame by the insertion of a paragraph announcing an elopement, in which they insinuate that themselves are parties; so that an elopement in high life may be considered as one of the sure roads to popularity."

"But not always a safe one," replied Bob.

"Life is full of casualties," rejoined Dashall, "and you are by this time fully aware that it requires something almost beyond human foresight to continue in the line of safety, while you are in pursuit of Real Life in London. Though it may fairly be said, 'That all the world's a stage, and all the men and women merely passengers,' still they have their inside and their outside places, and each man in his time meets with strange adventures. It may also very properly be termed a Camera Obscura, reflecting not merely trees, sign-posts, houses, &c. but the human heart in all its folds, its feelings, its passions, and its motives. In it you may perceive conceit flirting its fan—arrogance adjusting its cravat—pedantry perverting its dictionary—vacuity humming a tune—vanity humming his neighbour—cunning shutting his eyes while listening to a pedagogue—and credulity opening his eyes and ears, willing and anxious to be deceived and duped."

"It is a strange world, indeed," said Tallyho; "and of all that I have ever heard or seen, this London of your's is the most extraordinary part."

"Yes,—

> "This world is a well-cover'd table,
> Where guests are promiscuously set;
> We all eat as long as we're able,
> And scramble for what we can get—"

answered his Cousin; "in fact, it is like every thing, and at the same time like nothing—

> "The world is all nonsense and noise,
> Fantoccini, or Ombres Chinoises,
> Mere pantomime mummery
> Puppet-show flummery;
> A magical lantern, confounding the sight;
>
> Like players or puppets, we move
> On the wires of ambition and love;
> Poets write wittily,
> Maidens look prettily,
> 'Till death drops the curtain
> —all's over—good night!"

By this time they were at Long's, where, upon inquiry, all trace of Sparkle had been lost for two days. All was mystery and surprise, not so much that he should be absent, as that his servant could give no account of him, which was rather extraordinary. Tom ascertained, however, that no suspicion appeared to have been excited as to Miss Mortimer, and, with commendable discretion, avoided expressing a word which could create such an idea, merely observing, that most likely he had taken an unexpected trip into the country, and would be heard of before the day was out.

On leaving Long's however they were met again by Mortimer in breathless anxiety, evidently labouring under some new calamity.

"I am glad I have found you," said he, addressing himself to Dashall; "for I am left in this d— — —d wilderness of a place without a friend to speak to."

"How," inquired Ton, "what the d— — —l is the matter with you?"

"Why, you must know that Merry well is gone—"

"Gone—where to?"

"To—to—zounds, I've forgot the name of the people; but two genteel looking fellows just now very genteely told him he was wanted, and must come."

"Indeed!"

"Yes, and he told me to find you out, and let you know that he must become a bencher; and, without more todo, walked away with his new friends, leaving me forlorn enough. My Sister run away, my Uncle run after her—Sparkle absent, and Merrywell—"

"In the hands of the Nab-men—I see it all clear enough; and you have given a very concise, but comprehensive picture of your own situation; but don't despair, man, you will yet find all right, be assured; put yourself under my guidance, let the world wag as it will; it is useless to torment yourself with things you cannot prevent or cure.

"The right end of life is to live and be jolly."

Mortimer scarcely knew how to relish this advice, and seemed to doubt within himself whether it was meant satirically or feelingly, till Dashall whispered in his ear a caution not to betray the circumstances that had transpired, for his Sister's sake. "But," continued he, "I never suffer these things, which are by no means uncommon in London, to interfere with my pursuits, though we are all somewhat at a loss. However, as the post is in by this time, some news may be expected, and we will call at home before we proceed any further.—Where do you think the Colonel is gone to?"

"Heaven only knows," replied Mortimer; "the whole family is in an uproar of surmise and alarm,—what may be the end of it I know not."

"A pretty breeze Master Sparkle has kick'd up, indeed," continued Tom; "but I have for some time noticed an alteration in him. He always was a gay trump, and whenever I find him seriously inclined, I suspect some mischief brewing; for rapid transitions always wear portentous appearances, and your serious files are generally sly dogs. My life for it they have stolen a march upon your Uncle, queered some country Parson, and are by this time snugly stowed away in the harbour of matrimony. As for Merrywell, I dare be sworn his friends will take care of him."

Expectation was on tiptoe as Dashall broke the seal of a letter that was handed to him on arrival at home. Mortimer was on the fidget, and Tallyho straining his neck upon the full stretch of anxiety to hear the news, when Dashall burst into a laugh, but in which neither of the others could join in consequence of not knowing the cause of it. In a few minutes however the mystery was in some degree explained.

"Here," said Tom, "is news—extraordinary news—an official dispatch from head-quarters, but without any information as to where the tents are pitched. It is but a short epistle." He then read aloud,

"Dear Dashall,

"Please inform the Mortimer family and friends that all's well.

Your's truly,

C. Sparkle."

Then handing the laconic epistle to Mortimer—"I trust," said he, "you will now be a little more at ease."

Mortimer eagerly examined the letter for the postmark, but was not able to make out from whence it came.

"I confess," said he, "I am better satisfied than I was, but am yet at a loss to judge of the motives which have induced them to pursue so strange a course."

"The motive," cried Tom, "that may be easily explained; and I doubt not but you will find, although it may at present appear a little mysterious, Sparkle will be fully able to shew cause and produce effect. He is however a man of honour and of property, and most likely we may by this time congratulate you upon the change of your Sister's name. What a blaze it will make, and she will now most certainly become a sparkling subject. Hang it, man, don't look so dull upon a bright occasion.

> *"To prove pleasure but pain, some have hit on a project,*
> *We're duller the merrier we grow,*
> *Exactly the same unaccountable logic*
> *That talks of cold fire and warm snow.*
>
> *For me, born by nature*
> *For humour and satire,*
> *I sing and I roar and I quaff;*
> *Each muscle I twist it,*
> *I cannot resist it,*
> *A finger held up makes me laugh.*
>
> *For since pleasure's joy's parent, and joy begets mirth,*
> *Should the subtlest casuist or sophist on earth*
> *Contradict me, I'd call him an ass and a calf,*
> *And boldly insist once for all,*
> *That the only criterion of pleasure's to laugh,*
> *And sing tol de rol, loi de rol lol."*

This mirth of Dash all's did not seem to be in consonance with the feelings of Mortimer, who hastily took his departure.

"Come," said Tom to his Cousin, "having gained some information respecting one friend, we will now take a stroll through Temple Bar, and have a peep at Merrywell; he may perhaps want assistance in his present situation, though I will answer for it he is in a place of perfect security."

"How," said Bob—"what do you mean?"

"Mean, why the traps have nibbled him. He is arrested, and gone to a lock-up shop, a place of mere accommodation for gentlemen to take up their abode, for the purpose of arranging their affairs, and where they can uninterruptedly make up their minds whether to give bail, put in appearance and defend the suit, or take a trip to Abbott's Priory; become a three months' student in the college of art, and undergo the fashionable ceremony of white-washing."

"I begin to understand you now," said Bob, "and the only difference between our two friends is, that one has willingly put on a chain for life—"

"And the other may in all probability (continued Tom,) have to chaff his time away with a chum—perhaps not quite so agreeable, though it really is possible to be very comfortable, if a man can reconcile himself to the loss of liberty, even in "durance vile."

By this time they were walking leisurely along Piccadilly,

> "And marching without any cumbersome load,
> They mark'd every singular sight on the road."

"Who is that meagre looking man and waddling woman, who just passed us?" inquired Tallyho.

"An old Bencher," was the reply; "there you see all that is left of a man of *haut ton*, one who has moved in the highest circles; but alas! bad company and bad play have reduced him to what he now is. He has cut up and turn'd down very well among the usurers and attornies; but it is impossible to say of him, as of his sirloin of a wife (for she cannot be called a rib, or at all events a spare rib) that there is any thing like cut and come again. The poor worn-out Exquisite tack'd himself to his Lady, to enable him to wipe out a long score, and she determined on taking him for better for worse, after a little rural felicity in a walk to have her fortune told by a gipsy at Norwood. He is now crippled in pocket and person, and wholly dependent upon bounty for the chance of prolonging a miserable existence. His game is up. But what is life but a game, at which every one is willing to play? one wins and another loses: why there have been as many moves among titled persons, Kings, Queens, Bishops, Lords and Knights, within the last century, as there are in a game at chess. Pawns have been taken and restored in all classes, from the Sovereign, who pawns or loses his crown, to the Lady whose reputation is in pawn, and becomes at last not worth half a crown. Shuffling, cutting, dealing out and dealing in, double dealing and double faces, have long been the order of the day. Some men's cards are all trumps, whilst others have *carte blanche*; some honours count, whilst others stand for nothing. For instance, did not the little man who cast up his final accounts a short time back at St. Helena, like a Corsican conjurer, shuffle and cut about among kings and queens, knaves and asses, (aces I mean) dealing out honours when he liked, and taking trumps as he thought fit?—did he not deal and take up again almost as he pleased, having generally an honour in his sleeve to be played at command, or *un roi dans le marche*; by which cheating, it was scarcely possible for any one to get fair play with him, till, flushed by success, and not knowing how to bear his prosperity, he played too desperately and too long? The tables were turned upon him, and his enemies cheated him, first of his liberty, and ultimately of his life."

At this moment Tallyho, who was listening in close attention to his Cousin, struck his foot against a brown paper parcel which rolled before him.—"Hallo!" exclaimed he, "what have we here?—somebody has dropped a prize."

"It is mine, Sir," said an old woman, dropping them a curtsey with a smile which shone through her features, though thickly begrimed with snuff.

"A bite," said Tom.

"I dropp'd it from my pocket, Sir, just now."

"And pray," inquired Tom, "what does it contain?" picking it up.

"Snuff, Sir," was the reply; "a kind, good-hearted Gentleman gave it to me—God bless him, and bless your Honour too!" with an additional smile, and a still lower curtsey.

Upon examining the paper, which had been broken by the kick, Tom perceived, that by some magic or other, the old woman's snuff had become sugar.

"Zounds!" said he, "they have played some trick upon you, and given you brimstone instead of snuff, or else you are throwing dust in our eyes."

The parcel, which contained a sample of sugar, was carefully rolled up again and tied, then dropped to be found by any body else who chose to stoop for it.

"This," said Dashall, "does not turn out to be what I first expected; for the practices of ring and money dropping{1} have, at various times, been carried on with great success, and to the serious injury of the unsuspecting. The persons who generally apply themselves to this species of cheating are no other than gamblers who ingeniously contrive, by dropping a purse or a ring, to draw in some customer with a view to induce him to play; and notwithstanding their arts have frequently been exposed, we every now and then hear of some flat being done by these sharps, and indeed there are constantly customers in London to be had one way or another."

"Then you had an idea that that parcel was a bait of this kind," rejoined Bob.

"I did," replied his Cousin; "but it appears to be a legitimate letter from some industrious mechanic to his friend, and is a curious specimen of epistolary correspondence; and you perceive there was a person ready to claim it, which conspired rather to confirm my suspicions, being a little in the style of the gentry I have alluded to. They vary their mode of proceeding according to situation and circumstance. Your money-dropper contrives to find his own property, as if by chance. He picks up the purse with an exclamation of 'Hallo! what have we here?—Zounds! if here is not a prize—I'm in rare luck to-day—Ha, ha, ha, let's have a peep at it—it feels heavy, and no doubt is worth having.' While he is examining its contents, up comes his confederate, who claims a share on account of having been present at the finding. 'Nay, nay,' replies the finder, 'you are not in it. This Gentleman is the only person that was near me—was not you, Sir? 'By this means the novice is induced to assent, or perhaps assert his prior claim. The finder declares,

> 1 The practice of ring-dropping is not wholly confined to London, as the following paragraph from the Glasgow Courier, a very short time ago, will sufficiently prove: — 'On Monday afternoon, when three Highland women, who had been employed at a distance from home in the harvest, were returning to their habitations, they were accosted by a fellow who had walked out a short way with them, 'till he picked up a pair of ear-rings and a key for a watch. The fellow politely informed the females that they should have half the value of the articles, as they were in his company when they were found. While they were examining them, another fellow came up, who declared at once they were gold, and worth at least thirty shillings. After some conversation, the women were induced to give fifteen shillings for the articles, and came and offered them to a watch-maker for sale, when they learned to their mortification that they were not worth eighteen pence!'

that sooner than have any dispute about it, he will divide the contents in three parts; recommends an adjournment to a public-house in the neighbourhood, to wet the business and drink over their good luck. This being consented to, the leading points are accomplished. The purse of course is found to contain counterfeit money—Flash-screens or Fleet-notes,{1} and the division cannot well be made without change can be procured. Now comes the touch-stone. The Countryman, for such they generally contrive to inveigle, is perhaps in cash, having sold his hay, or his cattle, tells them he can give change; which being understood, the draught-board, cards, or la bagatelle, are introduced, and as the job is a good one, they can afford to sport some of their newly-acquired wealth in this way. They drink and play, and fill their grog again. The Countryman bets; if he loses, he is called upon to pay; if he wins, 'tis added to what is coming to him out of the purse.

"If, after an experiment or two, they find he has but little money, or fight shy, they bolt, that is, brush off in quick time, leaving him to answer for the reckoning. But if he is what they term well-breeched, and full of cash, they stick to him until he is cleaned out,{2} make him drunk, and, if he turns restive, they mill him. If he should be an easy cove,{3} he perhaps give them change for their flash notes, or counterfeit coin, and they leave him as soon as possible, highly pleased with his fancied success, while they laugh in their sleeves at the dupe of their artifice."

"And is it possible?" inquired Tallyho—

> "Can such things be, and overcome us
> Like a summer's cloud?"

"Not without our special wonder," continued Dashall; "but such things have been practised. Then again, your ring-droppers, or practisers of the fawney rig, are more cunning in their manoeuvres to turn their wares into the ready blunt.{4} The pretending to find a ring being one of the meanest and least profitable exercises of their ingenuity, it forms a part of their art to find articles of much more

1 *Flash-screens or Fleet-notes*—Forged notes.

2 *Cleaned out*—Having lost all your money.

3 *Easy cove*—One whom there is no difficulty in gulling.

4 *Ready blunt*—Cash in hand.

value, such as rich jewelry, broaches, ear-rings, necklaces set with diamonds, pearls, &c. sometimes made into a paper parcel, at others in a small neat red morocco case, in which is stuck a bill of parcels, giving a high-flown description of the articles, and with an extravagant price. Proceeding nearly in the same way as the money-droppers with the dupe, the finder proposes, as he is rather short of *steeven*,{1} to *swap*{2}his share for a comparatively small part of the value stated in the bill of parcels: and if he succeeds in obtaining one-tenth of that amount in hard cash, his triumph is complete; for, upon examination, the diamonds turn out to be nothing but paste—the pearls, fishes' eyes—and the gold is merely polished brass gilt, and altogether of no value. But this cannot be discovered beforehand, because the *bilk*{3} is in a hurry, can't spare time to go to a shop to have the articles valued, but assures his intended victim, that, as they found together, he should like to *smack the bit*,{4 }without *blowing the gap*,{5} and so help him G—d, the thing wants no *buttering up*,{6} because he is willing to give his share for such a trifle."

1 Steeven — *A flash term for money.*

2 Swap — *To make an exchange, to barter one article for another.*

3 *A swindler or cheat.*

4 Smack the bit — *To share the booty.*

5 Blowing the gap — *Making any thing known.*

6 Buttering up — *Praising or flattering.*

This conversation was suddenly interrupted by a violent crash just behind them, as they passed Drury Lane Theatre in their way through Bussel Court; and Bob, upon turning to ascertain from whence such portentous sounds proceeded, discovered that he had brought all the Potentates of the Holy Alliance to his feet. The Alexanders, the Caesars, the Buonapartes, Shakespeares, Addisons and Popes, lay strewed upon the pavement, in one undistinguished heap, while a poor Italian lad with tears in his eyes gazed with indescribable anxiety on the shapeless ruin—' Vat shall me do?—dat man knock him down—all brokt—you pay—Oh! mine Godt, vat shall do! ' This appeal was made to Dashall and Tallyho, the latter of whom the poor Italian seemed to fix upon as the author of his misfortune in upsetting his board of plaster images; and although he was perfectly unconscious of the accident, the appeal of the vender of great personages had its desired effect upon them both; and finding themselves quickly surrounded by spectators, they gave him some silver, and then pursued their way.

"These men," said Dashall, "are generally an industrious and hard-living people; they walk many miles in the course of a day to find sale for their images, which they will rather sell at any price than carry back with them at night; and it is really wonderful how they can make a living by their traffic."

"Ha, ha, ha," said a coarse spoken fellow following—"how the Jarman Duck diddled the Dandies just now—did you twig how he queered the coves out of seven bob for what was not worth *thrums*.{1} The *Yelper*{2} did his duty well, and finger'd the *white wool*{3} in good style. I'm d————d if he was not up to slum, and he whiddied their wattles with the velvet, and floored the town toddlers easy enough."

"How do you mean?" said his companion.

"Why you know that foreign blade is an ould tyke about this quarter, and makes a good deal of money—many a *twelver*{4} does he get by buying up broken images of persons who sell them by wholesale, and he of course gets them for little or nothing: then what does he do but dresses out his board, to give them the best appearance he can, and toddles into the streets, *touting*{5} for a good customer. The first genteel bit of flash he meets that he thinks will dub up the possibles,{6} he dashes down the board, breaks all the broken heads, and appeals in a pitiful way for remuneration for his loss; so that nine times out of ten he gets some Johnny-raw or other to stump up the rubbish."

"Zounds!" said Dashall, "these fellows are smoking us; and, in the midst of my instructions to guard you against the abuses of the Metropolis, we have ourselves become the dupes of an impostor."

 1 Thrums—*A flash term for threepence.*

 2 The Yelper—*A common term given to a poor fellow subject, who makes very pitiful lamentations on the most trifling accidents.*

 3 White wool—*Silver.*

4 Twelver — A shilling.

5 Touting — Is to be upon the sharp look out.

6 To dub up the possibles — To stand the nonsense — are nearly synonimous, and mean — will pay up any demand rather than be detained.

"Well," said Tallyho, "it is no more than a practical illustration of your own observation, that it is scarcely possible for any person to be at all times secure from the arts and contrivances of your ingenious friends the Londoners; though I confess I was little in expectation of finding you, as an old practitioner, so easily let in."

"It is not much to be wondered at," continued Tom, "for here we are in the midst of the very persons whose occupations, if such they may be termed, ought most to be avoided; for Covent Garden, and Drury Lane, with their neighbourhoods, are at all times infested with swindlers, sharpers, whores, thieves, and depredators of all descriptions, for ever on the look out. It is not long since a man was thrown from a two-pair of stairs window in Charles Street,{1} which is just by, having been decoyed into a house of ill fame by a Cyprian, and this in a situation within sight of the very Police Office itself in Bow Street!"

"Huzza! ha, ha, ha, there he goes," vociferated by a variety of voices, now called their attention, and put an end to their conversation; and the appearance of a large concourse of people running up Drury Lane, engrossed their notice as they approached the other end of Russel Court.

On coming up with the crowd, they found the cause of the vast assemblage of persons to be no other than a Quaker{2} decorated with a tri-coloured cockade, who was

1 A circumstance of a truly alarming and distressing nature, to which Dashall alluded in this place, was recently made known to the public in the daily journals, and which should serve as a lesson to similar adventurers.

It appeared that a young man had been induced to enter a house of ill fame in Charles Street, Covent Garden, by one of its cyprian inmates, to whom he gave some money in order for her to provide them with supper; that, upon her return, he desired to have the difference between what he had given and what she had expended returned to him, which being peremptorily refused, he determined to leave the house. On descending the stair-case for which purpose, he was met by some men, with whom he had a violent struggle to escape; they beat and bruised him most unmercifully, and afterwards threw him from a two-pair of stairs window into the street, where he was found by the Watchman with his skull fractured, and in a state of insensibility. We believe all attempts have hitherto proved fruitless to bring the actual perpetrator or perpetrators of this diabolical deed to punishment.

2 Bow-street.—Thursday morning an eccentric personage, who has for some time been seen about the streets of the Metropolis in the habit of a Quaker, and wearing the tri-coloured cockade in his broad white hat, made his appearance at the door of this office, and presenting a large packet to one of the officers, desired him, in a tone of authority, to lay it instantly before the Magistrate. The Magistrate (G. R. Minshull, Esq.) having perused this singular paper, inquired for the person who brought it; and in the next moment a young man, in the garb of a Quaker, with a broad-brimmed, peaceful-looking, drab-coloured beaver on his head, surmounted by a furious tri-coloured cockade, was brought before him. This strange anomalous ' personage having placed himself very carefully directly in front of the bench, smiled complacently upon his Worship, and the following laconic colloquy ensued forthwith:—

Magistrate—Did you bring this letter?

Quaker—Thou hast said it.

Magistrate—-What is your object in bringing it?

Quaker—Merely to let thee know what is going on in the world—and, moreover, being informed that if I came to thy office, I should be taken into custody, I was desiroiis to ascertain whether that information was true.

Magistrate—Then I certainly shall not gratify you by ordering you into custody.

Quaker—Thou wilt do as seemeth right in thy eyes. I assure thee I have no inclination to occupy thy time longer than is profitable to us, and therefore I will retire whenever thou shalt signify that my stay is unpleasant to thee.

Magistrate—Why do you wear your hat?—are you a Quaker?

Quaker—Thou sayest it—but that is not my sole motive for wearing it. To be plain with thee, I wear it because I chose to do so.   Canst thee tell me of any law which compels me to take it off?

Magistrate—I'll tell you what, friend, I would seriously recommend you to retire from this place as speedily as possible.

Quaker—I take thy advice—farewell.

Thus ended this comical conversation, and the eccentric friend immediately departed in peace.

The brother of the above person attended at the office on Saturday, and stated that the Quaker is insane, that he was proprietor of an extensive farm near Ryegate, in Surrey, for some years; but that in May last his bodily health being impaired, he was confined for some time, and on his recovery it was found that his intellects were affected, and he was put under restraint, but recovered. Some time since he absconded from Ryegate, and his friends were unable to discover him, until they saw the account of his eccentricities in the newspapers. Mr. Squire was desirous, if he made his appearance again at the office, he should be detained. The Magistrate, as a cause for the detention of the Quaker, swore the brother to these facts. About three o'clock the Quaker walked up Bow-street, when an officer conducted him to the presence of the Magistrate, who detained him, and at seven o'clock delivered him into the care of his brother.

very quietly walking with a Police Officer, and exhibiting a caricature of himself mounted on a velocipede, and riding over corruption, &c. It was soon ascertained that he had accepted an invitation from one of the Magistrates of Bow Street to pay him a visit, as he had done the day before, and was at that moment going before him.

"I apprehend he is a little cracked," said Tom; "but however that may be, he is a very harmless sort of person. But come, we have other game in view, and our way lies in a different direction to his."

"Clothes, Sir, any clothes to-day?" said an importunate young fellow at the corner of one of the courts, who at the same time almost obstructed their passage.

Making their way as quickly as they could from this very pressing personage, who invited them to walk in.

"This," said Tom, "is what we generally call a *Barker*. I believe the title originated with the Brokers in Moor-fields, where men of this description parade in the fronts of their employers' houses, incessantly pressing the passengers to walk in and buy household furniture, as they do clothes in Rosemary Lane, Seven Dials, Field Lane, Houndsditch, and several other parts of the town. Ladies' dresses also used to be barked in Cranbourn Alley and the neighbourhood of Leicester Fields; however, the nuisance has latterly in some measure abated. The Shop-women in that part content themselves now-a-days by merely inviting strangers to look at their goods; but Barkers are still to be found, stationed at the doors of Mock Auctions, who induce company to assemble, by bawling "Walk in, the auction is now on," or "Just going to begin." Of these mock auctions, there have been many opened of an evening, under the imposing glare of brilliant gas lights, which throws an unusual degree of lustre upon the articles put up for sale. It is not however very difficult to distinguish them from the real ones, notwithstanding they assume all the exterior appearances of genuineness, even up to advertisements in the newspapers, purporting to be held in the house of a person lately gone away under embarrassed circumstances, or deceased. They are denominated Mock Auctions, because no real intention exists on the part of the sellers to dispose of their articles under a certain price previously fixed upon, which, although it may not be high, is invariably more than they are actually worth: besides which, they may be easily discovered by the anxiety they evince to show the goods to strangers at

the moment they enter, never failing to bestow over-strained panegyrics upon every lot they put up, and asking repeatedly—"What shall we say for this article? a better cannot be produced;" and promising, if not approved of when purchased, to change it. The Auctioneer has a language suited to all companies, and, according to his view of a customer, can occasionally jest, bully, or perplex him into a purchase.—"The goods must be sold at what they will fetch;" and he declares (notwithstanding among his confederates, who stand by as bidders, they are run up beyond the real value, in order to catch a flat,) that "the present bidding can never have paid the manufacturer for his labour."

In such places, various articles of silver, plate, glass and household furniture are exposed to sale, but generally made up of damaged materials, and slight workmanship of little intrinsic value, for the self-same purpose as the Razor-seller states—

> *"Friend, (cried the Razor-man) I'm no knave;*
> *As for the razors you have bought,*
> *Upon my soul! I never thought*
> *That they would shave."*

> *"Not shave!" quoth Hodge, with wond'ring eyes,*
> *And voice not much unlike an Indian yell;*
> *"What were they made for then, you dog?" he cries.*
> *"Made! (quoth the fellow with a smile) to sell."*

Passing the end of White Horse Yard—"Here," continued Tom, "in this yard and the various courts and alleys which lead into it, reside numerous Girls in the very lowest state of prostitution; and it is dangerous even in the day time to pass their habitations, at all events very dangerous to enter any one of them. Do you see the crowd of squalid, half-clad and half-starved creatures that surround the old woman at the corner?—Observe, that young thing without a stocking is stealing along with a bottle in one hand and a gown in the other; she is going to put the latter *up the spout*{1} with her

> 1 *Up the spout, or up the five*—Are synonymous in their import, and mean the act of pledging property with a Pawnbroker for the loan of money—most probably derived from the practice of having a long spout, which reaches from the top of the house of the Pawn-broker (where the goods are deposited for safety till redeemed or sold) to the shop, where they are first received; through which a small bag is dropped upon the ringing of a bell, which conveys the tickets or duplicates to a person above stairs, who, upon finding them, (unless too bulky) saves himself the trouble and loss of time of coming down stairs, by more readily conveying them down the spout.

accommodating *Uncle*,{1} in order to obtain a little of the enlivening juice of the juniper to fill the former."

> 1 *Uncle*, sometimes called the *Ferrit*, or the *Flint*—Cant terms for Pawnbroker, though many of these gentlemen now assume the more reputable appellation of Silversmiths. They are willing to lend money upon all sorts of articles of household furniture, linen, plate, wearing apparel, jewellery, &c. with a certainty of making a very handsome profit upon the money so circulated.
>
> There are in this Metropolis upwards of two hundred and

thirty Pawnbrokers, and in some cases they are a useful and serviceable class of people; and although doubtless many of them are honest and reputable persons, there are still among them a class of sharpers and swindlers, who obtain licences to carry on the business, and bring disgrace upon the respectable part of the profession. Every species of fraud which can add to the distresses of those who are compelled to raise temporary supplies of money is resorted to, and for which purpose there are abundance of opportunities. In many instances however the utility of these persons, in preventing a serious sacrifice of property, cannot be denied; for, by advancing to tradesmen and mechanics temporary loans upon articles of value at a period of necessity, an opportunity of redeeming them is afforded, when by their industrious exertions their circumstances are improved. Many of them however are receivers of stolen good.s, and, under cover of their licence, do much harm to the public. Indeed, the very easy mode of raising money by means of the Pawnbrokers, operates as an inducement, or at least an encouragement, to every species of vice. The fraudulent tradesman by their means is enabled to raise money on the goods of his creditors, the servant to pledge the property of his employer, and the idle or profligate mechanic to deposit his working tools, or his work in an unfinished state. Many persons in London are in the habit of pawning their apparel from Monday morning till Saturday night, when they are redeemed, in order to make a decent appearance on the next day. In low neighbourhoods, and among loose girls, much business is done by Pawnbrokers to good advantage; and considerable emolument is derived from women of the town. The articles they offer to pledge are generally of the most costly nature, and the pilferings of the night are usually placed in the hands of an Uncle the next morning; and the wary money-lenders, fully acquainted with their necessities, just lend what they please; by which means they derive a wonderful profit, from the almost certainty of these articles never being redeemed.

The secresy with which a Pawnbroker's business is conducted, though very proper for the protection of the honest and well-meaning part of the population, to shield them from an exposure which might perhaps prove fatal to their business or credit, admits of great room for fraud on the part of the Money-lender; more particularly as it respects the interest allowed upon the pawns. Many persons are willing to pay any charge made, rather than expose their necessities by appearing before a Magistrate, and acknowledging they have been concerned in such transactions.

Persons who are in the constant habit of pawning are generally known by the Pawnbrokers, in most instances governed by their will, and compelled to take and pay just what they please. Again, much injury arises from the want of care in the Pawnbroker to require a proper account, from the Pledgers, of the manner in which the goods offered have been obtained, as duplicates are commonly given upon fictitious names and residences.

Notwithstanding the care and attention usually paid to the examination of the articles received as pledges, these gentlemen are sometimes to be duped by their customers. We remember an instance of an elderly man, who was in the habit of bringing a Dutch clock frequently to a Pawnbroker to raise the wind, and for safety, generally left it in a large canvass bag, till he became so regular a customer, that his clock and bag were often left without inspection; and as it was seldom deposited for long together, it was placed in some handy nook of the shop in order to lie ready for redemption. This system having been carried on for some time, no suspicion was entertained of the old man. Upon one occasion however the Pawnbroker's olfactory nerves were saluted with a smell of a most unsavoury nature, for which he could by no means account—day after day passed, and no discovery was made, till at length he determined to overhaul every article in his shop, and if possible discover the source of a nuisance which appeared rather to increase than

abate: in doing which, to his utter astonishment, he found
the old man's Dutch clock trans-formed into a sheep's head,
enclosed in a small box similar in shape and size to that of
the clock. It will scarcely be necessary to add, that, being
in the heat of summer, the sheep's head when turned out was
in a putrid state, and as green as grass. The Pawn-broker
declared the old gentleman's works were out of repair, that
he himself was out of tune, and eventually pledged himself
never to be so taken in again. After all, however, it must
be acknowledged that my Uncle is a very accommodating man.

"My Uncle's the man, I've oft said it before,
Who is ready and willing to open his door;
Tho' some on the question may harbour a doubt,
He's a mill to grind money, which I call a spout.
Derry down.

He has three golden balls which hang over his door,
Which clearly denote that my Uncle's not poor;
He has money to lend, and he's always so kind,
He will lend it to such as leave something behind.
Derry down.

If to music inclin'd, there's no man can so soon
Set the hooks of your gamut to excellent tune;
All his tickets are prizes most carefully book'd,
And your notes must be good, or you're presently hook'd.
Derry down.

Shirts, shoes, and flat-irons, hats, towels, and ruffs,
To him are the same as rich satins or stuffs;
From the pillows you lay on, chairs, tables, or sacks,
He'll take all you have, to the togs on your backs.
Derry down.

Then ye who are needy, repair to your friend,
Who is ready and willing your fortunes to mend;
He's a purse full of rhino, and that's quite enough,

Tho' short in his speech, he can shell out short stuff.
Derry down.

What a blessing it is, in this place of renown
To know that we have such an Uncle in town;
In all cases, degrees, in all places and stations,
'Tis a good thing to know we've such friendly relations.
Derry down.

"Surely," said Tallyho, "no person could possibly be inveigled by her charms?"

"They are not very blooming just now," answered his Cousin—"you do not see her in a right light. It is impossible to contemplate the cases of these poor creatures without dropping a tear of pity. Originally seduced from a state of innocence, and eventually abandoned by their seducers, as well as their well-disposed parents or friends, they are left at an early age at large upon the world; loathed and avoided by those who formerly held them in estimation, what are they to do?—It is said by Shakespeare, that

"Sin will pluck on sin."

They seem to have no alternative, but that of continuing in the practice which they once too fatally begun, in which the major part of them end a short life of debauchery and wretchedness.

"Exposed to the rude insults of the inebriated and the vulgar—the impositions of brutal officers and watchmen—to the chilling blasts of the night during the most inclement weather, in thin apparel, partly in compliance with the fashion of the day, but more frequently from the

Pawnbroker's shop rendering their necessary garments inaccessible, diseases (where their unhappy vocation does not produce them) are thus generated.

"Many are the gradations from the highest degree of prostitution down to the trulls that parade the streets by day, and one or two more steps still include those who keep out all night. Some of the miserable inhabitants of this quarter are night-birds, who seldom leave their beds during the day, except to refresh themselves with a drop of Old Tom; but as the evening approaches, their business commences, when you will see them decked out like fine ladies, for there are *coves of cases*,{1} and others in the vicinity of the Theatres, who live by letting out dresses for the evening, where they may be accommodated from a camesa{2} to a richly embroidered full-dress court suit, under the care of spies, who are upon the look-out that they don't brush off with the stock. Others, again, are boarded and lodged by the owners of houses of ill-fame, kept as dirty and as ragged as beggars all day, but who,

"Dress'd out at night, cut a figure."

It however not unfrequently happens to those unhappy Girls who have not been successful in their pursuits, and do not bring home with them the wages of their prostitution, that they are sent to bed without supper, and sometimes get a good beating into the bargain; besides which, the Mistress of the house takes care to search them immediately after they are left by their gallants, by which means they are deprived of every shilling."

Approaching the City, they espied a crowd of persons assembled together round the door of Money the perfumer. Upon inquiring, a species of depreciation was exposed, which had not yet come under their view.

It appeared that a note, purporting to come from a gentleman at the Tavistock Hotel, desiring Mr. Money to wait on him to take measure of his cranium for a fashionable peruke, had drawn him from home, and that during his absence, a lad, in breathless haste, as if dispatched by the principal, entered the shop, stating that Sir. Money wanted a wig which was in the window, with some combs and hair-brushes, for the Gentleman's inspection, and also a pot of his Circassian cream. The bait took, the articles

1 *Coves of cases*—Keepers of houses of ill fame.

2 *Camesa*—A shirt or shift.

were packed up, and the wily cheat had made good his retreat before the return of the coiffeur, who was not pleased with being seduced from his home by a hoaxing letter, and less satisfied to find that his property was diminished in his absence by the successful artifices of a designing villain. This tale having got wind in the neighbourhood, persons were flocking round him to advise as to the mode of pursuit, and many were entertaining each other by relations of a similar nature; but our heroes having their friend Merrywell in view (or rather his interest) made the best of their way to the Lock-up-house.

CHAPTER XXIII

"The world its trite opinion holds of those
That in a world apart these bars enclose;
And thus methinks some sage, whose wisdom frames
Old saws anew, complacently exclaims,
Debt is like death—it levels all degrees;
Their prey with death's fell grasp the bailiffs seize."

ON entering the Lock-up House, Bob felt a few uneasy sensations at hearing the key turned. The leary Bum-trap ushered the Gemmen up stairs, while Tallyho was endeavouring to compose his agitated spirits, and reconcile himself to the prospect before him, which, at the moment, was not of the most cheering nature.

"What, my gay fellow," said Merrywell, "glad to see you—was just going to scribble a line to inform you of my disaster. Zounds! you look as melancholy as the first line of an humble petition, or the author of a new piece the day after its damnation."

"In truth," replied Bob, "this is no place to inspire a man with high spirits."

"That's as it may be," rejoined Merrywell; "a man with money in his pocket may see as much Real Life in London within these walls as those who ramble at large through the mazes of what is termed liberty."

"But," continued Tom, "it must be admitted that the views are more limited."

"By no means," was the reply. "Here a man is at perfect liberty to contemplate and cogitate without fear of being agitated. Here he may trace over past recollections, and enjoy future anticipations free from the noise and bustle of crowded streets, or the fatigue of attending fashionable routs, balls, and assemblies. Besides which, it forms so important a part of Life in London, that few without a residence in a place of this kind can imagine its utility. It invigorates genius, concentrates ingenuity, and stimulates invention."

"Hey dey!" said Tallyho, looking out of the window, and perceiving a dashing tandem draw up to the door—"who have we here? some high company, no doubt."

"Yes, you are right; that man in the great coat, who manages his cattle with such dexterity, is no other than the king of the castle. He is the major domo, or, in other words, the Bailiff himself. That short, stout-looking man in boots and buckskins, is his assistant, vulgarly called his Bum.{1} The other is a Gentleman desirous of lodging in a genteel neighbourhood, and is recommended by them to take up his residence here."

"What," inquired Bob, "do Bailiffs drive gigs and tandems?"

"To be sure they do," was the reply; "formerly they were low-bred fellows, who would undertake any dirty business for a maintenance, as you will see them represented in the old prints and caricatures, muffled up in îreat coats, and carrying bludgeons; but, in present Real life, you will find them quite the reverse, unless they find it necessary to assume a disguise in order to nibble a queer cove who proves shy of their company'; but among Gentlemen, none are so stylish, and at the same time so accommodating—you are served with the process in a private and elegant way, and if not convenient to come to an immediate arrangement, a gig is ready in the highest taste, to convey you from your habitation to your place of retirement, and you may pass through the most crowded streets of the city, and recognise your friends, without fear of suspicion. Upon some occasions, they will also carry their politeness so far as to inform an individual he will be wanted on such a day, and must come—a circumstance which has the effect of preventing any person from knowing the period of departure, or the place of destination; consequently, the arrested party is gone out of town for a few days, and the matter all blows over without any injury sustained. This is the third time since I have been in the house that the tandem has started from the door, and returned with a new importation."

By this time, the gig having been discharged of its cargo, was reascended by the Master and his man, and bowl'd off again in gay style for the further accommodation of fashionable friends, whose society was in such high

1 *See Bum-trap), page 166.*

estimation, that no excuse or denial could avail, and who being so urgently wanted, must come.

"'Tis a happy age we live in," said Merry well; "the improvements are evident enough; every thing is done with so much facility and gentility, that even the race of bailiffs are transformed from frightful and ferocious-looking persons to the most dashing, polite and accommodating characters in the world. He however, like others, must have his assistant, and occasional substitute.

"A man in this happy era is really of no use whatever to himself. It is a principle on which every body, that is any body, acts, that no one should do any thing for himself, if he can procure another to do it for him. Accordingly, there is hardly the most simple performance in nature for the more easy execution of which an operator or machine of some kind' or other is not employed or invented; and a man who has had the misfortune to lose, or chuses not to use any of his limbs or senses, may meet with people ready to perform all their functions for him, from paring his nails and cutting his corns, to forming an opinion. No man cleans his own teeth who can afford to pay a dentist; and hundreds get their livelihood by shaving the chins and combing the hair of their neighbours, though many, it must be admitted, comb their neighbour's locks for nothing. The powers of man and the elements of nature even are set aside, the use of limbs and air being both superseded by steam; in short, every thing is done by proxy—death not excepted, for we are told that our soldiers and sailors die for us. Marriage in certain ranks is on this footing. A prince marries by proxy, and sometimes lives for ever after as if he thought all the obligations of wedlock were to be performed in a similar manner. A nobleman, it is true, will here take the trouble to officiate in the first instance in person; but there are plenty of cases to shew that nothing is further from his noble mind than the idea of continuing his slavery, while others can be found to take the labour off his hands. So numerous are the royal roads to every desideratum, and so averse is every true gentleman from doing any thing for himself, that it is to be dreaded lest it should grow impolite to chew one's own victuals; and we are aware that there are great numbers who, not getting their share of Heaven's provision, may be said to submit to have their food eat for them."

Tallyho laugh'd, and Dashall signified his assent to the whimsical observations of Merrywell, by a shrug of the shoulders and an approving smile.

"Apropos," said Merrywell—"what is the news of our friend Sparkle?"

"O, (replied Tom) he is for trying a chance in the Lottery of Life, and has perhaps by this time gained the prize of Matrimony:{1} but what part of the globe he inhabits it is impossible for me to say—however, he is with Miss Mortimer probably on the road to Gretna."

"Success to his enterprise," continued Merrywell; "and if they are destined to travel through life together, may they have thumping luck and pretty children. Marriage to some is a bitter cup of continued misery—may the reverse be his lot."

"Amen," responded Dashall.

"By the way," said Merrywell, "I hope you will favour me with your company for the afternoon, and I doubt not we shall start some game within these walls well worthy of pursuit; and as I intend to remove to more commodious apartments within a day or two, I shall certainly expect to have a visit from you during my abode in the county of Surrey."

"Going to College?" inquired Tom.

"Yes; I am off upon a sporting excursion for a month or two, and I have an idea of making it yield both pleasure and profit. An occasional residence in Abbot's Park is one of the necessary measures for the completion of a Real Life in London education. It is a fashionable retreat absolutely necessary, and therefore I have voluntarily determined upon it. What rare advice a young man may pick up in the precincts of the Fleet and

1 It has often been said figuratively, that marriage is a lottery; but we do not recollect to have met with a practical illustration of the truth of the simile before the following, which is a free translation of an Advertisement in the Louisiana Gazette:—

> "A young man of good figure and disposition, unable though
> "desirous to procure a Wife without the preliminary trouble of
> "amassing a fortune, proposes the following expedient to obtain the
> "object of his wishes:—He offers himself as the prize of a Lottery
> "to all Widows and Virgins under 32: the number of tickets to be
> "600 at 50 dollars each; but one number to be drawn from the
> "wheel, the fortunate proprietor of which is to be entitled to
> "himself and the 30,000 dollars."—New York, America.

the King's Bench! He may soon learn the art of sharp-shooting and skirmishing."

"And pray," says Tallyho, "what do you term skirmishing?"

"I will tell you," was the reply. "When you have got as deeply in debt every where as you can, you may still remain on the town as a Sunday-man for a brace of years, and with good management perhaps longer. Next you may toddle off to Scotland for another twelvemonth, and live in the sanctuary of Holyrood House, after seeing the North, where writs will not arrive in time to touch you. When tired of this, and in debt even in the sanctuary, and when you have worn out all your friends by borrowing of them to support you in style there, you can brush off on a Sunday to the Isle of Man, where you are sure to meet a parcel of blades who will be glad of your company if you are but a pleasant fellow. Here you may live awhile upon them, and get in debt (if you can, for the Manx-men have very little faith,) in the Island. From this, you must lastly effect your escape in an open boat, and make your appearance in London as a new face. Here you will find some flats of your acquaintance very glad to see you, even if you are indebted to them, from the pleasures of recollection accruing from past scenes of jollity and merriment. You must be sure to amuse them with a good tale of a law-suit, or the declining health of a rich old Uncle, from either of which you are certain of deriving a second fortune. Now manage to get arrested, and you will find some, who believe your story, ready to bail you. You can then put off these actions for two years more, and afterwards make a virtue of surrendering yourself in order to relieve your friends, who of course will begin to be alarmed, and feel so grateful for this supposed mark of propriety, that they will support you for a while in prison, until you get white-washed. In all this experience, and with such a long list of acquaintances, it will be hard if some will not give you a lift at getting over your difficulties. Then you start again as a nominal Land-surveyor, Money-scrivener, Horse-dealer, or as a Sleeping-partner in some mercantile concern— such, for instance, as coals, wine, &c. Your popularity and extensive acquaintance will get your Partner a number of customers, and then if you don't succeed, you have only to become a Bankrupt, secure your certificate, and start free again in some other line. Then there are other good chances, for a man may marry once or twice. Old or sickly women are best suited for the purpose, and their fortunes will help you for a year or two at least, if only a thousand or two pounds. Lastly, make up a purse» laugh at the flats, and finish on the Continent."

"Very animated description indeed," cried Dashall, "and salutary advice, truly."

"Too good to be lost," continued Merrywell.

"And yet rather too frequently acted on, it is to be feared."

"Probably so—"

"But mark me, this is fancy's sketch," and may perhaps appear a little too highly coloured; but if you remain with me, we will clip deeper into the reality of the subject by a little information from the official personage himself, who holds dominion over these premises; and we may perhaps also find some agreeable and intelligent company in his house."

This proposition being agreed to, and directions given accordingly by Merrywell to prepare dinner, our party gave loose to opinions of life, observations on men and mariners, exactly as they presented themselves to the imagination of each speaker, and Merrywell evidently proved himself a close observer of character.

"Places like this," said he, "are generally inhabited by the profligate of fashion, the ingenious artist, or the plodding mechanic. The first is one who cares not who suffers, so he obtains a discharge from his incumberances: having figured away for some time in the labyrinths of folly and extravagance, till finding the needful run taper, he yields to John Doe and Richard Roe as a matter of course, passes through his degrees in the study of the laws by retiring to the Fleet or King's Bench, and returns to the world with a clean face, and an increased stock of information to continue his career. The second are men who have heads to contrive and hands to execute improvements in scientific pursuits, probably exhausting their time, their health, and their property, in the completion of their projects, but who are impeded in their progress, and compelled to finish their intentions in durance vile, by the rapacity of their creditors. And the last are persons subjected to all the casualties of trade and the arts of the former, and unable to meet the peremptory demands of those they are indebted to; but they seldom inhabit these places long, unless they can pay well for their accommodations. Money is therefore as useful in a lock-up-house or a prison as in any other situation of life.

"Money, with the generality of people, is every thing; it is the universal Talisman; there is magic in its very name. It ameliorates all the miserable circumstances of life, and the sound of it may almost be termed life itself. It is the balm, the comfort, and the restorative. It must indeed be truly mortifying to the opulent, to observe that the attachment of their dependents, and even the apparent esteem of their friends, arises from the respect paid to riches. The vulgar herd bow with reverence and respect before the wealthy; but it is in fact the money, and not the individual, which they worship. Doubtless, a philosophic Tallow-chandler would hasten from the contemplation of the starry heavens to vend a farthing rushlight; and it therefore cannot be wondered at that the Sheriffs-officer, who serves you with a writ because you have not money enough to discharge the just demands against you, should determine at least to get as much as he can out of you, and, when he finds your resources exhausted, that he should remove you to the common receptacle of debtors; which however cannot be done to your own satisfaction without some money; for if you wish a particular place of residence, or the most trifling accommodation, there are fees to pay, even on entering a prison."

"In that case then," said Tallyho, "a man is actually obliged to pay for going to a prison."

"Precisely so, unless he is willing to mingle with the very lowest order of society. But come, we will walk into the Coffee-room, and take a view of the inmates."

Upon entering this, which was a small dark room, they heard a great number of voices, and in one corner found several of the prisoners surrounding a Bagatelle-board, and playing for porter, ale, &c; in another corner was a young man in close conversation with an Attorney; and a little further distant, was a hard-featured man taking instructions from the Turnkey how to act. Here was a poor Player, who declared he would take the benefit of the Act, and afterwards take a benefit at the Theatre to reestablish himself. There a Poet racking his imagination, and roving amidst the flowers of fancy, giving a few touches by way of finish to an Ode to Liberty, with the produce of which he indulged himself in a hope of obtaining the subject of his Muse. The conversation was of a mingled nature. The vociferations of the Bagatelle-players—the whispers of the Attorney and his Client—and the declarations of the prisoner to the Turnkey, "That he would be d————d if he did not sarve 'em out, and floor the whole boiling of them," were now and then interrupted by the notes of a violin playing the most lively airs in an animated and tasteful style. The Performer however was not visible, but appeared to be so near, that Merrywell, who was a great lover of music, beckoned his friends to follow him. They now entered a small yard at the back of the house, the usual promenade of those who resided in it, and found the Musician seated on one of the benches, which were continued nearly round the yard, and which of itself formed a panorama of rural scenery. Here was the bubbling cascade and the lofty fountain—there the shady grove of majestic poplars, and the meandering stream glittering in the resplendent lustre of a rising sun. The waving foliage however and the bubbling fountain were not to be seen or heard, (as these beauties were only to be contemplated in the labours of the painter;) but to make up for the absence of these with the harmony of the birds and the ripplings of the stream, the Musician was endeavouring, like an Arcadian shepherd with his pipe, to make the woods resound with the notes of his fiddle, surrounded by some of his fellow-prisoners, who did not fail to applaud his skill and reward his kindness, by supplying him with rosin, as they termed it, which was by handing him the heavy-wet as often as they found his elbow at rest. In one place was to be seen a Butcher, who upon his capture was visited by his wife with a child in her arms, upon whom the melody seemed to have no effect. She was an interesting and delicate-looking woman, whose agitation of spirits upon so melancholy an occasion were evidenced by streaming tears from a pair of lovely dark eyes; and the Butcher, as evidently forgetful of his usual calling, was sympathising with, and endeavouring to soothe her into composure, and fondling the child. In another, a person who had the appearance of an Half-pay Officer, with Hessian boots, blue pantaloons, and a black silk handkerchief, sat with his arms folded almost without taking notice of what was passing around him, though a rough Sailor with a pipe in his mouth occasionally enlivened the scene by accompanying the notes of the Musician with a characteristic dance, which he termed a Horn-spike.

It was a fine scene of Real Life, and after taking a few turns in the gardens of the Lock-up or Sponging-house, they returned to Merrywell's apartments, which they had scarcely entered, when the tandem drew up to the door.

"More company," said Merry well.

"And perhaps the more the merrier," replied Tom.

"That is as it may prove," was the reply; "for the company of this house acc as various at times as can be met with in any other situation. However, this appears to wear the form of one of our fashionable, high-life Gentlemen; but appearances are often deceitful, we shall perhaps hear more of him presently—he may turn out to be one of the prodigals who calculate the duration of life at about ten years, that is, to have a short life and a merry one."

"That seems to me to be rather a short career, too," exclaimed Bob.

"Nay, nay, that is a long calculation, for it frequently cannot be made to last half the number. In the first place, the Pupil learns every kind of extravagance, which he practises en maitre the two next years. These make an end of his fortune. He lives two more on credit, established while his property lasted. The next two years he has a letter of licence, and contrives to live by ways and means (for he has grown comparatively knowing.) Then he marries, and the wife has the honour of discharging his debts, her fortune proving just sufficient for the purpose. Then he manages to live a couple of years more on credit, and retires to one of his Majesty's prisons."

By this time Mr. Safebind made his appearance, and with great politeness inquired if the Gentlemen were accommodated in the way they wished? Upon being assured of this, and requested to take a seat, after some introductory conversation, he gave them the following account of himself and his business:—

"We have brought nine Gemmen into the house this morning; and, though I say it, no Gemman goes out that would have any objection to come into it again."

Tallyho shrugg'd up his shoulders in a way that seemed to imply a doubt.

"For," continued he, "a Gemman that is a Gemman shall always find genteel treatment here. I always acts upon honour and secrecy; and if as how a Gemman can't bring his affairs into a comfortable shape here, why then he is convey'd away without exposure, that is, if he understands things."

With assurances of this kind, the veracity of which no one present could doubt, they were entertained for some time by their loquacious Host, who, having the gift of the gab,{1} would probably have continued long in the same strain of important information; when dinner was placed on the table, and they fell to with good appetites, seeming almost to have made use of the customary grace among theatricals.{2}

"The table cleared, the frequent glass goes round, And joke and song and merriment abound."

"Your house," said Dashall, "might well be termed the Temple of the Arts, since their real votaries are so frequently its inhabitants."

"Very true, Sir," said Safebind, "and as the Poet observes, it is as often graced by the presence of the devotees to the Sciences: in point of company he says we may almost call it multum in parvo, or the Camera Obscura of Life. There are at this time within these walls, a learned Alchymist, two Students in Anatomy, and a Physician—a Poet, a Player, and a Musician. The Player is an adept at mimicry, the Musician a good player, and the Poet no bad stick at a rhyme; all anxious to turn their talents to good account, and, when mingled together, productive of harmony, though the situation they are in at present is rather discordant to their feelings; but then you know 'tis said, that discord is the soul of harmony, and they knocked up a duet among themselves yesterday, which I thought highly amusing."

"I am fond of music," said Merry well—"do you think they would take a glass of wine with us?"

> 1 *Gift of the gab—Fluency of speech.*

> 2 *It is a very common thing among the minor theatricals, when detained at rehearsals, &c. to adjourn to some convenient room in the neighbourhood for refreshment, and equally common for them to commence operations in a truly dramatic way, by ex-claiming to each other in the language of Shakespeare,*

>> "Come on, Macbeth—come on, Macduff,
>> And d————d be he who first cries—hold, enough."

"Most readily, no doubt," was the reply. "I will introduce them in a minute." Thus saying, he left the room, and in a very few minutes returned with the three votaries of Apollo, who soon joined in the conversation upon general subjects. The Player now discovered his loquacity; the Poet his sagacity; and the Musician his pertinacity, for he thought no tones so good as those produced by himself, nor no notes—we beg pardon, none but bank notes—equal to his own.

It will be sufficient for our present purpose to add, that the bottle circulated 'quickly, and what with the songs of the Poet, the recitations of the Player, and the notes of the Fiddler, time, which perfects all intellectual ability, and also destroys the most stupendous monuments of art, brought the sons of Apollo under the table, and admonished Dashall and his Cousin to depart; which they accordingly did, after a promise to see their friend Merry well in his intended new quarters.

CHAPTER XXIV

"All nations boast some men of nobler mind,
Their scholars, heroes, benefactors kind:
And Britain has her share among the rest,
Of men the wisest, boldest and the best:
Yet we of knaves and fools have ample share,
And eccentricities beyond compare.
Full many a life is spent, and many a purse,
In mighty nothings, or in something worse."

THE next scene which Tom was anxious to introduce to his Cousin's notice was that of a Political Dinner; but while they were preparing for departure, a letter arrived which completely satisfied the mind of the Hon. Tom Dashall as to the motives and views of their friend Sparkle, and ran as follows:

"Dear Dashall,

"Having rivetted the chains of matrimony on the religious anvil of Gretna Green, I am now one of the happiest fellows in existence. My election is crowned with success, and I venture to presume all after-petitions will be rejected as frivolous and vexatious. The once lovely Miss Mortimer is now the ever to be loved Mrs. Sparkle. I shall not now detain your attention by an account of our proceedings or adventures on the road: we shall have many more convenient opportunities of indulging in such details when we meet, replete as I can assure you they are with interest.

"I have written instructions to my agent in town for the immediate disposal of my paternal estate in Wiltshire, and mean hereafter to take up my abode on one I have recently purchased in the neighbourhood of Belville Hall, where I anticipate many pleasurable opportunities of seeing you and our friend Tallyho surrounding my hospitable and (hereafter) family board. We shall be there within a month, as we mean to reach our place of destination by easy stages, and look about us.

"Please remember me to all old friends in Town, and believe as ever,

Your's truly,

"Charles Sparkle."

"Carlisle."

The receipt of this letter and its contents were immediately communicated to young Mortimer, who had already received some intelligence of a similar nature, which had the effect of allaying apprehension and dismissing fear for his Sister's safety. The mysterious circumstances were at once explained, and harmony was restored to the previously agitated family.

"I am truly glad of this information," said Tom, "and as we are at present likely to be politically engaged, we cannot do less than take a bumper or two after dinner, to the health and happiness of the Candidate who so emphatically observes, he has gained his election, and, in the true language of every Patriot, declares he is the happiest man alive, notwithstanding the rivets by which he is bound."

"You are inclined to be severe," said Tallyho.

"By no means," replied Dashall; "the language of the letter certainly seems a little in consonance with my observation, but I am sincere in my good wishes towards the writer and his amiable wife. Come, we must now take a view of other scenes, hear long speeches, drink repeated bumpers, and shout with lungs of leather till the air resounds with peals of approbation.

"We shall there see and hear the great men of the nation, Or at least who are such in their own estimation."

> "Great in the name a patriot father bore,
> Behold a youth of promise boldly soar,
> Outstrip his fellows, clamb'ring height extreme,
> And reach to eminence almost supreme.
> With well-worn mask, and virtue's fair pretence,
> And all the art of smooth-tongued eloquence,
> He talks of wise reform, of rights most dear,

Till half the nation thinks the man sincere."

"Hey day," said Tallyho, "who do you apply this to?"

"Those who find the cap fit may wear it," was the reply—"
I leave it wholly to the discriminating few who can discover what belongs to themselves, without further comment."

By this time they had arrived at the Crown and Anchor Tavern, in the Strand, where they found a great number of persons assembled, Sir F. B——— having been announced as President. In a few minutes he was ushered into the room with all due pomp and ceremony, preceded by the Stewards for the occasion, and accompanied by a numerous body of friends, consisting of Mr. H———, Major C———, and others, though not equally prominent, equally zealous. During dinner time all went on smoothly, except in some instances, where the voracity of some of the visitors almost occasioned a chopping off the fingers of their neighbours; but the cloth once removed, and 'Non nobis Domine' sung by professional Gentlemen, had the effect of calling the attention of the company to harmony. The Band in the orchestra played, 'O give me Death or Liberty'—'Erin go brach'—'Britons strike home'—and 'Whilst happy in my native Land.' The Singers introduced 'Scots wha hae wi' Wallace bled'—'Peruvians wake to Glory'—and the 'Tyrolese Hymn.' But the spirit of oratory, enlivened by the fire of the bottle, exhibited its illuminating sparks in a blaze of lustre which eclipsed even the gas lights by which they were surrounded; so much so, that the Waiters themselves became confused, and remained stationary, or, when they moved, were so dazzled by the patriotic effusions of the various Speakers, that they fell over each other, spilt the wine in the pockets of the company, and, by making afterwards a hasty retreat, left them to fight or argue between each other for supposed liberties taken even by their immediate friends.

POLITICAL DINNER, Tom & Bob taking a lesson on the Constitution, & not neglecting their own.

Unbridled feelings of patriotic ardour appeared to pervade every one present; and what with the splendid oratory of the speakers, and the deafening vociferations of the hearers, at the conclusion of what was generally considered a good point, a sufficient indication of the feelings by which they were all animated was evinced.

At the lower end of the table sat a facetious clerical Gentleman, who, unmindful of his ministerial duties, was loud in his condemnation of ministers, and as loud in his approbation of those who gave them what he repeatedly called a good hit. But here a subject of great laughter occurred; for Mr. Marrowfat, the Pea-merchant of Covent-Garden, and Mr. Barrowbed, the Feathermonger of Drury Lane, in their zeal for the good cause, arising at the same moment, big with ardour and sentiment, to address the Chair on a subject of the most momentous importance in their consideration, and desirous to signalize themselves individually, so completely defeated their objects by over anxiety to gain precedence, that they rolled over each other on the floor, to the inexpressible amusement of the company, and the total obliteration of their intended observations; so much so, that the harangue meant to enlighten their friends, ended in a fine colloquy of abuse upon each other.

The bottles, the glasses, and the other paraphernalia of the table suffered considerable diminution in the descent of these modern Ciceros, and a variety of speakers arising upon their downfall, created so much confusion, that our Heroes, fearing it would be some time before harmony could be restored, took up their hats and walked.

"Now," said Dashall, as they left the house, "you have had a full view of the pleasantries of a Political Dinner; and having seen the characters by which such an entertainment is generally attended, any further account of them is almost rendered useless."

"At least," replied Tallyho, "I have been gratified by the view of some of the leading men who contribute to fill up the columns of your London Newspapers."

"Egad!" said his Cousin, "now I think of it, there is a tine opportunity of amusing ourselves for the remainder of the evening by a peep at another certain house in Westminster: whether it may be assimilated, in point of character or contents, to what we have just witnessed, I shall leave you, after taking a review, to determine."

"What do you mean?" inquired Tallyho.

"Charley's, my boy, that's the place for sport, something in the old style. The Professors there are all of the ancient school, and we shall just be in time for the first Lecture. It is a school of science, and though established upon the ancient construction, is highly suitable to the taste of the moderns."

"Zounds!" replied Bob, "our heads are hardly in cue for philosophy after so much wine and noise; we had better defer it to another opportunity."

"Nay, nay, now's the very time for it—it will revive the recollection of some of your former sports;

For, midst our luxuries be it understood,
Some traits remain of rugged hardihood."

Charley is a good caterer for the public appetite, and, to diversify the amusements of a Life in London, we will have a little chaff among the Bear-baiters."

Tally-ho stared for a moment; then burst into laughter at the curious introduction his Cousin had given to this subject. "I have long perceived your talent for embellishment, but certainly was not prepared for the conclusion; but you ought rather to have denominated them Students in Natural History."

"And what is that but a branch of Philosophy?" inquired Dashall. "However, we are discussing points of opinion rather than hastening to the scene of action to become judges of facts—Allons."

Upon saying this, they moved forward with increased celerity towards Tothill-fields, and soon reached their proposed place of destination.

On entering, Tallyho was reminded by his Cousin to button up his toggery, keep his ogles in action, and be awake. "For," said he, "you will here have to mingle with some of the queer Gills and rum Covies of all ranks."

This advice being taken, they soon found themselves in this temple of torment, where Bob surveyed a motly group assembled, and at that moment engaged in the sports of the evening. The generality of the company bore the appearance of Butchers, Dog-fanciers and Ruffians, intermingled here and there with a few Sprigs of Fashion, a few Corinthian Sicells, Coster-mongers, Coal-heavers, Watermen, Soldiers, and Livery-servants.

The bear was just then pinn'd by a dog belonging to a real lover of the game, who, with his shirt-sleeves tuck'd up, declared he was a d————d good one, and nothing but a good one, so help him G———d. This dog, at the hazard of his life, had seized poor Bruin by the under lip, who sent forth a tremendous howl indicative of his sufferings, and was endeavouring to give him a fraternal hug; many other dogs were barking aloud with anxiety to take an active share in the amusement, while the bear, who was chained by the neck to a staple in the wall, and compelled to keep an almost erect posture, shook his antagonist with all the fury of madness produced by excessive torture. In the mean time bets were made and watches pull'd forth, to decide how long the bow-wow would bother the ragged Russian. The Dog-breeders were chaffing each other upon the value of their canine property, each holding his brother-puppy between his legs, till a fair opportunity for a let-loose offered, and many wagers were won and lost in a short space of time. Bob remained a silent spectator; while his Cousin, who was better up to the gossip, mixt with the hard-featured sportsmen, inquired the names of their dogs, what prices were fix'd upon, when they had fought last, and other questions equally important to amateurs.

THE COUNTRY SQUIRE taking a peep at CHARLEY'S THEATRE WESTMINSTER, ere the performance of the Old Bait

Bruin got rid of his customers in succession as they came up to him, and when they had once made a seizure, it was generally by a hug which almost deprived them of life, at least it took from them the power of continuing their hold; but his release from one was only the signal for attack from another.

While this exhibition continued, Tom could not help calling his Cousin's attention to an almost bald-headed man, who occupied a front seat, and sat with his dog, which was something of the bull breed, between his legs, while the paws of the animal rested on the top rail, and which forcibly brought to his recollection the well-known anecdote of Garrick and the Butcher's dog with his master's wig on, while the greasy carcass-dealer was wiping the perspiration from his uncovered pericranium.

Bob, who had seen a badger-bait, and occasionally at fairs in the country a dancing bear, had never before seen a bear-bait, stood up most of the time, observing those around him, and paying attention to their proceedings while entertaining sentiments somewhat similar to the following lines:—

> *"What boisterous shouts, what blasphemies obscene,*
> *What eager movements urge each threatening mien!*
> *Present the spectacle of human kind,*
> *Devoid of feeling—destitute of mind;*
> *With ev'ry dreadful passion rous'd to flame,*
> *All sense of justice lost and sense of shame."*

When Charley the proprietor thought his bear was sufficiently exercised for the night, he was led to his den, lacerated and almost lamed, to recover of his wounds, with an intention that he should "fight his battles o'er again." Meanwhile Tom and Bob walk'd homeward.

The next day having been appointed for the coronation of our most gracious Sovereign, our friends were off at an early hour in the morning, to secure their seats in Westminster Hall; and on their way they met the carriage of our disappointed and now much lamented Queen, her endeavours to obtain admission to the Abbey having proved fruitless.

> "Oh that the Monarch had as firmly stood
> In all his acts to serve the public good,
> As in that moment of heartfelt joy
> That firmness acted only to destroy
> A nation's hope—to every heart allied,
> Who lived in sorrow, and lamented died!"

It was a painful circumstance to Dashall, who was seldom severe in his judgments, or harsh in his censures. He regretted its occurrence, and it operated in some degree to rob a splendid ceremony of its magnificence, and to sever from royalty half its dignity.

The preparations however were arranged upon a scale of grandeur suited to the occasion. The exterior of Westminster Hall and Abbey presented a most interesting appearance. Commodious seats were erected for the accommodation of spectators to view the procession in its moving order, and were thronged with thousands of anxious subjects to greet their Sovereign with demonstrations of loyalty and love.

It was certainly a proud day of national festivity. The firing of guns and the ringing of bells announced the progress of the Coronation in its various stages to completion; and in the evening Hyde Park was brilliantly and tastefully illuminated, and an extensive range of excellent fireworks were discharged under the direction of Sir William Congreve. We must however confine ourselves to that which came under the view of the Hon. Tom Dashall and his Cousin, who, being seated in the Hall, had a fine opportunity of witnessing the banquet, and the challenge of the Champion.

A flooring of wood had been laid down in the Hall at an elevation of fourteen inches above the flags. Three tiers of galleries were erected on each side, covered with a rich and profuse scarlet drapery falling from a cornice formed of a double row of gold-twisted rope, and ornamented with a succession of magnificent gold pelmets and rosettes. The front of the door which entered from the passage without, was covered with a curtain of scarlet, trimmed with deep gold fringe, and looped up on each side with silken ropes. The floor, and to the extremity of the first three steps of the Throne, was covered with a splendid Persian-pattern Wilton carpet, and the remainder of the steps with scarlet baize.

The canopy of the throne, which was square, was surrounded by a beautiful carved and gilt cornice, prepared by Mr. Evans. Beneath the cornice hung a succession of crimson-velvet pelmet drapery, each pelmet having embroidered upon it a rose, a thistle, a crown, or a harp. Surmounting the cornice in front was a gilt crown upon a velvet cushion, over the letters "Geo. IV." supported on each side by an antique gilt ornament. The entire back of the throne, as well as the interior of the canopy, were covered with crimson Genoa velvet, which was relieved by a treble row of broad and narrow gold lace which surrounded the whole. In the centre of the back were the royal arms, the lion and the unicorn rampant, embroidered in the most costly style. Under this stood the chair of state, and near the throne were six splendid chairs placed for the other members of the royal family. These decorations, and the Hall being splendidly illuminated, presented to the eye a spectacle of the most imposing nature, heightened by the brilliant assemblage of elegantly dressed personages. The Ladies universally wore ostrich feathers, and the Gentlemen were attired in the most sumptuous dresses.

About four o'clock, his Majesty having gone through the other fatiguing ceremonies of the day, entered the Hall with the crown upon his head, and was greeted with shouts of "Long live the King!" from all quarters; shortly after which, the banquet was served by the necessary officers. But that part of the ceremony which most attracted the attention of Tallyho, was the challenge of the Champion, whose entrance was announced by the sound of the trumpets thrice; and who having proceeded on a beautiful horse in a full suit of armour, under the porch of a triumphal arch, attended by the Duke of Wellington on his right, and the Deputy Earl Marshal on his left, to the place assigned him, the challenge was read aloud by the Herald: he then threw down his gauntlet, which having lain a short time, was returned to him. This ceremony was repeated three times; when he drank to his Majesty, and received the gold cup and cover as his fee.

The Grand Coronation Banquet

The whole of this magnificent national pageant was conducted throughout with the most scrupulous attention to the customary etiquette of such occasions; and Tallyho, who had never witnessed any thing of the kind before, and consequently could have no conception of its splendour, was at various parts of the ceremony enraptured; he fancied himself in Fairy-land, and that every thing he saw and heard was the effect of enchantment. Our friends returned home highly gratified with their day's amusement.

CHAPTER XXV

"Behold the Ring! how strange the group appears
Of dirty blackguards, commoners and peers;
Jews, who regard not Moses nor his laws,
All ranks of Christians eager in the cause.
What eager bets—what oaths at every breath,
Who first shall shrink, or first be beat to death.
Thick fall the blows, and oft the boxers fall,
While deaf'ning shouts for fresh exertions call;
Till, bruised and blinded, batter'd sore and maim'd,
One gives up vanquish'd, and the other lam'd.
Say, men of wealth! say what applause is due
For scenes like these, when patronised by you?
These are your scholars, who in humbler way,
But with less malice, at destruction play.
You, like game cocks, strike death with polish'd steel;
They, dung-hill-bred, use only nature's heel;
They fight for something—you for nothing fight;
They box for love, but you destroy in spite."

THE following Tuesday having been appointed by the knowing ones for a pugilistic encounter between Jack Randall, commonly called the Nonpareil, and Martin, as well known by the appellation of The Master of the Rolls, from his profession being that of a baker; an excellent day's sport was anticipated, and the lads of the fancy were all upon the "*qui vive.*"

Our friends had consequently arranged, on the previous night, to breakfast at an early hour, and take a gentle ride along the road, with a determination to see as much as possible of the attractive amusements of a milling-match, and to take a view as they went along of the company they were afterwards to mingle with.

"We shall now," said Dashall (as they sat down to breakfast) "have a peep at the lads of the ring, and see a little of the real science of Boxing."

"We have been boxing the compass through the difficult straits of a London life for some time," replied Bob, "and I begin to think that, with all its variety, its gaiety, and

its pride, the most legitimate joys of life may fairly be said to exist in the country."

"I confess," said Dashall, "that most of the pleasures of life are comparative, and arise from contrast. Thus the bustle of London heightens the serenity of the country, while again the monotony of the country gives additional zest to the ever-varying scenes of London. But why this observation at a moment when we are in pursuit of fresh game?"

"Nay," said Tallyho, "I know not why; but I spoke as I thought, feeling as I do a desire to have a pop at the partridges as the season is now fast approaching, and having serious thoughts of shifting my quarters."

"We will talk of that hereafter," was the reply. "You have an excellent day's sport in view, let us not throw a cloud upon the prospect before us—you seem rather in the doldrums. The amusements of this day will perhaps inspire more lively ideas; and then we shall be present at the masquerade, which will doubtless be well attended; all the fashion of the Metropolis will be present, and there you will find a new world, such as surpasses the powers of imagination—a sort of Elysium unexplored before, full of mirth, frolic, whim, wit and variety, to charm every sense in nature. But come, we must not delay participating in immediate gratifications by the anticipations of those intended for the future. Besides, I have engaged to give the Champion a cast to the scene of action in my barouche."

By this time Piccadilly was all in motion—coaches, carts, gigs, tilburies, whiskies, buggies, dog-carts, sociables, dennets, curricles, and sulkies, were passing in rapid succession, intermingled with tax-carts and waggons decorated with laurel, conveying company of the most varied description. In a few minutes, the barouche being at the door, crack went the whip, and off they bowled. Bob's eyes were attracted on all sides. Here, was to be seen the dashing Corinthian tickling up his tits, and his bang-up set-out of blood and bone, giving the go-by to a heavy drag laden with eight brawney bull-faced blades, smoking their way down behind a skeleton of a horse, to whom in all probability a good feed of corn would have been a luxury; pattering among themselves, occasionally chaffing the more elevated drivers by whom they were surrounded, and pushing forward their nags with all the ardour of a British merchant intent upon disposing of a valuable cargo of foreign goods on 'Change. There, was a waggon, full of all sorts upon the lark, succeeded by a donkey-cart with four insides; but Neddy, not liking his burthen, stopt short on the way of a Dandy, whose horse's head coming plump up to the back of the crazy vehicle at the moment of its stoppage, threw the rider into the arms of a Dustman, who, hugging his customer with the determined grasp of a bear, swore d———n his eyes he had saved his life, and he expected he would stand something handsome for the Gemmen all round, for if he had not pitched into their cart, he would certainly have broke his neck; which being complied with, though reluctantly, he regained his saddle, and proceeded a little more cautiously along the remainder of the road, while groups of pedestrians of all ranks and appearances lined each side.

At Hyde-Park Corner, Tom having appointed to take up the prime hammer-man, drew up, and was instantly greeted by a welcome from the expected party, who being as quickly seated, they proceeded on their journey.

"This match appears to occupy general attention," said Tom.

"I should think so," was the reply—"why it will be a prime thing as ever was seen. Betting is all alive—the Daffy Club in tip-top spirits—lots of money sported on both sides—somebody must make a mull{1}—but Randall's the man—he is the favourite of the day, all the world to a penny-roll."

The simile of the penny roll being quite in point with the known title of one of the combatants, caused a smile on Dashall's countenance, which was caught by the eye of Tallyho, and created some mirth, as it was a proof of what has frequently been witnessed, that the lovers of the fancy are as apt in their imaginations at times, as they are ready for the accommodating one, two, or the friendly flush hit which floors their opponents.

The morning was fine, and the numerous persons who appeared travelling on the road called forth many inquiries from Bob.

"Now," said he, "I think I recollect that the admirable author of the *Sentimental Journey* used to read as he went along—is it possible to read as we journey forward?" "Doubtless," replied Tom, "it is, and will produce

   1 *Mull—Defeat, loss, or disappointment.*

a fund of amusing speculation as we jog on. Lavater founded his judgment of men upon the formation of their features; Gall and Spurzheim by the lumps, bumps and cavities of their pericraniums; but I doubt not we shall be right in our views of the society we are likely to meet, without the help of either—do you see that group?"

Bob nodded assent.

"These," continued Tom, "are profitable characters, or rather men of profit, who, kindly considering the constitution of their friends, provide themselves with refreshments of various kinds, to supply the hungry visitors round the ring—oranges, nuts, apples, gingerbread, biscuits and peppermint drops."

"Not forgetting *blue ruin and French lace,*"{1} said the man of fist; "but you have only half done it—don't you see the *Cash-cove*{2} behind, with his stick across his shoulder, *padding the hoof*{3} in breathless speed? he has *shell'd out the lour*{4} for the occasion, and is travelling down to keep a *wakeful winker*{5} on his retailers, and to take care that however they may chuse to lush away the profit, they shall at least take care of the principal. The little Dandy just before him also acts as Whipper-in; between them they mark out the ground,{6} watch the progress, and pocket the proceeds. They lend the money for the others to traffic."

"I confess," said Tom, "I was not exactly up to this."

"Aye, aye, but I know the *Blunt-monger*,{7} and am up to his ways and means," was the reply.—"Hallo, my eyes, here he comes!" continued he, rising from his seat, and bowing obsequiously to a Gentleman who passed them in a tandem—"all right, I am glad of it—always good sport when he is present—no want of sauce or seasoning—he always *comes it strong.*"{8}

"I perceive," replied Tom, "you allude to the noble Marquis of W———."

1 French lace—*A flash or cant term for brandy.*

2 Cash-cove—*A monied man.*

3 Padding the hoof—*Travelling on Shanks's mare, or taking a turn by the marrow-bone stage, i.e. walking.*

4 Shell'd out the lour—*Supplied the cash.*

5 Wakeful winker—*A sharp eye.*

6 Mark out the ground—*Is to place his retailers in various parts of the Ring for the accommodation of the company, any where he may expect to find them himself.*

7 Blunt-monger—*Money-dealer, or money-lender.*

8 Comes it strong—*No flincher, a real good one.*

Travelling gently along the road, they were presently impeded by a crowd of persons who surrounded a long cart or waggon, which had just been overturned, and had shot out a motley group of personages, who were being lifted on their legs, growling and howling at this unforeseen disaster. A hard-featured sailor, whose leg had been broken by the fall, brandished a splinter of the fractured limb, and swore—"That although his timbers were shivered, and he had lost a leg in the service, he would not be the last in the Ring, but he'd be d————d if he mount the rubbish-cart any more." It is needless to observe his leg was a wooden one.

Upon examining the inscription on the cart, it was found to contain the following words:—"Household Furniture, Building Materials, and Lumber carefully removed." As it was ascertained that no real injury had been sustained, our party speedily passed the overturned vehicle and proceeded.

The next object of attraction was a small cart drawn by one poor animal, sweating and snorting under the weight of six Swells, led by an old man, who seemed almost as incapable as his horse seemed unwilling to perform the journey. A label on the outside of the cart intimated that its contents was soap, which created some laughter between Tom and Bob. The man in the front, whose Jew-looking appearance attracted attention, was endeavouring to increase the speed of the conveyance by belabouring the boney rump of the *prad*{1} with his hat, while some of their pedestrian *palls*{2} were following close in the rear, and taking occasionally a *drap of the cratur*, which was handed out behind and returned after refreshment.

"These," said Tom to his Cousin, "are also men of profit, but not exactly in the way of those we passed—second-rate Swells and broken-down Gamesters, determined, as the saying is, to have a shy, even if they lose their sticks, and more properly may be termed men of plunder; desperate in their pursuits, they turn out with intent to make the best of the day, and will not fail to nibble all they can come easily at."

"They are not worth the blood from a broken nose," said the Pugilist, with a feeling for the honour of his profession which did him credit.—"They are all prigs, their company

1 Prad—*A cant term for a horse.*

2 Palls—*Partners, accomplices, colleagues.*

spoils all genteel society, and frequently brings disgrace upon others with whom they are unworthy to associate, or even to be seen— there's no getting rid of such gentry. Is it not d————d hard a man can't have a pleasant bit of a turn-up, without having his friends filched?—But here comes the gay fellows, here they come upon the trot, all eager and anxious to mark the first blow, start the odds, and curry the coal.{1} These are the lads of life—true lovers of the sport—up to the manouvre—clear and quick-sighted, nothing but good ones—aye aye, and here comes Bill Gibbons, furnished with the fashionables."

"What do you call the fashionables?" inquired Bob.

"Why, the Binders."

Here he was as much at a loss as ever, which the other perceiving, he continued—"The Binders are the stakes and ropes, to fence in the Ring."

Bill Gibbons, who was well known on the road, and was speeding down pretty sharp, was followed by crowds of vehicles of all descriptions; as many to whom the place of meeting was but conjectured, upon seeing him felt assured of being in the right track. Here were to be seen the Swells in their tandems—the Nib Sprigs in their gigs, buggies, and dog-carts—and the Tidy Ones on their trotters, all alive and leaping. Mirth and merriment appeared spread over every countenance, though expectation and anxiety were intermingled here and there in the features of the real lads of the fancy; many of whom, upon this very interesting occasion, had bets to a considerable amount depending upon the result of the day. The bang-up blades were pushing their prads along in gay style, accompanied by two friends, that is to say, a biped and a quadruped. The queer fancy lads, who had hired hacks from the livery-stable keepers, were kicking up a dust, and here and there rolling from their prancers in their native soil; while the neck or nothing boys, with no prospect but a whereas before their eyes, were as heedless of their personal safety as they were of their Creditor's property. Jaded hacks and crazy vehicles were to be seen on all sides—here lay a bankrupt-cart with the panels knock'd in, and its driver with an eye knock'd out, the horse lamed, and the concern completely knock'd up, just before the period when the hammer of the Auctioneer was to be called in, and his effects knock'd down. There was another

1 Curry the coal—Make sure of the money.

of the same description, with a harum-scarum devil of a half-bred, making his way at all risks, at a full gallop, as unmanageable in his career as his driver had been in his speculations; dust flying, women sprawling, men bawling, dogs barking, and the multitude continually increasing. Scouts, Scamps, Lords, Loungers and Lacqueys—Coster-mongers from—To the Hill Fields—and The Bloods from Bermondsey, completely lined the road as far as the eye could reach, both before and behind; it was a day of the utmost importance to the pugilistic school, as the contest had excited a most unparalleled degree of interest!

It would be scarcely possible to give a full and accurate description of the appearances as they went along; imagination would labour in vain, and words are altogether incapable of conveying a picture of the road to this memorable fight; the various instances in which they could discover that things were not all right were admirably contrasted by others, where care and good coachmanship, with a perfect management of the bloods, proved the reverse—while the single horsemen, whose hearts were really engaged in the sport, were picking their way with celerity, and posting to the point of attraction.—The public-houses were thronged to excess, and the Turnpike-keepers made a market of the mirth-moving throng.

Our party arrived in the neighbourhood of Copthorne about half-past twelve, where all was bustle and confusion. The commissary in chief, Mr. Jackson, being out of town, some of the subalterns, who had taken the command *pro tempore*, had, for divers weighty reasons, principally founded on a view to the profits of certain of the Surrey Trusts, and to accommodate the sporting circles at Brighton, fixed the combat to take place in a meadow belonging to a farmer named Jarvis, near this place.

Drawn & Etched by H. Alken, Esqr

7. Bankrupt Carts.
8. Not all right.
9. All right.

ROAD TO A FIGHT. Plate 2.

10. Real dealers in the Sport
11. Tom and Bob bang-up.
12. The Ring.

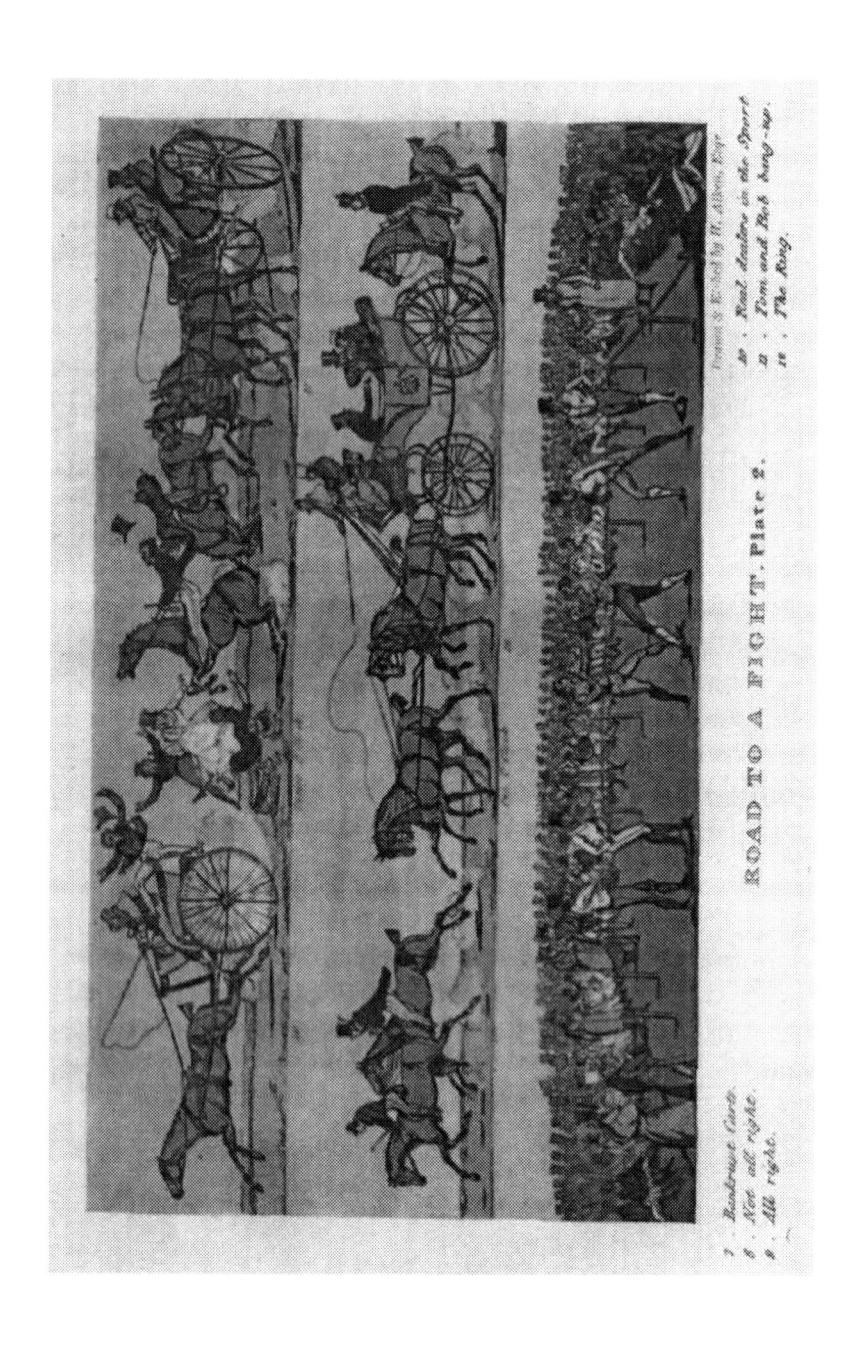

On this spot accordingly the ring was formed, and an immense mass of all descriptions of vehicles was admitted, not much, it may naturally be supposed, to the prejudice of the owner of the premises, whose agents were praise-worthily active in levying proper contributions. Some Gentlemen however in the neighbourhood, observing that the strictest delicacy was not maintained towards the sacredness of their fences, insisted that the place was too confined, and intimated that a move must be made, or they should make application to the Magistrates; and at the same time suggested Crawley Downs, the site of so many former skirmishes, as the most convenient spot for their accommodation.

In this state of things, a move immediately took place, and a fresh ring was established on the spot alluded to; but, in effecting this new lodgment, much mortification was experienced, not alone by those, who, after a dreadful drag up one of the worst by-roads in England, had obtained a comfortable situation, but by those, who, speculating on the formation of the ring, had expended considerable sums in the hire of waggons for their purpose from the surrounding farmers. The waggons it was found impossible to move in due time, and thus the new area was composed of such vehicles as were first to reach the appointed ground.

The general confusion now was inconceivable, for, notwithstanding the departure of connoisseurs from Jarvis's Farm, Martin still maintained his post, alleging, that he was on the ground originally fixed, and that he should expect Randall to meet him there; in which demand he was supported by his backers. This tended to increase the embarrassment of the amateurs; however, about one, Randall arrived at Crawley Downs, in a post-chaise, and took up his quarters at a cottage near the ground, waiting for his man; and at two, General Barton, who had just mounted his charger, intending to consult the head-quarters of the Magistrates, to ascertain their intention in case of proceeding to action at Jarvis's Farm, was suddenly arrested in his progress by an express from the Martinites, announcing that their champion had yielded his claim to the choice of ground, and was so anxious for the mill, that he would meet Randall even in a saw-pit. Bill Gibbons arriving soon after, the Ring, with the assistance of many hands, was quickly formed; by which time, Tom and Bob had secured themselves excellent situations to view the combat.

About twenty minutes before three, Randall entered the outer Ring, attended by General Barton and Mr. Griffiths. He was attired in a Whitehall upper Benjamin, and *threw his hat into the Ring* amidst loud applause. In a few minutes after, Martin approached from an opposite direction, accompanied by Mr. Sant and Mr. Elliott; he was also warmly greeted.

The men now passed the ropes, and were assisted by their immediate friends in peeling for action. Martin was attended by Spring and Thurton; Randall, by Harry Holt and Paddington Jones.

The men stript well, and both appeared to be in excellent health, good spirits, and high condition; but the symmetry of Randall's bust excited general admiration; and the muscular strength of his arms, neck, and shoulders, bore testimony to his Herculean qualities; the whole force of his body, in fact, seem'd to be concentrated above his waistband. Martin stood considerably above him, his arms were much longer, but they wanted that bold and imposing weight which characterized those of Randall. They walked up to the *scratch*, and shook hands in perfect good fellowship. Every man now took his station, and the heroes threw themselves into their guard.

It was rumoured that Martin intended to lose no time in manoeuvring, but to go to work instanter. This however he found was not so easily to be effected as suggested, for Randall had no favour to grant, and was therefore perfectly on his guard. He was all wary caution, and had clearly no intention of throwing away a chance, but was evidently waiting for Martin to commence. Martin once or twice made play, but Randall was not skittishly inclined, all was "war hawk." Randall made a left-handed hit to draw his adversary, but found it would not do. Martin then hit right and left, but was stopped. Randall was feeling for Martin's wind, but hit above his mark, though not without leaving one of a red colour, which told "a flattering tale." Randall returned with his left, and the men got to a smart rally, when Randall got a konker, which tapped the claret. An almost instantaneous close followed, in which Randall, grasping Martin round the neck with his right arm, and bringing his head to a convenient posture, sarved out punishment with his left. This was indeed a terrific position. Randall was always famous for the dreadful force of his short left-handed hits, and on this occasion they lost none of their former character. Martin's nob was completely in a vice; and while in that hopeless condition, Randall fibbed away with the solid weight of the hammer of a tuck-mill. His aim was principally at the neck, where every blow told with horrible violence. Eight or ten times did he repeat the dose, and then, with a violent swing, threw Martin to the ground, falling on him as he; went with all his weight. The Ring resounded with applause, and Jack coolly took his seat on the knee of his Second. Martin's friends began to look blue, but still expected, the fight being young, there was yet much to be done.

All eyes were now turned to Martin, who being lifted on Spring's knee, in a second discovered that he was done. His head fell back lifeless, and all the efforts of Spring to keep it straight were in vain. Water was thrown on him in abundance, but without effect: he was, in fact, completely senseless; and the half-minute having transpired, the Nonpareil was hailed the victor.

Randall appeared almost without a scratch, while poor Martin lay like a lump of unleavened dough; he was removed and bled, but it was some time before he was conscious of his defeat.

Nothing could exceed the astonishment which so sudden and complete a finish to the business produced. The round lasted but seven minutes and a half, of which four minutes and a half had elapsed before a blow was attempted. Thus ended one of the most extraordinary battles between two known game men on the pugilistic records. Very heavy bets had been made upon it in all parts of the kingdom. One gentleman is said to have had five thousand pounds, and another one thousand eight hundred guineas. The gains of the conqueror were supposed to be about a thousand pounds.

The amusements of the day were concluded by a second fight between Parish and Lashbroke, which proved a manly and determined contest for upwards of an hour, and in which the combatants evinced considerable skill and bravery, and was finally decided in favour of Parish. All amusement which might have been derived from this spectacle, however, was completely destroyed by the daring outrages of an immense gang of pickpockets, who broke in the Ring, and closed completely up to the ropes, carrying with them every person, of decent appearance, and openly robbing them of their watches, pocket-books and purses. And the lateness of the hour, it being five o'clock, and almost dark, favoured the depredators.

In the midst of this struggle, Tom Dashall had nearly lost his fancy topper,{1} and Tallyho was secretly eased of his clicker.{2} From the scene of tumult and confusion they were glad to escape; and being again safely seated in the

1 Topper—A flash term given to a hat.

2 Clicker—A flash term given to a watch,

barouche, they made the best of their way home; in doing which, they found the roads almost as much clogg'd as they were in the morning. The Randallites were meritorious, and, flushed with good fortune, lined the public-houses on the road to *wet their whistles*, singing and shouting his name in strains to them equally inspiring as

"*See the conquering hero comes!*
Sound your trumpets, beat your drums;"

while the Martinites rolled along the road in sullen silence; and, by the time they reached town, an account of the Battle was hawking about the streets, and songs singing to the praise of the successful combatant in all the melodious cadences of a last dying speech and confession: such is the promptitude of London Printers, Poets, and News-venders.

"Well," said Dashall, as they re-entered the house, "the events of this day have completely disappointed some of the knowing ones."

"That may be," replied Bob, "but they have been too knowing for me, notwithstanding your previous instructions. However, I don't regret seeing the humours of a Prize Ring; and the next time you catch me there, I must take a lesson from the man of profit, and keep a wakeful winker on the possibles. Really, I could not help feeling astonished at the immense number of persons assembled on such an occasion."

"Zounds!" said Tom, "'tis the real centre of attraction, the thing, the tippy, and the twig, among the Lads of the Fancy. Why, it is pretty generally known, through the medium of the newspapers, that a certain Nobleman paid the debts of one of these Pugilists, amounting to 300L. that he might be released from Newgate in order to fight a prize battle; and it is not long since that the Marquis of T—ed—e, whilst entertaining a large party, after dinner introduced the subject with so much effect, that a purse of 100 guineas was subscribed among them for a turn up between two of the *prime hammermen*; who, being introduced, actually set-to in his drawing-room for the amusement of his friends. Nor is it less true, that this sporting Nobleman gloriously took up the conqueror, (as the saying is) and evinced his patronage and his power at once, by actually subduing his antagonist, proving to certitude, that if his Lordship would but practise this sublime art, he could hardly fail of adding to his present title that of the Champion of England! It is the theme of constant conversation, and in many cases there is more anxiety about contests of this sort than there is about the arrival of a Monarch on the Irish coast among the lads of *praties*, whiskey, and buttermilk—thoughts are busy, energies are active—and money in galore is circulated upon it."

Bob laughed heartily at these observations of his Cousin upon what he termed the sublime art.

A PRIVATE TURN-UP, in the Drawing Room of a Noble Marquis

"You don't appear to enter into the spirit of it," continued Tom; "but I can assure you, it is a very animating subject, and has occupied the attention of all classes, from the peer to the prelate, the peasant and the pot-boy; it is said that one of the lower order of ranting Preachers, not many miles from Bolton-on-the-Moors, lately addressed his auditory in the following metaphorical language, accompanied with striking and appropriate attitudes:—'I dare say, now, you'd pay to see a boxing-match between Randall and Turner, or Martin—yet you don't like to pay for seeing a pitched-battle between me and the Black Champion Beelzebub. Oh! my friends, many a hard knock, and many a cross-buttock have I given the arch bruiser of mankind—aye, and all for your dear sakes—pull—do pull off those gay garments of Mammon, strike the devil a straightforward blow in the mouth, darken his spiritual daylights. At him manfully, give it him right and left, and I'll be your bottle-holder—I ask nothing but the money, which you'll not forget before you go.' "

"The true spirit moved him," said Bob, "and a very laudable one too; but he very emphatically deprecated the votaries of Mammon."

"Certainly, he being called, would have been unworthy of his calling if he had not."

This conversation was carried on over a glass of generous wine, and, dwindling into indifferent subjects, is not necessary to be detailed; suffice it to say, that, fatigued with the day's exertions, they sought repose in the arms of Morpheus at an early hour, determined on the pursuit of fresh game with the dawn of the morning.

CHAPTER XXVI

"See yonder beaux, so delicately gay;
And yonder belles, so'deck'd in thin array—
Ah! rather see not what a decent pride
Would teach a maiden modestly to hide;
The dress so flimsy, the exposure such,
"twould almost make a very wanton blush.
E'en married dames, forgetting what is due
To sacred ties, give half clad charms to view.
What calls them forth to brave the daring glance,
The public ball, the midnight wanton dance?
There many a blooming nymph, by fashion led,
Has felt her health, her peace, her honour fled;
Truss'd her fine form to strange fantastic shapes,
To be admir'd, and twirl'd about by apes;
Or, mingling in the motley masquerade,
Found innocence by visor'd vice betrayed."

AN agreeable lounge through the Parks in the morning afforded them an opportunity of recalling in idea the pleasures of the past Real Life in London, of which Tallyho had been enabled to partake, and during which he again signified a desire to change the scene, by a departure at an early period for his native vales, to breathe, as he observed, the uncontaminated air of the country—to watch the wary pointer, and mark the rising covey—to pursue the timid hare, or chase the cunning fox; and Dashall finding him inflexible, notwithstanding his glowing descriptions of scenes yet unexplored, at length consented to accompany him to Belville Hall, upon condition that they should return again in a month. This mode of arrangement seemed perfectly satisfactory to Bob; and a view of the Panorama and a peep at the Tennis Court would have finished their rambles for the day, but at the latter place of amusement and healthful exercise, meeting with young Mortimer, a further developement of facts relative to Sparkle and his Bride transpired; in which it appeared that they had arrived at their place of destination, and had forwarded an invitation to his brother-in-law to pay them an early visit, and who proposed starting in a few days.

"Well," said Dashall, "we will all go together, and no doubt with our old friend Sparkle we shall be able to endure the unchanging prospects of a country life."

> "In the Country how blest, when it rains in the fields,
> To feast upon transports that shuttle-cock yields;
> Or go crawling from window to window, to see
> An ass on a common, a crow on a tree.
>
> In the Country you're nail'd, like some pale in your park,
> To some stick of a neighbour, crammed into the ark;
> And if you are sick, or in fits tumble down,
> You reach death ere the Doctor can reach you from town."

"Never mind," cried Tallyho, "a change of scene will no doubt be useful, and, at all events, by enduring the one, we may learn more judiciously to appreciate the other."

"True," said Tom, "and I shall like myself all the better for being in good company. But pray, Mr. Mortimer, what do you mean to do at the approaching masquerade?"

"Not quite decided yet," was the reply.

"You go, of course?"

"Certainly—as Orpheus, or Apollo. But pray what character do you intend to sustain?"

"That's a secret—"

"Worth knowing, I suppose—well, well, I shall find you out, never fear."

"Time's a tell-tale," said Dashall, "and will most likely unfold all mysteries; but I always think the life and spirit of a masquerade is much injured by a knowledge of the characters assumed by friends, unless it be where two or more have an intention of playing, as it were, to, and with each other; for where there is mystery, there is always interest. I shall therefore propose that we keep to ourselves the characters in which we mean to appear; for I am determined, if possible, to have a merry night of it."

> "On the lightly sportive wing,
> At pleasure's call we fly;
> Hark! they dance, they play, they sing,
> In merry merry revelry;
> Hark! the tabors lively beat,
> And the flute in numbers sweet,
> Fill the night with delight
> At the Masquerade.
> Let the grave ones warn us as they may,
> Of every harmless joy afraid;
> Whilst we're young and gay,
> We'll frolic and play
> At the Masquerade."

Tom's observations upon this subject were in perfect accordance with those of. Mortimer and Tallyho; though he had intended to consult his Cousin as to the character he should appear in, he now determined to take his own direction, or to have advice from Fentum in the Strand, whose advertisements to supply dresses, &c. he had observed in the newspapers.

These preliminaries being decided upon, as far as appeared needful at the moment, Mortimer departed towards home, where he expected to meet his Uncle upon his return from the chase after the fugitives, Sparkle and Miss Mortimer, now Mrs. Sparkle; and Tom and Bob to Piccadilly, where a select party of Dashall's friends were invited to dinner, and where they enjoyed a pleasant evening, drank rather freely, and had but little to regret after it, except certain qualmish feelings of the head and stomach the next morning.

The anticipated Masquerade had been the principal subject of conversation, so long as reason held her sway; but the hard exercise of the arm, and the generosity of the wine, had an early and visible effect upon some of the party, who did not separate till a late hour, leaving Bob just strength and intelligence enough to find the way to his dormitory.

By the arrival of the appointed evening for the grand Masquerade at Vauxhall Gardens, Tom Dashall, who had a particular view in keeping his intended proceedings a secret, had arranged all to his wishes, and anticipated considerable amusement from the interest he should take in the safety of his Cousin, whom he entertained no doubt of quickly discovering, and with whom he determined to promote as much mirth as possible.

Tallyho, in the mean time, had also made occasional calls upon Merrywell in his confinement, and, under his direction, been preparing for the occasion, equally determined, if possible, to turn the laugh on his Cousin; and it must be acknowledged, he could scarcely have found a more able tutor, though he was doomed rather to suffer by his confidence in his instructor, as will hereafter be seen; for, in escaping the intended torment of one, he was unexpectedly subjected to the continual harassing of another.

It was about half after eleven o'clock, when Tallyho, duly equipped in his country costume, as a Huntsman, entered this splendid and spacious scene of brilliancy. The blaze of light which burst upon him, and the variety of characters in constant motion, appeared almost to render him motionless; and several of the would-be characters passed him with a vacant stare, declaring he was no character at all! nor was he roused from his lethargic position till he heard a view halloo, which seemed to come from a distant part of the Garden, and was so delivered, as actually to give him an idea of the party being in pursuit of game, by growing fainter towards the close, as if receding from him. The sound immediately animated him, and answering it in a truly sportsman-like style, he burst from his situation, and cracking his whip, at full speed followed in the direction from which it came, under the impression that he knew the voice of Dashall, and should discover him. In his speed, however, he was rather rudely attacked by a small dandy personage, whose outward appearance indicated some pretensions to manhood, with a "Demmee, Sir, how dare you be rude to my voman! for egad I shall have you clapped in the Round-house—here, Vatchman, take this here man in charge— Vatch! Vatch!" The voice however soon told him he had a lady to deal with, and he entered into a long harangue by way of apology. This not being acceptable to the offended party, he was surrounded by a host of Charleys springing their rattles all at once, and, notwithstanding the dexterous use of his whip, he was obliged to yield. At this moment, Tallyho was again sounded in his ears, issuing from another quarter; but his struggles to pursue the party from whom it came were ineffectual. A rough-hewn Sailor with a pipe in his mouth, and an immense cudgel in his hand, however, arrived to his assistance, accompanied by an Irish Chairman in a large blue coat, and a cock'd hat bound with gold lace, armed with a chair-pole, who effected his liberty; and he again scoured off in pursuit of his friend, but without success. He now began to think his situation not altogether so pleasant as he could wish. He listened to every voice, examined every form that passed him in rapid succession; yet he felt himself alone, and determined not to be led away by sounds such as had already occupied his attention, but rather to look about him, and notice the eccentricities with which he was surrounded. Sauntering along in this mood, he was presently assailed by a voice behind him, exclaiming, "Bob—

"Bob, if you wish to go safely on,
Tarn round about, and look out for the Don."

Upon hearing this, he turned hastily around, and encountered a group of Chimney-sweepers, who immediately set up such a clatter with their brushes and shovels, dancing at the same time in the true May-day style round him and a strapping Irish fish-woman, that he was completely prevented from pursuit, and almost from observation, while a universal laugh from those near him bespoke the mirth his situation excited; and the Hibernian damsel, with true Irish sympathy, attempted to allay his chagrin by clasping him in her brawny arms, and imprinting on his ruddy cheek a kiss. This only served to heighten their merriment and increase his embarrassment, particularly as his *Cher ami* swore she had not had a buss like it since the death of her own dear dead and departed Phelim, the last of her four husbands, who died of a whiskey fever, bawling for pratees and buttermilk, and was waked in a coal-shed.

This mark of the Lady's favour was not so favourably received by Tallyho, and, determined to make his escape, he gave Moll a violent fling from him, overturned her and her basket, knock'd down two of the Chimney-sweepers, and then with a leap as if he had been springing at a five-barred gate, jumped over his late companion, who lay sprawling among the flue-fakers, and effected his purpose, to the inexpressible amusement of those, who, after enjoying a hearty laugh at him, now transferred their risibility to those he left behind. Finding himself once more unshackled, he smack'd his whip with enthusiasm, and repeated his Tallyho with increased effect; for it was immediately answered, and, without waiting for its final close, he found the person from whom it was proceeding to be no other than a Turk, who was precipitately entering one of the rooms, and was as quickly recognized by him to be the Hon. Tom Dashall. The alteration which a Turkish turban and pelisse had effected in his person, would however have operated as an effectual bar to this discovery, had he not seized him in the very moment of vociferation; and although his Cousin had been the chief cause of the adventures he had already met with, he had at the same time kept an eye upon Bob, and been equally instrumental in effecting his release from embarrassment.

"Come," said Tom, "I am for a little gig in the Room—how long have you been here?—I thought I should find you out, very few can disguise themselves from me; we will now be spectators for half an hour, and enjoy the mirth excited by others."

"With all my heart," rejoined Bob, "for I am almost as tired already as if I had spent a whole day in a fox-chase, and have run as many risks of my neck; so that a cool half hour's observation will be very acceptable."

They had scarcely entered the Room, as a Priscilla Tomboy passed them at full speed with a skipping-rope, for whose accommodation every one made way; and who, having skipped round the room to shew her fine formed ancle and flexibility of limbs, left it for a moment, and returned with a large doll, which she appeared as pleased with as a child of eight or ten years of age. A Jemmy Jumps assured Tom, that his garments were altogether unsuitable to the nation in which he was residing, and recommended that he should not exist another day without that now very fashionable appendage of a Gentleman's dress called stays—An excellent Caleb Quotem, by his smartness of repartee and unceasing volubility of speech in recounting his labours of a day—"a summer's day," as the poet says, afforded much amusement by his powers of out-talking the fribble of a Staymaker, who, finding himself confused by his eternal clack, fled in search of another customer. A Don Quixote was conferring the honour of knighthood on a clumsy representative of the God of Love, and invoking his aid in return, to accomplish the object of finding his lost Dulcinea. An outlandish fancy-dressed character was making an assignation with a Lady, who, having taken the veil and renounced the sex, kindly consented to forego her vows and meet him again; while a Devil behind her was hooking the cock'd-hat of the gay deceiver to the veil of the Nun, which created considerable laughter, for as they attempted to separate, they were both completely unmasked, and discovered, to the amazement of Tallyho, two well-known faces, little expected there by him—no other than Merrywell as the Dandy Officer, and his friend Mr. Safebind as the Nun. The exposure rather confused them, while Tom and Bob joined the merry Devil in a loud burst of laughter—they however bustled through the room and were quickly lost.

A French *Frisseur*, without any knowledge of the language of the nation from which he appeared to come, could only answer a question *a la Françoise* from the accomplished Tom Dashall, by a volume of scented powder from his puff, which being observed by a Chimney-sweeper, was returned by dust of another colour from his soot-bag, till the intermixture of white and black left it difficult to decide which was the Barber and which the Sweep. They were now suddenly attracted by a grotesque dance between a Clown of the Grimaldi school and a fancy Old Woman in a garment of patch-work made in an ancient fashion. A red nose, long rows of beads for ear-rings, and a pair of spectacles surmounted by a high cauled-cap, decorated with ribbons of various hues, rendered her the most conspicuous character in the room: and notwithstanding her high-heeled shoes, she proved herself an excellent partner for the Clown.

MASQUERADE. *Tom and Bob, keeping it up in real characters.*

By this time, Bob, who was anxious to carry his plan into execution, began to be fidgetty, and proposed a walk into the open air again. As they left the room, his ears were attracted by the following song by a Watchman, which he could not help stopping to catch, and which afforded his Cousin an excellent opportunity of giving him the slip:

> "Fly, ye prigs,{1} for now's the hour,
> (Tho' boosey kids{2} have lost their power,)
> When watchful Charleys,{3} like the Sun,
> Their nightly course of duty run
> Beneath the pale-faced moon;

1 Prigs—Pickpockets.

2 Boosey kids—Drunken men.

3 Charleys—A cant term for watchmen.

> But take this warning while ye fly,
> That if you nibble, click,{1} or clye,{2}
> My sight's so dim, I cannot see,
> Unless while you the blunt{3} tip me:
> Then stay, then stay;
> For I shall make this music speak,{4}
> And bring you up before the Beak,{5}
> Unless the chink's in tune.
>
> Now, ye rambling sons of night,
> Or peep-o'-day boys{6} on your flight,
> Well prim'd with Jack or Child Tom's juice,
> While you the silver key{7} produce,
> Your safety then is clear.
> But snuffy,{8} and not up to snuff,{9}
> You'll And your case is queer enough;
> Shell out the nonsense;{10} half a quid{11}
> Will speak more truth than all your whid:{12}
>
> Then go, then go;
> For, if you linger on your way,

You'll for my music dearly pay,
I'll quod you, never fear."

Turning round with laughter from this character, who had attracted many hearers, he look'd in vain for Dashall, and was not displeased to find he had fled. He therefore hastily withdrew from the scene of merriment, and according to the instructions previously received, and for which he had prepared, quickly changed his dress, and appeared again in the character of a Judge, under the impression hinted by his counsellor, that the gravity of his wig and gown, with a steady countenance,

1 *Click*—*A contraction of the word clicker, for a watch.*

2 *Clye*—*A pocket-handkerchief.*

3 *Blunt*—*Money.*

4 *Music*—*Alluding to the rattle.*

5 *Beak*—*A magistrate.*

6 *Peep-o'-day boys*—*Staunch good ones*—*reeling home after the frolics of the night.*

7 *Silver key*—*Money which is thus termed, as it is supposed to open all places, and all hearts.*

> *"If you are sick and like to die,*
> *And for the Doctor send,*
> *Or have the cholic in your eye,*
> *Still money is your friend*—*is it not?"*

8 *Snuffy*—*Drunk.*

9 *Up to Snuff*—*Elevation of ideas.*

10 *Shell out the nonsense*—*To pay money.*

11 *Half a quid—Half a guinea.*

12 *Whid—Words or talk.*

would be a quiet and peaceable part to get through, and shield him from the torment of those whom Bob suspected willing to play tricks with him should he be discovered. Here however he again found himself at fait, for he had scarcely entered the Gardens, before a host of depredators were brought before him for trial. The Charleys brought in succession, drunken Fiddlers, Tinkers and Barbers; and appeals were made to his patience in so many voices, and under so many varying circumstances, that Justice was nearly running mad, and poor Tallyho could find no chance of making a reply. An uproar from the approaching crowd, announced some more than ordinary culprit; and, in a moment, who should appear before him but a Don Giovanni, and the hooking Devil, Here was a fine case for decision; the Devil claimed the Don as his property, and addressed the Representative of Justice as follows:—

"Most learned and puissant Judge!

"Protect my rights as you would the rights of man; I claim my property, and will have my claim allowed."

"Hold," replied Bob, "if that is the case, you have no occasion to appeal to me—begone, black wretch, and in thy native shades yell forth thy discordant screams."

"Most righteous Judge!—a second Daniel!" cried a bearded Shylock, with his knife and scales, "he shan't escape me—I'll have my bond—so bare his bosom 'next the heart'—let me come near him."

"This is playing the Devil, indeed," said the Don.

"By the Powers!" cried a 'Looney Mackwolteb,' "he's jump'd out of the fire into the frying-pan; and, when the Smouchee has done wid him, he may be grill'd in his own fat."

At this moment, a Leporello, who caught the last words of the Irishman, burst into the presence of the Judge, singing—

"Zounds, Sir, they'll grill you now, lean or fat, I know what games you were always at, And told you before what harm you would hatch: Now the old Gentleman's found you out, He'll clap us all in the round-about; Let us be off, ere they call for the Watch."

The word Watch was re-echoed in a thousand voices; the vociferations of the callers, the noise of the rattles, and the laughter of those immediately surrounding the judgment-seat, offered so good an opportunity for escape, that Giovanni, determining to have another chance, burst from the grasp of the arch enemy of mankind, to pursue his wonted vagaries, to the no small gratification of Bob, who, without actually acquitting the prisoner, rejoiced at his own escape.

He had however scarcely time to congratulate himself, before he was annoyed by a Postman, in the usual costume, whom he had already seen delivering letters to the company; the contents of which appeared to afford considerable amusement; and who, presenting a letter addressed to The Lord Chief Justice Bunglecause, in a moment disappeared. Breaking open the envelope, he read with astonishment the following lines:—

> *"Tho' justice prevails*
> *Under big wigs and tails,*
> *You've not much of law in your nob;*
> *So this warning pray take,*
> *Your big wig forsake,*
> *And try a more modern scratch, Bob."*

"Go along Bob—Lord Chief Justice Bob in a scratch," cried a Waterman at his elbow, (who had heard him reading) in a voice loud enough to be heard at some distance.

"There he'll be at home to a hair," squeaked a little finicking personification of a modern Peruquier, sidling up to him, picking his teeth with a tortoise-shell comb.

Bob, in bursting hastily away, under the reiterated cries of "Go along Bob—Lord Chief Justice Bob," with the idea of overtaking the Postman, found himself in a moment lock'd in the close embraces of a Meg Merrilies; while a little bandy-legg'd representative of the late Sir Jeffery Dunstan, bawling out, Ould wigs, Ould wigs, made a snatch at the grave appendage of Justice, and completely dismantled the head of its august representative. This delayed him in his progress, but it was merely to witness the wig flying in the air, with as much mirth to the surrounding company as when the greasy night-cap of the Rev. George Harvest was toss'd about the pit at the theatre, each one giving it a swing who could get within reach of it. Thus mutilated in his apparel, and probably conceiving, according to the song,

"*The wig's the thing, the wig, the wig,*
The wisdom's in the wig,"

Bob Tallyho took flight into a dressing-room, declaring justice was abroad and propriety not at home. He was however rather at a loss, as in his last character he had not been able to meet with the Turk, but determined to resume the search in a 'Domino. Having therefore equipped himself as a spectator, he again sallied forth with intention to explore the room, and for a time remained comparatively unmolested; but as he could no where find his Cousin, he strolled indiscriminately among the characters, viewing whatever appeared amusing or interesting in his way. The fineness of the weather greatly animated the scene, and gave increased brilliancy and effect to the illuminations, which were disposed in a numerous variety of splendid devices, representing national trophies, stars, wreaths, and crowns of laurel. It was the first moment he had found an opportunity of viewing the place in which he had been acting.

The amusements of the evening were judiciously varied, and protracted by a constant succession of entertainments of various descriptions. Mr. Chalons exhibited many of his most surprising deceptions in the rotunda; where also young Gyngell displayed some capital performances on the slack-wire. In the long room the celebrated fantoccini exhibition, with groupes of quadrille dancers, enlivened the scene. In one walk of the garden, Mr. Gyngell's theatre of arts was erected, where were exhibited balancing, the *Ombres Chinoises*, gymnastic exercises, and other feats, and Mr. Gyngell performed several airs on the musical glasses; in another,

Punchinello delighted the beholders with his antics; in a third a very expert Juggler played a variety of clever tricks and sleight-of-hand deceptions, and a couple of itinerant Italians exhibited their musical and mechanical show-boxes; in another part of the gardens the celebrated Diavolo Antonio went through his truly astonishing evolutions on the *corde volante*. The Duke of Gloucester's fine military band occupied the grand orchestra; an excellent quadrille band played throughout the night in the long room, while a Scottish reel band in the rotunda, and a Pandean band in the gardens, played alternately reels, waltzes, and country dances.

This interval of peace was truly acceptable to Bob, and he did not fail to make the most of it, roving like the bee from one delight to another, sipping pleasure as he went, almost regretting he had not taken the last dress first, though he was every now and then importuned by Mendicants and Servant girls, very desirous to obtain places of all work. The introduction of a Dancing Bear, who appeared to possess more Christian qualities than his Leader, attracted his attention; but, in pressing to the scene of action, he received a floorer from a Bruiser in gloves, who mill'd indiscriminately all who came in his way, till the Bear took the shine out of him by a fraternal embrace; and his Leader very politely asked those around which they thought the greater bear of the two. Upon rising, Bob found himself in the hands of two itinerant Quack Doctors, each holding an arm, and each feeling for his pulse. One declared the case was mortal, a dislocation of the neck had taken place, and there was no chance of preserving life except by amputation of the head. The other shook his head, look'd grave, pull'd out his lancet, and prescribed phlebotomy and warm water.

Bob, who had received no injury, except a little contusion occasioned by the blow, seized the ignorant practitioners by the throat, and knocking their heads together, exclaimed with a stentorian voice,

"Throw physic to the clogs, I'll none on't." "Go along Bob," was repeated again, as loud and as long as before; he however burst from those around him in pursuit of fresh game; nor was he disappointed, for he presently found a dapper young Clergyman in gown and surplice, and who, with book in hand, was fervently engaged in exhortations and endeavours to turn from the evil of their ways a drunken Sailor and a hardened thief, (the Orson of the Iron Chest,) when the group were surrounded by a detachment of the Imps and Devils of Giovanni in London, a truly horrid and diabolical crew, who, by their hideous yells, frantic capers, violent gestures, and the flaring of their torches, scared the affrighted Parson from his task, made his intended penitents their own, and became an almost intolerable nuisance to the rest of the company for the remainder of the evening.

While he was thus engaged, the supper-boxes were thrown open, and the company appeared to be all on the move towards the more substantial entertainments of the evening. He was next suddenly detained by a Jew Pedlar, who was anxious to shew him his wares.

"Get out, Smouchee," said Bob.

"Ant is dat all vat you can say to a poor honesht Jew, what vants to live by his 'trade, for vye you trow my religionsh in my teeth? I'm so honesht vat I never cheats nobody—vill you puy a gould———l Vat you take for your gown? I shall puy or sell, it's all the same to me.

"Now whatsoever country by chance I travel through, 'Tis all the same to I, so the monies but comes in; Some people call me tief, just because I am a Jew; So to make them tell the truth, vy I tinks there is no sin. So I shows them all mine coots vid a sober, winning grace, And I sometimes picks dere pockets whilst they're smiling in my face."

Bob laugh'd, but declared he'd have nothing to do with him.

"Then," said the Hon. Tom Dashall, "you may go along Bob."

"What! is it possible? I have been looking for you these two hours."

"I can't eat pork," said Dashall, resuming his character.

"Come along," said Bob, happy to find his relation; and catching him by the arm, they proceeded to refreshment, and partook of an excellent supper of cold viands plentifully supplied, and accompanied with a profusion of ices and jellies, served up in a style highly creditable to the managers.

Here they were joined by Mortimer, who had been as frolicsome as any imp in the Gardens, in the character of the Devil, but who had lost sight of the Dandy Officer and the Nun, whom he had so ingeniously hooked together. The wine was good, and after enjoying their repast, Tom and Mortimer enshrined themselves in dominos for the remainder of the evening. The usual masquerade frolics and dancing were afterwards continued, and about five in the morning they left this region of fun, mirth and good humour.

CHAPTER XXVII

That Life is a picture of strange things and ways,
A grand exhibition, each hour displays;
And for London there's no place can with it compare,
'Tis a jumble of every thing curious and rare.
Cheap-side Bustlers—Fleet Street Hustlers,
Jockeys, Doctors—Agents, Proctors,
Bow Street Slangups—Bond Street Bangups,
Hide and Seekers—Opera Squeakers,
Lawyers, Tailors—Bailiffs, Jailors,
Shopmen, Butlers—Alderman Gutters,
Patriot Talkers—Sunday Walkers,
Dancers, Actors—Jews, Contractors,
Placemen, Croakers—Boxers, Brokers,
Swindlers, Coroners—Spies, and Foreigners,
And all, all to keep up the bubble of strife,
And prove ways and means—is the picture of Life.

THE bustle and merriment of the Masquerade were long remembered in the mind of Bob Tallyho, and furnished frequent conversations between him and his Cousin; and the laughable occurrences of the evening, in which they had been engaged, were re-enjoyed in recollection, notwithstanding the preparations they were making for an excursion of another kind in the country, which though not exactly to the taste of Dashall, was inflexibly persevered in by Tallyho.

Tom tried every effort in his power to prolong the appointed period of departure in A'ain. The heart and mind of his Cousin appeared to be occupied with anticipated delights, which he described in the most glowing colours of imagination. The healthful fields, the enlivening fox chase, and the sportive exercises of a country life, were detailed with ecstacy; and though last, not least, the additional zest for the more attractive scenes (in Tom's idea) that would present themselves for inspection upon a return to the Metropolis. At length it was finally arranged that their country excursion should not exceed one month in duration, and that they would leave London time enough to reach Belville Hall on or before the first day of September.

Dashall, after consenting to this arrangement, finding there was not much time to spare, was anxious to improve it in the pursuit of such lively and interesting amusements as chance and accident might throw in their way. "Come," said he, a few mornings after the masquerade, "it must not be said that you have been so long in London without viewing as many of its important curiosities as the time would admit; though I am sure we shall not have an opportunity of glancing at all those I could point out, and I am pretty sure that persons from the country frequently see more in a few days residence in the Metropolis, than those who have inhabited it for their whole lives. We will therefore take a stroll out, without any determined line of pursuit, and survey what chance may bring in our way; for the places deserving of particular inspection are so numerous, and lay in so many directions, that it is scarcely possible for us to turn round without finding some objects and subjects yet in store.

Thus saying, and taking the arm of his Cousin, they walked along Piccadilly in a direction for the City; for as it was a clear morning, Tom, although he had not mentioned the road he meant to take, still had an object in view.

"It is certainly much to be deplored," said he, as they were just entering Leicester Square by Sydney's Alley, "that the abominable nuisance of barrows being driven on the pavement cannot be removed; it is a great shame that lusty and able fellows should be wheeling foul linen, hogwash, and other filthy articles along the street, to the annoyance and inconvenience of pedestrians."

"I am of your opinion," replied his Cousin; "but during the short time I have been here, I have discovered many other equally objectionable annoyances. There is, for instance, the carrying of milk pails, which, unless great care is taken, are so likely to break people's shins; and in dirty weather the trundling of boys' hoops, to the discomfiture of many a well-dressed Lady."

At this moment a butcher was passing with a tray heavily loaded, and Bob narrowly escaped a blow from the projecting corner, which immediately induced him to add that to the number of what he termed street grievances, and almost to overturn both the carrier and his load.

"A lucky escape," said Dashall, "for you might have lost an eye by coming in contact with that tray, and I wonder a stop is not put to the probability of such fatal accidents. It is related that a certain City Alderman, whose constitution, it may be presumed, is rather of a combustible nature, by the alarms he spread during his mayoralty, of the intention to burn the City of London, and destroy all its peaceable inhabitants, thrashed a butcher who ran against him in the public street. This it must be admitted was a summary mode of punishment, although it was not likely to remove the nuisance; but there are still many that are not enumerated in your list. Both by day and night in the most frequented streets of the Metropolis and its environs, the unoffending passengers of either sex are frequently obstructed on, or absolutely pushed off the pavement by a trio of arm-in-arm puppies; nay they will sometimes sweep the whole of the space from the wall to the curb stone, by walking four abreast, a practice brutally infringing the laws of civil society in pedestrian excursions through a crowded Metropolis.

"I have however with pleasure, upon some occasions, seen these vile trespassers meet with a just resentment in the unexpected pugilistic exertions of the insulted party; and have almost rejoiced to see them packed into a coach and sent home with bruises, black eyes, and bloody noses, serving, it is to be hoped, as wholesome lessons for their future conduct. In some cases duels have arisen from this violation of decorum in the King's highway, and by this means, scoundrels have been admitted to the undeserved honour of being met on a level by gentlemen.

"These," continued he, "are the polite encroachers on the pavé.. There are, however, many others, but of a less censurable, though certainly of a finable description; such as journeymen bakers wheeling barrows conveying the staff of life—publicans' boys collecting pewter pots—lady drivers of similar vehicles, containing oysters, inferior or damaged fruit, delicate prog for pug dogs, cats, &c.

"After all, the most prominent offenders, or at least obstructors of the public way, in my opinion, are those sturdy John Bulls, brewers' servants, by means of ropes and pulleys affixed to their drays, lowering down beer into, or drawing up empty casks from the cellars of public-houses. Now although this may be unavoidable, ask one of these bluff bipeds to let you pass, the consequence frequently will be, instead of rough civility, an insolent reply accompanied with vulgar oaths; in short, a torrent of abuse, if not a shove into the kennel; perhaps a grimy rope thrown against your white stockings. Private, emolument and convenience certainly ought to give way to public accommodation."

"Confound that dustman's bell," said Bob, as they passed down Wych-street; "it is as bad as any thing we nave mentioned yet; it absolutely deafens one."

"Oh, if you call noises nuisances, we may go on with a list from this time to this day month, and scarcely comprehend them. The cries of London are many of them very laughable, and many very lamentable, and by way of contrast to the deafening dustman, take care of the bespatterings from the mud cart. The garlick-eating rogues, the drivers of these inconvenient conveniences, grinning horribly their ghastly smiles, enjoy a most malicious pleasure in the opportunities which chance affords them, of lending a little additional decoration from the contents of their carts, by way of embellishment to a cleanly dressed passenger. Therefore keep, if possible, at such a respectful distance as to avoid the effects of this low envy, and steer clear of the mudlarks."

By this time they had passed through the line of leading thoroughfares, and had St. Paul's in their view, when Tom took occasion to remark, "He was sorry the scaffolding was not removed, or," continued he, "we would soon have mounted above these petty considerations, and looked down upon the world. However, we can take a tolerable survey of the metropolis from the Monument, and as it is not much farther, we may as well extend our walk to that celebrated pillar, said to be one of the finest in the world, and erected by Sir Christopher Wren in memory of the great fire which in 1666 broke out at a house on the spot, and destroyed the metropolis from Tower Hill to Temple Bar. From this pillar you will have a fine panoramic view of London, Westminster, and Southwark; and as we are about to leave its noise, its bustle, and its inconveniences in a day or two, we may as well take a general survey."

Bob having signified his consent to this proposal, they made the best of their way to the Monument, where having deposited the customary entrance money with the door-keeper, they were allowed to ascend by the winding staircase to the top, when a prospect was presented to the eye of Tallyho, of which he could not have formed any previous conception. The view of the river as far as the eye could reach, each way, the moving of the boats, the bustle and activity of the streets, and the continued hum which arose to their ears, formed altogether a subject of delightful contemplation; while the appearance of being as it were suspended in the air, rendered it awful and terrific. Bob had almost grown giddy in his ascension, and for some time took care to keep a fast hold of the iron railings at top, in order to secure himself from falling; till Dashall drew from his pocket a telescope, and directed his attention to Greenwich Hospital, Shooter's Hill, and the public buildings at a distance, where they were scarcely discernible by the naked eye. Bob was delighted with the view of Greenwich Hospital, and the account which his Cousin gave him of the establishment; and upon descending they took a complete walk round this celebrated pillar, marking its decorations and reading the inscription.

"It is," said Tom, "a fluted column of the Doric order; the total height is 202 feet, the diameter at the base 15 feet, and the height of the column 120 feet; the cone at the top, with its urn, are 42 feet; the height of the massy pedestal is 40 feet; there are 345 steps inside; but," continued he, "it is really a great pity that this beautiful Monument should be in such a confined situation, for in a proper place it would form one of the most striking objects of the kind that architecture is capable of producing.

"The inscription, it is true," continued Dashall, "had better be erased, it contains a libel, or more properly a lie, which almost contradicts itself, for no rational being can entertain the notion that the Catholics, or indeed any religious sect, could wilfully have perpetrated so horrible a deed as this pillar was intended to impute to them; nor can so much credit be given to human foresight as for it to be concluded that a fire, which broke out in a single house, could upon this, rather than upon other occasions, have extended its ravages in so extraordinary a manner.—

While we arc on the spot we will take a peep at a curious piece of antiquity; not that I am so great a lover of such curiosities, but it would appear almost unpardonable for you to have been in London without seeing London Stone."

"I have heard of it," said Tallyho, "and if we are near, let us have a view."

"Come on then," said Dashall; "This same London Stone is at present fixed close under the south wall of St. Swithin's Church, Cannon Street. It has by some been supposed of British origin, a kind of solemn boundary, or some other object probably of a religious nature, which through every change and convulsion of the State has been preserved with reverential care. But this is the very place," said he.

Bob stared about him with surprise, to discover this curious and apparently valuable relic, without finding it, till at length his Cousin directed his attention to the spot, which at present is under a pitching-block, or resting-place for persons carrying heavy loads, and almost burst into laughter, for he had raised his Cousin's expectation by the previous description.

"How!" said Tallyho, "and is this your curiosity?"

"Even so," replied Tom, "that is the celebrated London Stone; it formerly stood nearer the middle of the street, was placed deep in the ground, and strongly fixed with iron bars. According to account, the first mention of it was in the reign of Ethelstan, king of the West Saxons, and it has been usually viewed by our antiquaries as a military stone, from which the Romans began the computation of their miles, a conjecture which certainly appears very reasonable, not only from the discovery of the Roman road after the year 1666, running directly to this stone from Watling Street, but from the exact coincidence which its distance bears with the neighbouring station, mentioned in Antonine's Itinerary, the principal of whose Journeys either begin or end with London."

The sound of a horn interrupted this conversation.

"Apropos," said Tom, "we can take the Post Office in our way, a place of considerable importance; so allons."

They now pursued their way to Lombard Street.

"This collection of buildings," said Dashall, as they entered, "important as its concerns are to the nation, claims no praise as a building. It stands behind Lombard Street, from which, on the south side of the street, there is a passage leading to it, under an arched gateway.

"A plan has, however, been adopted for erecting a building worthy of this great establishment, on the site now called St. Martin's-le-grand, and to improve the access to it by pulling down the east ends of Newgate Street and Paternoster-Row. It is now proceeding rapidly.

"The Post-office system is, however, one of the most perfect regulations of finance and convenience existing under any government. It has gradually been brought to its present perfection, being at first in the hands of individuals, and replete with abuses. In its present form it not only supplies the government with a great revenue, but accomplishes that by means highly beneficial to the persons contributing.

"The Post-office is the most important spot on the surface of the globe. It receives information from all countries; it distributes instructions to the antipodes; it connects together more numerous and distant interests of men than any similar establishment. It is in the highest degree hitherto realized, the seat of terrestrial perception and volition—the brain of the whole earth; and hitherto it has been in a narrow valley, misshapen even to deformity, and scarcely accessible to the few mail coaches which collect there for their nightly freights.

"The present Post-office was erected in 1660; but great additions have been made to it from time to time, though the whole is disjointed and inconvenient.

"The mode of carrying letters by the General Post was greatly improved a few years since, by a most admirable plan, invented by Mr. Palmer. Previously to its adoption, letters were conveyed by carts, without protection from robbery, and subject to delays. At present they are carried, according to Mr. Palmer's plan, by coaches, distinguished by the name of mail-coaches, provided with a well-armed guard, and forwarded at the rate of eight miles an hour, including stoppages. Government contracts with coach-keepers merely for carrying the mail, the coach-owner making a profitable business besides, of carrying passengers and parcels. It is not easy to imagine a combination of different interests to one purpose, more complete than this. The wretched situation, however, of the horses, on account of the length of the stages which they are frequently driven, is a disgrace to the character of the British nation, and requires the interference of the legislature. No stage should exceed twelve miles in length.

"The rapidity of this mode of conveyance is unequalled in any country, and the present rate of charge for each passenger is little more than sixpence per mile.

"Houses having boxes, for receiving letters before five o'clock, are open in every part of the Metropolis; and after that hour bell-men collect the, letters during another hour, receiving a fee of one 'penny for each letter. But, at the General Post-office, in Lombard Street, letters are received till seven o'clock: after which time, till half an hour after seven, a fee of sixpence must be paid; and from half after seven till a quarter before eight, the postage must also be paid, as well as the fee of sixpence."

"Well," said Tallyho, "for a place of such public utility and constant resort, I must confess I expected to see a building of the most magnificent kind; but I am also puzzled to conceive how such extensive business can be carried on with so much regularity as it is."

"Your observation," replied his Cousin, "exactly coincides with that of many others; but you will some day or other be as much surprised on other subjects, for there are places in London where mercantile and legal business is conducted in situations of obscurity, of which you can have no conception; but as a national establishment, though its internal regulations are good, its external appearance is no recommendation to it. But come, let us proceed towards home, I have a call or two to make on the road, for as we depart quickly for the open fields, and are to bid adieu to London smoke as well as London Stone, we have but little time to spare, so let us post away."

Bob, alive to this subject, did not require a second hint, but taking the arm of Dashall, they proceeded along Cheapside, made a call at Mortimer's, the Gun-smith's on Ludgate hill, provided themselves with all necessary shooting apparatus; and Tom, ever mindful of the variety which he conceived would be needful to render rusticity agreeable on their way, purchased a pair of boxing gloves, a backgammon board, and other amusing articles, to provide, as he said, against a rainy day.

On arrival at home, they were presented with a letter from Sparkle, announcing his arrival at his new mansion, and expressing a hope that he should have the pleasure of meeting his friends within a day or two; expatiating with great apparent delight upon the happiness of his own situation, and promising lots of amusement, in detailing to them the events of his peregrinations. This operated as an additional spur to the speed of their departure, and it was agreed that they should start the next morning.

"I don't know," said Bob, "whether I should really like a continued Life in London; I have seen many of its comforts and many of its inconveniences." "Then," replied Tom, "you may certainly, by the exercise of your reason, and the decision of your judgment, upon mature reflection, strike the balance; and if you do not give it in favour of the former, I shall entertain doubts upon your sagacity."

"Well," continued Bob, "I shall now have a fine opportunity for drawing out a distinct account, and when done, I will submit the result to your inspection."

Every thing being prepared, they were on the road to Belville Hall at an early hour the next morning.

As the occurrences of a Country excursion, or the delineation of a Country Life, form no part of the intended plan of this Work, we shall not enter into any detailed account; but leaving our Heroes in the pursuit of fresh game, under new circumstances, and in somewhat new situations, bear in our minds their intended return, to engage, contemplate, and enjoy a future review of the complicated, yet ever new and ever varying scenes of a Real Life in London, with a determination to meet them on arrival, and not lose sight of them in their future rambles.

END OF VOL. I.

Printed in the United Kingdom
by Lightning Source UK Ltd.
123579UK00001BA/6/A